The Secrets of Sterling Shearin

The Noblest Cause

by **W. Ferrell**

This book is a work of fiction. Names, characters, places, and incidents are products of the author's imagination or are used fictitiously.

Cover art and illustration on page 179 are by Anna Lyon.
Interior book design by Judy Jordan, Sir Speedy Printing.

All Rights Reserved, 2013. No parts of this publication may be reproduced or transmitted in any form without prior permission of the author in writing (except for brief quotations as in critical articles or reviews).

>Willard Doral Ferrell
>221 Bear Run Lane
>Kernersville, NC 27284
>bearrun3@triad.rr.com

Additional copies of this book may be acquired
via Amazon.com

ISBN 1481060759

Preface

What follows is a remarkable, provocative journal that I have uncovered. It is written primarily by the brother of my ancestor Frederick Kenchen Shearin (1761-1845). I have endeavored to change as little as possible in the way of wording, punctuation, etc., in the process of rendering the journal accessible to modern readers. The [brackets], footnotes, and four of the six illustrations are my additions.

Chapter One

Sun. 22 Apr' 1787

 I have committed a shameful act. A woeful act that throws my soul into utter disorder. Whenever has it been my nature to be so bold? Have I not ruined my life when it is only upon the wing of beginning?

 My insides are stirred & agitated beyond containment. Yet there is none to whom I can unbosome myself. I must put my quill to paper in an attempt to order these shafts of emotion that project in all directions.

 I have such little in way of excuse. I am the best educated of my family, having read every book in Mr. Macon's collection these past three years to improve myself. My mind has been thereby focused on nobler issues. Most especially the wondrous uniqueness of the experiment we embarked upon in 1776. I talk with Mr. Macon & Kenchen &c. about the quintessential entertwining of liberty, virtue, & happiness. Now with what I have done, I feel the pompous jade.

 The only mitigating aspect was how buoyant & gay I felt upon leaving Mr. Macon's. I had gone to his place to return the compilation of *Cato's Letters*. By good fortune, he was holding a meeting of the trustees of the newly chartered Warrenton Academy. There in his front yard, beneath the canopy of his white oaks, I met some of the most illustrious gentlemen of our country. There was the rich, respected, but radical Wylie Jones[*], who wrote a Bill of Rights for our State *before* the writing of its Constitution. There was war hero William R. Davie, who caused Gen'l Cornwallis to style Charlotte "a hornet's nest". There was Benjamin Hawkins, who was a member Gen'l Washington's staff as his French translator & more recently a member of Congress from North-Carolina. Of course my mentor Nathaniel Macon & his brother were there.

 Mr. Davie is to leave shortly for Philadelphia to attend the convention to amend the Articles of Confederation. Rumor has it that Wylie Jones & Nathaniel Macon had declined the legislature's appointment to that convention, expressing fear that the convention's object was to limit the independency & freedom won for North-Carolina in the war.

 These prominent, famous gentlemen met me warmly when Macon introduced me. I was filled with optimism & pride. Mr. Jones took note of the book I returned & engaged me in some little intercourse regarding the thoughts of Gordon & Trenchard. He offered to lend me books from his

---

[*] Wylie actually spelled his name 'Willie' (named for a Rev. Willie), but it was pronounced 'Wylie'.

considerable library at his home in Halifax. To be treated with such respect by these leaders of our country, men of education & substantially more property than my family—well it filled my breast with gladness. How ashamed I feel now. I am a sorry, graceless varlet.

But as I rode homeward, it was with the feeling that I live in a time when all manner of things are possible. Even the cloudless azure of the sky & the near perfect mildness of this Spring day—the feeling of the air against my skin eminently agreeable—were in harmony with my optimism. The soft sounds of Aristotle's hooves, the creak of my saddle leather, & the distant birds desirous of mating played as music to my ear. I must at least partially attribute my subsequent brazenness to that spirit. Never before have I been guilty of such a transgression.

As it happened, I stopped at a spring for water. And there was a young mulatto girl kneeling at the spring. As I got down from Aristotle, my eyes were drawn to her as she leaned over the spring to drink. Her loose homespun garment hung so loose as to reveal almost completely her small breasts. As I said hello to her, I thought to myself 'she is more than passing fair'.

"Nothing like good cold spring water for a healthy thirst."

She nodded agreement.

Given my state as a near virgin, I own that three quarters of all white women & half of colored women inspire a degree of lust in me. It is a truth I cannot deny. When she leaned over for another drink, I confess I swelled. This day when all things seemed possible.

She was slender with a white woman's thinner features, a slight aquilinity to her nose, light brown skin, and long, glistening black, tightly curly hair drawn into a wild pony's tail. A very fetching negress with sweetness about her.

"The dogwoods are really beautiful just now, aren't they?" I said.

"Um-hmn, they are. I loves 'em."

"I've never seen you before. Where are you from?"

"Hawkins plantation."

"Which?"

"Master Benjamin's." She spoke like a slave, but with just a touch of demureness & without coarseness.

"If I had seen you before, I think I would have remembered. You are very pretty."

She smiled & looked down reflexively. "You don't mean dat. You just funnin'," she replied. She looked back at me with a little twinkle in her eye that told me she liked my having said it. Then she thought better of it & said, "I best be gettin' along."

"I wish you wouldn't. I think you are enchanting."

I took her hand, still wet with spring water, & kissed it like I would a lady's. She did not pull away. I looked her in the eye & slowly pulled her into a light embrace. I kissed her on the lips.

"I best be gettin' along. I…be missed," she said. But she did not really pull away. And I kissed her more wholeheartedly. She returned my kiss. Several times.

"I be missed," she repeated as she finally pulled away.

"Please, don't run off. What's your name?"

She turned back toward me & I asked her name again. She looked at me as to discover the violence of my intent. I must have looked more beseeching, more pleading than demanding. She could have run off. After a long moment she said, "Sarah."

"Sarah," I repeated, like a poem in one word. "Such an appositely beautiful name. Perfect… for you." We stared at one another. "Can I have one more kiss?" She stood still & we kissed. And kissed. When she felt me against her, she pulled away again & ran several steps.

She stopped & turned & muttered, "We can't…dis ain't…" She stood there looking at me with vulnerability in her countenance. There stood a profusely blooming dogwood right at her back, the sublimely white blooms framing her dusky beauty.

"Sarah, you are so enchanting." I rushed to her & kissed her forcefully. I kissed her on her neck & put my hand under her homespun to caress her breast. And then she did something that sealed my fate: She let out a little feminine moan that bespoke pleasure. And soon thereafter, when she pulled away again, I took her by the arm with more confidence than is my nature deeper into the woods. I pulled her coarse garment off her, laid it down on the thick leaf mulch, & forcefully laid her down on it as she weakly protested. I kissed her breasts & touched her between her legs where it was wet. When I stood to take off my breeches, she started to get up, but I own that I was on her as a flash of lightning.

Would that the ecstasy of those next minutes could be captured better in memory, given the price of the rashness, the wrongness. I try to remember now. I remember the sweet smell of the rotting leaves upon which we lay. And then our musky sexual smells. I remember the waves of remorse that swept over me. Had we been observed? Would Hawkins find out? Sarah did not seem as pretty. Indeed she was not cleaner than would be expected of a farm slave.

She wept quietly. She had given to me that of which I had but dreamed. I kissed her cheek & feelings of tenderness slowly returned. I hugged her naked body & forced myself to say, "Sarah, you have made me happy."

She did not respond. In a little, when she got up to put her clothes on, I said to her that I would like to do something for her. I suggested bringing her some corn, but she said they might be accused of stealing it. We settled on my bringing her some venison. Then she asked "What's yo' name?"

I hesitated for an uncomfortable, long moment. "Sterling...Sterling Shearin. My father & brothers farm east of here."

I reached out & hugged her & kissed her on both cheeks & hugged her again. Whatsoever anger she might feel toward me did not seem apparent in her expression. I estimate her to be 16. Yet I do not think she bled. I reckon her no virgin.

We agreed to meet at this place Saturday evening next for me to bring her some venison. I do not know if I am guilty of rape, but I am sensible that I have done wrong. There can be no doubt that I will have to pay, but just what will be the price?

Tues. 24 Apr' 1787

In some ways I am normal. I am the eleventh of the thirteen children of Joseph Shearin. Papa came to North-Carolina with his father & grandfather from Brunswick Co. Virginia about 1750. Papa's grandfather came to Virginia many years earlier as an indentured servant. We are indentured to no one now, and we take great pride in our independence. In this we are like most folk in the Roanoke River valley and in North-Carolina.

But in many ways am I out of step with my fellows. Why, men do sometimes fornicate with slaves. But discreetly, & not with someone else's slave. And I think it is for them totally a fleshly thing. While I feel something akin to affection. Affection for the sweetness about her eyes, for the fact that she did embrace me, did put her arms about my waist. Even an honorable & free-thinking man like Macon would laugh at me.

When I go to take her venison, will she bring agents of revenge? Master Benjamin or slave brothers? A vengeful sweetheart or even husband? In [Alexander] Pope's words,
 "*What dire offence from am'rous causes springs,*
 What mighty contests rise from trivial things!"

I wish there were someone to whom I could unbosome myself. I know the one I am closest to in this world, my brother Kenchen, would not approve. Lewis & my other brothers & sisters would be worse & doubly damn me for confessing it. Journal, you are my confessor.

Fri. 27 Apr' 87

In a few days I will be a man of nineteen years. I gain title from Grandpa & Papa to sixty-two acres. By agreement & affection, I shall owe Papa a goodly portion of labor until I am one-&-twenty. That aside, I am exceedingly grateful to the liberality of Grandpa & Papa.

Of course not so much of it is made land. Nine acres are well-cleared of trees and have been farmed by Papa, Kenchen, & me for 4 or 5 years. I am building my house on the edge of that clearing. On two more acres we have cut the trees but the stumps are left, and I will cultivate corn around the stumps. On an additional 2 acres, me and Will and Beck cut the trees this past winter and have them piled for burning the stumps next fall.

I have planted corn, cabbage, stringbeans, peas, and carrots; I am preparing to plant tobacco. If all goes well, we will complete the roof on my house by June. If I work dawn till dusk, have some help from connexions and friends, and have fortuitous weather, I should be able to afford to marry in a couple of years. In consideration of what I am feeling for this negress, imagine what fulfillment there might be in the love of a wife.

Tomorrow even: will my brown beauty be there? The thought heats my blood. In spite of working sun up to sun down for Papa and on my land, I am made awake with alacrity for her.

Saturday 28 April 1787

She came.

Naturally we met at dusk, just before the twilight thickened into darkness. The air was as perfect as Spring could render it, tho' a few clouds had started to roll in. When she espied me, her eyes widened—interest? surprise?—but then she lowered her countenance. I looked about. She seemed alone.

She stole another glance at me, her eyes studying to go hard or soft. I put forth the large basket I had brought her & took from it a cutting of a Sweetbay Magnolia branch with the first 2 blossoms of the season upon it. I presented it to her. The lemon sweet smell filled the space between us. A hint of a smile appeared & then broadened as I put the basket full to the brim with venison, salted pork, pickles, honey, bread, & dried apples at her feet. She inspected it & was visibly pleased.   Mayhap her expectations of white men were not high. She hesitantly kissed me on the cheek and said thank you.

"You are very welcome." I hid the agitation I felt by sitting down on a fallen tree. I hoped she would not just take the basket & go.

She went back to the basket & played through it for a moment. She glanced at me. I did not speak for I knew not what to say. Then she took one of the pickles from its crock. She put it to her lips.

"Um. Good." Her countenance seemed at that moment to turn something mischievous. I smiled. "Taste?" she asked. I stood & went to let her put the remnant of the pickle in my mouth. Her fingers lingered there. I kissed them. She smiled at me so warmly.

I embraced her slowly with the gentlest tenderness a man could do. Such that she knew she could if she chose run off from me. Her hands lightly touched my waist. We held each other with the barest, lightest touch for several delicious moments. Barely touching...still… touching. This delicate embrace was as pleasurable as….it was inexpressible. I kissed her mouth and anon she was kissing me back.

We continued kissing for a time. I fondled her perfectly shaped little breasts and she began to press herself against my leg. I undressed her slowly. Then she removed my shirt & breeches. She touched me where my admixture of lust & affection for her was displaying itself in its true & natural colors. I apprehend that she delighted in something about it from the mischievous smile she cast up at me. And that she delighted even more in the moans she elicited from me. Of the noises of the forest still much awake in this warm cloudy Spring twilight, I fear ours were the loudest. We bathed in each others' warm perspiration; we bathed in carnal knowledge one of the other. It was even more pleasurable than our first encounter, perhaps because we both felt safer with each other. We intended good each for the other.

I may die tomorrow, or more likely, be afflicted with a severe cost for this action. Verily, I have failed to achieve that rectitude of conduct from which departure is fatal. Yet let me recollect that this action, this experience, was very fine.

Then, some few moments after we finished, we were startled by a noise. I jumped up entirely naked and grabbed my gun. An animal? A man? Who or what had seen us? If it intended harm, we had been nakedly vulnerable. I walked in what I thought to be the direction of the sound with nothing on but my gun. How reassuring 'twould have been to have seen a pair of deer. I walked some little way before I encountered a rabbit. I was left uneasy.

But when I returned, Sarah laughed gleefully at my appearance. I had to laugh in return. How fetching, how very agreeable is her laugh.

We dressed. We shared some of the honey and bread. I asked her about herself.

She and her mother had been bought in Halifax seven winters ago. Her mother had married a slave on Hawkins plantation a year later and she had a young half-sister and half-brother. She reckoned her father was the mother's previous master; several of her features seemed of a piece with her conjecture.

She asked what the word "enchanting" meant. What had I meant at our first meeting when I called her "enchanting"?

I was caught off guard. I read too much for a farmer of small means. "It means to cast a spell or to charm." I looked down, embarrassed. Then I smiled & said "Isn't that what you do?"

She answered my smile & giggled. "Never heard such but from you. 'Spect you be butterin' up plenty of 'em."

"No, that's not true at all."

An easy silence followed...but then the silence grew awkward as thoughts of practicality re-emerged. I asked what she or her family needed that I might be able to discreetly provide.

"Mo' apples and pig meat. I loves honey. Some milk?" Her answer came eagerly.

"I think I can do that, Miss Sarah." She smiled, tho' I couldn't collect whether it was at the ironic courtesy of my address or the prospect of good food. "Can we meet here again Saturday next? Twilight?"

"Probably 'bout d'only time. Don't know if it lies in my way e'en then." She speaks as a slave, but with a lilt, a feminine melody to her voice. "May be a hard month for most o' us. You know dat. I be no house servant. E'en now, I shouldn't tarry."

"Have you confided, have you told anyone?"

She hesitated for full half a minute. "Not Mama...but a friend."

"There is danger on all sides of our meeting. I am possessed of a thousand fears on its account. Tell no one else, please."

Without answering or the least ceremony, she started off. I stopped her and kissed her affectionately. "You are not just..." an allurement of guilty pleasure I thought but did not say. "You are sublime."

"How you do go on," she responded in a whisper, her countenance possessing a natural demure expression like a fine white lady might have. I flatter myself that she understood me as well—or as poorly—as I understand myself where she is concerned.

At this moment, my mind fills with a thousand thoughts, at least half of them worries. This, my last candle, is spent. But sleep will not come quickly tonight.

Sunday 6 May 1787

Pshah! Pshah! Pshah! Fie upon it! It rained all day & night Saturday. We mucked out the stalls of a morning, but with most of Papa's blacks and me working on it, it was done pretty quick. I managed to get Will to venture out in the rain to my spread to chop trees. Will is strong and a hard worker.

But I tried to outwork him to deaden my frustration, knowing what the rain would likely mean to our plans. I went in the cold, driving rain to our rendezvous spot on the remote chance that Sarah would come. Of course, she did not come. I am sensible that she did not actually promise to come. What a dark, drenched treacherously muddy ride home. I came in wet skin out & shivering. Kenchen and Mama asked what in tarnation is wrong with me.

Sun 13 May '87

  The rain did stop hours after my last entry. I thought I worked hard before for Papa, but I work much harder now that it is <u>my</u> farm. Kenchen came over one day to help. We got all the tobacco to the fields. I was heartily tired last night when I went to see if Sarah would come — and much more so when she did not. If she could read, a note could be left or gotten to her.

  I spent all day today cutting red oaks, hickories, poplars & pines and sawing them for my house. When I got back to Papa's, he and Macon and Lewis had just returned from Halifax, where they went naturally to trade, but also for the great pleasure of the May horse races. They couldn't get money for my deerskins, but they got corn whiskey, which trades nearly as well.

  They were in good spirits after a visit to a real town and the races. I was delighted they brought the Petersburg newspaper. I read its entirety to Mama, sisters, &c. I asked for all the particulars of the race-meeting. Macon said Col. Davie's & Wylie Jones' horses were dominant. Macon said Jones had a good word for me and repeated his offer of lending books. Bless my stars! How singular to be remembered by such an illustrious gentleman.

  Also the Persons are having a birthday ball Saturday next.

15 May

  Papa, Kenchen, Lewis, and Macon each brought a slave and the nine of us completed my roof and more. (Note: owe Kenchen, Lewis & Macon two days labor each.)

  Macon's negro was an exceedingly skilled carpenter whom he is renting for the summer from Mr. Person. This man has an axe—of his own design—with a subtle curve to the handle & more metal on the side opposite the blade; never have I cut with an axe of such prodigious efficiency. This slave is an exceptional man & a strong argument against the inherent inferiority of blacks. Of course he is not full-blooded.

  Macon has not allowed his ownership of several slaves to soften him.

Tho' at thirty he already looks the part of the refined Roman senator (a firm jaw, slightly deep set eyes under heavy, oft-wrinkled brows, & very little hair), he employed his tall, well-proportioned, sturdy frame to my great advantage—as if 'twere his home we worked upon.

I esteem Nathaniel Macon as no other man. I took him into my confidence to some degree. I have a plan: At the Persons' ball I want him to be present as I try to finesse Benjamin Hawkins.

"Suffer me to say to you, Sterling, that you're more full of tricks than a hare in a thicket," Macon declared. He is no friend to deception. But he was intrigued. He agreed to help.

Sunday 20 May 1787

The Persons' affair was about as grand as we have seen in Warren Co. 'Twas a very large assembly, due in some measure to Squire Person's liberality in inviting a number of smaller freeholders such as myself. Not indiscriminant. Only the diligent & literate amongst our number who might conceivably aspire in time to the level of the genteel.

I flatter myself that several maidens from these families—and especially Patsy Williams—flirted with me somewhat more now that I have my own farm *and* a near completed house. I have always found it agreeable to be around Patsy at a husking or frolic because of her alert (& now solicitous) green eyes & pleasing figure.

There was a warmly-contested horse race, 4 circuits about a half mile course. Then a bountiful spread for dinner at four with everyone contributing a dish. Then lots of hard cider and whiskey and toasting. To the Lady Person's birthday. To each of the thirteen republics of America in our noble experiments in freedom—may we be beacons to the world. To the Governor. To the Fair Sex & so on.

The dancing was gay & exciting with a large band of negro and white musicians. I love it all, but I only know the country dances. Patsy dances with an excellent carriage but not so fine an ear for the movement.

The genteel dances that the Persons, Hawkins, and Macons know put us poorer planters in our place on such an occasion. Their minuets, danced with great ease & propriety, could leave no one indifferent. Most impressive.

Now that some goodly imbibing had transpired, I endeavored to hatch my tenuous scheme. It would require good fortune. The Hawkins have four or five times as many slaves as my entire family and are inclined to rent a few out from time to time. With Macon by my side, I encountered Benj. Hawkins as casually as possible and inquired how many gallons of whiskey he would take to rent a young teenage negro for the next five months through the October harvesting, to help me weed and what not. He offered liberal terms as I hoped — no doubt encouraged by drink and the desire not to appear niggardly in the presence of Macon. Macon is after all probably his chief rival in Warren Co. in terms of education (they both attended college of New Jersey [later known as Princeton Univ.]) and respect.

Then I asked if a teenage negress might be a little cheaper.

Again Hawkins answered amiably. "Yes, yes. Two gallons less for the five months. Glad to help a young novice farmer get going."

I shook his hand and said I would bring the whiskey over the first of June and fetch my first slave. I hate being surreptitious but, verily, it would not do for Benjamin Hawkins to know how desperate I am for his slave girl.

Chapter Two

Sunday 27 May 1787

I flatter myself that my house is something of which to be proud. At 17'x 23', it is slightly bigger than Macon's (although Macon & his wife, especially she, contemplate improvements). It has a stone foundation and a stone hearth & chimney with some capacity for a nice oven. I have a pine floor; I believe I am the only farmer in Warren Co. with less than 200 acres who does not have dirt for a floor. In due course, I design to have a cellar.

For now I will make do with two hinged wooden windows which I will replace with glass as I prosper. And I will make do with a ladder to the loft in lieu of a stair. Two grand white oaks in front will have to serve in place of a covered front porch. The oaks and then two columns of six young apple trees each will give my front door a most esthetic avenue of approach as the apple trees mature. Kenchen helped me obtain and plant them when I was fifteen. He inherits Papa's small orchard.

There is a price for everything. I forego glass windows to have a dry wooden floor. I will go the rest of the year without whiskey to have Sarah for five months. 'Tis received wisdom that a week without strong drink is unhealthy; hence I may well be giving up my health as well.

Well, my scheme is not a *fait accompli* as our French allies in the revolution would say.

Sunday 3 June

I did not go over to the Hawkins's place on June 1st because I learned from my brother Lewis that Benjamin would be going to Halifax early on Saturday the 2nd. This improved my odds a little. By going over mid-morning I hoped to be able to deal with Benjamin's redoubtable mama, Delia Hawkins.

There is no polite way around it: Delia is corpulent. But she is indeed a very good sort of women, magnanimous & kind. She is possesst of greater understanding than most men & is properly influential in Warren Co. politics in spite of her sex. An unabashed Whig,[*] Delia Hawkins rightfully counts us Shearins as voting allies. But what signifies most in this instance: I flatter myself that she is partial to me.

---

[*] The late 18th-century Whig believed in the natural tendency of government to become the enemy of freedom, based on their reading of history—especially Roman history.

But as I indicated, she is intelligent, and I feared she would detect my design. Still, I reckoned my prospect of success better in dealing with her genial self than with her son. I told her of the deal agreed to by Benjamin.

"Well, sounds like to me you got to Benjamin when he was in his cups, Sterling. Kind of mischievous of you." She paused. "Well." She paused again. "You're not having any of my skilled people. Come on…let's see. Sookie here would be good for weeding, easy field work, shelling peas…"

"She's only eleven or twelve!"

"That's about right for what you are paying."

"I've heard one named Sarah is well-behaved."

"Where did you hear aught of that scrawny thing?"

"I'm not sure. Is it a fact? Or would she be troublesome?"

"She's alright. She would probably be suitable for what you will need. Garden work. She's small-boned and skinny; not good for anything heavy. She's right smart making soap, candle-dipping, so forth."

She paused and then continued, more to herself than to me: "As I think on it, we probably ought to have her spinning, weaving, sewing, and doing house servant work. Well…when you bring her back. She is probably weedin' in the south cornfield. Ride down and fetch her. But Sterling!" said she as she cast a serious eye upon me that gave me pause. "A pox on you if you don't return her as good as you find her."

I quietly exhaled a sigh of relief & rode off before she could contemplate further.

How can I describe that strange scene when I came upon her? The shock, the utter confusion evident in her expression when first she espied me was—to our good fortune—only observed by me, but only because the others present were not looking directly at her. She hid her face cleverly as she wiped perspiration with her sleeve. By degrees she suppressed the excitement in her countenance. As I was able to suppress the exhilaration which I felt. We went back to her family's mean hut for her to get her few possessions and bid her mama adieu. I promised her mama monthly visits if she worked well. Once over her surprise, her mother was not easy & gave me a look remarkably similar to Delia's.

I mounted her up behind me on my horse Aristotle. She naturally held her arms around my middle. I was possessed of an inexpressible fine feeling. It was all as if in a dream. No words were spoken. When we were off Hawkins land and assuredly alone, I patted her hand and said "I missed you sorely." She squeezed her embrace and laid her head against me in a comfortable, affectionate way.

Then we talked a little. She had not been able to sneak away the Saturday night after we were rained out. But she had come the following Saturday when I was at Persons' ball and assumed she would never see me again.

We worked the rest of the day at the farm until the barest of light streaked the western sky. Every now and then one would catch the other's eye and smile. We supt on a soup of sorrel, potatoes, corn and venison while water heated on the fire for bathing.

We took each others' clothes off and bathed each other. We stood nude before each other by the light of the fire. The light of the fire illuminated one side of her. It made her glow near halo like...the side in shadow no less beautiful. There was silence, but for the crackle of the fire. I felt an ineffable sense of awe. We embraced. We kissed and kissed and kissed. And finally lay upon my bed to do the wondrous dark deed. Then we slept embracing through the night. It was light unusual sleep with many mild awakenings that brought thoughts of how blessed I was to be able to touch her—yet also twinges of anxiety. Surely this is too wondrous good and the other shoe will drop upon us at any moment.

Today we have worked well. Sarah takes initiative, and I do not have to tell her much. She will free me to hunt more, which will improve our diet and allow me to have some skins to sell. With luck there will be enough to share meat with Macon and Kenchen to repay their frequent favors.

Sunday 1 July

Almost a month has passed. We have had good weather and worked steadily. Got our first stringbean crop harvested and our second planted. We took something of a break yesterday, fishing for a few hours in the Roanoke. I have to remind myself that we are master and slave. She is better than obedient in that she looks for what needs doing. Hence I am rarely commanding her to do anything. Rather I find myself praising her work.

Last week after a typical long day, she came over unsolicited and rubbed my back in a most relaxing manner. I felt compelled to return the favor and asked what I could do for her. She had ready answers. She asked me to teach her to read and to allow her to carry some food to her family.

She has learned the alphabet and to write her name already. Sarah is bright. She is good. She is kind. She is absolutely as wonderful & human as any white woman. She deserves better than the fate Providence has cast upon her.

I rode her over to Hawkins plantation with some fish and squirrels for her family last night. I have cut oak all afternoon. A new saw mill has started not far down the Roanoke from here. Oak barrel staves will fetch ready money in Halifax, and there is a little more land cleared but for stumps. It has been peculiar her not being here today.

Sunday 15 July

 It has been exceedingly hot. Tobacco is doing well, but the corn wants rain. Sarah and I swam in our creek where it swells close to the Roanoke. Sarah joked about how "It's mighty good you be washin' some of dat white smell off'n you."

 Afterward, we explored each other in yet another way—this one unspeakable even to my journal. It explodes the capacity of my imagination that husbands and wives might engage in such intimate exploration of one another. Does this actually occur or is Sarah an aberration...a uniquely free individual in contradistinction to her slave state?

Sun' 22 July

 My first independent trading trip was successful beyond my hopes. Everything sold for either real coin or North-Carolina or Virginia money. My good fortune was due to the timely arrival of two schooners at Halifax. The oak barrel staves went for Spanish silver. The skins went for Virginia money. I sold Kenchen's and my extra produce to one of the schooners for N.-C. money. Normally produce is so plentiful this time of year even in Halifax, with its several thousand souls, that we only hoped for a poor barter trade.

 I used the worst (to wit, North-Carolina) money to buy gunpowder, flour, coffee, and sugar for Kenchen and me. I was tempted to buy Sarah a fine cotton shift. 'Twould be certain to raise an eyebrow when next she visits her family. I settled for one of a little finer weave than that to which she is accustomed but not better than what the Hawkins' house servants would wear.

 I feared Mr. Wylie Jones would not remember me, but he was hospitable and lent me Joseph Addison's *Cato*[*] and some back issues of the *Virginia Gazette*. His house surpasses any that I have ever seen. From the quality of the linen he wears to the refinement of his address, there is no superlative that is excessive. By comparison, a Mr. Person or Mr. Macon or Mr. Hawkins seems near indifferent. Nay, they are gentlemen, but not of his stamp. He was gracious in conversation without a trace of haughtiness to despise in his manners. He is an admirable gentleman and proof that opulence, when accompanied by virtue and knowledge, need not lead to dissipation.

---

[*] Addison's popular 1713 play contributed to the subsequent naming of the previously mentioned Cato's Letters. George Washington so favored the play that he had it performed for the troops at Valley Forge. Phrases from it can be found in numerous pronouncements made by founding fathers from Patrick Henry to John Adams.

Sunday 12 Aug'

When Sarah came back from her second visit to her family, they teased her that her speech and manner are getting "high falutin" after two months of living with a white man who reads books & has a wooden floor in his house. She has gone through the primer that Grandpa and Kenchen used to teach me early reading. She possesses a fine intelligence. We are starting to

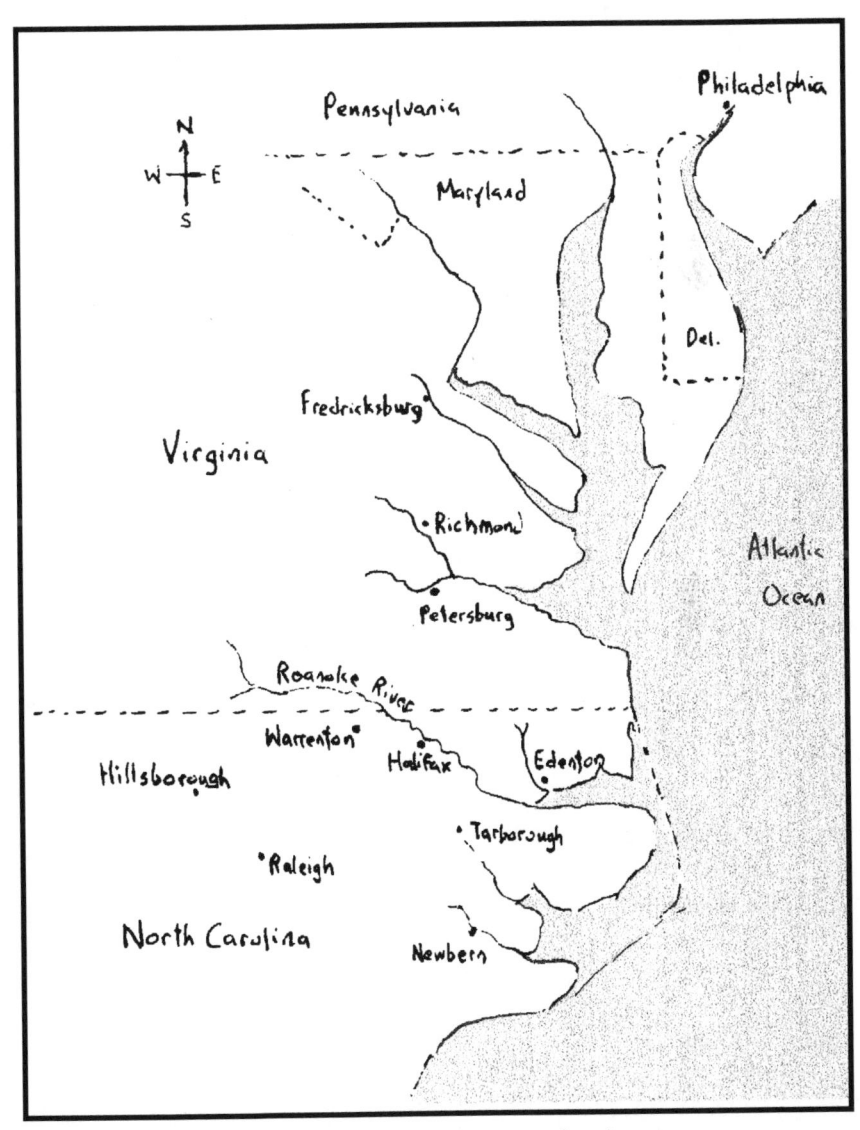

Map Relevant to Sterling's travel and entries.

find humor in many of the same things. (I wonder would she see humor in an Irish joke.)

She seems as happy to be here as I am happy to have her. I have gleaned from little things she has said that her treatment at Hawkins plantation is generally pretty harsh, the more so since the hiring of an overseer. Except when their little patch is yielding, they hardly get enough to eat. Her stepfather has been beaten severely once. In my family, injuring a slave by beating him is thought of as similar to injuring a horse from which you expect service. I remember Grandpa whipped Dick once when Dick pushed him to it. But not such a whipping as would send a man to bed. It was what a miscreant sailor, mechanic, student, or apprentice might get from his master.

My family's philosophy has always been reward good work with food, clothes, and privileges; if that does not yield satisfaction, sell them. Of course we do not have many. Amongst Grandpa, Papa, and my four living grown brothers (Kenchen, Gardner, Lewis, and Isham), we total only nineteen adult slaves. Perhaps larger slaveholders face a more complicated situation. At best, slavery is a vulgar, nay, a wretched thing.

I could never have succeeded so well in keeping worms off the tobacco, keeping critters out of the corn and beans, gotten so much wood cut and to the mill, gotten so many skins, repaid a day's labor to Macon, and on and on without Sarah's diligent work.

I asked her one day "If you worked so well for the Hawkins, why would they have consented to rent you out? Did Delia just not know?"

"I 'spect I don't work so hard fo' dem."

Sun' 26 Aug'

The tobacco priming, handing, and tying are going well. I only wish I had a more sizeable crop. Macon, Kenchen, and I hunted together, and I had them over to my place for watermelon. They are the only folks with whom I am on sufficiently intimate terms to be able to ask them over when I could only offer spring water to drink. I must note, however, that the Dog Days of August are well upon us, and neither Sarah nor I have come down with any of the sickness so common this time of year. So much for the lack of strong drink.

Macon said rumors abound that Davie and the bunch in Philadelphia are trying to throw out the Articles of Confederation and substitute an entirely new constitution. He is alarmed.

Nathaniel Macon has served in North-Carolina's House of Commons & Senate off and on since 1781. He was elected by Warren Co. whilst he was serving in Genl Greene's army. So patriotic a Whig was Nathaniel that he was refusing any pay for serving in the army, and except for Gen⟨sup⟩l⟨/sup⟩ Greene's command, would have refused his election. Such is his character.

Nearly losing his beautiful and devoted consort Hannah at the birth of their son Plummer in the Spring of '86 persuaded him to honor her request that he attend closer to his family and farm and eschew politics. With about 700 acres and nineteen slaves, he is not so rich as the Persons or Hawkins, but he is respected in very high degree for his absolute integrity, his erudition, & his understanding.

Kenchen complimented me on the progress of my house and farm in Sarah's presence, and I credited her. Kenchen told this Irish joke: An Irishman, newly arrived in Philadelphia, was approached by an aggressively barking dog. He tried to pull up a pavement stone to throw at the dog but it was too snugly placed. The Irishman exclaimed "What kind of country is this? The dogs run loose but the stones are tied down." Was Sarah's smile just at seeing us laugh or did she think it funny? Probably the former: like me she has never seen a paved street, but where I have heard and read of them, she probably has not.

Out of her hearing Kenchen said with a sly smile that she was quite easy on the eye. She has filled out a little, which is agreeable to his tastes.

I was awakened in the middle of the night last Wednesday night. Sarah's Mama, half-sister, and a girl-friend had sneaked over to see her. A long ways on foot. If they stayed long at all, they would get very little sleep before dawn. I gave them a watermelon and a knife and told them as long as they were up to make sure there were no animals in the corn. (They had their own knife.) I am sure Sarah misses her folk.

It pains me not to be able to read the Harrington and Gordon from the *Virginia Gazette*—concerned as they are with liberty and rights—to Sarah. And Addison's tragedy about Cato attempting to establish a virtuous republic only to be obliterated by despotic Julius Caesar. Of great interest to me but no doubt alien to her world. (At least we do not treat slaves as badly as did the ancients.) Would she get stoic inspiration from Addison's lines?

Content thyself to be obscurely good.
When vice prevails, and impious men bear sway.
The post of honour is a private station.

Sun '16 Sept.

Harvesting & curing going well. Including the tobacco, a pittance from produce and from Sarah's candles, more barrel staves after harvest, and last July's fortuitous trades, prospects are good that I will have amassed over £40 by the end of the year.

Now the quandary arises. My prime need is a male slave. It is essential if I am to get my land cleared and productive. £40 would suffice to pay down on a good male. If I may acquire him on good terms (and weather favors the farmer), I may be able to have him paid for in two years. Then my prospects would soar.

On the other hand, £40 might pay for Sarah outright. Or I could buy her partially on credit and buy some livestock. But what can become of Sarah. I cannot marry her. What life would we have amongst our neighbors? What life would our mullato children have?

And a white wife would not tolerate one such as her around. Nor could I tolerate it. I cannot afford to spend every shilling I have on her and then manumit her. I could hunt for her a kind master. Perhaps one of the four or five free negro families in Halifax Co. who own slaves. But that is no guarantee of good treatment, and it still separates her from her connexions. I own I am very uneasy on all these matters.

She is fascinated by *Gulliver's Travels*, as best she understands it.

Friday 21 Sept.

Sarah thinks she is with child.

Chapter Three

Thursday 11 Oct'r 1787

I had a great pain in my viscera for days. Finally I endeavored to lessen it by confessing to my closest brother, Kenchen. After some little scolding, he said:

"Many men would just buy her & simply view it as a quick start to their slave holdings."

"I couldn't do that."

"When a child is black or mulatto, one can easily fall into putting it in another category. Seeing it as not your own. Seeing it as…seeing it as just a slave."

I shook my head. "Kench, it would be the child of someone for whom I must own I have genuine feelings. To make matters worse, Sarah is not that dark-skinned to begin with: Our child could well be lighter still. It is inconceivable to me to proceed in that manner."

"Brother, brother. What is to be done with ye? I can imagine how you feel, but you are the veriest puddinghead to have got yourself in such a fix." After thinking for a while, he said: "Mayhap Mother Walker will know some way."

We visited his mother-in-law, who is a venerable mid-wife. Mrs. Walker nursed me through the putrid malignant sore throat* three years back; she is a woman of considerable wisdom & experience. Kenchen hath not the regard for her that I have; he claims his mother-in-law has a propension to treat every symptom with an emetick. Yet she is my only hope.

She produced a solution of many ingredients. Bark, stinkweed, savine, and tansy were mentioned. She said that it seems to work about half the time and that I owe her 1 shilling, 2 pence—and a quantity of snuff later if it works.

I gave the potion to Sarah and she drank it down. Nothing happened, except that she got a little nauseous. My hopes should not have risen. I must face this squarely now, whatsoever the consequences.

Sat' 13 Oct'r

Untoward events come in a train. Today I was over at Kenchen's repaying some labor I owe him. I was squaring a beam with a broad-axe. Like so many before me, I cut my leg. I can work but poorly & there is much to do. Still,

---

* strep throat; "bark" was probably quinine from cinchona bark.

'tis no heavier weight upon my mind than Sarah. What I have implanted in her implants thorns in my heart. Palpable thorns.

Wed' 17Oct'

On Tuesday I went back to Mrs. Walker.

"With all your vast experience & store of knowledge of physic, isn't there something, Mrs. Walker, is there not something that can be done?" I implored.

She looked at me in steely silence, letting my beseeching plea—nay, she must see it as even as pandering & obsequious—lay out there…for me to bathe in how much I deserved this fate. Mrs. Walker, about as affable as a broody settin' hen on her best days, was on this day possesst of a posture & countenance utterly devoid of sympathy.

She looked away from me & replied, "Not anything that I know how to do."

I collected that there was no point in pressing her more. I nodded humbly, apologized for troubling her, & bid her good day.

I walked out & mounted Aristotle, the soul of melancholy. Mrs. Walker came to her door to watch me depart. When I was nearly out of earshot, she hollered:

"Young man! Come back here."

She mixed up a second potion, much heavier on the bark this time and a larger dose. As she mixed it, she gave me a scornful piece of her mind.

I hurried home to administer the potion to Sarah. Again she drank it down and little happened. Then late this afternoon out in the cornfield, Sarah started having cramping pains. The second time she bent over clutching her abdomen, I helped her back to the house. She was in pain and I wanted to comfort her but she insisted I leave. I asked should I get Mrs. Walker.

"Jes' leave me alone."

I worked for a little but was agitated to distraction. I went to Mrs. Walkers but she was birthing a baby near Warrenton. It was dark when I got home. Sarah was not there. When I found her she was walking toward the house with the shovel. She said "'Tis done." She would say nothing more. While this represents the severest chastening of my life, what it represents for Sarah I cannot fathom. She has something of the Stoic about her. A reserve. Perhaps a whole person is in her that I do not know. Alas, a fearful knot of dread is from both our stomachs gone.

Sun' 28 Oct^r

All the Shearin tobacco filled three hogsheads. Papa, my brother Isham, and I carried it the 25 miles to Halifax, timing our trip to catch the last day of the fall races. The Roanoke valley has the fastest horses in America. How gratifying it is when rich Virginian planters condescend to come down and enter their horses; ours always win. It is not simply the care and attention we lavish, but also that the quality of our horses suffered less detriment from the War than most. Lord Cornwallis, having met my brothers at Guilford Ct. House, was not so confident when he came through here on his way to Yorktown and did not tarry. (The bloody Englishman killed my brother Joseph and gave Kenchen his limp.)

One story has it that when the British took over Wylie Jones' home, "The Grove," for their brief sojourn, Col. Tarleton had some rather pointed intercourse with Mrs. Jones, who in the spring of 1781 was a young wife & must have been even more beautiful than she is now, to wit now that she is several times a mother.

One of the orphans she kept even then inquired of Col. Tarleton how he had injured his hand.

"I acquired this wound at the battle of Cowpens," answered he in his supercilious manner. "In the service of my King, I was cut by the sabre of one Col. Wm. Washington, a common, illiterate traitor. Scarce able to write his name I'll warrant."

Hearing this, Mrs. Jones could not help herself:

"Colonel, forgive me for saying so, but you ought to know better. For you bear upon your person proof that he knows very well how to make his mark."

Col. Tarleton espied her with contempt. "Pray thee of the sharp tongue, where is your brave husband?"

"I'm sure I don't know."

"If you ever see him again in this life, warn him that if we meet I will make my mark on him."

"Indeed?" answered the feisty Mrs. Jones. "Col. Tarleton, could you turn around facing away from me so that I might properly describe you to my husband?" The implication being clear, Tarleton looked upon the point of violence, but Lord Cornwallis sent him from the room.

I would have liked to confirm the story when I returned Addison's *Cato*. Mr. Wylie Jones, Esq., was entertaining a gathering of notables in his front yard—a truly magnificent grove of majestic white oak trees from which his home derives its name. The well-married Edenton lawyer James Iredell was expounding upon the virtues of the new Constitution, seconded by Wm. R. Davie & Benj. Hawkins.

Iredell spoke flamboyantly, undeterred by something of a lisp. In contrast to the heroic Davie, Iredell hired a substitute to fight for him in the Revolution.

"In spite of your assurances, Mr. Iredell," protested Mr. Jones, "this new government has little chance of enduring as a **federal** government – to wit, a con**fed**eration of thirteen sovereign republics. It will gradually consolidate the States into mere administrative departments. Without a bill of rights, the so-called 'federal' government will eventually become tyrannous."

Hawkins grunted. "Certainly North-Carolina or Virginia would both take up arms if the Central government interfered with our rights!"

The handsome Davie with his sonorous voice said much the same thing as Hawkins; his delivery is so commanding as to generally leave the issue as settled when he speaks. Something I could not abide.

With three against one I ventured without ceremony into the fray. "If you will indulge my boldness,"—they all looked at me in amazement—"please allow me to interject what every Whig knows: In the course of time it is the nature of every government to oppress its people. To what standard should we appeal if we have no declaration of our rights?"

I drew an appreciative smile from Jones. A bewildered start from the others, who from my dress knew themselves to be my betters.

"Think you an elected government would trifle with our rights to free speech, our rights to bear weapons of self-defense, our rights to trial by jury?" asked lawyer Iredell, his hands gesticulating quickly & finally dismissively as if I were suggesting something ridiculous.

"In all countries at all times the ambitions and avarices of particular men—sometimes well-intentioned men—are forging chains for men who are simply minding their own business." I startled myself with my own eloquence. "It may take a spell, but in time most governments will trifle with the rights of the governed."

"Bravo! young Sterling!" acclaimed Jones. "Excellently stated. And what about the new government having unlimited power to borrow? The power to borrow should require a 2/3 majority of congress or some other constraint. Nothing furthers the 'ambitions and avarices of particular men' as does easy debt. Witness our Carolina since 1776."

"*Touché*" granted Davie.

"With borrowed money, the politician may purchase good will & votes, while obscuring the costs," added Mr. Jones. "It is an inviting dissemblance left eligible, nay wide-open by this Constitution!"

"But the best characters from all states will furnish the highest quality of men to lead this union," offered Hawkins. "Men like Washington, Madison, Hamilton, Edmund Randolph, Jefferson."

"These are fine men, Benjamin, but we need a constitution that better harnesses the self-love of the leaders to the preservation of our liberty and property. For protection of liberty and property is the *raison d'être* for government, and yet history manifests the abject, consistent failure of governments to achieve this essence. Government is invariably captured and used by the politically powerful against the liberty and property of everyone else."

"You know, Wylie, you are almost alone among the *gentlemen* of North-Carolina in your anti-federalism," said Iredell, his lisp more prominent in his agitation. "You cast your vote with the ruffians, the Baptist and Presbyterian preachers; the lower sorts." The portly Iredell looked at me as he spoke. "All of the best characters are with us."

Jones answered with obvious irritation at Iredell's inconsiderateness toward me. "Sir, you use me ill with such an observation. Please have the complaisance to speak to the issue. This constitution is not federal: It will lead to the consolidation of the States into weaklings incapable of protecting our rights!"

I feigned not noticing the slight and used the opportunity to ask Hawkins under what terms he would sell Sarah.

"I have heard you were well pleased. I'd say £65."

I was dumbfounded. Around £40 would have been fair for a female of her age. "What? £65 for a teen-aged female? Did I hear you properly?"

"Indeed you did," said Hawkins. "£65."

Jones put Iredell in his place by turning to our conversation: "I will sell you a good young buck for £10 or £12 more than that."

I turned to Mr. Jones as he continued. "The boy I have in mind is maybe 20. Short but well-made. I believe he would behave for *you*, but my overseer and he are like oil and water."

"I would like to have the girl."

"A wife for a slave you have?"

"Nay. She would be my only slave."

"Young Sir, you are getting the cart before the horse."

"You are probably right."

"Come back after the horses race and look at him. £76. Half initially, two years for the balance, no interest first year, 5% thereafter."

Good terms from a man I can probably trust ... to do what I should do. Versus Hawkins' perverse obstruction of an obviously unworkable situation.

I thought of little else but this choice as the day wore on. We were not so fortunate as in July in trade. Tobacco was right plentiful this fall. The candles and produce sold poorly as well. My total profit for the year was £39, seven shillings.

Still wracked with doubt, I went with Papa to see the slave. I questioned him; he would not say much. Looked strong enough. His face was scared from small pox, he was missing an upper fore tooth, and his back showed signs of severe whipping. Maybe, as with Sarah, better treatment would pay a dividend. Papa felt strongly this slave was a good investment and urged me on. I perceive that Kenchen had shared my situation with him.

This was the worst dilemma of my life. Mr. Jones started to lose patience with me. Then he good-naturedly said "I will throw in a young pig if that will move you. But deliberate no more. I have other matters."

I felt distresst at annoying Mr. Jones in my uncertainty. I said I appreciated his indulgence, shook his hand, and gave him the £38 down payment—tho' I was uncertain still. (Also borrowed a volume of Shakespeare.) Papa and I took the slave (named Marmaduke) and the pig and went to trade at the market square. I spent my last pence on necessities and a pair of shoes for Sarah to have for the winter. There was no money for sugar or a Gazette—luxuries I love.

We collected the inebriated Isham from Mr. Johnson's tavern as he was on the verge of a fight with a pretentious fellow named Abner Whitaker. To his credit, Isham's trouble was connected with asserting that all folks wanting to give up North-Carolina's hard-won independence were Tories.

I left Marmaduke at Kenchen's that night and carried Sarah back to the Hawkins' today. I talked to her awkwardly and tried to express the reality I see facing me...us. I gave her the shoes. I told her that I cared very much for her, that she deserved better, but that we could never marry. Nor would her being my continual paramour be tolerable. How could we continue? She thanked me for the shoes. For a moment I could not discern her; then she broke down weeping. It tore my heart out.

Sunday 18 Nov '87

Sarah has been gone 3 weeks now. Each of the last 3 nights I have tried to draw her. Mayhap this last attempt captures some semblance of her.

This is how I recall her in my mind's eye right after she had cut her wild pony's tail in the heat of the summer. Against all custom, she loved to go bare-headed to display that her hair was possesst of less kink than most of her race. I miss her.

Sarah

Sun' 25 Nov.

 This has been the hardest month of my life. The best I can say is that Marmaduke and I have succeeded in cutting a good bit of wood for the sawmill, with obvious prospects for future cultivation. And we planted a bit of winter wheat. Everything else is bad. I hurt every time I think of Sarah, which is most of the time.

 In place of the easy rapport between Sarah and me is a deep-seated fear and mistrust betwixt myself & Marmaduke. I slept very lightly with my guns and knives in the bed with me the first week. I told him I would endeavor to treat him well in proportion to the goodness of his work. While I would have an extreme aversion to whipping, I told him I would whip him if he pushed me to it. I told him if he were loyal and industrious (in so many words), I would help him have a family of his own. Still, I do not trust him and he does not trust me.

Clearing stumps is very hard work even when you have been able to burn them some. I have stayed tired, heavy-hearted, and several days literally sick. As such I will return the Shakespeare vol. to Mr. Jones but little read. I read *Romeo and Juliet* with much distraction and it deepened my gloom. These lovers were not weak or faint of heart as was I.

Sunday 2 Dec^r

I left Marmaduke with Kenchen to keep an eye on him and to return some of the labor I owe Kenchen. Macon made the trade trip with me to Halifax. It was an exceedingly cold journey. Biting cold winds cut right through our cloaks; what sun there was seemed distantly frail & icy.

In lieu of commenting again on the unseasonableness of weather so bitterly cold in early December, I told Macon about my intercourse with Wylie Jones, Davie, & James Iredell at the previous visit.

"I'm very sorry to hear Iredell has taken that position so strongly," said Macon. "I remember being inspired by something he wrote early in the Revolution. A piece, 'To the Inhabitants of Great Britain', I think it was. I remember he wrote something like 'the noblest of all causes is the struggle for freedom'".

Several silent minutes later, Macon added "I suppose being a customs collector, a judge, attorney general…well, you end up a creature of government. How could Iredell avoid ending up a Tory?"

We were more than delighted to find Mr. Jones at home and to be invited into his magnificent, warm mansion. It was a distinct pleasure to share a warm drink with him sitting in comfort about his crackling hearth. He shared with us a compelling essay (from the *New-York Journal*) by one Brutus on the proposed new constitution.

This new constitution stipulates that congress may make all laws which are necessary and proper … to promote the general welfare. The men who framed this document no doubt meant thereby that no laws could be passed except those that **generally** affect all of the thirteen republics. For instance Congress could not build a canal in New York or send money to victims of flooding here on the Roanoke.

But as time passes, a very broad interpretation will prevail. Congress— as the judge of what promotes "The **general** welfare"—will make any law it pleases. The constitution will provide no restraint on Congress whatsoever.

The inevitable ambitious men of the future will consolidate our thirteen states into provinces, ignore our rights, and tax us without limit.

"This essayist Brutus," said Macon, "sounds to me like a man who knows which way the tree will fall."

The trading ended up being mostly barter with the store for needed goods and credit. I was able to pay Mr. Jones a few shillings more on Marmaduke and to buy Sarah a blanket and a little book, *Aesop's Fables*, that her reading should not be quenched. (I was glad to find a used copy that I could afford.) I am determined to see her again. On the way home Macon purposefully invited me over for dinner next Sunday. My kind mentor & friend is obviously sensible of my want of cheering.

Sun' 9 Dec^r

Patsy Williams was at Macons today. Her amiableness and her pleasing manner lifted my spirits. Indeed, I own she is not without allurements. What of her hair not covered by mobcap & hat is such a light brown as to be near flaxen. And tho' much obscured by the panniers of her skirt, every hint suggests a tidy figure. She hath a way of turning her head to her right & looking at me with a little sideways smile, her lips a little pouty, her pointed chin, her small green eyes sparkling mischievously...

Marmaduke did fine left at home. Perchance my house is warmer & dryer than that to which he is accustomed, and therefore he apprehends that he could fare worse. I begin to grow easy on that account, I hope with justice.

Sun' 16 Dec^r

It was a milder December day after many very cold ones. I boldly rode over to Hawkins plantation, inducing something of a stir. I gave Sarah's mama some venison and the blanket and asked if Sarah might be spared for a ride on my horse. Sarah took the blanket, wrapped it about her, & climbed up on Aristotle with the merest glance at her mama.

We rode to our spot. She said it was hard to go back to the treatment at Hawkins plantation. I said I did not know what I could do, but with time perhaps something could be done. "Master Benjamin knew I wanted you badly and was just mean about it. Presently, I stew in the juices of his disfavor. But circumstances change ... I have missed you more that I can say. I am afraid I love you."

We sat silently holding each other for a while. We had not lain together since well before her miscarriage. She said it was her time of month and that people said it was safe. If I wanted her. While we made love, I thought she said, but in the faintest voice, "I love you too."

When we returned I gave her the little book. Inside I had inscribed:

"Sarah, the country and the society of which I am a part is—except for the odious institution of slavery—the best and noblest the world has known. To my eternal discredit, my love for you can not overcome the expectations of everyone else who is dear to me. Still I will seek opportunities to help you. With tenderest affection, Sterling."

Chapter Four

New Years Day 1788

'Tis a New Year. 1788. I resolve to concentrate on my farm and avoid Hawkins plantation for at least the next three months. After all, I can do much about my farm and little about Sarah. Her plight and mine were put in perspective by considerable tragedy and sickness that has befallen hard by in the last few days.

Isham's two-year-old fell into the fire and likely will not live. Isham and his wife were taking advantage of the cold weather to slit hog throats and prepare them for smoking; their only slave was deathly sick and the five-year-old was in charge of the two-year-old.

Midwife Walker's old husband has the same sickness as Isham's slave. Kenchen asked me to visit them & help out, which I did. A pretty fair snow was falling, and Mrs. Walker asked me to carry her to Macon's where a slave was in horrible pain. The pain had started in his upper right and then moved with great intensity to his lower right abdomen. We found him in a perspiration lying with his right knee bent towards his stomach. Three days previous this twenty year old negro man was the picture of health. Mrs. Walker said she has seen this pattern before, & that it always seemed to lead to a very painful and certain death.[*]

All the laudanum and whiskey he could keep down was all she could advise. It was very sad to watch his agony helplessly. He died the next day. Macon still owed money on him.

Then today the sheriff came around. A man was found dead down where the Halifax-Warrenton road borders Kenchen's and Isham's farms. Dead from knife wounds. Probably happened before the snowfall on the 28th of December.

Sunday 6 Jan^y

The Williams invited me over for Sunday dinner. Their place is humble, but they have a fine oven—their pride and joy. (I brought them extra fire wood.) The genial Patsy displayed an intelligent interest, not only in the murder, but also in the new Constitution. Her manners aspire to refinement, especially in comparison with the rest of her family. One might collect

---

[*] probably appendicitis

merely from the attention that she pays to her hat that she has ambition. Patsy's features, tho' not so striking at first, at second glance shine soft & alluring. Indeed, aside from some little crowding of her teeth, she is a beautiful maiden.

Our legislature has gone along with the ruse put on by the convention in Philadelphia (which was only authorized to amend the Articles of Confederation) by calling elections in March for a ratifying convention in July. It is everywhere the subject of intercourse.

The new Constitution would allow standing armies during peace time! Throughout history standing armies have been the tools of tyranny—involving countries in needless war, providing patronage and force to gird the despotic elite. Was not a standing army the tool of King George III in keeping us in bondage to him? Is not all of Europe thus kept tamed? Our militias provide fervid self-defense. More than that is pernicious.

The murdered man was Abner Whitaker, brother-in-law to the overseer the Hawkins hired in October and cousin to the prominent Halifax planter Col. John Whitaker, who is even more prominent as the chief tax collector of our vicinage (a pox upon him). During the last couple of years he had worked as an overseer like his brother-in-law in Halifax and Northampton Counties. There being no more vulgar & negligent race of mortals than overseers, I shall not shed a tear. He was likely a Tory as well, for he is the very same man with whom Isham quarreled on our visit to Halifax.

Much suspicion is cast upon Isham <u>and</u> Kenchen: the public quarrel, where the body was found, and Kenchen's possession of Abner Whitaker's horse and saddle. Kenchen said the horse wandered up riderless. Kenchen also said the sheriff eyed suspiciously the bad cuts on his wrist and hand and did not seem satisfied by his explanation that they derived from an encounter with a wild turkey.

Isham's wife is distraught over the child's terrible death. He is quiet and withdrawn. At least his slave is recovered. A bilious fever with much regurgitation. Many folks have taken it, but most seem to recover in three days.

These events, the progress Marmaduke & I are making clearing my land, and the flirtatious interest Patsy has shown have distracted me and helped me with my resolution not to think of Sarah. But sometimes…well…today I stumbled in the woods & fell upon the rotting leaves that blanket the ground. I smelled the sweet fragrance of their decay, that same fragrance as when Sarah & I first lay on the ground under the blooming dogwood trees. It sticks much in my stomach.

Sun' 27 Jan^y

Marmaduke & I are making land furiously. I have hopes of having twenty-two or 23 acres under cultivation this summer. We have sold wood at the saw mill for whiskey and North-Carolina money. Papa sold me some pigs and chickens at discount for the money; I traded the whiskey at Person's Ordinary* for necessities.

I have lost my taste for whiskey—which may bring me some ridicule. Patsy eschews it as well in favor of hard cider or apple brandy. Perhaps we are well-suited. I went over to see her yesterday. I flatter myself that she has set her cap at me. She cooks delicious chicken dumplin' stew.

However today when we were clearing land, I came upon a pair of dogwoods standing like two lovers embracing. I decided to leave the two lovers in the middle of what is to be my osh [Irish] potato field as a memorial to Sarah. I will never forget first seeing her last spring framed by white dogwood blossoms.

Little new on the Abner Whitaker murder. I fear malignant rumors circulate about Kenchen and Isham. Kenchen said the sheriff came snooping around again. Naturally this agitates him exceedingly.

Isham remains distant. The work necessitated by their farm— which is only a few years ahead of mine—will pull him and his wife through. They are not the only family to endure such a tragedy.

Sun' 3 Feb^y

Nathaniel Macon, his brother John, my brother Lewis, and I had good success hunting yesterday. John is going to allow himself to be nominated for the ratifying convention. The Macons had a copy of George Mason's "Objections to the Constitution," which we discussed at length.

Mr. Geo. Mason is exactly correct that Congress would only be a "shadow of representation." The legislature of a republic should have <u>annually</u> elected representatives so numerous that they possess the same interests, feelings, and opinions which the people themselves would possess were they assembled. In North-Carolina every voter may easily know his legislator. On the other hand, a Congressman will represent 30,000 people! Congress will become an elite corps whose small numbers will facilitate bribery.

George Mason's suggestion that "regulation of commerce" require a two-thirds majority was not so obvious to me: "I don't understand. Insuring that commerce is regular, that the individual States do not erect barriers to

---

* part of this old inn is still standing in Littleton, N.C.

trade amongst themselves...Why should that require any voting at all?"

"Well, it shouldn't," answered Nathaniel. "But George Mason sagely conceives that the eight northern States will eventually vote for high tariffs so they can raise the prices on their manufactured goods. They may vote for high shipping duties so that it will cost us more to export our agricultural products to anyone but them. The five southern States will disproportionately pay the federal tax. Why should farmers be forced to subsidize ship owners and manufacturers? Observe: the northern States oppose Mason's suggestion."

With reference to the murder, Nath' has learned through one of his servants that there was a meeting or party of men at Hawkins' place right after Christmas. Macon conjectures from the description that the meeting had something to do with running pro-Constitution candidates. He is making inquiries.

Wedn' 6 Feb^y

The sheriff has been questioning everyone hereabouts on the subject of the murder. Turns out that Isham and Kenchen have had warm altercations with this Abner Whitaker before when he was doing duty as a part-time tax collector under his cousin's authority. At a minimum, we Shearins will face close scrutiny from the tax gatherer.

I observed to the sheriff that tax collectors and overseers would by nature have numerous enemies.

We break from clearing land tomorrow to plant tobacco, then cabbage and yams in their respective protected beds.

Sun' 10 Feb^y

We carried rabbits and eggs over to Patsy and enjoyed her fine cooking. Marmaduke especially.

Patsy's father said the murdered man's brother-in-law, Caleb Brown, is making, shall we say, ungenerous insinuations about Isham and Kenchen. On a pleasanter note, Mr. Williams —intermittently devout since his baptism six years ago—heard an itinerant Baptist preacher in Warrenton denounce the Constitution as dangerous to our freedom and independency.

A cold hard rain fell before we could leave. To speak the truth, their home is not so water tight as mine. Not that mine is perfect in that regard either, if the rain be hard enough.

Sunday 17 Feb '88

 Macon has learned who most of the people at the Hawkins meeting were, and Abner Whitaker was one of them. The slaves took particular note of a pompous stranger, apparently a friend of Benjamin Hawkins, named Robert Goodloe Harper. A South-Carolinian. Benjamin and his brother Philemon were there. Solomon Green, John Ward, & Caleb Brown (Abner's brother-in-law) were probably there.

 He talked to Benjamin's mama, Delia. She confirmed that it was a covey of Federalists. She volunteered that she told them it was pointless to run Constitution candidates in Warren Co. Somehow Delia did not properly educate her sons in Whig philosophy.

 Macon also had learned an intricate secret from the closed deliberations whereby this new Constitution was hatched. Wylie Jones has it by a letter from George Mason that a devil's bargain was struck between the New England States and South-Carolina & Georgia: New England agreed to insure 20 years of further importation of slaves provided that S.-C. & Georgia would agree to a simple majority to "regulate" commerce, rather than the more prudent two-thirds majority. Jones expresses regret that he did not accept his appointment to the Convention so as to support Mason's efforts. Was there ever a more evil bargain?

Sunday 24 Feb^y

 Mama and Papa came over and stayed three days. Papa talked considerably about how times had changed. How twenty-five years ago he would make good money from carving spoons during winter from the wood of yellow poplar trees. But now people with ready money to spend can afford better. I told him he exaggerated, pointing out that I have but five pewter spoons and that our Sunday guests, the Williams, I believe have only wooden spoons.

 When Papa was a boy, wheelbarrows that you push were unknown. Nor did anyone have rocking chairs. Progress.

 Papa recollects Abner Whitaker and Caleb Brown being coopers [barrel makers] for a spell in Halifax 2 or 3 years back. Theirs was a cooperage of low degree & like many a partnership, theirs ended badly.

 I enjoyed hosting the Williams with Mama's help. When Patsy and I went down to the spring to fetch pails of water, we kissed. And then again with an embrace. The faint scent of rosemary about her was enticing. Feminine & welcoming. Her full breasts against my chest filled me with yearning.

Sunday 2 March

We got most of the potatoes planted around Sarah's dogwoods. Then heavy rains came so that we cannot plough.

My mind keeps wandering back to Sarah. I think back on her reserved nature (except at such times as we were loving), and I wonder whether she really cared for me or whether she was just being pragmatical. Was she a slave making the best of her circumstance? Was the intimacy I felt predominantly one-sided? The powerful lust and all that had to be accomplished on the farm last summer may have obscured the truth from me.

She probably would have a preference for a man of her own race. When Sarah spoke of "washing some of that white smell off," was she jesting or was that an oblique complaint? Certainly Patsy's white skin, her pretty green eyes, her fine soft near flaxen hair, and other subtleties of being white are pleasing to me.

I would like to see Sarah. There is another month before my resolution would permit it. Maybe I could stand to marry her to Marmaduke if I were married. He is turning out to be a likely negro. He confided to me that he would very much "like a woman" and he would like a fiddle. He was learning the fiddle when the altercations between him and the overseer put an end to it. I would like to get us one and learn myself, but we will not be able to afford that any time soon.

Marmaduke is good with his hands; he is presently carving pieces to make a fish basket. I reckon I ought to go out in the chilly drizzle to chip stumps. A few swings of the axe and I will be oblivious to the wet, to the cold, and (I hope) to Sarah.

Sunday 12 April

I believe the Irish provide the correct pronunciation of the word "lawyer." "Lyer." The unctuous lawyer James Iredell (the very one I audaciously debated in Halifax) has published answers[*] to George Mason's "Objections to the Constitution."

He calls a bill of rights which would constrain the federal government "ridiculous." He claims a large legislature—the sort which any Whig of understanding would regard as safe from being bought—would be too expensive. He is not in the least concerned that the Southern States will be abused by the system of tariffs and shipping duties. He is not concerned that

---

[*] *Norfolk and Portsmouth Journal* (Va.) Feb. 20 - March 19, 1788, and subsequently in North Carolina.

farmers would profit less from their work, so that northern manufacturers and ship-owners can profit more.

I must admit that Iredell writes with specious cleverness. I give him credit for agreeing with Mr. Mason that the new constitution errs in not allowing the prohibition of further importation of slaves. The slave trade "has already continued too long for the honor and humanity of those concerned in it." But I suspect him of working for a plum appointment in the new general government should he lure our country into that union.

John Macon, Wylie Jones, and several other patriots won election from Warren and Halifax to the convention in Hillsborough. Davie is the only Federalist elected around here. And Col. Davie is a special case.

He possesses a beauty of person & a reputation of true valor during the War that render him very agreeable in everyone's eyes. After receiving a severe wound in his thigh at the battle of Stone Ferry in 1779, he spent his last shilling raising & equipping a body of cavalry—with which he heroically assailed & harried Cornwallis & Tarleton as they moved from South Carolina to Charlotte.

Indeed, in the fall of 1780 after Gates' disastrous defeat at Camden & Sumter's rout by Tarleton, South-Carolina was at the mercy of the British, and North-Carolina appeared virtually defenseless. Cornwallis' ability to march through our state & into Virginia made our cause appear hopeless. Defeat hung upon us in eminent degree. Tories everywhere were beating their chests. When Cornwallis initially moved into North-Carolina, Col. Davie lead a bold, nay temeritous action of defiance:

He infested Charlotte, a town of 20 houses & a courthouse, with his 3 companies of NC militia & defied Cornwallis' entire army to enter! The British were astonished & flummoxed. Numerous charges by the British Cavalry resulted in only losses for the Cavalry. Cornwallis was stymied as he reasoned that this could only be an ambuscade [ambush]. Finally Col. Davie led his brave men in a deft retreat before Cornwallis' huge army surrounded the entire village. The people of Mecklenburg & Rowan Counties, strong Whigs already, were thereby encouraged to every possible harassment & defiance of the invaders—this at a time when Cornwallis, nay perhaps everyone, had every reason to think he had the War virtually won.

How could you vote against such a one, Federalist tho' he be? Why, even his manners are so graceful that his natural hauteur is not unattractive. Col. Davie is a singular man, not one elected because of his federalism.

The murdered Abner Whitaker's cousin, federalist John Whitaker, was defeated, as was former Gov. Martin. Alexander Martin isn't even a true federalist but merely one whose principles are less than firm: He was one of the delegates with Davie at Philadelphia where we were sold out. Such is the prevailing sentiment that I am optimistic that North-Carolina will remain free and independent.

Sunday 19 April

By the time the three months moratorium on seeing Sarah had passed, I had gotten her out of my daily thoughts. We have been diligently planting corn, carrots (a gamble), butterbeans, stringbeans, black-eyed peas, watermelon, and a little cotton. Papa says I am a little early; he says that the soil is not warm enough till the oak leaves are the size of a squirrel's ear. Well, the cabbage next.

Then there is Patsy Williams. We get on famously. When we are alone, there is kissing. It is not so fluid as with Sarah, but I love to slip my hand inside her shift to fondle her lush bosom. I am afraid something shall transpire if a real opportunity presents itself.

But then the dogwoods started blooming, and I have Sarah on my mind—with such a mixture of feelings. Sometimes there is a pain in my gut like a hunger pain. Was she a saint or a pragmatical actress? I am disgusted with myself on several counts. How little I know this girl I loved.

Sun' 3 May

I started this day full of glee: It was a clear blue day. And weather has been generally good. At this point I have prospects of harvests nearly thrice last year's. I contemplated having Marmaduke two-thirds paid for after harvest and being in decent position to marry.

There is an energetic affection betwixt Patsy and me. She would be a most eligible helpmate. And God's teeth, I want her in my bed! I must own that I am possessed by the curse of wanton instinct.

With these buoyant thoughts, I carried some fish freshly caught in our fish baskets over to Macon's. I recognized one of Hawkins' slaves, who was visiting some of Macon's. I asked him how it fared with Sarah and her family. His reply smote me like a club: Sarah and her family were sold abruptly the first of the year! No one knows where they are.

Wed' 6 May

Now that I had nothing to gain from disguising my interest in Sarah, I went over to Hawkins plantation to see if I could find out where she is. Benjamin was up north. Delia remembered the girl (and seemed to know already of my attachment).

"Sterling, I don't remember exactly how they happened to be sold. I had nothing to do with it. Her papa had been trouble from time to time. Don't go pursuing her. It will be nothing but trouble for you."

I persisted and we found Caleb Brown the overseer. The tall & handsome olive-skinned Mr. Brown insisted on selling Sarah's papa because he was repeatedly insolent. Hawkins policy was not to break up families, so with Benjamin's permission, he sold them to a trader at the New Year's slave trade at Halifax. He doubted they had been re-sold locally. I perceive Caleb Brown's manner to possess a glimmer of deviousness. Nay, I apprehend that suggestions of dissemblance infused his every gesture. Yet I was much in the thrall of sensibility & emotion. I may be prejudiced by his malicious insinuations about my brothers. My contempt for his vulgar vocation further colors my view. I trust not my judgment.

In need of sympathetic advice, I stopped by Nathaniel Macon's on the way home. He is a good mentor and friend. He listens calmly, sharpens my thinking and settles my mind.

"Think you, Sterling," asked my sage neighbor "that you could ever enjoy the happy home and family that I enjoy with Mrs. Macon and our children if this Sarah were a part of your life?" The necessary, compelling question that brings it all back into perspective.

"Cast off this fancy like an old snake skin," said he, yet calmly & sympathetically.

Still I am bound to inquire about her when we go to Halifax again.

Thursday 21 May

It is hard to justify this trip to Halifax. None of the family has much to sell. There are few necessities we have to have at this juncture.

There *is* a broken wagon wheel for which we need the wheelwright. I may be able to borrow a book from Mr. Wylie Jones. According to Macon, Jones is hosting a ball after the horse races.

Halifax during the fall and spring horse races is the gayest, most festive place I have ever been. Macon had little difficulty instigating the trip. Papa has some cured hams to sell, and loving the horses as he does, was quick to join us. John Macon is going too.

It has turned unseasonably warm and dry these last three weeks: I should stay home with Marmaduke to tote pails of water to irrigate the weaker young crops. He promises to apply himself diligently to it all day Saturday. I have written him a pass to visit with Grandpa's slaves Saturday evening. If there is no trace of Sarah in Halifax, maybe I can close this painfully unresolved chapter of my life.

Chapter Five

Sunday 24 May 1788

    Naturally we attended to the trading first. Whiskey for gun powder, nails, coffee, sugar & fine flour for all of the family. I sold some of the salted pork that Isham had prepared at such a dear cost. Papa's pork sold well too as there were boats docked that were in want of such.

    We were privileged to enjoy the last day of the race-meeting, which included both the one-mile heats and 'the heroic distance' [4 mile heats]. It was the most prodigious assemblage I have ever witnessed in one place. A very large portion of the population of Halifax & Northampton Counties was surely present.

    We were all sorely tempted to wager, especially for Mr. Jones' magnificent stallion. Prudence & necessity restrained us (more the prudence in Nathaniel's case). Yet when the exciting 4 mile contest required a 3rd heat to produce a winner, John Macon & my brother Isham could not help themselves. John Macon lost 3 shillings on the 2nd place Edenton mare. Isham won a half-gallon of whiskey on Jones' triumphant stallion. When we congratulated Mr. Jones, he was upon the wings of ecstasy; he invited us to his ball. (We all had worn our best in hopes of such an invitation.)

    I made several inquiries about Sarah. Not a trace. I did not even encounter anyone with any recollection of her or her family. 'Tis as if they were effaced from the earth. Of course the trail is nearly five months cold. One fellow volunteered that there were a couple of traders who were not regulars. I resolve to take this as a sign from whatever divine providence that may exist.

    In the late afternoon, we headed for the ball at 'The Grove.' Except for Papa & Isham who went to the cocking main. I reminded Papa of his promise to Mama to refrain from wagering on this trip. I do not own to just anyone that cock fighting repulses me. Even more than the common views on slavery, it makes me feel out of step with my countrymen. Papa mentioned later that my debate opponent, the flamboyant James Iredell, was a warm participant at the cocking main. Papa said that he cursed like any ruffian, lisp & all, when he lost.

    The ball was the most brilliant affair I have ever attended! Such a wealth of candles, the fine playing of the musicians, the beautiful & exquisitely-adorned genteel ladies, the wondrous dancing, the grandness of the mansion, and the delicious apple brandy punch—all of us were drawn into a state of mirth & conviviality. Indeed, of the brilliancy of this assembly, too much cannot be said. I was sensible of some little delight by the mere fact of my being thought worthy of inclusion amongst this company. And the fairness of several belles of my class inspired me in particular. Surely I have done right to move beyond Sarah.

Buoyed by the brandy punch, I danced the country dances and had a wonderful time at it. I declared to Macon my warmth for the dancing, & he offered to teach me one of the politer dances when next I visit.

"A deftly performed minuet elevates the spirit of those observing as well as the spirit of the dancers," spake Macon justly.

"So true, Mr. Macon. 'Tis a portion of why many regard dancing as the rudiment of a genteel education," offered Wm. Davie, who was standing close by. My immediate thought was of the impracticality of my affording the expense of a dancing master, but 'twould have been mortifying to mention. I smiled & nodded agreement. I could not discern if Col. Davie intended condescension. But I thought that Col. John Whitaker, who was also standing there, smiled with a veneer that hid not his haughty disdain.

"I have heard our host say that one of the reasons Gen[l] Washington is so generally admired is his grace of movement," Macon said. "And that dancing is the source of this grace."

"I warrant that he is right in both conclusions," answered Col. Davie.

"Those whose feet have never been under the guidance of a dancing master, are apt to discover a want of grace in their every motion, nay, even when they sit or stand," said Col. Whitaker, looking directly at me. "Such folk will often seem over-burdened with limbs, which they know not how to use."

I own that if he intended to discomfit me, to intimidate me, to make me awkward, & to induce a want of confidence on my part, Whitaker succeeded admirably. For there was some justice in these remarks in general. And as applied to me in particular, no doubt.

Whitaker at that moment inhaled with genteel dexterity a tiny portion of snuff from his thumbnail, displaying the exquisitely decorative lid of his fine diminutive snuff box as he did so. His countenance then exhibited a smile expressing the frisson of pleasure from the tobacco. Or was it from the deftness & elegance of his insouciant one-handed performance? Mayhap both.

Momentarily Whitaker & Davie were drawn off from us by a group warmly discussing horses that excel at the heroic 4 mile distance. As casually as I could manage, I said to Macon: "Col. Whitaker looked direct at me when he spoke of those in want of a dancing master. Am I so conspicuously uncouth?"

Macon laughed heartily. "Not at all, Sterling. Whitaker is puff'd up with importance, his wealth, his fine horses, his always managing appointment to various offices & emoluments through his connexions. He takes any opportunity to place himself above others, and that lack of complaisance evinces that he is not a real gentleman. During the War, I always wondered that he wasn't a Tory. Pay him no mind."

"We both could use some punch."

With Macon's kind words, additional punch, and the exercise of a couple of country dances, I overcame the intimidation of Whitaker & many others in that brilliant company whose finery & deportment were surely superior to my own.

It was my good fortune that John Macon has an easy way with the fair sex. He introduced me to several pretty & eligible maidens. One was very easy of conversation, but she lives a good ten miles east of the Roanoke in Northampton Co. Above 40 miles from my home to hers makes an impossible barrier to courting.

Another girl shot an arrow through my heart with her look & her manner. There was a subtle delicacy to her movements & expressions. It was indeed a pleasure to observe her upon the dance floor. In some ways she reminded me much of Sarah. Her nose was like Sarah's, possessing a hint of aquilinity but still with feminine charm. Her frame was similar, tho' she was a little taller. Her hair was dark and curly—though not as tightly curled as Sarah's and with a glimmer of redness. Her movement perhaps possessed a refinement that Sarah's lacked, but once when she opened her eyes very wide like Sarah, it set my heart aflutter. On the other hand her eyes were blue and she had a light smattering of freckles on her sunburned face. From her sunburn and the moderately coarse weave of her clothes I knew her not to be above me in station. Alas, I was unable to gain an introduction.

Ah! I love women! And strong drink and dancing and music. Who could fail to find joy on such an occasion? Life is again full of adventure & possibility.

There was a great deal of discussion of the proposed Constitution. Most were against it, though Davie, John Whitaker, and a few well-heeled gents made some good points. They seemed confident it will prevail, even though sentiment amongst freeholders around here is overwhelmingly against it.

Already seven states have ratified. Only Massachusetts had a close vote (187-168). This seems insanity to me. Of the seven, only Massachusetts recommended amendments. The only encouraging news is that 6000 Pennsylvanian farmers signed petitions to their legislature asking that their ratification be overturned.

Mr. Jones believes South Carolina will be the eighth state. He said they think the federal government will help them with their war debt. Mr.

Davie assured us that the States' debts will not be assumed by the federal government. Let us hope Mr. Davie is correct since we in North Carolina have already borne much of the pain of reducing our debt.

Mr. Jones expressed disappointment that so few honest Whigs throughout our thirteen heretofore sovereign States are sounding the alarm over the loss of our freedom. It falls to New-York, Virginia, and North-Carolina.

John Macon observed that the meretricious opening of the constitution "We The People..." is most improper. The handful of delegates at Philadelphia who composed this dangerous document were mere representatives of the legislatures. By what right do they style themselves "We The People?" These so-call federalists expose their real intention of consolidating our thirteen republics into one huge empire, which must over time gravitate to despotic governance.

Mr. Jones' formidable home inspires awe! His mansion is the only house of which I am cognizant (including Mr. Johnson's long room) which could accommodate so large an affair primarily *indoors*. Large rooms with high ceilings. Elaborate and beautifully carved paneling and mantels. A huge, marvelous group of windows (the middle ones bowed out) look out over what constitutes their back yard: their own race track.

The front yard, from whence the Jones estate derives its name, The Grove, consists of an immense park of magnificent, majestic White Oaks. When I spoke to Mr. Jones of the beauty & serenity of this grove, he said:

"Mr. Shearin, I see that on yet another subject we are in perfect accord. I've told Mrs. Jones that when I die, she has the liberty of getting firewood for her own use from any of my land except this grove. These oaks are to be held sacred from the axe."

They also have a side yard which possesses a garden for *flowers* alone. Even now I can still smell the delicious musky fragrance of the milk-white roses in that garden. There are other plants of ornamental nature, such as mock orange & dogwood. The Joneses are truly paragons of gentility.

Toward the end of the evening, Mr. Jones invited me into his library to borrow another book. In this smaller room there was a fine-weave carpet—not on a table—but on the floor!

As I was selecting a volume to borrow, the angel who had wounded me with her arrow walked into the room. She greeted Mr. Jones and commenced pointing out to a young man books she had read. Alas, they made a likely couple. Her young man was tall & well-made, resplendent in clothes of a weave as fine as that of our host. Indeed, the elegance of his silk stockings & the fastidious care to his hair with rolls & plaited queue made me apprehend him as one of the first fashion.

She gestured I think to a volume of *Spectator*. But then to Shakespeare!

And then to a volume of Jonathon Swift. The young man, whose handsome face was unmarked with lines of thinking, looked incredulous.

" 'Tis true," volunteered the sensitive Mr. Jones. "Just last night, she and I chatted concerning Swift's 'An Argument Against Abolishing Christianity.' She begs a candle or even a dim rush-light and reads for hours after all the work is done and everyone else is asleep. She will go blind some day I fear."

The handsome Col. Davie came in with others, and overhearing what Jones said, jovially needled him. "So Wylie, now you are subverting even orphans with your deist ideas?"

"William, as different as are our views—political and religious—we both revel in the dessemination of ideas and knowledge. 'Tis little more than that. As I get older, I get less and less concerned with persuading anybody of anything."

Mrs. Jones entered right behind Col. Davie. "Colonel Davie, my husband has simply gravitated to the comforting illusion that if people broadly are educated they will properly value reason and liberty and he will not have to persuade. He ignores the truth that the simple, superficial people are always more fruitful. Ignorance ever multiplies faster than thoughtfulness."

"Mrs. Jones, you eloquently make the case for a more energetic government to guide the masses. You have a federalist heart," responded Col. Davie.

"I leave that debate to you gentlemen—as is fitting. Wylie dear, I need you for a moment." Mrs. Jones demanded her husband's attention to some detail and all the others moved along gaily.

I wondered if the angel might be one of the orphan girls Mrs. Jones keeps. That would be consistent with Col. Davie's remark & the modest simplicity of her clothing. 'Tis irrelevant: she seemed smitten with the handsome & self-assured young man by her side. I selected her Swift volume, and when Mrs. Jones was finished with her husband, I asked his permission.

"Why Swift, yes by all means," Mr. Jones replied. "'Whoever could make two ears of corn or two blades of grass to grow upon a spot of ground where only one grew before, would deserve better of mankind, and do more essential service to his country than the whole race of politicians put together.' Jonathon Swift was an excellent, nay, brilliant man."

Before thanking Mr. Jones for all of his kindness and hospitality, I asked him if the extraordinarily literate and pretty young girl was one of his wife's orphans.

"You think she is pretty do you?" he asked in a tone that possesst the possible intimation that he did not. "Yes, she's Mrs. Jones' star pupil."

Edwin Hodgkin's illustration of "The Grove" in Halifax, North Carolina.
(Courtesy of the North Carolina State Archives)

Another guest accosted him before he said her name, and then I had to bide my time just to express my gratitude and farewell.

That night we so slept in the arms of copious libations that we might have been in fine feather beds rather than on the ground under our wagons. A snort of whiskey in the morning eased our sore heads a little. While we were less than robust on our homeward journey, all agreed it was a very fine time. Nathaniel lamented not having known for a surety of invitations to such a brilliant ball; he would have brought his wife as she is not currently swelled with child.

Most of all, I am looking forward now to a world of possibilities, not depressed into the gloom of fainthearted guilt and thoughts of things implausible.

Monday 25 May

A most welcome drenching rain.

Sunday 7 June

 We have been models of industry these past two weeks to make up for my less than necessary trip to Halifax. Crops are mostly coming along well. The corn is looking vibrant & is well-weeded; stringbeans, excellent. On the other hand, I need more experience or better knowledge of cultivating yams. Papa blames the soil, but his approach has never been scientific. Mastering winter wheat is not a matter of falling off a log either.

 This morning my thoughts were upon the fair sex. Or should I say they kept returning to the fair sex in spite of me. Having resolved to be positive & pragmatical, I guided them to Patsy Williams, whom I have not seen in some time. I was working on a stump and trying to think of an excuse to visit her, when behold! There she was traipsing up to our place. With a basket of fresh-baked bread, no less! A most soothing sight for these eyes. She hath not that modesty of gait esteemed by some but rather moves with a certain… obvious feminine motion that inspires, to speak the bold truth, a lustful yearning.

 Though it was after ten o'clock, we had yet to break our fast. The aroma of that fresh-baked bread was irresistible. We roasted eggs in the hot ashes and made coffee (a special occasion) to go with the fresh bread. Nor did we skimp on the butter. What a fine breakfast!

 We engaged in a deal of idle chit chat. All very amiable. She could have had no doubt of how pleased I was to see her for I did not endeavor to hide the truth. She had on no short-gown, only her shift. Surely this was merely because of the warmth of the day, but I must own that she conjured, well, wanton thoughts in eminent degree.

 I told her about the gay time in Halifax. She seemed as full of glee at the telling as I was at being there. Patsy confessed that she has never been out of Warren Co. in her life, except for one memorable occasion when for some reason the whole family had gone on the trip to Halifax after a particularly good harvest.

 "A man works from sun to sun, but a woman's work is never done." An apposite description of any family with less than ten slaves. And of course Patsy's family has none. By my reckoning, her father's farm is a few acres shy of the fifty required to vote. When Patsy is not helping with farm work, cooking, or cleaning, she is harvesting cotton and flax, combing, spinning, reeling, boiling, spooling, warping, quilling & weaving cloth—then sewing garments from it. When a genius of the future invents machines to make cloth, he will be deified by womankind. He will introduce the concept of leisure to ordinary women.

 But alas, a cloth-making apparatus is just a dream. Thus Patsy was soon saying she must go. I did not want her to go. I remembered the Virginia newspaper acquired at Halifax. I knew she would enjoy hearing it read, even though it was nearly four weeks old now.

I sent Marmaduke to the river to check the fish baskets. (It would not do for him to hear me read the runaway slave notices.) After reading her the first of the four pages, I paused for a drink of water.

As I lowered my cup I saw her looking at me in an admiring, perhaps even...loving way. For once it was not that coquettish smile of hers with her head turned a little to the side. Her countenance was brazenly fixed upon me, not looking away. Our eyes kissed for several moments; then did our lips. She smelled alluring—as if she might have rubbed crushed lemon verbena upon her skin. We kissed and kissed and embraced and touched each other. This went on...was it minutes?...was it an hour? I was warm—no, afire—with yearning. I took off her cap, that her fine fair hair might fall upon her shoulders. I untied her apron and petticoat*; they fell to the floor.

She had on the freshest, nicest cotton shift I had ever seen her wear. With merely the sheer cotton between her voluptuousness and me, the touching drove me wild. Her breasts felt full and beautiful. I would have killed to see them & touch them flesh to flesh. I slipped the shift off over her head. Only at this point did Patsy say something like "Sterling, this isn't right. We cannot do this."

How could we do any other? All the water in the ocean could not douse this fire. She did not resist at all as I ushered her down onto my bed. She spread her legs for me. Delicious, wanton sin. Voluptuous. Like a luxurious feather bed. Like Mother Earth. I sigh now as I recall it.

We were dressed and somewhat composed when Marmaduke returned with fish for her. I rode her most of the way to her home on Aristotle. We talked hardly at all. But when I bid her adieu with a kiss, I felt close to her. My heart fluttered all afternoon. The axe and the hoe floated effortlessly in my hand.

Sun' 14 June

I rode over to Patsy's last night with some game and supt with them. They insisted I accompany them today to hear a preacher speak at Person's Ordinary. I am as deist as Jones & more so than Macon, but since no one possesses all of the truth and it was an excuse to be with Patsy, I agreed.

---

* petticoat at this time meant skirt.

Unbeknownst to Mr. Williams, the speaker turned out to be a well-educated Presbyterian, a teacher, physician, and farmer from Guilford Co. And a delegate to the Hillsborough convention. Dr. David Caldwell announced that South-Carolina had become the eighth state to ratify the proposed constitution.

He insisted this federal constitution should be analyzed with reference to the lengthy declaration of rights that is part of North-Carolina's 1776 constitution. He insisted especially that North-Carolina's tradition of religious tolerance and diversity be guarded. (I have heard Macon boast to a Virginian that North-Carolina never entertained the notion of an established church in 1776, whereas Virginia nearly established one.)

A surprisingly edifying and rational speaker. Not the Bible-thumping Baptist I had anticipated. Williams and others are struggling to get a church organized in this part of the country; Dr. Caldwell was not tailor-made to their purposes.

Patsy and I had no time alone, and I am getting behind with the farm work.

Sunday 28 Jun

Warrenton is nearly half as big as Halifax now and half the distance; hence Kenchen & I decided I should take our mid-summer trading there during court session.

I went by the Williams on the way to see if I could do any trading for them. I think if Patsy's father were more industrious, he could have raised himself. He was napping after breakfast with a whiskey jug by the bed. It gave me a chance to speak with a modicum of privacy to Patsy. I asked her if she could come over for Sunday breakfast again. She gave me a sly mistrustful smile. I promised to read her something interesting from the Jonathon Swift book. She said she might try in a teasing way—but that I should court her at her home.

Trading was fair. I obtained necessities for produce and had a shilling credited to me & two to Kenchen at Mr. Person's store in the bargain.

Nath' Macon & two of his slaves were working on the Warrenton Academy with one of Hawkins' slaves. A good example of why he is admired by many besides me. He confided to me that there is a rumor: Some unnamed black saw men fitting Kenchen's & Isham's description in the vicinity where Abner Whitaker was found in the same time frame.

Plausible: It was near their homes. Whose negro spoke thus? (Nearly all the freed ones are around Halifax.) Of what value would this be in court?

'Tis probably merely some effort to blacken their character, their reputations. Who might be behind it? Caleb Brown?

On the other hand, Macon has heard through the slave grapevine that Hawkins' guest, a Mr. Robert Goodloe Harper, had bitter words with Abner Whitaker. Will the sheriff get wind of this information?

Sun' 5 July

Patsy did not come. I am beset with doubt as to what I should do. I reckon that I should court her at her home—though the limitations to our pleasure there make me prefer it here instead. If another swain should approach her seriously and marry her, it would pain me to no end. I am sensible that some deep residue from my relationship with Sarah restrains me from feeling unbridled love. I do not trust myself to act decisively.

It seems Marmaduke suffers no such indecision. He is asking me about marrying Papa's slave Fanny. I have written him a pass for all of Saturday & Sunday next.

Sun' 12 July

'Duke sang all day Friday as we weeded corn & picked butterbeans. Eager & energetic after a full day's work, he took off for Papa's with good portions of butterbeans, fish, and high hopes.

Patsy came this morning! With her fine baked bread. With 'Duke not around, we were kissing in no time. As before, touching her is like striking flint so that fire is emitted & the dry kindling blazes. But she resisted with religious-tinged protestations of sinfulness.

We drank a good bit of hard cider with the bread. Soon I had her out of her shift & in my bed. After the flood of physical intercourse, we lay together for awhile naked—though she pulled her shift up to cover most of her. Pleasure beyond compare followed by this easy closeness. I must marry her.

Sun' 19 July

On a lark late yesterday, I went over to Patsy's with some venison; I was hoping she would invite me to stay to supper. It was with a gratified smile that she introduced me to another suitor. Her father seemed very fond of him and emphasized that he was a member of the church they were starting. His manners were not handsome. This Baptist blade had the audacity to ask me if I thought my brothers killed the murdered man. I expressed some umbrage, and Patsy came to his defense to the extent of saying Isham's temper was known.

I quitted their place abruptly; ceremony is not my talent. I headed for the river (rather than directly home) with the thought of cooling my hot body & head with a swim. Before I got there I realized it was getting too dark & turned back homeward. Just then I was hailed by a fellow in the distance laboring under the weight of a saddle & bags.

As I approached I saw by his fine clothes & superb saddle that he was a prosperous gentleman. He introduced himself as John Taylor of Caroline Co., Va. He was on his way to visit his ailing father-in-law John Penn of Williamsboro.* His horse broke its leg in fording the Roanoke—a desperate endeavor even when the river is as low as it is now.

It sounds as tho' he came across at the neck haunted by Mordecai's ghost. Several years ago a runaway slave by the name of Mordecai (or '*Mor*deky' as most pronounce it) died mysteriously attempting to ford the Roanoke. It is not clear whether he drowned or hit his head on a rock in trying to cross, but what everyone remembers is that he was found on the north bank of the neck with his knife clutched so tightly in his hand that he had to be buried with it. Many blacks believe his ghost lives under the huge rocks evident in the river when it is low & that he is capable of using his knife on whites who are particularly abusive to slaves.

I carried Mr. John Taylor home for the night and before long found him to be an especially engaging guest. Various & extensive were the conversations that filled the measure of his visit. He was as much a lover of music & literature as I am. A very successful lawyer & planter, yet not the least condescending in regards to the humble home & bed I shared with him. There was not a tincture of hauteur in his character, tho' his manners were pleasingly dignified.

The news he carried was not good. Virginia has ratified the constitution in a very close vote. Mr. Taylor was suspicious that Robt. Morris, the stockjobber [financier] who made a vast fortune off the Revolution and who just happened to be in Richmond for the convention, may have greased the palms of crucial delegates. Quite a coincidence that the Pennsylvanian Morris should be in Richmond at that critical juncture.

---

* John Penn (1740-14 Sep 1788), signer of the Declaration of Independence. Williamsboro, near present-day Henderson, NC, flourished until it was bypassed by the railroad; little remains there today except North Carolina's oldest wood-frame church (1758).

New-Hampshire also ratified by a slim margin. Both states proposed amendments, but as Mr. Taylor said, "It is imperative that New-York & North-Carolina hold out to force the new government to add amendments guaranteeing our rights."

After supper my guest did an interesting thing; He cut a small dogwood twig and with my hammer beat on one end of it to fray that end into something of a brush. Then he commenced to clean his teeth with it, finally swishing with apple brandy. He claims this regimen is beneficial to teeth & gums. I am inclined to emulate him henceforth.

Mr. Taylor is also a keen student of agriculture as a science. He had advice for me in growing sweet potatoes and a useful approach to creating a red cedar hedge as effective, durable fencing. My farm will benefit from fencing as my livestock multiply.

Mr. Taylor thumbed through my volume of Jonathon Swift with "property of Wylie Jones" inside the cover. We discussed our admiration for both Swift & Jones. Indeed, he has letters for Wylie Jones connected with their shared goal of North-Carolina rejecting the constitution.

I was delighted to be able to contribute to nature's harmony, for Mr. Jones is to rendezvous with John Macon tomorrow on their way to the Hillsborough convention.

Toward the end of our exceedingly agreeable evening, I appositely observed that Swift's line "If heaven had looked upon riches to be a valuable thing, it would not have given them to...a scoundrel" was not supported by the example of Messrs. John Taylor and Wylie Jones.

He responded that only in America would one find such a literate yeoman farmer. "Indeed, I'm reminded of what my friend, the famous Mr. Jefferson, the very one who was formerly Gov. of Virginia & author of the Declaration, is want to say on this subject. Something to the effect that only in America does one find farmers who can read Homer."

The acceptance of such a fine gentleman assuages in some measure my disappointment with Patsy.

Mon 20th July

I fed my guest the best I had to offer and rode him over to John Macon's. John did not have a suitable horse to sell him either and so I lent him Aristotle to ride to Warrenton. Nathaniel will fetch him for me next Saturday when he labors on the Academy building.

Mr. Jones arrived, and I returned his book with profuse thanks. He is suggesting that the anti-federals refrain from debating at the convention.

The topic has been thoroughly thrashed; people often talk of nothing else. Jones has assessed that the anti's have a two to one majority. "Let's save the taxpayer by simply voting and going home."

Sunday 16 Aug'

It seems initially that Mr. Jones' plan for a frugal convention might obtain. For a while, Iredell & Davie simply talked unanswered. But apparently some anti-federalists considered that Iredell had hired a man to take down and publish the proceedings and so felt compelled to express our side. Dr. Caldwell was one of them. Wm. Goudy of Guilford and Joseph MacDowell of Burke ably expressed the Whig mistrust of government.

In the end ratification of the Constitution was overwhelmingly rejected 183-83. We remain free & independent!

Also, Jones & Macon hired a teacher for Warrenton Academy while in Hillsborough.

I resolved after the disappointment at Patsy's and the inspiration of John Taylor to be the epitome of diligence. Marmaduke complains I will kill us both. I goad him that he has a wife now that needs purchasing. We have accomplished much in terms of skins & raw lumber to be sold. Tobacco is looking fair, but corn could benefit from rain.

And then today came an invitation to sup next Saturday with Patsy's family.

Chapter Six

Sunday 23 Aug' 1788

Patsy was cordial. We were never alone except for a few moments. I asked her about her Baptist suitor. She owned that she had attempted to inspire a degree of jealousy. She admitted having hoped I would be a more ardent suitor, considering the liberties I had taken.

"There is some justice in your complaint, Patsy," I responded. "But please rest assured that I in no way intended to use you ill. Indeed, I have missed you very much. Very much."

She favored me then with a charming smile, perhaps a little coy, but encouraging enough. That little sideways tilt of her head as she smiles at me somehow frames the femininity of her lips & her cheeks with just a little suggestion of wanton thoughts…either her own or her insight into mine. I am not sure I could say which.

I continued with my excuse that a fledgling farm demands constant attention, an excuse with more than a color of truth to it. I wish that we could have had more private converse. I do not know her as well as I would like.

Marmaduke has had a falling out with his wife. This is not all bad in light of the exigencies of drought: We both make trip after trip with buckets of water to irrigate the corn and garden crops lest we lose them. We have been doing this by moonlight after working tobacco by day. (Need to make a second neck yoke this winter*; the one we have fits me poorly.)

Sun' 30 Aug'

Yesterday a light rain fell at last. More is wanting, but 'twas sufficient to render me more hopeful.

I carried a watermelon over to Patsy's and visited for an hour. I invited her over for dinner next Sunday; she countered by inviting me to a church barbecue instead.

Mon' 7 Sept'

The church barbecue was quite pleasant—until the end. An excellent attribute of Christianity is the encouragement of people to be good to one another. Neighborly folk.

---

* Neck yokes were made to facilitate carrying two buckets of water or other burdens of nearly equal weight and were made to fit different size people.

Towards the end, Patsy and I went for a stroll. Our intercourse was the essence of amiable conversation. Indeed, I could not remember Patsy ever being so flattering to me as on this occasion.

We strolled by a pretty bevy of the bright yellow fall-blooming wildflowers, tickseed I think they are called, & I exclaimed to Patsy on the brilliancy of the yellow that nature had produced. "'Tis wondrous after the August drought, Patsy, don't you think? How good-looking they are!"

"Sterling, have I ever told you how very good-looking *you* are...with your curly hair & your trim physique?"

Who could not smile at such a declaration?

"And there. You are too slow to smile, but when you do it is so charming."

Our stroll having carried us to some degree of privacy, nothing could have been more of an inducement to take her into my arms & kiss her right there & then. And so we continued doing for some moments, until Patsy loosed my embrace & asked:

"Sterling...do you care for me?"

"Yes, Patsy. I can easily say that I do. Have I given you reason to think otherwise? Otherwise than expresst by my present caresses?"

"Well...no. And well...Sterling, I think that I am with child."

I was utterly thunderstruck. Emotions ran thru' all my vital frame, as if the lightning had come with the thunder. This I warrant is what our French allies would have styled a *coupe de foudre*. I was unable to speak.

How I would have wished to consider this circumstance for a while. Was I ready for marriage? Was Patsy's character fully known to me & of optimal quality?

Yet if Patsy and I are to marry and spend our lives together, it would be unseemly to poison the beginning of our marriage thus. For the act of extended deliberation would express a half-heartedness on my part that would be profoundly hurtful to Patsy.

I endeavored to vanquish my heavy heart and my mixed stew of feelings. With as much equanimity as I could muster I spoke:

"Patsy...dearest, will you be my wife?"

After a pause that was disconcertingly long, she broke into a very big smile and hugged and kissed me, and alas, said "Yes."

Later I attempted to dwell upon the many positive and pragmatical facets of this marriage. There are many. Still, I will delay the wedding a month to ensure that she truly is with child. To ensure 'tis no invention.

Sunday 13 Sept^r

We have debated making the long trip up into Virginia to Petersburg to sell tobacco and the scant produce we will have this fall. Their market is larger and on a better waterway. Our more southern produce will be a bit ahead of theirs. Macon says we may have to pay tariffs since we have stayed out of the union. If we must pay extra tax, then we will go to Halifax as usual.

I go to see Patsy Saturday next. If she is verily pregnant, we will plan for our marriage.

Thursday 17 Sept^r

Marmaduke awakened me late last night. He had been bitten on the back of his leg by a cottonmouth. I tried to suck what of the venom I could out of his wound. I tried to reassure him and get him to stay still and then rode to Mrs. Walker's. I arrived before the rooster announced the dawn and had to awaken them. Since we did not have the snake to use his fat, she gave me a fermented poultice made from crushed chestnut bark and leaves. She also gave me thyme to add to a sorrel broth.

Marmaduke has been deathly sick. I have kept him still and made him drink much sorrel broth and spring water. As I write this, I believe he has rounded the corner. God's teeth! I would have mourned him and missed him. We are both sorely relieved.

It seems he was returning from a midnight visit to a girl on Mr. Person's plantation several miles east. I had no idea he even knew any of the Persons' negroes. Apparently, his "marriage" is over.

Many a master would discipline a slave for slipping off. But Marmaduke generally puts in as hard a day's work as I do with a little prodding. I cannot blame him for wanting a life beyond working. I am too glad he will live to be harsh with him.

Sunday 20 Sept^r

Well, I am to be a married man come October. And surely the better for it. We will carry our produce to market early and once that is done, we will be married at her house.

'Duke tells an interesting detail about his lady friend at Person's plantation. She has lately been given the care of a light-skinned young mulatto boy. The boy had been bought from a free black man near Halifax (the sale being forced by the hardship of our lack of rain).

The interesting part is how the black seller acquired the light-skinned pickaninny. The boy was *given* as a newborn to the black master by none other than Caleb Brown!

Sunday 4 Oct^r

Ready money was scarcer this fall. The schooners buying in Halifax mostly sell to bigger boats in Norfolk; thus our prices are reduced by union tariffs in Virginia.

I had more tobacco to sell than last year but less of everything else. My total profit was barely £28. (Hope to raise a little with wood and skins later.)

When I went to Mr. Jones to pay some of what I owe on Marmaduke, I had a fine surprise. There was a note of thanks from Mr. John Taylor.

Dear Sir [Sterling],

I wish to thank you earnestly for your hospitality at the time of my dire circumstance. You were the essence of kindness & generosity. The trusting loan of your only horse without recompense obliges me in particular. Allow me to add that I enjoyed your company beyond measure. Self-educated farmers such as yourself, men whose property may be modest but whose intelligence is as expansive as your own, these give me faith that our grand republican experiment has wings.

I surreptitiously measured your front window opening and commissioned our excellent friend Mr. Jones to have a window with glass panes done for your home. Please accept it as a token of my gratitude.

Yr mst obedient & humble servant,
John Taylor

My heart swelled with pride. I am blessed.

I paid Mr. Jones £18 on Marmaduke. (Next fall I will be paying 5% on the balance of £20 that I still owe him.) The other £10 was sorely needed since the corn yielded so little. I did acquire two very fine hens that can set sixteen eggs each.

Also purchased a looking glass as a wedding present for Patsy. Mama and Papa have one, but it is nearly two years since I had seen myself. Produces a peculiarly queer sensation. Thanks to nature's God that men are not required to be handsome. Patsy says I am handsome, but I doubt her. I do think she likes the curl of my hair. Perhaps also the leanness & muscle earned by honest hard work.

This afternoon I put freshly washed straw in the clean ticking, tightened the bed ropes, and generally tried to tidy our home for Patsy. Following advice from Mama, I have strewn pennyroyal about the floor. It provides a nice mint smell, and many claim it repels ticks and chiggers—an exceedingly useful function.

Patsy has seemed happy on each occasion when I have seen her since our engagement, and that makes me happy. She is a fetching belle when she smiles. We marry Sunday.

Sunday 25 Oct'

Matrimony is a checkered surface, a mingling of pleasures and regret. During the first week we enjoyed episodes of physical intimacy. Patsy manifested her culinary skills and took pleasure in becoming the mistress of our home. 'Tis a finer abode than she has known. (I am proud that our glass window will so lighten our house on cold winter days). She re-arranges what we have, but I confess that the proverbial woman's touch is largely a blessing.

Yet in our second week of marriage, Patsy was beset by sickness, especially in the mornings. Her mood grew as sour as her stomach. I began to miss that solitude I had previously enjoyed in abundance.

Even now I bring my journal, quills, and ink well to the banks of the Roanoke to write and think peacefully. Alas, Kenchen says such tribulations are familiar to him in his four years of marriage. 'Twill encourage me to waste no daylight hours lounging about the house.

Following John Taylor's suggestion, I have started an incipient cedar hedge. I have extended a taut rope line between two sizeable red cedars. Birds perching upon the line will plant many cedar seeds. I will help the hedge along by transplanting a few medium size cedars as time allows. Taylor suggests topping them at shoulder height to encourage dense growth. He has me convinced that—for the patient farmer—such hedges are more durable and less labor-consuming than normal wood fencing. I cannot be terribly patient tho' unless I delay acquiring more livestock.

Sun' 29 Nov'

Patsy's wretched illness has passed. Hallelujah! I think we progress. At times Patsy possesses that sweetness of disposition which any man would wish in his consort.

I resolved a dilemma rightly yesterday and I own that I feel satisfaction. Three cows wandered in. One had Nath'. Macon's brand; the other two were younger and did not have brands. By convention the unbranded ones belong to me, but in truth, they are likely Macon's cows. I returned all three cows to him and enjoyed his gratitude. (Macon initially insisted I keep the unbranded ones.) The respect of your friends and the respect you feel for yourself cannot be over-valued. May I ever have the sagacity to do the honorable action.

20 Dec^r

I had hoped Macon's fine logical mind would rescue me from the throes of melancholia on this cold, gray winter's day. Verily, his truth made it worse.

It started when Patsy spied me staring at Sarah's bare-leaved dogwoods. She testily asked why I left those two trees standing in the middle of the field as if it were something a puddin' head would do.

"'Twill be plain to thee come the blooms in April" I replied mildly, endeavoring both to ameliorate her spirit and hide my emotional attachment to Sarah's memorial. But as a few more words passed, a resentment built in me.

The thought that I might not be the babe's father had crept into my mind more than once. I do not think Patsy bled at our first encounter and thus was likely no virgin. Her Baptist suitor seemed ardent. Against my better judgment, I gave vent to these fears. Her ways of answering soothed me little. The altercation grew warm & left much bitterness betwixt us.

A few days later I apologized profusely for my doubts. I made considered efforts to be a kind husband. Matters improved briefly. Then two days later another argument erupted over something paltry. I was surely blameless in this one. Her disposition is wickedly mercurial.

I went to Macon's in hopes of sympathy and guidance. But Macon says his relationship with Hannah possesses what our French allies would call *"joie de vivre."*

"Mrs. Macon hath the talent of growing more amiable the longer I know her," quoth he.

I thought of the fluid interaction between Sarah and myself. Unlike Kenchen, Nathaniel describes matrimonial bliss as one part work and four parts natural and divine affection. Indeed he claims he would never marry again should he lose his wife. The only issues over which they contend are her desire for a finer home like the Hawkins & Persons. And he is even now stocking up materials to build such.

I had hoped he would speak more like Kenchen; to wit, marriage involves many tribulations and is made good as is your farm by ardent effort. He did not. And this day is the grayest of winter days. My melancholia mounts & my wits grow more disordered.

I know not what to do but to throw myself into clearing land of trees and stumps by day and making useful items from animal skins (moccasins &c.) by candle light. Hard work and prosperity may salvage my spirit.

Chapter Seven

Sunday 25 Jany 1789

    Time, shared purposes, persistent industry: These elements improve our lives. Patsy has mellowed as she has swelled. We have worked together to produce a fertile raised bed for her kitchen garden. The fish-baskets yield fish enough with little labor so that some may be used as an excellent green manure—especially catfish & herring. We both anticipate fondly the results with the herb seeds we are acquiring from connexions.
    Patsy has taught me to make tolerable coffee from chestnuts. She enjoys my reading to her some evenings from the Shakespeare volume I borrowed last month from Macon. As a matter of course, I pause to clarify the words & story for both Patsy and Marmaduke. (In truth, I have difficulty understanding this 200-year-old language myself.)
    'Duke is a contented servant I believe. He relishes Patsy's considerable improvements to our cuisine even more than I. Duke would do anything for a serving of her pudding, even this time of year when there is no berry sauce to go on't. And I suspect him of getting on with more than one neighbor's wench by night. I am making him some high lacing leather boots for when the snakes come back out. Last summer he was without moccasins from frost to frost.
    Actually I believe they enjoy Shakespeare more than do I. His characters are always ruled by fate and never win or lose by their own cleverness or effort. But Shakespeare can turn a phrase.

Sunday 19 Apr'

    I await the birth of our child. Mama, my sisters, Mrs. Walker, & all the women of the vicinage are attending Patsy—all sewing without ceasing. I work with my younger brother Daniel on his reading. At almost sixteen, he should be doing better: He is an obtuse student, lacking the spring that moved Sarah to eagerness.
    If 'tis a boy, we will name the babe John for Patsy's father, for my grandfather, & for John Taylor. I wrote Mr. Taylor a long letter of thanks and requested him to kindly share with me any further thoughts—especially agricultural advice—which he might care to. I was exceedingly pleased that this superb gentleman condescended to do so. He has it on good authority that James Madison of Virginia will bring forth amendments to the Constitution so that North-Carolina may safely enter the federation of States. And he

cautioned against night soil,* which is a temptation with so much of our abject clay soil.

We now have over thirty-eight acres cleared for cultivation. By this time next year I hope to acquire oxen & plough and be able to plough ten acres of it rather than planting everything in hills amongst stumps. The plowed fields of established planters with numbers of slaves are beautiful to behold. I aspire to no less. As Macon says, North-Carolina is a meritocracy, where a man can improve his life by his efforts.

Sis' just came out and said Patsy was cursing me so mightily that she was sure to be a Baptist no longer. A good sign suggesting no fear of dying.

Back to

Monday 20 April

A healthy boy. We are blessed. What a fascinating little creature. I had only two shillings for Mrs. Walker. She agreed to take 2 more shillings worth of corn when it comes in.

Sunday 19 Jul' 1789

On the road to Warrenton I overtook Mr. Person, Benj. Hawkins, & one Mr. Robt. Goodloe Harper of S.-Carolina. They were less than genial. Perhaps these wealthy "federal" gentlemen view me as beneath them. Have I given offense to Mr. Person by way of Marmaduke's dalliance or to Mr. Hawkins by boldly debating him in Halifax? Or something to do with Sarah? Or are we Shearins slandered behind our backs as the probable murderers of Abner Whitaker?

I had hoped that malignant suspicions of that nature had died away. The sheriff no longer seems to be investigating. I wished to inquire of Mr. Harper in some manner regarding Abner Whitaker. Little is known of Mr. Hawkins' foreign guest hereabout. I wish the rumor of his harsh words with Whitaker at that previous visit were more widespread. Dampt as my spirit was by their coolness, I chose to leave the whole subject alone. Wisdom or timidity?

Before we reached Warrenton however, Harper himself asked "Have they found the rogue who killed poor Abner Whitaker? He was such an excellent & eligible fellow."

Harper possesses a self-assuredness bordering on pomposity. Quite the macaroni with his hair rolled on the sides, fine silver buckles on his cobbler-made shoes, fine cotton shirt, coat & breeches of excellent weave. Indeed he

---

* "Night soil" referred to human feces used as fertilizer. It has been associated with intestinal parasites or "worms", a common affliction of the time.

was dressed finer than Person & Hawkins, tho' some intuition suggests to me he may be more affectation than substance. 'Tis not rare for such dandies to be dressed to the very edge of their finances.

He went on to assert that North-Carolina must cease its foolishness and join the American union. He seemed to take satisfaction in predicting the U. States will be a great empire. By the way he speaks the word "empire," I know he has not the heart of an Honest Whig.

Person & Hawkins seemed confident that the convention called for November in Fayetteville will ratify—if the Federal Congress follows thru' with a Bill of Rights. They noted that having to pay tariffs on all our goods flowing into or thru' Virginia would be devastating to our economic well-being; thus remaining outside would simply be untenable. I fear they are right. I can only hope the Bill of Rights is well-fashioned.

In Warrenton I saw copies of the debates of the convention in Hillsboro where North-Carolina rejected the Constitution. They are dominated by the pronouncements of Iredell & Davie, who paid for their publication. I warrant not a disinterested expenditure.

Trading in Warrenton was tolerable. Acquired nails for building 'Duke's house and a corn crib. If weather continues this good, my crop will justify a separate corn crib.

Today I asked Kenchen if he knew anything of my having offended either Person or Hawkins. He said I "likely allow my imagination too big a pasture to roam in"—imagining slights where mere indifference prevails.

Sunday 18 Aug

The dog days are upon us. The humid heat oppresses. Marmaduke is sickly, and our cow's bag is badly swelled.

Patsy berates me for not pushing myself & 'Duke harder that we might rise in the world. She claims I spend too much time reading. (How rarely I make a journal entry now-a-days.) I would never have imagined that she would berate me as lazy; compared to her father I am a Trojan. I grow sensible that Patsy is more ambitious than I am, and in a different way.

I have felt close enough to her to be intimate only twice in the four months since little John's birth. In the field the other day I thought of suggesting taking a nude swim like Sarah & I did—perhaps even followed by the dark musky deeds after the swim. I am sure Patsy would scowl at my suggestion of the swim; she views bathing (as many do) as less than conducive to good health. But I totally submerge in the creek as often as once per week in the hot months and I am rarely ill. I own it is quite a pleasing, fresh feeling.

My relations with Patsy are a far cry from the easy physical closeness & fluid intercourse with Sarah. Perchance when her figure is tidy again she will display more penchant to share herself with me.

Our crops thrive, especially the corn planted down near the Roanoke. In July I would swear you could literally *hear* it grow. My first acre of flax even shows promise.

Sunday 13 Sept'

My setter had puppies and Marmaduke asked for one of his own. When I said "sure," he seemed disproportionately gleeful. Curious, I engrossed him today in conversation as we picked cotton.

It happens that 'Duke had only been in Halifax a short while (not above 3 months) before I bought him. He had had some difficulty making friends with Jones' slaves. A little stray dog he adopted was his only close confidant. The overseer had killed his dog one day in a fit of anger. Marmaduke had attacked the overseer & was subsequently whipped severely. Hence the poison betwixt them.

Jones apparently bought 'Duke from a trader who acquired him near Edenton. He assumes his mama is still there. He revealed that his mama was born in Africa, where she was a slave in the tribe to which she belonged. African warriors from the coast attacked & captured the whole tribe. They were marched a long distance to the coast. While they were held there, the rumor spread that they would be sold to white devils who would eat them. They were convinced that this was so, because it was said these white devils had taken off great multitudes & none had <u>ever</u> come back. He said his mama said that as long as she lived she would remember her relief when she got to North-Carolina & observed many older blacks, who obviously had not been eaten. She cited this to him more than once as a lesson in not believing every tale you hear.

Sunday 18 Oct'

Through Mama's influence, we went to Halifax to trade the week *preceding* the horse races. Less temptation of drink, gambling, fights, &c. A good woman is a salubrious influence.

Concerning Papa's influence, I am less certain. He found what he regards as an excellent bargain in a fourteen-year-old male slave & persuaded me to buy. I am now 48 pounds in debt (£15 to Mr. Jones for 'Duke at 5%; £33 to Col. Whitaker for Dick at 6%). I am not easy with the debt or the difficulty of managing a new slave. Nay, it leaves me **very** uneasy. But there is no other way to fully develop my farm & progress beyond subsistence.

    I was sorely embarrassed just after the transaction. Nay, it is more apposite to say I was mortified. Mr. Person confronted me roughly over Marmaduke sneaking on to his plantation and cavorting with his slaves. This transpired in front of Col. Whitaker & other respectable folk. If it were his design to heighten his intimidation of me, he completely succeeded; the incident has plagued my mind ever since.

    Mr. Jones was tolerant of my not paying off 'Duke. —On the subject of our staying out of the union, Mr. Jones says it now appears impossible. It is too dear for us to pay tariffs to trade with Virginia, or to pay tariff on goods simply going thru' Virginia (as most must, given our small ports). Furthermore, Gen. Washington's administration seems mild thus far. A Bill of Rights appears eminent.

    Jones did not permit himself to be nominated as a delegate to the Fayetteville convention. Numerous Federalists (Davie, Col. Whitaker, Benj. Hawkins, & Solomon Green) were elected.

    Jones lent me *Notes on the State of Virginia* by Thomas Jefferson, the author of The Declaration of Independence. Like John Taylor, Jones is also acquainted personally with Jefferson and holds him in very high regard. Macon & Hawkins have made mention of this popular new book, and thus I anticipate the free moments I may read therein.

    Baby John & Patsy are in good health. Patsy's garden infinitely enhances the quality of our repasts. No one yet hath said that John in any way resembles me. Nor do I think it. Yet he is a precious babe.

Sunday 1 Nov[r]

    On Friday, Patsy & I had coarse words over some small matter and later in the day I did something I hoped never to do. I whipped the new slave Dick.

    I felt it degraded us both. It stirred my insides fiercely, tho' I could not allow this to be perceived. He had lied to me I discovered; & then cursed me when confronted.

    Still I secretly wished Patsy or Marmaduke would volunteer that I was justified. Indeed, last night Patsy did so in an oblique manner by saying that she was glad to see I was man enough. Then she initiated intimacy for the first time since our wedding.

Naturally I have kept a sharp eye on Dick. Both he & 'Duke have watched their p's & q's since the whipping. I can envision becoming the type of slave master I have ever abhorred.

Late today in Jefferson's excellent book, I encountered these painful truths which few reflective men would contradict.

> *"There must doubtless be an unhappy influence on the manners of our people produced by the existence of slavery among us. The whole commerce between master and slave is a perpetual exercise of the most boisterous passions, the most unremitting despotism on the one part, and degrading submissions on the other.*
>
> *"Deep-rooted prejudices entertained by the whites; ten thousand recollections, by the blacks, of the injuries they have sustained; new provocations; the real distinctions which nature has made; and many other circumstances, will divide us into parties, and produce convulsion, which will probably never end but in the extermination of the one or the other race."*

Sunday 8 Nov^r

I have had an extraordinary adventure. It fills me with equal portions of exuberance & agitation. Nay, foreboding or worry may be more nearly the word for that latter portion—at least till some time hath past. Yesterday is one cloudy autumn day which I shall never forget.

I rode over to a farm a little east of Person's Ordinary, endeavoring to trade skins for a linen wheel for Patsy. The farmer's wife insisted I negotiate with her husband, who was pursuing rumors of a bevy of wild turkeys. There being no tastier game than the turkey, I readily quitted her place to ride after the husband—with hopes of hitting two birds with one ball.

Tho' I found neither turkey nor the husband, I happened upon something else. I heard & was drawn to some heated talking, nay even shouting there in the dense forest. As I came closer, I detected the coarse voice of an angry man. Hopefully not the owner of the linen wheel I thought to myself. I dismounted Aristotle to approach cautiously. The words of warmest anger came from the other side of several large boulders there deep in the woods. Durst I intrude on such a scene? I climbed on to the largest boulder to peer over at what I might be walking into with very little welcome.

As I climbed the boulder I heard a scream, a scream of a girl or young woman. Reaching the top, I espied before me a man striking a young woman. He sent her sprawling with the back of his hand. He was large & well-made.

She seemed some little familiar, tho' from whence I had no idea. She moved to get up for he looked as tho' he might kick her. What a foul blackguard! Instinct drove me to grab a loose stone. His next blow knocked the slender young woman back to the ground.

In that instant I recognized her. The loose auburn curls, the delicate but freckled features, the fine blue eyes. It was her. She was the Jones' orphan, the one whom I had seen but that once, more than a year ago. My last thought of restraint evaporated: I pounced from the boulder & smote the back of the odious blackguard's head with all vigor. From equal portions of anger & fear of his greater size in a mere fist fight, I laid into him with every ounce of force. The villain fell to the ground. His tricorn fell off & there was blood on the back of his head.

He lay still there; I was relieved given his size. But then I feared that I might have killed him. My gut churned in turmoil. I turned him on his back, stone still in hand. He breathed but was not conscious.

I turned to her. Her lip bled and she appeared, well, beyond disconcerted… dazed. She covered her face with her hands. I offered my hand to help her to her feet & asked her if she were alright. As she stood she nodded affirmatively. She smoothed her garments, & attempted to regain her composure.

"I…I am surely in your debt, sir. I…thank you. I am mortified by this. I am embarrassed and ashamed."

"It is he who should be ashamed," I answered.

"I don't know what to say. I am ashamed, for he is my husband just above four months." She paused & opened her eyes very wide like Sarah used to do. "He should be ashamed…But this is the second time, so he clearly perceives no shame in it."

We stood there for several awkward moments, neither of us knowing what to do or say, both our wits in a degree of disorder. Her words "he clearly perceived no shame in it" brought to mind a phrase pregnant with co-incidence.

"I never wonder to see men wicked, but I often wonder to see them not ashamed," I said.

She looked at me with amazement in her countenance—beautiful, the more beautiful for her eyes seemed to look into me. I apprehend that none had looked at me in such a manner. I have never felt so visible.

"As Mr. Swift would put it," I appended.

"Swift…why…you have read Jonathon Swift. Such an impossible coincidence! You quote the very book. The very book I was reading yet again in the shelter of this great rock." She looked about her & managed to retrieve the familiar volume (which I later determined we both had borrowed from Mr. Jones) from whence it lay on the ground.

An expression of wonderment forced its way upon her traumatized face, engendered I reckon by the sensation of having found one who shared her peculiar interest. "You have read this?"

"Upon your recommendation, gentle lady," I answered cryptically. She looked at me with yet greater confusion.

I explained. "A year & half ago at Wylie Jones' Spring ball, I saw you in Mr. Jones' library. I overheard you speak of reading this book by Swift. Tho' I did not get to make your acquaintance, I thought you were sublimely charming. The beauty of an angel, yet with an intellect. At that juncture in my life, having lost someone dear to me, it lifted my spirit merely to know that such as you existed. Obviously I borrowed the very book from Mr. Jones & enjoyed it beyond measure."

She nearly swooned and held to the boulder with one hand. Was it what I said or the blows she had absorbed? I took her other arm to steady her.

She seemed to recover. We stood perilously close to an embrace and looked into each others eyes. I own I sighed a sigh of pleasure. Did I imagine that she did too? But then she shook her head, perhaps expressing disbelief.

She stepped back. She looked at her husband there on the ground. He was very still.

"Sir, I am not accustomed to such flattering & flowery words...Perhaps, Sir, at such a time as this, you use me ill. I'm sorry. I-I am in disorder; I am confused quite proper."

"Madame, I apologize. It is natural under these circumstances to be disconcerted, nay even distresst. And I did not wish to add to your distress with words less than complaisant. Perhaps...well, I apologize." I paused. "Still, none of my words were intended as flattery."

A silence lay between us. We both looked down. Then I spoke a bold truth.

"Tho' you be married to a man...a man of a vulgar aspect & tho' blood trickles from your lip, you are no less the vision of an angel to my eye."

It was not apposite for me to speak thus. She wiped at her chin with her bare fingers. I had no handkerchief to offer her; it descended upon me at that moment that I was no gentleman, nor ever would be.

"I...I do not even know you...To hear such sweet words from a stranger who has rescued me from...I feel as tho' I am in some strange dream. I have heard no good word from any quarter...since..." She looked down. Another awkward silence. Which drove me to blurt something else inappropriate:

"Alas, I would that I could be a part of some dream of yours. But were this a dream, it would not be my duty to inform you that I too am married. Yet this is a reality that I hope will place in proper context my praise of you."

"I pray you are married better," she muttered, almost to herself.

There followed another silence. I espied the villain, monitoring his unconsciousness. He had not stirred in the least. I began to wonder again had I done him mortal harm.

"What...what can I do to ameliorate your circumstance?" I asked, ignoring that fear.

She did not answer immediately. Then she started to cry. Through her tears she whispered "I've not heard such a...fine word..." She cried harder & I put my arm around her shoulders. "...such a word as *ameliorate* ...none such...since I left Mr. Jones' household."

She cried hard & I comforted her as best I knew how. Alas, after a few moments she recovered her composure & apologized profusely. I tried with little success to assure her that she had nothing for which to apologize. Then there was yet another awkward silence. We both looked at the ground & then we both looked at her assailant, her husband there upon the ground. She kneeled by him, her face expressing an admixture of concerns. We decided to lay him across his horse & carry him to their home.

I hoisted him with some difficulty upon his horse. His queue was caked with blood, but his breathing was steady. I grew hopeful that I had done no mortal damage to the villain. Yet surely he must rouse at any moment. There was considerable liquor on his breath.

I asked if she had been one of the Jones orphans just to make conversation, to calm myself as much as her. She replied affirmatively as she led the horse in the direction of home. I whistled for Aristotle and asked if she would like me to lead the horses & she ride Aristotle.

"I believe I am better off walking," she replied.

We walked in silence. Then I awkwardly asked "So you have been married just above four months?"

"Yes. Mrs. Jones and I both thought we had married me well. Asa makes a fine impression—tall, handsome, quite genial in public, two hundred acres, three negroes."

"I fear you valued yourself too little."

"Indeed?" she questioned. "An orphan with nothing in her pocket & modest appearance cannot have but modest expectations. We thought our expectations had been exceeded."

"Fie upon it. How can you speak in that strain? Ma'am, your pleasing appearance & your learning, why they would be agreeable to any man."

"How you do go on. You flatter me shamelessly." She colored still more & then shook her head. "I own I could warm to such rattling. 'Tis a pleasant change from being teased or criticized for my nose, for my many, many shortcomings. I am not so well-trained to manage a farmhouse as I should be. There is some justice to Asa's complaints. Our acres & slaves are steeply mortgaged. I suppose that justifies him driving me so hard."

I thought of my mounting debts. And indeed a skillful, diligent wife is essential to the economy of a farm. I did not know what to say. I glanced at Asa to ascertain whether he might be rousing. I knew not whether to worry more that his stillness implied permanent harm or that he might awaken angrily at any moment.

"Many tribulations are overcome with persistence and patience," I offered.

"You are right." she replied. We walked on a ways. She began to weep again silently.

"It will work out." I tried to reassure.

"Asa denies me any time of my own, *especially* for reading. I know 'tis not serviceable to the fortune of one such as myself. But can it not afford a woman an innocent entertainment?

"I own I fear he will destroy this book when he wakes unless I make it very plain to him it is Mr. Jones' property. I had kept it secretly. He can barely read and has forbidden me to have books. Unsuitable for women, he says, leading them to the devil. My every moment must be devoted to making cloth, tending the garden, leaving no stone unturned for our plantation to yield profit. While fully a quarter of his labor is lost to drink & gambling on cocks and horses."

She spoke through her tears. "It would all be bearable if it weren't for his scorn & roughness toward me. He even forbids me to sing. He claims my voice vexes him."

I put an arm around her, and she turned and cried upon my shoulder. I wished again I were a rich gentleman with the luxury of a clean handkerchief to offer her.

"How can I feel affection for a husband who is brutal to me and shows me no affection?" she asked thru' her tears. "And how can one live without feeling affection?"

"I feel perfect sympathy for what you are saying. It likely is not as bleak as it seems this moment."

"I shouldn't be pouring my heart upon you so. Sir, I am so sorry. I am abject. I am ashamed. I have…I've just been so alone…these months. —And you seem…you seem like…" She wanted the right word.

"Like a kindred spirit?"

"Why…yes. I think."

I said nothing for a moment. It was a moment that I had no desire to hurry.

"A phenomenon too rare," I almost whispered. "You do nothing wrong.

You speak but justice," I spake in the tenderest tones a man might utter.

"I own my want of some bit of kindness or sympathy these months has dampt my spirit so…I am not sure of what I am saying…& saying to you, a stranger."

She wiped her tears and regained her composure again & apologized yet again.

We resumed walking in silence. I tried to think of something comforting to say. "Unsettling events are doubtless a part of every life."

She said "yes" quietly & smiled just a little in appreciation of my casting it in that benign light. We walked on a little further & I asked how far it was to her home.

"Half a mile, maybe less."

"Should I be present when he wakes up, or gone?"

"Gone, I think."

"Will you be alright?"

"I think so. He will be more sober. I may tell him God smote him down for his conduct."

I chuckled. "I heartily hope that invention is a success. Such a belief could only improve his conduct. Perhaps I was God's agent & thus you do not dissemble." She almost smiled.

"I wish it were seemly for me to try to protect you." She looked me in the eye. "But in truth I am…" What I was thinking I could not say:—to wit, I am too moved by your presence to be around you, married as I am to my wife.

"Well…Ma'am, gentle lady, please allow me to bid you adieu."

With a touch of the gallant, I took her hand and touched it to my lips and then turned & mounted Aristotle. From my saddle, I saw her husband was starting to stir, weakly moving a hand toward his bludgeoned head.

"Wait, sir. What is your name?"

I looked down from Aristotle into her upturned countenance. How wonderful to have a portrait of her: she did not look away, nay she held my gaze. If ever I see her again, it would never be like this.

"Sterling Shearin." Aristotle was suddenly restless, intuiting perhaps that I really should be gone; I had to wheel him around sharply.

"If your need is dire enough, those at Person's Ordinary know where I farm."

"Mr. Shearin…do you know my name?"

I thought it might be better if I did not. I shook my head & murmured "no".

"Emily…Johnson."

Chapter Eight

Friday 1 Jan. 1790

 Mrs. Emily Johnson was in my mind continually. That is, until last week: little John got quite sick. His illness devastated both Patsy & me. We feared his death. Only now that he seems to recover do I feel the earth beneath my feet to be solid.

 I have kept close to home to keep watch on Dick, and thus mid-wife Walker was a great source of news. There has been no mention of anyone dying or pressing charges of assault over in the vicinage of the incident. I own that I am heartily relieved!

 North-Carolina has joined the Union & been among the first states to ratify a Bill of Rights, though Mrs. Walker knew little of their contents. Mrs. Walker said she had been called to Patsy's homeplace & that all her family had worms. I told her of Mr. Taylor's comments regarding night soil.

 Patsy & I converse little except about little John or farm matters. I suppose I have been somewhat withdrawn; my mind had been much occupied by the fair angel Emily Johnson until little John shook it loose.

 Patsy seems to take no notice. But then our fewer interactions are possessed of less asperity. She seems happy. She takes pleasure in ordering & ruling the household. She is better at commanding the blacks than am I; I perceive that it gratifies her.

 Hope to sell a little wood, some skins, and (for the first time) some smoked pork to reduce my debt. Increasing the productiveness of our farm and reducing my indebtedness: these must be my goals for 1790.

Sat^y 9 Jan '90

 Went hunting with the Macons and my brother Lewis. I got a 12-point buck.

 We enjoyed provocative conversation. I learned that the Bill of Rights contains no constraint upon the Federal government's power to tax, borrow, or regulate commerce. That tiny knot of men in congress can do any of that to us with a simple majority. And they do so without the accountability of the annual elections we use to keep our Carolina legislators in line.

 I brought up Jefferson's condemnation of slavery in his book, knowing that Nathaniel was reading it. John Macon commented that a few Whigs (he mentioned Joseph M'Dowall of Burke Co.) & Federalists spoke at Hillsborough & Fayetteville of the Constitution being a missed opportunity to do something about slavery.

I spoke boldly: "Our Country is peculiar for its understanding of and fondness for liberty. We have fought & bled for it. How can we indefinitely deny it to our negroes?"

"You are a puddin' head, Sterling" Lewis replied bluntly. "You talk as if negroes were our equals. Their minds are beneath ours. They need to be led. They were even more primitive where they came from than they are here. Besides, who could imagine developing the land here without them?"

"How could we live with them free amongst us after the history we have with them?" John Macon added. "Many the former master who had disciplined a slave might be found by the side of the road murdered."

"Half the worth of most prosperous folk is in their slaves. And the other half, their land, would be worth piddlin' little without the slaves. Sterling, this should all be obvious to you. Can you weigh nothing in common scales? Use your sense & get your head out of so many books." My pragmatical brother was irritated with me.

"Lewis there is much to recommend Jefferson's book. I agree with him and with Sterling that slavery is a cursed thing. That it is at root unjust. But you are right. If all the investment we have made in them is wiped away, we would be devastated. We would not be remotely able to provide for them. All but the most resourceful of them would starve." Nathaniel spoke reasonably.

"I know you are all right in all you say. But are you not troubled that we so easily become tyrants in our households much like the King Georges—the tyrants in government—we despise? And our slaves become sneaky, devious beings. Both we & they are degraded by this institution," I responded.

"Many young men who reflect at length have your same thoughts, Sterling. But freeing the slaves is simply beyond the realm of the possible & practical. Content yourself with being a benevolent master & good steward. We must confine our hopes & striving to what is possible." Nathaniel's calm words furnished a good benediction on the subject.

Nath' is acquainted with Emily's husband, Asa Johnson, but I had no opportunity to inquire further as Macon was anxious to get home to his ailing wife.

Wed^{y} 13 Jan.

Hannah Macon has died! We are bereft of a fair & noble lady. How will Nathaniel bear it? Patsy has made a corn-meal cake which I am about to carry over. How to console him? Cruel Providence.

Sunday 24 Jan'

Kenchen & Lewis are making haste to Halifax where a man named Reynolds is buying everyone's certificates for what the state gov't owes them for fighting in the Revolution. He is paying only five shillings on the pound but pays in gold or silver.

Kenchen is returning the Jefferson book to Jones for me. I have asked him to ask Jones to lend me something that his former ward, Mrs. Emily Johnson, would like.

Nath' Macon has been the stoic when I have been with him. I believe he may have already cried himself dry.

Friday 5 Feb^y

Kenchen sold his certificate (and traded two skins for some necessities for us). When he made my book exchange with Jones, he said Jones said there was something that smelled about Reynolds buying up all the certificates. Jones says Reynolds knows something we do not know.

Kenchen said Mr. Person made a point of confronting him about Marmaduke still sneaking on to his plantation. Person says he shot at him just the other night and that he best stop if he wants to continue breathing.

I have talked to 'Duke about this twice in stern terms. This is an embarrassment. How much worse if it became a mortal embarrassment?

Patsy says I ought to try whipping some sense into him. I have never whipped him, and I feel for his predicament. When I confronted him this time he said:

"Massa, she the one you gotta buy fo' me. Cain't live widout dat woman."

I started to bring up that he has been married one time already but I considered the fact that he knowingly risked his life—my wrath he fears not at all—to see this negress. After working hard dawn to dusk.

I grow sensible of a certain respect and, dare I say, affection that I feel for Marmaduke. I am tempted to try to trade Dick (who is often troublesome) for 'Duke's woman. 'Tis the only way I could afford to get her any time soon. I might be able to reduce my debt slightly: Dick should be worth 4, 5, or 6 pounds more. Except for chopping stumps & lumber, I can imagine her labor nearly matching the value of his.

Sunday 14 Feb^y

The book that Kenchen borrowed for me, *The Life & Opinions of Tristram Shandy*, is quite eccentric. The author Mr. Sterne is ever playing his reader—I am ever so far into the book & Tristram has yet to be born. 'Tis perhaps the central jest of the book that the author cannot explain anything simply, but must make explanatory digression after explanatory diversion. Alas, remember Tristram? But it has made me laugh & diverted me from— What am I to do about 'Duke, whose bed was empty in the middle of last night?

Sunday 7 March

I rode over to Person's plantation to make the proposition to him. He knows he has me over a barrel and would only go for an even trade—Dick for 'Duke's woman. I cannot afford to throw away five pounds.

Benj. Hawkins' older brother Philemon was there sharing some apple brandy with Person. He teased me that I was always trying to acquire women slaves. Now that the legislature has elected Benjamin Senator, the Hawkins seem more conciliatory in their Federalism. Philemon had a bound copy of the Federalist propaganda, and he insisted I read several passages he had marked.

One passage from Federalist essay #26: "…The State Legislatures… will always be…suspicious and jealous guardians of the rights of the citizens against encroachments from the federal government…and will be ready enough…to sound the alarm to the people and not only be the VOICE, but, if necessary, the ARM of their discontent." Hawkins said the author of the passage was Washington's Secretary of the Treasury, Alexander Hamilton.

Another from Federalist #39 (by James Madison he thinks): "Each state in ratifying the constitution is considered a sovereign body, independent of all others, and only to be bound by its own voluntary act."

"In other words," said Hawkins, "North-Carolina may leave the union as voluntarily as she joined. Therefore you may expect the Federal government will treat the individual states with proper respect. Firm anti-federalists such as yourself & our friend Macon should be soothed."

'Tis reassuring. And Mr. Person was more convivial in manner than last time, which also made me feel better. Yet his last taunting words, while said in a jesting mode, were more than half serious: "You better make that trade 'fore your slave ends up with a ball in him."

On a lark, I went to nearby Person's Ordinary and inquired of the barkeep whether one Asa Johnson was a regular patron. The barkeep said he came in frequently, especially Saturday evenings.

I have nearly finished & enjoyed the novel that Kenchen borrowed for me, *Tristram Shandy*. 'Twill be weeks before I can get it back to Jones in

Halifax. Time for Mrs. Johnson to read it.

I suffer a thousand reservations. I had asked Kenchen to ask for a book that Mr. or Mrs. Jones thought Mrs. Johnson would enjoy. Some of this humor…might bring vermillion shades to her countenance. Kenchen said that Mr. Jones selected it because it was famous & unusual. "Highly regarded in London for its satire." Mr. Jones has not read it himself.

Having been forbidden by her blackguard of a husband, I warrant Mrs. Johnson would relish the luxury of almost any book. But what if she finds it offensive? What if she finds the veriest notion my smuggling a book to her rude? Durst I clandestinely deliver it to her?

Wednesday 10 March

We now will have over fifty acres in cultivation. My family is impressed with what we have accomplished. Patsy's family too (they all *look* like they have worms). There is much to be said for being off your pillow when the cock crows. But, will our progress continue if I trade Dick for Duke's woman?

Sunday 14 March

Yesterday I set out to go hunting over toward the Ordinary. I was full of uncertainty, but I washed up and wore the nicest of my three shirts (the cotton one). And I put *Tristram Shandy* in my saddle bags.

It was a fine crisp clear day, the sky a beautiful rich blue without a cloud. I got two rabbits & traded them for a few pence credit at Person's Ordinary. Asa Johnson was not there. I heaved a sigh of relief and started homeward. But at the last instant I espied him from a distance coming toward the tavern. With an agitated heart I turned Aristotle back eastward. Emily—Mrs. Johnson deserves this small favor, I insisted to myself.

I found the Johnson place with little effort. Except for their smoke house, I reckon their farm & home no better than my own, in spite of three slaves and more acres. However, as agitated as I was, my powers of observation were not keen.

Mrs. Johnson was out in her yard at work by a small fire. When she saw me, I detected a hint of discomposure; she momentarily smoothed her apron & adjusted her mob cap & straw hat. A negro came from behind the corn crib.

I greeted her and asked if Aristotle & I could have some water.

"Why of course. Mr. Shearin isn't it?" It's been above 4 months now since our "meeting" back in early November.

"Yes, Mrs. Johnson. I am flattered you remember me." Better that little be said of that meeting.

"'Tis ever a pleasure to see any friends of Mr. Jones. Patty, you can go about your business. I am acquainted with this gentleman." The slave hesitantly returned from whence she came.

"Come over to the well, Mr. Shearin."

I drew up a bucket. She handed me a dipper for myself. We were both a little sheepish about looking at one another. But then Mrs. Johnson did look at me with a little smile. I smiled back & held her gaze as long as propriety would allow. Perhaps an instant longer.

I asked her how she had been. There were frissons of pleasure each time she permitted me to look into her blue eyes. She is not a perfect beauty I suppose. She has a minor scar or two in her complexion not perfectly hidden by her light freckling. A childhood case of small pox possibly. Not everyone would love her nose. (Mayhap I like it for being not unlike Sarah's.) Her figure is tidy but perchance a little too slender for some. But she is possessed of some intangible inner beauty. There is modesty & sweetness in her every gesture, her voice, her movements. I thought again of the indelicate nature of some of the humor in the book I intended to deliver. I had second & third thoughts.

"I am just fine, sir," she answered. "And you?" Her back to the corn crib & the slave, she continued to look at me and shot an arrow through my heart. I was not sure if the slave was out of earshot.

"We have had serious illness in our family, but all are well now."

"Oh! pardon me. It won't do not to stir the pig fat & lye into an emulge." She hurried back to the pot and, once stirring, replied, "I am glad everyone is well. Please come sit and visit for a spell."

"Thank you kindly, Ma'am. Just a few minutes for Aristotle to rest." It was like that *instant* before lightning to be in her presence. Simply to exchange these banalities with her warmly excited my blood.

"Who was sick?"

"My infant son, little John. He gave us a scare." There followed a silence. Then I awkwardly asked "How do you feel about our being in the Union now?"

She laughed. "What a curious a question. Do you jest with me?"

I would have felt ridiculous except that she answered so sweetly. It was hardly the normal question for a man to ask the fair sex—perhaps even one so uniquely literate. "'Tis a long while since anyone asked me anything of that nature. When I was in Mr. Jones' household, the luxury of such questions entertained me, even though they lie well beyond the sphere in which we, to wit we women, have any dominion."

She paused. "I cannot say that I see any difference thus far."

"I hope you will be able to say the same in later years when men less honorable than Gen'l Washington hold sway."

"Mr. Shearin, I collect that you are a strong Whig like Mr. Jones," she said; I adore the sweet femininity of the very tone of her voice.

"I plead guilty, Mrs. Johnson. I beg your indulgence."

"Indulgence granted," she said, laughing. "I used to enjoy hearing these ideas debated at the Grove, and I own I almost always agreed with Mr. Jones."

"I'm delighted to hear that," I responded.

She paused from stirring the soap emulsion & looked up at me. When she finally spoke again it seemed out of a need of avoiding a more embarrassing silence.

"Isn't it a beautiful crisp day?"

"Indeed. 'Tis my favorite kind of weather."

"Mine too. Just a pleasant degree of coolness in the air."

After another awkward little pause, she asked if there were any news from Warrenton or Halifax. I told her of a quotidian thing or two. She listened all attention. But then she seemed to grow sensible that she was looking at me too direct & started to glance about, discomfited, for Patty or whoever might observe us.

"Has your husband been kinder?" I spoke as quietly as I could that a snooping slave might not hear. I wanted to ask what her husband remembered of *the event* but refrained.

"Mostly." She spied Patty peering from a corner of the corn crib. "Patty, you get back to work." Her bark of command was as impotent as my own.

As Patty went back behind the corn crib I took the opportunity to fetch *Tristram Shandy* from my saddle bag. I handed it to her discreetly.

"I borrowed this from Mr. Jones on the advice that this novel would give you pleasure. Would you care to borrow it for a month or so?" I tried to be casual in case Patty was peeking through a slat & kept my voice low.

She quickly hid the book in a pocket of her petticoat. "I don't know what to say. I am so surprised…and flattered by your thoughtfulness. Mr. Shearin, you are so kind." She lowered her voice to a whisper. "You are…Thank you. I…"

I looked to the ground in embarrassment before saying she was most welcome. When I looked up, her initial smile at the surprise favor had faded subtly to possess shades of worry. Alas, I may have done her no favor after all. Yet what could I do but forge ahead?

"How shall I retrieve it? I don't go to Halifax again before mid-April." She looked uncertain. We both hesitated. "We could rendez—I could fetch it from you at the boulders in the woods where we…where we met."

She smiled & nodded yes.

"About this time of day four Saturdays hence, April 10th?" She nodded assent again. "I better go now," I said. At that moment one of the other two negroes appeared from the fields.

She extended her hand. The simple touching her hand with mine for that moment was sublime; I wished that moment could have been extended. I yearned to lift her hand to my lips to kiss it, without regard to the staring negroes. Instead I released her hand. I mounted Aristotle and rode off at a gallop.

Brisk trotting & slow thorough reasoning, like wit & judgment, being two incompatible movements, I chose brisk trotting.

4 April

I have never seen the Redbud trees bloom so beautifully. Nor have I ever seen Macon so bitter. The immediate subject of his bitterness was the federalist double-cross: Sec. of Treasury Hamilton is pushing federal assumption of the States' debts. Davie & other Federalists assured us this would never happen when they wanted our consent to the Constitution.

Virginia, North-Carolina, & other states have substantially paid down their debts. Where is the fairness that we now should have to pay South-Carolina's & Massachusetts's?

"Fairness is not what Hamilton is after" said Macon. "He wishes to strengthen the central government by gaining the allegiance of the wealthy creditors of the individual states. First he leaks his plans to his friends—lawyers, rich merchants, eastern patricians—so they may gather all the state bonds for a pittance. Then he binds this new aristocracy to himself & to his schemes with liberal interest rates paid by the taxpayer."

"So James Reynolds, who bought my brothers' bonds for less than a quarter their face value, was an agent of Hamilton or his rich friends?"

"So it seems. What's more, taking on the States' debts will so balloon the federal debt as to make it a perpetual thing, ever there to feed the Federalist aristocrats, ever there to justify— not just impostes & shipping duties—but also federal excise taxes directly upon us. Hamilton is a treacherous rogue." Macon was usually a calmer voice, even when aroused.

"Is it a certainty? So honorable a man as Gen'l Washington should surely veto it." I said.

"My hope is that the North-Carolina men who are just now joining congress will tilt the vote against it."*

Though I fully agree with Nathl that this Federal gov't is off to an ominously treacherous beginning, I have never seen him so agitated. I believe the enduring hurt of losing Hannah contributes to the emotion of his reaction.

My mind remains much with Mrs. Johns—Emily is such a beautiful word. My young son (I hope he is mine) is an inspiration to me in the face of the reality that there is not real love betwixt my wife & myself.

Sun^y 11 April

I arrived at the boulders in the woods early. It is a pretty place, gently sloping down towards a creek. It is especially nice at this time of year, with the smell of greenness & April's budding growth in the air. A few dogwoods had started blooming, & there was some sort of shrub with a whitish pink tubular flower possesst of a light fragrance [*Rhododendron atlanticum*?] that I had not noticed before. I could see why she had chosen this place. I was there for some spell with no sign of her, and I despaired of a confusion of times or difficulty for her getting away. I knew she would not forget. Then I worried that perhaps my initiative or the book itself hath given offence; she may have told her husband of my effrontery after reflection. She may have decided that was the right path & given him the book to return to its owner.

More time passed & I grew by degrees more persuaded she had taken offense. I walked down to the creek, hoping movement would assuage my agitation. I walked toward their place. Back to the intended rendezvous spot. I grew sensible, nay certain she would not come.

Alas, my heart danced up into my throat as I caught glimpse of her approaching on foot. That admixture of the subtle redness of her dark auburn hair, her spare freckles, & her eyes—bluer than robin eggs—enchants me more each time I espy her. There was a little bulge in her stomach & her face looked fuller. Was she with child? No less beautiful to my eye.

"Mr. Johnson did not get off to Person's Ordinary as early as is his habit. I hope I did not detain you."

"To see you is a pleasure worth any wait, Mrs. Johnson." Gauche gallantry came out of me like a jackrabbit. Appropriate calm reason deserted me.

She blushed. "Mr. Shearin, you embarrass me with your flattery. You put

---

* This is precisely what happened: North Carolina Congressmen arrived just in time to defeat assumption 29-27 on 29 March 1790.

me at a disadvantage. If I were a great beauty I would with all naturalness say thank you for your compliment."

"But you are," said I. "You must endure the truth." I smiled at her. To my relief, she returned my smile, placing a generous construction on my lack of restraint. Perhaps she took it as the silly flirtations of a rattle. That I was speaking entirely & helplessly from the heart to one I hardly know was entirely inapposite. With some little trepidation, I continued:

"Mrs. Johnson, I wish I had had an opportunity to warn you that some of the humor in *Tristram Shandy* is…has a degree of indelicacy to it. I hope that you were not offended."

Oh then how she did giggle & smile so agreeably that I became easy. She opened the book & read from the dedication:

"I live in constant endeavour to fence against the imfirmities of ill health, & other evils of life, by mirth; being firmly persuaded that every time a man smiles,—but more so, when he laughs, that it adds something to this Fragment of Life." She smiled right at me with a twinkle in her eye. "Now how, Mr. Shearin, could my mind take offense from such a one as this writer?"

While we pointedly did not speak of when Tristram's Mother at just that extraordinary moment, the deed of his *conception,* cried out "Husband, did you remember to wind the clocks?"—or of Tristram's accidental circumcision as he was relieving himself out a window (the window closing on him), we did both of us laugh heartily together at many other parts of the book. Humor aside, I apprehend that Mrs. Johnson relished reading this famous book & being able to discuss it with someone beyond measure. Her eyes shined so as we went on that she might have swallowed candles. Perhaps mine did as well, for never have I had more harmonious intercourse as our discussions of said book.

"Digressions, incontestably, are the sunshine;—they are the life, the soul of reading!" quoth Mrs. Johnson from *Shandy*. Quintessentially true of the book…and also of us here clandestinely in the woods. This could be nothing but a digression, but what sunshine it provided.

"You know, Mrs. Johnson, I liked this book when I read it, but the longer I converse of it with you, the better it gets. 'Tis funnier to think back on than the first reading," said I laughing.

At that moment she produced from her small basket a pair of muffins & offered me one. Before it touched my lips, I smelled its pleasing aroma.

"It smells of sweet potato & spice," said I with a smile. She beamed. And indeed it was delicious. We ate the muffins in silence, which at first was pleasant. But then neither of us could think of anything to say. I did not want her to leave. I asked her of her antecedents.

"My parents & my only sister died of small pox when I was nine or ten. I nearly died as well. You no doubt have noticed the scars," said she as she gestured to her left cheek & neck.

I lied complaisantly & said I had not noticed them till she pointed to them. Indeed, they are nothing compared to the pockmarks suffered by Sis & by Isham.

The Joneses had been a godsend to her as she had no other family in the vicinage of Halifax and those back in Virginia were quite poor. Mrs. Jones taught those of her orphans to read who had aptitude for it, and with Mr. Jones' great library, a flame was set ablaze in her life.

"And thanks to you there is still a candle lit."

"I am glad." A silenced followed. We were sitting close together there on the rock. The silence now was easy. I took her hand in mine & slowly raised it to my lips. She started to speak, but then did not. She looked into my countenance. As did I to her.

I sighed with pleasure. We spontaneously put our arms around each other and held each other in a long embrace. We looked into each other's eyes again. I was moved ineffably & felt her to be with my spirit. We kissed. So natural & sublime. I was aroused, but more than that, my soul soared. Never had a kiss so run through me. I shan't forget that moment.

Such harmony as were in those few kisses exceeded anything in my life. In fear that the rising lust might conquer the affection &...awe I felt, I pulled away, walking a few paces away. When I turned, I wanted to drink in her gaze, to live in it. But she had turned away.

"You must think me wanton."

"No!" cried I. "I do not think any such thing."

"'Tis wrong. I know it. Mr. Shearin...You've engendered such feelings of affection in me with your kindness & understanding. My life is entirely devoid of affection, entirely wanting in kindness, entirely empty of anyone's interest in my thoughts or feelings."

I went to her & kissed her again. Hugged her tight. We looked in each other's eyes. So nearly as sweet as kissing her, even tho' there were now twinges of despair in hers.

"But you must know I am torn by a thousand thorns of guilt."

"Yes. I am not entirely easy either. I am not without obligations." This was nothing that could be sifted to the bottom in our present states. Nay, nor did I want to. "There is only one solution." Lo!—all of a sudden, I tickled her shamelessly (twice grazing the side of her breast!) till she laughed helplessly & beseeched me to stop.

"So you see also that 'every time a *woman* laughs, that it adds something to this Fragment of Life,'" quoth I.

Still laughing, she said: "I have not been tickled in ages. You are something incorrigible." She caught her breath. "Far be it for me to be crossways with *Shandy*'s author...or with you."

"Let me tell you a related story." Then I commenced to tell her my favorite convoluted Irish joke, to which she laughed gleefully. Then we talked a little longer of every day things. Time passed quickly. The sun started to set.

"I will make it my quest to get you another book. To safely do it, 'twill have to be a month hence. My farm I can barely manage, and my sickly father-in-law looks to need my help on his farm." I left unsaid other reasons for not seeing her again soon. Have I not mounted a fiery steed without a bridle?

As I took my leave she asked "When I think of you & if we might again at some instance have a few moments alone again, may I style you... Sterling?"

I replied yes if I might call her Emily — Emily, such a sweet word.

Chapter Nine

Sunday 25 Apr' 1790

At the behest of Patsy, Mama, & Isham, I participated today in the raising of the roof at the new church. Absalom Jenkins, Patsy's old swain was there. (Little John's hair is light brown & straight just like Absalom's, rather than dark & curly like mine. Of course Patsy's is light brown too.)

The comradery & community that the church seems to be providing is a good thing. The leader, who has been holding meetings at his home, is a full time farmer with a Deist streak. He used to have a slave but sold him, he avers, on ethical grounds (he has five sons to help him farm). He is a literate planter, and I anticipate good conversation & exchange of books & newspapers betwixt us.

Since I have withdrawn any emotional aspect of myself from Patsy, we have in large measure gotten along better. She is more often actually solicitous of me than ever she was before. Except for her intermittent shrewish moods, she is a good manager of the household, kitchen garden &c. It goes without stating, this is invaluable to our well-being. I wish she would watch little John closer as too many young ones are seriously injured in mishaps. Isham's toddler, a cruel example.

Rains have been timely; all goes well. We are planting considerable tobacco & flax this year. Marmaduke's woman, Priss, can help Patsy with linen production.

I hope I have done right. 'Duke & Priss started meeting in the woods to keep him from getting shot. Person caught on and punished her by cutting her rations, saying she'll get no shoes next winter, & locking her up at night. Why he was so against their having entertainment of an evening I cannot fathom—unless it was to smoke me out.

Alas, I pleaded with Person at length to trade her to me for Dick with the five pounds allowance for his greater value. He finally relented to give me Priss & £2 for Dick, quite a good bargain for him.

Well 'Duke is most happy. I hope their affection will endure now that there is no barrier to it. Whilst I freely own that being rid of the troublesome Dick feels like being rid of a pocket full of rocks, I know very little of Priss' character aside from Marmaduke's attachment.

Wed[y] 28 April

My secret, my inner life…invisible to all & unshareable. Emily is ever with me. The thought of her & the affectionate glint in her eye lifts my spirit continually & lessens the weight of daily cares. Only when I am very involved or very tired is she not in my mind.

There is also a little place inside me that belongs to Sarah. I wonder what they would think of each other; I love them both. Neither can be a part of my tangible, physical life. Yet they are part of me. Hardly what the preachers mean by "spiritual" life.

'Tis not altogether hidden, this inner life; I am a different man. It should be visible to Patsy except that I am not really visible to her at all—save as a means to a better station in life. Tho' she is a tolerable mama & loves our little John, I sense not in her that capacity for relating characterized by depth of feeling. Or if it is there, I have not been able to elicit it. I have been a fool! God verily did not give man enough blood to operate his head & his next most important appendage at the same time.

Sunday 10 May

Good fortune smiled on me. On the return journey from Halifax, I took a chance detouring from the main road to the Johnson farm. Emily was weeding with the slaves & Asa was absent. Again I was able to discreetly convey a book (Shakespeare) I had borrowed from Mr. Jones and arrange for its retrieval. I am sure she is with child.

Sunday 24 May

When I went to help Patsy's father with farm work yesterday I found him in great pain with a toothache. I took him to mid-wife Walker.

None of the teeth had obvious holes in them, but the roof of his mouth was swollen on his left side. Mrs. Walker attempted to drain the swelling by jabbing her smallest knife into the swollen area with little success; Patsy's father howled in obvious dire pain. The fourth jab drew some blood & pus, but poor father-in-law gained only slight relief.

Mrs. Walker was reluctant to do more for him. In her experience, no poultices are effectual. She said bone-setting, blood-letting, & tooth-drawing were men's work & that I should carry him to Halifax to a doctor. Father-in-law pleaded with her. His farm could ill-afford that much lost time. Nor was he certain he could endure another day's worth of excruciation. He was pitiful.

Mrs. Walker tapped on his teeth on that side to identify the sorest. My father-in-law howled terrible. Mrs. Walker had him drink a good bit more whiskey, and while waiting for it to have effect, she gave me some rudimentary instruction in using a small pair of pliers she had. (A substance she called laudanum would have helped she said, but the trader in Halifax wanted considerable silver for it—would not consider paper money, whiskey or produce in trade. She had none.)

Such a procedure I could never repeat, lest my patient were King George or Asa Johnson or some other foul villain. Though very drunk, my father-in-law was in ear-splitting agony (Mrs. Walker forewarned) as I worked the tooth out. Part of one of the three roots seems to have broken & stayed in his gum. Yet in a few minutes he said the pain was subsiding. He fell asleep in the wagon going home; got considerable blood everywhere.

Mrs. Walker suggested I study physic that I might practice it when I have more slaves to tend my farm. An interesting idea, but I am not sure I could endure inflicting such pain—even to relieve it. I did keep the tooth with the thought that a deft smithy might be able to fashion pliers shaped to actually fit the shape of a tooth to be removed.

Sun' 7 June

My rendezvous with Emily was as poignant as previous meetings. She told me the story of *Macbeth*. (Having lent it to her first, I had yet to read it.) The story induced me to say: "Emily, you can see in this story why Mr. Jones & I are such staunch Whigs. Many men—and women—thru' all ages—have been ambitious for power over other men. The ambitious blackguards most drawn to rule are those who may least be trusted."

"But *we* can vote out villains" Emily rejoined.

"Republics can be corrupted. Especially with so weak a Constitution as our own. Unless we all remain jealous of our liberties, ambitious rogues will use patronage & deceit to gain dominion over us. Should we be so fortunate as to elect a good man—Gen'l Washington for instance— you may be sure his character will not be improved by the power he attains. Isn't the change in Mr. Johnson's behavior after he became your husband a small example of power's corrupting effect?"

"You speak so persuasively, Sterling. I own that I think Warren Co. would be smart to elect you to something."

"Now *you* are the flatterer. Besides I would need more slaves & land to be able to afford the time away from my farm. I hope we can get Macon to allow himself to be nominated."

"As honorable as farming is, Sterling, I see an intelligence in you that can contribute even more to this world than drawing substance out of the earth. *Macbeth* is a tragic play, but I lifted some lines from it that I have written down & hidden in my secret place:

'Our doubts are traitors,
And make us lose the good we oft might win,
By fearing to attempt.'
"You should not close the door to your future hopes."

How could I not love such a virtuous beauty as Emily. Her pregnant state made it easier not to want to touch & kiss her. But after a spell of conversation about everyday things, something got the better of me and I embraced her and kissed her fully on the lips. Her kiss is divine.

After a moment she pulled away and started to cry. I tried to comfort her, but she took my hand & held it away.

Thru' sobs said she "I care for you…over much."

"Emily, I—"

"We cannot see each other again."

Her words, spoken firmly, stunned me and wafted between us like a coil of smoke from a gentleman's pipe. I wanted to fan them away but knew not how. In the distance a dog barked. Faint sounds suggested an accompanying horseman. The worry that our meeting should in all prudence conclude quickly hindered my capacity to speak as much as the shock of her words.

"We cannot, Sterling. Tragic consequences are all that can come of it if… if we continued…our friendship." She wiped her tears but ceased her crying. She stood tall, her chin suddenly stiff with purpose. "We've consulted our wishes rather than our reason in meeting as we have." One could not be insensible that Emily had deliberated in earnest & was resolved.

"I must build my life around the children I will have & the management of my household. Otherwise I will…I will end up like Lady Macbeth."

What could I respond?

Emily looked back over her shoulder as she heard the horseman with his dog getting nearer. We expressed with a wordless glance that we needed to part instantly. We kissed one last brief kiss. And moved swiftly in opposite directions.

I feel despair. Yet it is leavened by, not simply the love, but more, the admiration & respect I feel for this angel. May I live as nobly as she in the face of imperfect realities.

Sun' 12 July

I allow the work of my farm to consume me. I take pleasure in simple things like cool spring water in the shade after worming tobacco in the feverish dusty July heat. I take pleasure in little John's frolics. When I get a breathing spell, I lend father-in-law a hand. Thru' the fatigue of industry I can sleep well and fight off fretting of things beyond my control. Still I think of her.

Sunday 26 July

 The worms on the tobacco are very bad this year. (I hope Prissy is better working flax than she is tobacco.) Tobacco burns too much of our labor. Kenchen has me about convinced to go with more corn next year. We can convert all the excess corn to the more transportable form of whiskey in his still; whiskey is accepted in trade better than North-Carolina paper money.

 Lewis brought by a Petersburg newspaper indicating that two Virginia congressmen were bribed into voting for Federal assumption of the States' debts. The bribe was the location of the permanent capital right near their districts on the Potomac. We agreed that the corrupting of the Federal gov't has begun.

 How blatantly hath they baited the hook & then effected a switch. Promise us one thing to gain ratification; then do the opposite. (That damned unctuous James Iredell got his reward for pushing ratification: an appointment to the Supreme Court. I remember Macon commenting when he learned that Iredell had paid to have the proceedings from the 1st ratifying convention published & distributed that "Iredell no doubt will be rewarded when the Federal gov't is appointed with a very nice emolument." The bulk of the proceedings were Iredell's & Davie's arguments.)

 After church, however, Philemon Hawkins made the reasonable argument that some States may have contributed more to the defeat of the British than others. Still honest Whigs should be on their guard.

 Isham said the slaves are saying the ghost of Mordecai killed Abner Whitaker, and he said with a laugh that satisfies him. Yes, a ghost! (Mordecai's name gets mentioned any time someone dies of a knife wound. I fear we are at the merest dawning of the scientific world view and that we have very far to go before reason generally prevails over superstition.)

Monday 3 Aug.

 Patsy's younger sister died of bilious fever & bloody flux[*]. Her mother is sick with it too. We need rain badly.

Sunday 23 Aug.

 The heat, the want of rain, my debts (which the lack of rain threatens to magnify), my distance from Patsy *and* from the angel who should be mine

---

[*] Apparently severe gastrointestinal infection and dysentery.

were it a perfect world—all these I claim as extenuating.

To speak the bold truth, it was hot as the hinges of Hell. I was weeding our plowed field with Prissy; you have got to stay with her to get good work out of her. For every 3 weeds we chopped we swatted 2 mosquitoes. Naturally after a spell, we paused in the shade for water. Her loose homespun, when she bent over, showed much of her breast, which appeared large & well-shaped. I think she noticed my glance and she gave me a smile. I construed its nature as…flirtatious is not the apposite word. There was mischief & pleasure in that smile.

I swelled with lust. In spite of heat & fatigue, my body suddenly came awake like the birds at dawn. She moved close by me. In reaching for the dipper, she brushed her breast against my arm. I collect that this was by design. After she drank deeply, she preened inches from me, arching her back to render her breasts more pert & prominent. I slid my hand under her garment and fondled her. Her only reaction was that knowing smile. To say I was aroused—nay, I was a covered pot boiling over a fire. I was about to be lost. Then I thought of the pain I would cause Marmaduke. The damage I would do a relationship of some value. I thought of the little marriage ceremony he had invited me to attend. I was disgusted with myself. I stood back abruptly.

"I respect your husband & your marriage. I apologize." I said. Whether she was disappointed or no, I did not study. I tore off to the house. Marmaduke was toting buckets of water for critical plants. I hollered at him to keep little John with him away from the house.

I went into the house, took the sewing from Patsy's hands & roughly took off her mob cap, bodice, petticoat & shift. How long since I had seen her naked by good light.

I kissed her forcefully. I pressed her down on the bed. She resisted. I held her arms above her head and entered her. I kissed her at the same time, invading her with my tongue. In spite of her resistance she grew wet. I humped her fiercely. On & on. She responded to my thrusts. I became so drenched with sweat that everything was lathered & lubricated with it. I felt like an animal.

I got up & took off the remnants of my clothing. I ordered her harshly to get on all four. She complied. I entered her from behind. I held her derriere in my hands and felt powerful as I thrust in & out of her. She began to squeeze me tighter & tighter, to emit moans, and then thrice she yelled "Oh God! Oh God! Oh God!" She squeezed me spasmodically & her arms collapsed as I reached crescendo.

We lay sprawled together. I thought how I needed this touching as much as the release. In a few moments she turned; there was a glimmer of a smile upon her face. The exact construction to place upon this—well, she was not mad. How little I apprehend. Exhausted, I kissed her forehead & thought "maybe there is hope for us" as I drifted into the arms of sleep.

Sat. 5 Sept.

At last we got rain. We are on the fourth day of intermittent torrents of rain & winds. Water leaks were minor and we have had the time to rectify all of them. Indeed we have accomplished every indoor chore we can do for now, and I have read everyone much of *Macbeth*. Time for writing in a journal.

In a moment of relative privacy I awkwardly tried to speak to Patsy of what transpired between us. I sought to apprehend the event itself, to better understand her nature, and to establish some kind of conduit to a real intimacy between husband & wife. She swatted at me with the fly broom (flies are terrible this year) and said something like "Hush your mouth, husband. Be ashamed before God & your wife to talk such." I had hoped for some assuagement of the guilt I felt for my animal lust. I had hoped for some verbal acknowledgement of her wanting me. She chooses to pretend nothing happened. She is just as before.

We begin to agitate one another in our two room home. I have suggested to a willing Marmaduke that we go out in the drizzle and make a little land. An area thick with hickories & chestnuts. We will lay aside the hickory for making pitchforks & tools during winter. I think we could trade a few well-made hickory pitchforks for a profit.

Sunday 6 Sept.

While chopping hickories in the rain yesterday, I determined to approach my brothers Lewis & Kenchen, Delia Hawkins, John Macon, our pastor and others about putting forth Nathl Macon's name for House Of Commons of North-Carolina. We could not have a better representative and it would perhaps benefit his spirit.

Sunday 23 Sept.

An eventful gathering today at church. An itinerant Baptist preached a hell-fire sermon which moved many. Our congregation swells.

Nathᷧ Macon did not come but sent a number of his slaves. All to whom I spoke (excepting one) agreed we should place Nathaniel's name in nomination. He is esteemed by all as learned & honest, a man of absolute integrity & independent Whig principles.

But most engaging of my interest was the presence of Mrs. Emily Johnson & her husband Asa. I would not be denied the opportunity for a few moments intercourse with her—even though entirely public it would be.

I had the advantage of seeing her first & observed in her countenance and posture dejection & tension. When she saw us approach she looked momentarily alarmed but then brightened & smiled.

I introduced Emily to Patsy as an acquaintance from my visits to Mr. Wylie Jones. Emily introduced Asa to us. There was not the least tincture in his expression that he had ever been in my presence before or had any knowledge of me.

Asa is a buck of the first stare; he is easily 3 or 4 inches my superior in height. He hath a thick chest. Strong teeth of good order. An easy smile. But for a weak chin, he is handsome enough. His manners were so polished & gallant as to discomfit me, tho' I have heard it said that he is inordinately fond of a certain species of wit practiced by the vulgar classes. None of this illumined his discourse on this occasion. Instead it was I who stumbled:

"You have a child now, Mrs. Johnson, isn't that right?" (She was obviously no longer pregnant.) Pain came into Emily's face. I felt yet more *gauche*. The baby, it turned out, had been born dead, and her travail was a life threatening ordeal from which she was still weak.

Turning away from the painful subject, I spoke to Asa about supporting Macon for the Gen'l Assembly, and he said "I wonder if Macon is forward-thinking enough. Is he a friend to the energy we need in government?"

"What do you mean, Sir? Perhaps you could be more specific." I responded.

"Well, think what benefits would accrue to us hereabouts were the government to build a canal allowing ships on the Roanoke beyond the rocks at Weldon's Orchard."

"Surely you do not mean the Federal government. The Constitution does not authorize the Federal government to do such a thing."

"Our State government then," said Asa.

"Hmn. Maybe. Is it right to tax all of North-Carolina for our specific benefit? Wouldn't it be better done by a private company? I mean, those most benefiting should put up the capital. Don't you think?"

"Well all I know is that a canal would raise the value of our lands & produce handsomely."

"Well sure. True enough. It would benefit us around here tremendously.

But the just way for it to happen is for a company of benefiting landholders to form and do it. If we allow the government to tax us higher & stick its fingers into such, be assured it will not stop there."

"You sound like all the old Whigs. A young man like you shouldn't be afraid of the government being an agent of progress," answered Asa Johnson.

"Old Whigs know history, Mr. Johnson. They know the nature of government. They know that government is the agent of power and force and hence prone to become corrupt & evil. At its best government is like fire—a very dangerous servant.

"Even a republican government, Mr. Shearin?"

"If history is our guide, yes."

"I think this is a new day. The past should not bind us."

"'Tis human nature that will bind us," I replied, too much a jackrabbit. I should have paused to give this profound truth more force.

"I see I'll never get the last word on you."

I forced a chuckle. "I'm sorry, Mr. Johnson. I get carried away. I'm sensible that I sometimes get overwrought on such subjects. I apologize. I just hope we do not relax our vigilance too much now that we are no longer beset by the obvious villainy of King George." I collect that Mr. Asa Johnson possesses an intelligence, not of philosophical depth, but of a nature that would render him formidable in many endeavors. After a moment's pause, I turned to a less controversial topic and asked Mr. Johnson how his crops were looking.

"Promising. The heavy rain was a mixed blessing. But I do not look for anyone to starve this winter."

Patsy & Emily were conversing amiably. Patsy invited Emily to her first quilting bee in November. Emily said she would love to come. Asa reckoned it excessively at nine miles by path & road (I knew it more like four or five through the woods.) He thought it might not be practicable.

"Mrs. Johnson, have you seen aught of Mr. Jones?" There was so little that I could say to her in this public circumstance. But I had to say something to prolong her presence.

"Alas, no, Mr. Shearin. Above a year I warrant. I've not returned to Halifax since my marriage."

Asa's gimlet eye subtly altered her expression. But she finished her thought. "Indeed, you remind me of my duty to write to him & Mrs. Jones, both of whom I deeply esteem & love. Both of whom I owe such gratitude."

Johnson covered his hardened eyes quickly with effusive expressions of his pleasure at having made our acquaintance & their need to be on their way. And too quickly she was gone.

Patsy & her old beau Absalom Jenkins also enjoyed some flirtatious conversation. Harmless enough I suppose. He is now wedded to an attractive buxom wife.

To his credit, he is literate, reading extensively in the Bible. I fear he may be helping to lead our congregation in a direction…less tolerant of deists such as myself, a narrowing direction with Hell an ever-present reminder.

A very few sentences Emily had spoken. And nothing that signifies. Yet as we rode home, it was not the noises of our horse or our cart that I heard so much as the music of her voice echoing sweetly within me.

Sunday 8 Oct.

The harvests & markets were fair. I paid the six percent interest on the loan to Col. Whitaker & paid off Mr. Jones completely. 'Twould have been to my advantage to pay down the higher interest loan to Col. Whitaker, but it would have been unfair to Mr. Jones. After buying necessities I have but seven shillings to cover any contingencies.

Macon was easily elected to the House of Commons.

Sun' 8 Nov^r

Patsy was quite proud of hosting the quilting bee. Shewing off the home we have made. Our house was bursting at the seams; slept twelve people including three kids. Duke & Prissy slept in the barn. Emily did not attend, tho' we have seen her at church once more.

Cold weather has come on hard & early. Many folks are very sick with great sweats.

There is talk of a Federal Tax on whiskey! How could Pres. Washington be a part to such odiousness? Whiskey is our currency. They justify it because assumption of the states' debts has so swelled the Federal debt.

Macon has lent me Adam Smith's *An Inquiry into the Nature and Causes of the Wealth of Nations.*

Sun' 29 Nov^r

Every member of Patsy's family is dead save herself and her brother Eli! Also our fine free-thinking pastor. This feverish plague has brought so much death & sadness. Prissy has it now. Mrs. Walker cannot do much. Onions applied to the feet do not assuage the fever in the least.

Sunday 6 Dec^r

Papa has died of the illness. I know fifty-five years is a good life. Still it is an awful blow. He was a fine man; may I live as good a life. Eleven people hereabouts in three short weeks. How precarious is our hold on life. Patsy & John have it. Woe unto us.

Sunday 13 Dec^r

Thanks be to heaven! John is himself again. Patsy is better as well. I am like everyone else. Our church is full of us, all looking for a divinity to sustain us. Absalom Jenkins is now pastor. Emily especially seems to have fallen under his spell. And I own that he has performed exceeding admirable service in comforting every one of us in our grief & mourning. He has earned my respect & esteem.

We have taken in eleven-year-old Eli. We will teach him to be a better farmer than his father. They auction the forty-five acre farm tomorrow. Patsy's father owed so much that Patsy & Eli will likely inherit nothing.

Sunday 20 Dec^r

I went to the auction to bid for their nice oven. Patsy had tried to get me to pilfer it before the auction—saying with some justification that it should belong to her. The auction was poorly attended, because ten acres of the farm is flood prone while the other thirty-five acres possess no spring or creek and are not very fertile. The home, corn crib, & c. are indifferent. The land possesses one advantage for me, & that is its contiguousness with my own.

I worked out a bargain with the creditor, Mr. Person. I make a down payment of £2 (Grand Papa will lend me one pound four shillings) & £3 worth of whiskey. Then I will owe him £90 at six percent with the stipulation that I pay at least £20 on the principal next fall.

The pressure of debt will be severe. But Patsy is overjoyed. We will have over one hundred acres. She will have her oven. Marmaduke & Prissy will have as good a house as any slaves in the county. I have hopes of inheriting a slave from Papa. If not, all of us—Eli included—will have to work ourselves to the bone.

Patsy shared with me an interesting rumor concerning Emily. Emily's baby was born dead & taken from her before she ever saw its face. Emily has had nightmares in which she can see her child from the back. She cries out to the child, but it never will turn toward her. She told no one of the dream save her immediate family.

At the end of one of Absalom's first services, he spoke to Emily thus: "Your babe is angry with you. When you turn truly to Christ and live as a virtuous biblical wife, the child will turn so that you may see its face." How could Absalom know of her dream? Sends shivers down my spine. Between this miraculous event and so many whom I have known all my life dying of the feverish plague, my deistic views are shaken. Maybe Mordecai's ghost did kill Abner Whitaker.

Chapter Ten

Sunday 9 January 1791

My spirits were sorely damp't after Absalom Jenkin's service: Not only my wife, but also Mrs. Emily Johnson, and much of the rest of the congregation are in the strong sway of this new holy man. (How much worse if he were the father of little John!) His well-received sermon today might be distilled to the premise that denial of yourself & service to others are *the* definition of virtue. Tho' I would be hard-pressed to debate the increasingly polished & confident Absalom, this wedges in my craw. Is this the only reason we exist?

My reading, the influence of Macon, my own thinking...these had led me to view the world as entering a new age of science & reason. The cruel deaths of many connexions & neighbors and the mystic powers of Absalom Jenkins fill me with doubt. To worsen matters the Hawkins' overseer, Caleb Brown, has become active in the congregation and gives Kenchen & me the evil eye. He is very friendly with Absalom. I am beset by a thousand fears.

I was lifted from this melancholy by the letter handed me by Nathaniel Macon's servant:

Dear Sterling,

In as much as you were instrumental to my re-entry into the political life, I wish to share with you a conversation pointedly visited upon me by our mutual friend Mr. Wylie Jones. As best as I recall it, Mr. Jones said unto me:

"Nathaniel, many men are virtuous in the Whig sense: They do not wish to control society but merely to enjoy its protection. The enterprising tradesman & the thriving farmer will be engrossed by the toils of their businesses and have scant time or inclination for the disquieting arena of politics. They want not to rule others but to be left alone.

"On the other hand, those who are drawn to political affairs are often the worst sorts: Those with a lust for power over others or those desirous of personal prestige or those hoping for something for nothing. In short it is those who least understand the nature & value of liberty who will generally seek office, while those possessing an honest Whig education will tend to simply mind their own business.

"For example, Richard Caswell* & I made a grave mistake in declining our appointments to the Constitutional Convention in Philadelphia in '87. We might have made the difference in my friend George Mason's efforts to make the Constitution a real guardian of freedom. As it is, 'tis a mere piece of wax—excepting the Bill of Rights.

"This is all too evident now that the arch-Federalist Hamilton & his Eastern friends have tipped their hand. First they have the Federal gov't assume the States' debts—to their tremendous personal enrichment. Then they have the Federal gov't create a National Bank, again enriching themselves at Taxpayer's expense. Never mind that the Constitution does not authorize Federal incorporation of anything—much less a National Bank with monopoly power & private stockholders.

"And now they are poised to inflict a whiskey tax upon us. They little realize how devastating this will be to those distant from good rivers: They mainly wish to establish the precedent of direct taxation upon the citizens of the formerly sovereign States.

"My thrust, Nathaniel, is that **you** must stand for Congress. The preservation of the liberty we have won is the noblest of causes. 'Tis worthy of you. I know of no man of true principles who is so widely respected as you. I implore you to allow your name to be placed in nomination."

Mr. Jones went on to confirm that Gen'l Washington is doing nothing to thwart Hamilton's schemes. He persuaded me of the advisability of his request. And so I hereby request your efforts on my behalf in this regard. I (and I flatter myself, N-C) owe you gratitude for my election to Commons.

Please relay much of this to Lewis, Kenchen, &c. I hope you and your family prosper. I remain
    Yr mst obdt & hmble srvnt,
      Nath' Macon

Buck Spring
January 8, 1791

Macon's intention and my ability to play a part alleviated in some degree my dejection.

---

* Richard Caswell (Governor in 1787) was a fellow Whig who also declined the appointment, thereby giving North Carolina's delegation a Federalist dominance.

Sunday 16 Jan^y

 Much has transpired of late. Lewis has had a daughter & Kenchen a son (Ezekiel). I did not get the one slave I need, a robust buck. Rather I got three poor ones: Lucy who is ancient (& valued at only £15), Suky who is valuable (£70) but married to Beck (who went to Mama), & little Will (£40) who is about 12-years-old.

 Papa left no will & the county has made a mess of the division of the slaves. I owe thirteen pounds nine shillings to various family members to equalize the division. More debt. It is a messy situation. Potentially I have more wealth but quite a large responsibility now.

 Macon came by with tidings that contribute more urgency to his being elected. He has it on firm authority that Sec. of Treasury Hamilton, when he was at the Constitutional Convention, proposed a <u>*permanent*</u> President & Senate and proposed that state Governors be appointed by the Federal gov't. 'Tis a dangerous man that runs Washington's administration!

"Buck Spring" was what Nathaniel Macon called his plantation. This is a representation of his home (a modification of a photo courtesy of North Carolina Archives). There was a second similar structure which housed his kitchen and upstairs bedroom for his daughters.

Sunday 13 Feb^y

  I arose early Thursday; it was brutally cold, eminently fit for hog-curing. I worked with haste on the farm till breakfast. Then I went to Warrenton to vote for Macon and to trade. At dusk Lewis & I set out for Franklin Co. for the second day of voting (Isham & Kenchen stayed behind for drink & carousing). We tried to sleep under our wagon but it turned so cold we had to get off the ground. The moisture in the air & the penetrating winds made for a rawness to the cold that we could not overcome. Then before dawn we were awakened by icy rain and sleet.

  We arrived at Franklin courthouse miserably cold & wet. We did our best to cajole voters to cast for Macon and to keep an eye on the sheriff as we promised Nathl. Naturally Macon is less well-known outside Warren Co., but I am hopeful.

20 Feb^y

  Macon won overwhelmingly! Our neighbor and friend is now our Representative to the union. His embarrassed opponent now claims that he withdrew his name from nomination once he realized who his opponent was, tho' I heard no mention of that before the election.

  We all fair well save a spat of sauciness from Priss. Patsy gave her a good slapping when she did it in front of the new ones and I hope that will quench it.

  The new slaves are manageable thus far. We have the stalls, front yard, &c. freshened with pine straw. Plenty of wood cut, ditches cleaned, fencing built & repaired. We are well prepared for spring (in fact two days of warm weather make me itch to go ahead & plant Irish potatoes) except that we have no money & little saleable surplus. We have just enough thread from the flax to clothe our bigger family; barely enough produce & seed to see us thru'. Achieving the £20 pay down on father-in-law's farm will require great industry & no little good fortune. Bad weather or sickness of any degree and we are ruined! It isn't as if I "ran in debt" as people are wont to say. Debt sought me out; it ran after me.

Sunday 10 April

  Much talk today at church of President Washington coming to Halifax. He is easily the most famed character to ever visit this vicinage. Many talk of going to see him. Asa Johnson & Caleb Brown for instance.

Others of us fear he is becoming a new King George III: He has been instrumental in bringing about our flimsy Constitution, our unnecessarily huge national debt, a tax on whiskey, and a national bank. The debt, the tax, & the bank will transfer our substance from us who till the soil to the Eastern stockjobber aristocracy. Alas, there are probably two men who respond to his fame & glorious reputation for every one of us who analyze his present governance.

After church as people were milling about, I turned & Emily was there at my side. She discreetly handed me a melancholy sack* and whispered:

"Mr. Shearin, you've seemed forlorn. I hope you are...faring well."

"Thank you," I whispered back. Asa approached & she turned to face him. Her caring made me feel better than the fragrances, tho' good they were.

Sun' 17 April

Having worked very hard and being low on meat, I took a little time to go hunting. Alas, something in the back of my mind pulled me in the wrong direction.

Going east I had scant luck. Nothing but pregnant does. By the time I managed a second bobwhite, I realized I was within a mile of Emily. And furthermore I considered how her husband was likely in Halifax rubbing elbows with the illustrious Washington.

Against my better judgment, I cautiously approached their place. No one seemed to be about. I had nearly dismounted at the front door before their dogs announced my presence.

Emily came out the front door, somewhat startled, with sewing still in her hand. She re-acted unhappily attempting to cover a blackened eye and a cut lip.

"Sterling! Of all times—you shouldn't..."

"Emily what happened?"

She retreated back into the house. I looked about again; I saw no one. I followed her inside without regard for nicety.

"What happened?" I repeated. She turned away and cried, not replying. "Has he hit you again?"

She gave a barely perceptible nod. I went to her and put my arm around her. She buried her tearful face in my shoulder. I comforted her as best I could.

---

* A melancholy sack was a tiny pouch with contents such as cloves, rose petals, & mint leaves.

Finally I said: "Emily your countenance cannot be so lachrymose or battered that it should fail to inspire me. Let me look at you. I cannot come here and leave without being thus inspired."

She evinced a tiny laugh. "Sterling, who would ever believe you?" I smiled at her. She returned a sheepish smile to me & started to become her calmer self.

"Asa has been better. This was probably my fault. I was dying his waistcoat purple as he insisted. He had been drinking & tripped & fell against me as I was pouring the pokeberry dye. You see the purple on my petticoat. I guess it fits with my other blemishes."

"Good gracious," said I. "No longer than pokeberry purple last, 'tis hardly worth anyone's time."

"I agree. But being seen looking splendid on such a fine occasion signifies to Asa."

I did not reply immediately. Asa's possession of that frivolity of character which leads one to pursue fashionable amusements was of a piece: It fit with all else I know of him. I asked "What signifies...what is important to you?"

"Usually I think I know. Today is not normal. This recent...altercation... and now your presence...are—none but you would ask me such a thing— and you shouldn't."

"I'm sorry."

"Anyway I could have avoided the...altercation had I been more alert."

I shook my head. "I would like to beat the living day lights out of him."

"No...that's not the Christian way," she said, but with little enthusiasm.

I looked at the bad purple stain on her unbleached linen petticoat. "I guess the best thing for that is bleaching it in the sun for awhile and then dying it with strong walnut dye."

"I warrant that you're right."

"I would be happy to keep you company while it is bleaching in the sun." I said with a mischievous smile.

"You would?" She answered with a smile. "You know I do have another petticoat, you naughty fellow, the one I wear to church."

"Tisk, tisk." She is an easy & natural presence for me. I have no natural deftness at flirtation or being the courtier. 'Tis not my talent. With Emily I can say what comes to my mind, be it teasing or serious, and she seems to place the construction upon it that I intended, or at least a charitable interpretation.

On the other hand, I am filled with malignant anger towards Asa Johnson when I view Emily's bruises & cut. What can be done?

We talked yet a short spell on idle subjects. She is still impressed &

awed by the minister. I hugged her & kissed her forehead to take my leave.

As I turned to exit the door, there stood their female slave! Who knows how long she had been there. I glanced back at Emily, who sighed a troubled sigh.

"Be gone. Maybe I can deal with this. He treats her worse than he treats me." Emily said. Alas, more difficulty was the last thing I intended her.

Sunday 24 Apr.

With trepidation I laid my eyes upon Asa at church today. I was relieved that he expressed not the slightest nuance of knowledge of my visit. Indeed he was full of telling all about exchanging salutations with the great Washington in Halifax.

Asa expresst some little indignation, nay, he was scornful of Wylie Jones for shunning Pres. Washington. Mr. Jones would not entertain him at his mansion, the Grove. The President put up at Martin's Tavern [subsequently called Eagle Tavern].

I was astounded. Still I defended Jones:

"Can you imagine any reasons Mr. Jones, who has shown great hospitality to so many—from orphans to humble persons such as myself to great characters such as John Paul Jones[*]—can you imagine reasons why Mr. Jones would shun the august President of the Union of our States? He must have had reasons."

"Well the word was that Jones thinks Gen' Washington is acting like the English King George. He is sore over all of what he terms 'usurpations of power' by the Federal government."

"You mean taking over the States' debts, the direct tax on whiskey, and the National bank."

"Yes, yes. Such a fuss. I figure we can get around paying the whiskey tax in these parts. How will they make us pay?" asked Asa Johnson.

"The assumption of debt & the National bank will end up costing us too; they just are more sophisticated thefts."

"I can see that you & Jones would get on well, Sterling Shearin. But you should have witnessed the great dignity with which the President conducted himself," said he expansively, holding his arms out to his sides & smiling as

---

[*] Legend and some evidence suggest that John Paul Jones stayed for months as Jones' guest in 1775 (much of it convalescing from typhoid fever) and that John Paul subsequently adopted the Jones surname. See *The John Paul Jones - Willie Jones Tradition* by Elizabeth H. Cotten (Chapel Hill, NC 1966). Alternately, see Samuel Eliot Morison's *John Paul Jones* for the conventional view.

if he had absorbed some of Washington's charm.

"Yes, I have heard that he touches no one to shake their hand but rather stiffly bows to them." I said.

"Yes, but if you had experienced his presence, you would not describe it with a belittling tone. He is the essence of gentility," Asa countered.

"I'm sorry, Mr. Johnson. I didn't mean to say that in a belittling tone. But I must own that I am troubled by similar things that I have heard."

"Such as?"

"I have heard that in the capitol he conducts formal levees like the King of England and rides about in a luxurious coach & six like the King of England," I said.

"Who are you to say we would not fare better with *him* as king?"

I was appalled to hear such un-Whiggish sentiment. Scratch a Federalist & you find a Tory underneath. "Only a peasant I suppose" I answered with quiet sarcasm.

I am in awe that Mr. Jones manifested such temerity. I hope that Washington will be affected rightly: That is, that he take notice of North-Carolinians' dislike of his kingly actions. I fear this could come back to haunt my worthy friend & benefactor.

The spring is unseasonably dry and I fear the specter of debtor's prison. I also fear Asa's slave eventually spilling her secret. I am too full of fears.

Sunday 6 Nov

Obvious to any reader is that my nice swan quills are no longer. Little two-year-old John cast them into the fire. This turkey quill must suffice.

During these last six months, woe has been our portion. So many things went against us. Tho' the weather was tolerable for most crops, we have no money & great debt. My calculations could hardly have been worse. I raised little tobacco, which was very profitable this year. Instead we raised more corn, which we naturally converted to the more transportable form of whiskey.

Although I know of more than one distiller who substantially escaped the Whiskey Tax, Kenchen & I felt its full force. 'Tis hard treatment. Mortified we are. Arch-federalist John Whitaker got the plum of Federal Tax collector. Who should get the position of his assistant but Asa Johnson!

About the middle of July, I had sensed a subtle difference in his attitude toward me. Given my proclivity to pessimistic imaginings in my social relations, I was uncertain until he visited this loathsome tax upon us. (I warrant it would have been better had he responded to my friendliness with his wife by challenging me to a duel, if that is the true spring behind it.) Tho' the Whiskey Tax be not uniformly applied, I apprehend from the quality of his raiments & his new steed that Asa must receive a handsome share.

Old Lucy & young Will were sick nigh unto death all of August. The cost of four visits from mid-wife Walker add up. Lucy recovered. Young Will did not; we were devastated by his death on Sept. 1st. There has been little mirth at this place since.

After paying our taxes & all our interest obligations and buying the minimal necessary supplies, I was 1 pound, six shillings short of paying the required £20 down on Patsy's father's farm. Squire Person had some knowledge of my situation and of the industry we had brought to bear; he accepted my excuses, but added a double interest on what I was short of the pay down.

So here I am well over £100 in debt at six percent per annum. So valuable an artisan as a skillful blacksmith would need near a full month's wage to pay that much interest. The farm will need several bountiful years without mishap to get out from under this debt.

We have but four pence for contingencies. We must produce some skins, wood, & wood products or live very poorly. (Little hope of surplus linen from the flax.)

I have seen Emily only three or four times at church over this half year. (We worked sun-to-sun several Sundays.) But last time I think she was hiding a bruise; inwardly I seethe.

Sunday 4 Dec^r

Word circulates that Preacher Absalom healed Asa Johnson's negress by placing on hands last Sunday. The second such event; his star ascends.

Even Macon attends the services on occasion, tho' I am not sensible of his ever taking communion. Over the past year, he has taken to reading & quoting the Bible, tho' not the more mystical parts.

Caleb Brown speaks of running for sheriff. I marvel now to recollect that on first acquaintance I thought Mr. Brown handsome; now I so perceive malice & dissemblance in his every feature, his every gesture, that I see no beauty of person in him at all. I will be interested to observe how voters see him. He criticizes our current sheriff for not solving the murder—the murder of Abner Whitaker.

"Our old sheriff might be up to handling an eye-gouging…when there are plenty of witnesses. But he plainly ain't up to solving a murder that wants investigation," says he on more than one occasion.

The sheriff has caught wind of this mouth of detraction against him, for he came snooping about Kenchen's & Isham's on Wednesday and my place on Thursday. He questioned Patsy & Marmaduke at length. I was working on fencing on the new land.

Now & then Patsy asks me a question that implies she thinks one of us committed the murder. Something like "Do you believe Kench's story of the wild turkey causing the cut on his hand?"

The bleakness of this cold gray day was worsened by seeing Emily at church today, again pregnant by her odious husband.

Alas I have blessings to count. Little John is a healthy & loveable young'un. The hunting has been good, and all my folks apply themselves so that we will not starve this winter.

Chapter Eleven

Sunday, 8 Jan' 1792

We worked out a complicated arrangement resolving the county's flawed division of Papa's slaves. I lose Sukie, my most valuable inheritance. At least she is reunited with her husband and she will owe us six weeks of labor per year for six years. In addition my debts to various family members are discharged, and I got a rifle, a quern,* a skein of linen thread, & three pigs out of the exchange. I did not fare well (getting no consideration for poor young Will's death), but Gardner & Lewis are very hardnosed about such things, and peace amongst family has some value.

I contemplate the advisability of giving Marmaduke the rifle. Occupying father-in-law's old house, he might need it for protection and he could supplement their diet with hunting. Dare I trust him to that degree?

At the New Year's slave trade, Asa Johnson bought a very expensive light-skinned mulatto wench. 'Tis said that she is exceeding fair & could very nearly pass.

Asa is able to make this purchase no doubt because of his profit from collecting the Whiskey Tax. He & Whitaker tread lightly in application of the tax and thereby avoid widespread contempt—for indeed, widespread contempt is what it would engender. But they collect enough from those whom they dislike to pay themselves handsomely.** Kenchen is trying to decide if he should sell his still.

Sunday 12 Feb^y

How events clump together. I had worried that some curse of fallowness lay upon us. (Tho' the infrequency of our relations explains it in Patsy's case.) Well, a week ago it became evident Pris is with child. And then today Patsy announced that she is. One must have faith. I have told Marmaduke that if the area of his primary stewardship (around father-in-law's old place) is well-tended as of July 4th, I will give him a rifle & train him in its use. And

---

* A "quern" was a small hand-driven mill for grinding grain into meal at home.

** The Federal government received virtually no revenue from the Whiskey Tax in North Carolina ("The Whiskey Rebellion in North Carolina" by Jeffrey Crow in the *North Carolina Historical Review*, January 1989). On 25 July 1792, Sec. of Treas. Hamilton wrote Edw. Carrington, inquiring about the possibility of using the Virginia militia to enforce "the Excise law in N Carolina."

further, that if he & Pris continue to apply themselves with industry, their private garden plot will be increased to a half acre beginning this fall.

Kenchen says Asa is a-whoring out his new possession for ready money. The lust stays upon my favorite brother as much as it does upon me: I wonder if he has partaken.

Dear Sterling,

Convey to all your connexions how I do miss you all. I miss my poor children & Buck Spring mightily. Yet it isn't for naught that I am here: Hamilton's latest scheme is to pay bounties to his favorite Eastern industries. He would have us, the farmers, subsidize his Yankee manufacturers & ship owners yet further.

James Madison of Virginia emerges as a leading voice of reason against Hamilton. Hamilton tries to get around the strictness of the functions enumerated for the federal gov't in the body of the Constitution by pointing to the "promote the **general** welfare" in the Preamble. Madison has the proper reply: If Congress can apply money indiscriminately for the purpose of promoting the general welfare, then it can take religion, education, road building, literally everything under its control. Why not reduce the Constitution to one phrase: The Federal government can do anything! I hope there are enough of us, planters & republican-minded Congressmen, to stall Hamilton's proposals. The tenor of this great city favors him. The rich, powerful residents of thriving Philadelphia view an energetic gov't as forward thinking & modern. They are ignorant of how Rome's original republic was gradually destroyed. Our federalist friend Justice Iredell is a fish in water amongst these elites.

Do they not see that as Hamilton spreads around favors that we taxpayers fund, he is building a corrupting web? Or are many already caught in his web?:—to wit, many of the affluent set here are holders of government bonds, holders of U.S. bank stock, holders of government jobs or contracts. I had the great honor of dining with Sec. of State Thomas Jefferson yesterday afternoon. He quotes Hamilton as saying "This constitution is a shilly shally thing of mere milk & water, which cannot last, and is only good as a step to something better."

In any case, it is utterly unjust to protect one set of industries at the expense of everyone else. When Hamilton & his corps in Congress say "for the good of the nation," what they generally mean is themselves.

Philadelphia is the grandest city I have ever seen. More than 60,000 souls! Goodly numbers of the homes are brick, many with considerable ornamentation. A few have iron stoves which sit out from the wall & heat the room much more effectually than a fireplace! Nice glass windows are taken for granted. The streets are paved with pebbles or stones & bordered by brick gutters & sidewalks—hence are never so muddy or dusty as Halifax. There are very grand public buildings. The library would overwhelm you. <u>Several</u> newspapers!

It is a vastly expensive place to visit. Hamilton's friend Robt. Morris charges the Pres. £700 a year for a house quite inferior to Wylie Jones'. If Morris greased palms in Richmond, he has made back his investment on this single transaction. Most folks in Warren Co. could not earn £700 [~$61,398 in 2012$'s] *in the seven best-crop years of their lives.*

Friend, Sterling, suffer me to plant the seed of your contemplating a visit to this brilliant city. Perhaps after a successful livestock drive up to Petersburg. You would have a good start on the trip: it would be the experience of a lifetime. You would be welcome to share my bed.

    Yr most obt ser't—
       Nathl Macon

Philadelphia
4 March 1792

                Sunday, 29 April

I am cheered by the prospect of pokeberry salad & bacon for our next meal. 'Tis three months since I ate our last leather britches [dried green beans]. Kenchen claims I am demented to care over much for green vegetables as I do. Their absence in winter is as bad to me as the leafless trees & the cold weather.

I've a mind to cease going to church. The sermons often rub me wrong and Emily is seldom there.

Corn, peas, beans, cabbage & carrots planted. Upwards of five acres of plowed rows this year—as pretty as any big planter's fields. All under my care are well. Patsy's brother has the makings of a good farmer, tho' I've given up teaching him to read.

                 20 May

Good tidings & bad. The good news is that republicans ("republican" seems to displace the old-fashion adjective "Whig") defeated Hamilton's program of bounties & high tariffs. The bad news is that Emily's baby was born dead; no news of how she fares.

Sunday, 19 August

Lewis brought Mama & Sis for a visit. They brought woeful news: Macon's six-year-old, his only son, has died in agony of jaw-fall [Lockjaw/Tetanus]. Earlier in the summer he had been struck severely by a headache stick* and lay senseless with a gashed head upon the ground for a spell; some conjecture a connection. Poor Macon.

The dog days of August are upon us; naturally many hereabout are ill. Old Lucy is again; she puts urine & cat blood in her chicken soup and claims it helps.

If we can keep the worms off the tobacco & sundry critters out of the corn, then our prospects are good.

Sun' 26 Aug'

Two great events, one delivered hither within the other. Firstly, Halifax now has its very own newspaper. Secondly, the French have suspended the monarchy; the greatest nation in the world has become a republic and affirmed the principles of our Revolution. Everyone—even federalists—drink toasts of celebration to the French—our allies, without whom we could hardly have achieved our own independence. To be joined by the French in our bold republican experiment gives us all pride & renewed confidence.

Sunday, 16 Sept.

Last week the finely-dressed Asa Johnson brought his harlot to church. I caught but scant glance of her since she sat in back with the other slaves. The most beautiful belles are those of whom you only get a glance. With Patsy so fat now, all the fair sex look most fetching to me. His harlot looked comely…and oddly familiar.

Asa taunted me privately, in a whisper: "For you Sterling, you can have her for three shillings." I suffered a tiny momentary temptation. Asa was not

---

* A "headache stick" was used to winnow wheat, and as the name suggests, could accidentally hit a careless person in the head.

doing me a favor; he merely wants to be able to tell Emily and reduce me in her eye.

I wonder that Asa seems to suffer no loss of respect in the congregation for profiting from his whore. Most probably do not know; he is discreet. However, I believe I heard Caleb Brown chide him today warmly for bringing her to church, altho' I am not certain he wasn't heated about something else altogether (I could not hear well).

Tues', 30 Oct^r

I have a daughter! Mama claims she looks like me when I was a baby. We were working feverishly to get all the crops ready to carry to market and were greeted with the good news when we came in to sup. Necessity happily kept me out of earshot of Patsy. Mother and child seem well, tho' all agree it was a difficult travail. We will name the babe Sarah.

Sunday, 4 Nov^r

I have paused here at Person's Ordinary, needing as I did to pay the three shillings credit extended to me in July. I tarry here over a mug of cider and savor a successful farming year and the prospect of a bit of rest.

Tobacco brought a fair price. We lugged what corn we could to market as corn rather than whiskey; results were at least better than last year when we paid Asa's tax.

I have paid all my interest plus £23 on my debt. I have bought all our essentials and *real* coffee per Patsy's request & the luxury of the new *N-C Journal*[*] newspaper. And I have £1, 15 shillings for contingencies. Progress. It has been a long while since I have had this much actual money.

The temptation of visiting Asa's harlot for three shillings presents itself within me & I swell. Kenchen has told me where her trysting hut lies; 'tis near. Fortuitously, Patsy's brother, Eli, accompanies me. As the preacher says, the flesh is weak.

Saw Wylie Jones. He said the Philadelphia papers have been full of vicious attacks upon Thomas Jefferson by Hamilton. Mr. Jefferson has not condescended to reply, though others have. Mr. Jones claims that Jefferson is merely rendered more famous by the attacks and is now seen as more the leader of republicans than Madison.

---

[*] *North-Carolina Journal* commenced publication in Halifax 26 July 1792. It was printed each Wednesday.

Tues, 6 Nov^r

    I returned to find Patsy gripped by a fever. She hurts in her head and below. Prissy had gone to fetch Mrs. Walker just as I arrived. She & Mama came and administered a clister [enema] of milk, water, & salt. This helped with the peculiarly foul odor of her discharge. They say this is very serious. Kenchen's wife & Priss take turns giving suck to the babe; little Sarah seems to be perfectly fine.

    The women are doing what can be done. I have made efforts to comfort her; she is one who when ill in body is also ill in spirit. The most I can do is pray and get the winter wheat planted.

11 Nov^r

    Patsy worsens. She is possesst by pain, fierce perspiration, & foul discharge. Kenchen's & Lewis' wives, Mrs. Walker, & Absalom Jenkins are here. Our home overflows; my bed will likely be in the barn tonight. Six days ago I was happier than I have been in a year. Now I feel helpless.

Tues. 20 Nov^r

We buried Patsy yesterday.*

---

* Patsy may have died from Puerperal fever, a strep infection that was a major cause of death associated with child bearing

Chapter Twelve

Sunday, 6 January 1793

If 'twere a more ordinary time, I would take much pleasure, as do all my friends & connexions, in the present events. No sooner had it been confirmed that France is now a republic than our sister in freedom found herself threatened by the powerful & intolerant monarchies of Prussia & Austria. News has arrived of the great French victory over these powers at Valmy. There was much celebration in Warrenton & Halifax—even an illumination at the latter. Kenchen drug me to Person's Ordinary on New Years where John Macon spoke for us all with the toast "May the tree of liberty planted in this country take root in France and spread over Europe."

Alas, this is no ordinary time: I drink from a bitter cup. I am continually in the grip of tortured thoughts. My soul is checkered by specious emotions mostly akin to guilt. My partner is dead; I am haunted by an irrational specter that tells me I failed her. By not providing for her better so that death would not take her? (I paid Mrs. Walker to do all the treatment she knew.) By not loving her as a spouse should? I could have been a better husband.

I miss that small degree of intimacy, nay, comfortable familiarity, we did possess. But when I am lucid I know I tried to love her & could not.

And as I may admit only here, I feel an admixture of guilt & foolish hope as from time to time the faint glimmer of Emily conjures itself in my breast. Here especially the admixture is more than 3 quarters guilt. What utter depraved foolishness. How one's own mind can be one's complex enemy.

I am finally managing to deal with the practical problems of the household without Patsy. Pris has stayed here this past week to give suck to little Sarah. When Marmaduke complains I will send the little ones to Mama's for a spell, then to Kenchen's wife. Old Lucy seems to have more vigor now that she is obviously more needed.

Sunday, 13 Jan^y

I was something taken aback today—nay, I was cut to the quick.

It is inconceivable to me now that on first acquaintance with Caleb Brown I thought him to have a handsome face. After church, that churl of an overseer of slaves, that man of wormwood & gall, spoke thus to Eli:

"Eli, it was a painful thing that your sister should survive the birthing & then die, what, above three weeks later?"

"It was above two weeks. But it wasn't three," said I.

"Hmn. Touchy, Shearin?" said he. "Tender of blame, are ye?" That man is brim full of malice for my family. He must really believe we killed his brother-in-law.

Later I attempted to discuss Mr. Brown's ungenerous insinuation with Eli. I tried to explain to him as Mrs. Walker has told me: A woman dying in the manner that his sister did is not uncommon. Lots of doubt in his countenance. Salt to the wound. The thought of Eli harboring blame toward me ran so in my head tonight, I could scarce taste my supper.

There are stumps to chop & fences to work. Hard work is the lone salve of my spirit. Without it I would not sleep at all.

Sunday, 20 Jan^y

Pres. Washington has been re-elected with little dissent. Vice-Pres. Adams lost many votes to Jefferson & other more republican characters. My great acquaintance John Taylor has been elected Senator from Virginia. I feel pride, and confidence for our U. States.

Our General Assembly has elected Alexander Martin to the Senate to serve in the room of James Iredell's aristocratical brother-in-law. Martin vows that his principle care will be to preserve the individuality & internal sovereignty of our State. He also vows to eliminate the dark councils of the Senate, who seem determined that their conduct shall never meet the eyes of the people.*

For want of a quiet mind, sound sleep I cannot attain; my bed is strewn with thorns.

Sunday, 3 Feb^y

Thus far my little ones do well enough with their alternate mothers, Pris, old Lucy, Mama, & Kenchen's Mary. At 3 years of age, John missed his mother heartily at first but now seems easy. I must apply my mind to our future. As I write these words, I am haunted by a multitude of memories which time cannot efface. Even wondering where is my little Sarah's secret namesake.

---

* At this time the U.S. Senate kept its proceeding secret.

Sunday, 24 Feb^y

The *N-C Journal* reports from a London paper of a British soldier being flogged for reading Thos. Paine's *The Rights of Man.* Expresses much about the nature of monarchical Britain.

Nathl Macon was unopposed in his re-election to Congress. Everyone knows he always does precisely as he declares.

'Tis 4 months since Patsy passed away. There is a quilting Saturday at Mrs. Person's. Several likely belles are sure to be in attendance. Perhaps I should also. To speak the truth, I don't have the fortitude. —Emily has been at church only once; our eyes barely met. I need little reminding that she is still bound & as remote as ever. She prudently avoids me.

Thurs', 28 Feb^y

Virginia Congressman Wm. Giles is on the cusp of delivering justice to the shrewd Sec. of Treasury Hamilton. He is charging him publically with illegally taking money borrowed in Europe to pay debts owed in Europe and depositing it in the Bank of the U.S., where it will earn interest for his corrupt corps of bank stockholders. Jefferson privately describes Hamilton to Macon as "The man who has the shuffling of millions backwards and forwards from paper into money into paper, from Europe to America, and America to Europe; the man who has the dealing out of treasury secrets among his friends in what time and measure he pleases, and who never slips an occasion of making friends with his means."

A quilting this late in winter is a bit unusual. Perhaps it is providence. 4 months. My grief has seasoned some little. My children need a mother & I need a wife; it is time I should start the process. I pray I am more fortunate this time, more perspicacious in my choice.

I was awakened from a dream in which I came upon Asa Johnson beating Emily & in my rage I killed him with my knife. The instant I pulled my knife out of him there was a rope around my neck & I was swinging from the gallows. I awoke in a sweat & panting.

Sunday, 3 March

Going into a den of women is never a comfortable undertaking. Hence I was glad of the company of another bachelor & one with whom I compare favorably. Over one hundred acres and three and a half slaves sound respectable. But only if you do not consider that my debt could bankrupt me in combination with a couple of crop failures. I reckon I am not alone in that predicament.

Struggling with my feelings of uncouthness, I managed some limited polite intercourse with a fair belle named Margaret Simpson at Mrs. Person's quilting bee. Miss Simpson is a pretty dark-haired girl. Mary & Kenchen Shearin speak of her merits including her good character & want of foolishness. However, I did not find her devoid of humor. Indeed, we had not been conversing long when she told me a little story of some capricious delicacy that induced her to lower her voice, which in turn required me to lean close to her, where I own I was enticed by the fragrant spices of her necklace. She & others were so cordial that in time I grew more easy in their midst.

"Mr. Shearin," spake Mrs. Person, the hostess, "You are known to be an excellent reader. We are very blessed to have acquired from a traveling peddler this very new book, *The Power of Sympathy* by Wm. Hill Hall. Would you be so kind as to read to our assembly whilst we sew?" She said this with some little pride, as she reverently handed me this new novel.

I read several pages. The story was engaging to me as well as the audience. Twice as I glanced up, Margaret Simpson's large brown eyes were fixed upon me, her countenance interested & amiable. A strangely worded thought crept from nowhere into my mind: This courting isn't as easy as a corpulent overseer breaking wind, but I *can* do it.

And then there came a knock at the door. Moments later, Mrs. Person ushered Mrs. Emily Johnson into the room. How, pray, could I have had the least presentiment of such a scene? My heart began to pound & refused to subside.

Emily avoided looking at me. I reckoned I should follow her example, yet her presence filled the room. To my further mortification, I had difficulty reading the next page smoothly in front of her of all people.

By force of mind, I concentrated on *The Power of Sympathy* rather than my compulsion to look into Emily's eyes & have her look back into mine. Just before the end of the chapter, I glanced at her evanescently, but her determined stare was fixed on her sewing.

At the end of the chapter, everyone sang out for me to continue. After a drink of water, I complied. This excellent novel will deserve notice. That I could apprehend this truth while my mind was so agitated by Emily's presence is remarkable.

Her cool reserve continued. She spoke with Mrs. Person, with Miss Simpson, with others, but she never squared her shoulders in my direction. The least mark of indifference or disregard from her gives me more pain than it is possible to express. Surely another construction could be placed upon her deportment, but my mind struggled.

At last I insisted Mrs. Person, who is proud with justice of her book & her own erudition, take a turn. As Mrs. Person read, Miss Simpson looked at me & smiled. I could not respond with the easiness that I had gained before Emily's arrival. Hiding my true feelings, my deep discomfiture, was never my talent. In due course, I took my leave, feeling quite as uncouth on quitting the quilting bee as when I had first arrived.

Filled with uncertainty, I wandered around on Aristotle for a spell. I endeavored to becalm myself, to little avail. I decided to hunt in the area of the probable path between Mrs. Person's place & Emily's. Pray, what was I about? I warrant that I was like a bird, whose nest has been robbed, who fears to come nigh, yet cannot determine how to leave. I was still too agitated to be effectual. I missed a buck. I missed a quail. Finally I just sat on a rock with my face in my hands.

As twilight approached, I surmised that she might spend the night. It started to get colder; I started for home. But then I thought I heard the hooves & snorting of a horse. I paused & turned. I held my breath & listened. It was a young woman riding side saddle. It was she.

When she espied me, she halted her cobb [small horse] but didn't speak. Then she expresst a...hesitant, uncertain smile.

"Hello" said I.

"Hello" she replied. We beheld each other for perhaps most of a minute in silence. She finally broke the silence. "I thought...I thought you'ld be most of the way home by now."

"I was distracted by a buck." I paused. "To tell the truth, I was really just distracted." I smiled helplessly. She returned my smile in her inveterate politeness.

"I'm glad to see you," said she. "You look well. I know you have been through a great deal of woe."

"Thank you" I said faintly. My thoughts were confused. Tho' I wanted to speak to her of all manner of particulars, I found myself thinking of how far she had to go at this late hour. "Night's coming on. I shouldn't detain you so distant from your home."

What was I saying? Had my wits deserted me? I needed to talk to her. For her to tell me to forget her & find a mother for my children.

She hesitated & looked at me as if discomfited by my presence.

"Yes," she said quietly. She clucked her cobb. My heart sank as she rode on. Alas, she turned back toward me. "Perhaps it is wrong to suggest...Why don't you ride with me a ways?"

We rode a ways in silence, my not knowing what to say.

"I'm sensible that Miss Simpson looks at you with some little favor," said she at last.

I did not know what to say. I looked at her questioningly.

"She is very pretty."

"Emily…"

"Perhaps you should call me Mrs. Johnson." Her reserve stung me.

"Mrs. Johnson, to speak the bold truth, Margaret Simpson's fairness & her friendliness were overwhelmed by your presence and my feelings for you."

She looked me in the eye for the 1st time this day. Then looked away. But turned back to me again with a glimmer of something more than politeness in her countenance before looking back the way we were traveling. We rode on in silence.

I spent a good quarter of a mile trying to think what I should ask of her, how I should phrase my desire for her guidance. Presently, she asked that I tell her of all the news from the *North-Carolina Journal*. In due course, our intercourse flowed more freely over these subjects of a non-personal nature. At the same instant, we both caught the sweet-betsy-like fragrance of a patch of early blooming burgundy trilliums. We looked at each other & found ourselves smiling at each other with abandon. Her cool reserve melted & her blue eyes revealed that she cared for me.

My heart swelled in my chest. The late winter coolness of the air no longer felt chill but rather perfectly suited to my inner warmth. It felt delicious against my skin. It was heaven to be able to be with her and to be myself, unrestrained by the eyes of others. And to sense her similar feeling.

I had thought to ask her to somehow release me so that I could pursue an eligible wife. But I could not manage such a question as our conversation took courses of its own. All thoroughly amiable & pleasing.

I recited to her these humorous lines from the newspaper:

Two Lawyers, when a knotty case was o'er
Shook hands, altho' they wrangled hard before,
Zounds, says the client who was cast, pray how,
Are you such friends that were such foes just now?
Thou fool says one, we Lawyers tho' so keen,
Like sheers, ne'er cut ourselves, but what's between.

She laughed freely. "Papa Jones used to say that lawyers were a necessary evil—but still evil."

She was very interested in all the news I could convey from the newspaper—including the French triumphs. She asked if I could smuggle her some reading materials again. Of course I can refuse her nothing. We settled on a concealed spot (between two rocks behind the Johnny house at church) as a place I could leave the contraband that she may then retrieve.

I noted the walnut dye of her petticoat, and she confirmed that it was the same one the pokeberry dye had been spilled upon & we laughed about it.

Then I probingly asked if the new mulatto was a help with linen production. Her countenance grew troubled. She was slow to answer.

"Not as much as one would wish."

I helped matters not at all by shifting the subject to my pretty little baby daughter. I could again read the sadness in her that she had no success in producing a healthy baby. Sometimes I am so utterly bereft of the skill of complaisance in spite of my intentions.

Regretting my thoughtlessness, I said "You will soon be enjoying a similar blessing, no doubt. I know you have consumed all your share of misfortune already."

"It is a lot less likely now, I'm afraid." I think that is what she replied for she spoke it almost under her breath. What does this whisper signify?

I managed to guide our intercourse into more genial subjects with her help. Then we rode awhile in silence. I took her hand in mine. We rode on like that. I adore her presence.

A mile from their place I leaned over to kiss her cheek & take my leave. She met me with her lips: I am a condemned man! How am I to court another when I am thus in her spell. Either God or Aristotle deserve the credit for my safely traversing that dark trail home; I was as if captured by Mr. Mesmer.*

Sun', 24 March

Much shocking news. Louis XVI has been executed. Seems to cool the ardor of some federalist types for the French revolution. Giles' resolutions against Hamilton were easily defeated! Two-thirds of the Congressmen finding Hamilton blameless were stockholders of the Bank of the U. States, writes Macon. The other one-third simply suffer a blind devotion to Pres. Washington.

Start planting corn tomorrow.

Friday, 12 April

Without opportunity to borrow a novel from Macon who is in Philadelphia or from Jones in Halifax, I had to settle for smuggling a much

---

* Franz Mesmer, 1734-1815, pioneer of hypnotism.

folded newspaper to Emily. Little Sarah thrives. Her name sake's dogwoods bloom profusely this year. Good weather for our planting.

Sunday, 28 April

Sometimes I think I should call upon fair Margaret; I need a wife in a great many respects. Then today at church, Emily's eyes kissed mine momentarily & I know I love her fiercely. She foments my soul. What am I to do?

Cabbage, beans, peas, melon all in the ground; all well thus far.

France is now at war with Great Britain as well!

Sunday, 12 May

Last Sunday, the new French ambassador, M. Genet, passed not far to the west of Warrenton. He landed in Charleston & is making his way—overland!—to Philadelphia. This less direct, more arduous route implies some design.

He spoke in great praise of republicanism. John Macon stated that he went further & used the word "democrat." How Federalists love to pejoratively style Republicans as "mobocrats" or "democrats." Genet uses the word as entirely positive.

Those who heard Monsieur Genet speak are talking of the bold move of forming a society and calling it the Granville-Warren Democratic Society, freely claiming the pejorative label. Many are sporting tricolor cockades, as they say we are all the "citizens" of France. Indeed, we could not have won our Revolution without them. Yorktown was a French victory & so much more.

Sun', 26 May

Nathl Macon is home from Philadelphia. He says the cunning Hamilton is triumphant. But Sen. John Taylor, whom Macon visited at his plantation near Fredericksburg on his homeward journey, is writing newspaper articles (over the name "Franklin")* and a pamphlet to alert the citizenry of the

---

* It was customary during this period to write letters to newspapers using pseudonyms such as "Brutus," "Cato," or "a Whig." It is perhaps significant that John Taylor chose the name "Franklin" since Benjamin Franklin was the lynchpin of French support in the Revolution and a proponent of such un-Federalist ideas as the importance of annual elections

corruptness of these matters:—to wit, 2/3 of the Congressmen supporting Hamilton are stockholders of the Bank and hence financial beneficiaries of his schemes.

Macon has words of praise for my brother Lewis, who with John Macon is managing his farm in his absence. If future congressional sessions are so long as this one, he will doubtless require an overseer. Perhaps he motivates his negroes to keenly heed Lewis & John with the threat of such; they have had no difficulty.

'Tis a month since Emily was at church.

Sunday, 9 June

I missed church last Sunday getting the sweet potatoes from bed to field & the corn weeded. Emily was absent again today, tho' Asa was there; I dare not inquire concerning her.

Amongst those present was Margaret Simpson, her sweet oval face with skin perfectly unblemished by pox, her big brown eyes, her fine, regular teeth. She was of a warm aspect and possesses a pleasing manner.

"Mr. Shearin, you look dashing & modern with the new style of hair & hat," said she. I had cut my queue & wore my round-brimmed hat cocked on one side with the French tri-color cockade.

"Thank you kindly, Miss Simpson. I'm cutting my hair shorter as those in the Roman Republic are said to have done. Have we not paid homage too long already to aristocratical forms? Pigtails & rolls & such," said I with a laugh, mocking styles that till recently had predominated. I did not say that the notion had first occurred to me when I espied similar on a young gentleman, a Virginian I think, on a handsome black stallion at the last Halifax race-meeting. Though I had eschewed a tricorn for a round-brimmed hat some time ago, cocking it with a French cockade does give it a certain flair.

"Suffer me to say that I like it right well, whatever your motive. The way your curls frame your face is so exceedingly different from pulling everything back into a queue. You will be cooler all summer too," said she, her voice, her manner, mild as buttermilk.

"Another benefit indeed."

"I've just succeeded in borrowing *The Power of Sympathy* from Mrs. Person to finish the story. I finished reading it & enjoyed it. But not nearly so much as when I listened to your reading of it at the quilting bee."

"Miss Simpson, you are something a flatterer I believe," said I with a smile. She gave me a mischievous smile back. "Of course, flattery is like perfume some say...ever so nice...as long as you don't swallow any of it."

She laughed. "No, no. You really read it so well, dramatizing each bit better than I could in my head. Changing your voice with the speakers. Really it was quite good."

I tarried there with her as she told me how the story developed. She is charming. I'll wager she will not remain unwed for long.

'Tis above 3 months since that quilting bee & my last intercourse [interaction] with Emily. But once have I lain my eyes upon her fleetingly, that one time at church in all that time. I must buck up. I must confront what is.

The fetching Miss Simpson. Well. I must examine her character more fully than did I with Patsy. I must wrestle with my soul. But alas, Miss Simpson is very pretty, and perhaps willing.

While there I received a flattering request: Several members of the Democratic Society asked me to suggest to Wylie Jones that he initiate a democratic society in Halifax. I am honored that they associate me with so fine a gentleman.

President Washington grows ever more monarchical: He has taken it upon himself to declare our States neutral in the war between France and all the kingly despots of Europe. France was our indispensable ally in the Revolution and is now our sister in the great republican experiment. (France was more important to the Revolution than Genl Washington, who in all the years of the Revolution never led us to a victory aside from Trenton.) We should at least afford French privateers safe harbor against the aggressive & formidable British navy. Does not our treaty with France guarantee them as much?

Monday, 17 June

Mary Walker Shearin, Kenchen's wife, is my favorite sister by marriage. She is handsome & amiable; she is less burdened by residual weight than most women after three children; and she possesses the strength & sympathy that all would wish in a wife or relation. Hence I was troubled Friday when I carried little John & Sarah to place them in her care. For I became sensible of gloomy thoughts preying upon her mind. Mary is less mercurial than most of red-hair & freckled complexion. As a rule, she is as solid as her strong bones.

I tarried there a spell under the pretense of doing some chores in partial return for all her care of my little children. I told her something of my dilemma of loving Emily Johnson yet obviously needing an eligible wife. She gave me practical advice. Yet again she gave Margaret Simpson a good word.

Confiding thus, I eventually drew forth from her that her concern was Kenchen: He has been absent from their farm a great deal. And if I may trust my inference, they were suffering a dearth of intimacy. I endeavored to reassure her of Kenchen's devotion to her & their family, and I said I would try to explore somehow whether there might possibly be something amiss.

Today I confronted Kenchen. After considerable hounding, he unloosed a tale of some little interest.

"I have been having relations with Louisa, Asa Johnson's mulatto."

"How can you afford that?" I asked.

"I only paid Asa the first couple of times."

My jaw dropped & I could not restrain a laugh: "Bless my stars, Kench! Your prowess is so great that she welcomes you on the sly?"

"'Tis not exactly so. But near enough," he answered with an irrepressible smile.

"Come on, Kenchen. Be candid. I'm Sterling, your brother."

"Well...as I said, I paid Asa once after harvest & once in December. She is so...Sterling, her comeliness & manner are irresistible. Then in late March I was over at my mother-in-law's (Mid-Wife Walker) when Asa's other female slave came asking for the potion for being rid of a baby. I was leaving as she was & I offered to give her a ride as far as my place.

"On the way I probed. She had a husband as well as a master who would both probably want her to have pickaninnies. And surely Miss Emily wants a child. Who was the potion for? It became clear it was for Louisa.

"The next day on a whim I sneaked over to Louisa's hut. I found her collapsed in the field, hoe still in her hand. I carried her back to her hut. When she came to, I tried to calm her in word & deed. In that vein, I told her it was probably normal for the potion to make her ill for a spell—tho' I was no more than guessing at that moment. I put a wet cloth to her forehead & asked what necessary chores I might do for her, what with her weak state. When I returned, she had discharged the contents of her stomach. I cleaned up & comforted her as I could. She was pitiful. I stayed with her till she felt she could walk to the Johnson house, which to my great relief was only an hour or so. For how mortifying might it have been for me to have to seek Mrs. Walker or even the Johnsons' aid for her had she worsened. Pray, how would I have explained my presence?"

"I do not remember Sarah being in such a woeful state as that," I said.

"Mrs. Walker has strengthened the potion I've learned since then—all the more when she thinks it for a negress—which Louisa really is but barely. I went back the next day, arriving just after the desired miscarriage had occurred. I comforted & aided her as I could. When finally I quitted her abode, I was sensible of a strong degree of appreciation on her part.

"Some time later, 6 weeks I guess, I returned clandestinely with gifts of apple brandy, fresh milk, & honey. She took me to her bed. I took a care to please her. I am kind to her & she to me. I love my Mary, but Louisa is… uhm…uhm."

"Iniquity was never so delicious?"

He nodded yes. "Sterling, she hath such…enthusiasm!"

I caught myself from laughing bawdily with him & endeavored to adopt a sternness apposite to what I needed to say to him for Mary's sake. With difficulty & awkwardness colored by my own feelings, I spoke to Kenchen of the shame of this dissipated pleasure, of the pain he was causing Mary, & of the vulnerability in which he was placing his family.

"The least you can do is to properly express to Mary your affection for her."

I fear my approach was too tepid, for before I left him he fell to talking about how it distresst his mind that Louisa must be shared with others.

"Of course, Asa charges enough that not just anyone can partake. And he is exceedingly discreet. Few know except such as might be patrons with ready money."

Kenchen also revealed that Asa himself has used her roughly on occasion. That odious wretch should burn in hell if there is a just God in Heaven.

Sun', 7 July

I journeyed to Halifax; the road has received no care & was lumpier than a diseased cow. I was able to sell my produce successfully to the large gathering and was then able to enjoy the grand & brilliant July 4th celebration. After the dinner at 3pm, there followed patriotic toast of great sentiment—each followed by discharge of cannon on the green.

A ball of some splendor followed the toasts. Dance elevates the spirit in eminent degree. I danced with Miss Simpson. How she hath bloomed in these last 2 or 3 years. She moves with a grace on the dance floor excelled only by the beauty of her face with those large brown eyes & their silken lashes. And her conversation, while confined to indifferent subjects, is so genial & illumined by humor as to cause her attractiveness to increase the longer you are in her presence. Nor am I the only man sensible of her charms. She had an ample supply of suitors in attendance at this ball. But I flatter myself she manifested a healthy interest in me.

Asa was there without Emily. I have seen virtually nothing of her now since early March.

I succeeded in broaching to Mr. Wylie Jones the subject of a democratic society. I did so with some trepidation: Democratic societies seem to have few characters of such gentility & wealth as he involved in them, in spite of their rapid proliferation in several states. Indeed, his rebuff was compelling:

"Sterling, I trust the people to a degree. They fought the Revolution to escape oppression, not to inflict a tyranny of the majority. But I fear—as does John Adams—that total democracy would lead to a tyranny of the majority.

"Never should prudent men allow a situation where those who pay little or no taxes can vote. The masses paying little tax would vote themselves benefits at the expense of the necessarily smaller number of affluent. Indeed the idle & poor will vote for the industrious & propertied to pay all the tax.

"The new states, Kentucky & Vermont, have adopted universal suffrage without property requirements. This will not produce a free & just society. A republic may; a full democracy will not. Count me as no democrat."

I tried to argue that he construed the word "democrat" as synonymous with "mobocrat" but to no avail.

Sunday, 21 July

After thirty-four years as a bastion of practical reason & deism, Halifax has succumbed to the growing popularity of religious sentiment: it has built its first church.

In a more liberal, disinterested, & patriotic exertion, Halifax—led by Wylie Jones & Wm. R. Davie—has raised more money for our State's new University than any other county in our State. Even chief tax gatherer Col. John Whitaker shared his bounty, donating £20 to the University of North-Carolina.

Crops fare well as the very hot weather has been adequately tempered by rain. The rumors are that prices are going up due to the European war.

Emily was at church for the first time in 2 & ½ months. (I have missed several services as well.) She averted her eyes from me. What does this signify? Is she saying, "I am married. Forget me. Get thy children a Mother."?

Sun', 28 July

The Democratic Society works to elect men of republican principles (such as John Macon) to our State General Assembly. We disseminate as we can John Taylor's writings exposing the corruption of the national Federalists & old copies of the few republican newspapers of Philadelphia & Virginia. Why do most newspapers lean toward federalism?

The alluring Miss Simpson & I enjoyed some conversation beyond the superficial at a frolic. I like her well. Who would not? Indeed, I was one of several suitors.

Sunday, 11 August

In spite of old Lucy's exertions, our farm & family miss greatly the presence of a competent wife. Even she urges me to get a wife.

I went to call upon Margaret Simpson. She was in a distinct perspiration from working in the field. I'm sensible that she suffered some little discomfiture from this circumstance, but in truth, it added to her charm in some sense to see her unprimped & ever so slightly flustered by it. Were I as pretty as she, I can never imagine ever being flustered. Indeed, her countenance glowed. And more. Her beautiful eyes were demurely solicitous.

It went as well as one could hope for. The intercourse betwixt Miss Simpson & her family and myself was exceedingly agreeable. Their cordial reception, enhanced more than a little by the welcoming aroma of baking bread that wafted through their abode, rendered me easy. Her family is respectable & of good character. Pray, who would not like them? If any can break me from forbidden Emily's spell, 'tis she. I am lacking in good sense if I dither.

She & I have been alone too little. It falls to me to have the initiative to remedy that defect.

Sunday, 18 August

Great success hereabouts for republicans & freedom at the elections. It was a good omen that so many at the courthouse sported the red, white, & blue cockade as all the French republicans are said to do. Conversed with Miss Simpson after church; we made some tentative plans.

Sat, 24 August*

Kenchen came to me today beaten severely. Covered with blood. The stick was wielded by Asa Johnson; Asa caught him with Louisa & went after him with a vengeance. No broken bones but numerous bad wounds. Clearly my arguments to him to mend his ways have been too meek-spirited. Alas, Asa has delivered a more effectual argument.

After old Lucy & I cleaned him up, he wanted me to help him concoct a story to tell Mary. He wanted to pretend he was knocked from his horse by a tree branch & fell down a ravine. I argued he should tell the truth and ask forgiveness.

Louisa had conveyed intelligence of particular interest; Asa has been Preacher Absalom's confederate in most of his occasional supernatural feats. For instance, the healing of Asa's slave & the knowledge of Emily's dream in which her dead baby will not show her its face! This information burns inside me.

I must see Emily. She must know. It has been above 5 months since our talk in the Spring after the quilting bee. Only 2 glances of her at church in all that time, & the latter time she didn't look at me. Pray, what has Asa done with her, to her? She may need my help for all I know. At the very least I must have her blessing to pursue Margaret Simpson. I sent Miss Simpson a note, postponing my visit. Damnation! Now, how to proceed. How to arrange a private intercourse with her.

Sunday, 1 Sept^r

Yesterday was a sweltering hot day. A thick cloud cover colored all with a gray aspect & could have & should have brought rain at any moment. When I arrived at Person's Ordinary, where I went to sell some garden produce, I was wet skin out with perspiration.

Asa was there. No flincher at the bottle is he. He was so in his cups that he seemed to pay me no notice. Alas, thought I, hath Providence done me this favor, provided me with this opportunity?

I headed west away from the Ordinary—suspicion is ever eagle-eyed—but then circled back. A lark or Providence guided my route to their farm by the boulders where I had first seen Emily being abused by her odious husband—& then where we had later rendezvoused. Would it not be an excellent co-incidence to find her at her secret place? I felt most agitated about the prospect of going again to their farm. Still I had to see if she was alright. Perhaps she would tell me in some manner to proceed with pursuing Margaret.

When I came around the huge boulder, I espied her. Emily had lain on this hot, humid day stretched out on a smaller shaded boulder in nothing but her shift. Not even her mob-cap on her head: her long auburn curls fell on her shoulders as she sat up, startled. How beautiful she was to me.

The little noise I had made approaching this spot in the woods had awakened her from a light, perhaps uneasy sleep.

"Sterling!" she exclaimed as she grabbed for her petticoat & bodice.

I jumped down from Aristotle and embraced her. I held her firmly for several moments, cherishing each one. She dropped the petticoat in her hand & put her arms around me as well.

"I worried about you. Are you all right? Have you been kept captive these many months?" I asked.

She sighed heavily. I waited patiently & made her look me in the eye.

"I received the worst beating of my life when he caught me with the newspapers. It was such a ridiculous, unlikely event that he should happen on me as he did that I took it as a sign from God."

"A sign of what? Pray tell, dearest one."

She smiled, amused at my flowery words. "A sign that obedience to one's husband is more valuable in God's sight than the entertainment of my feminine pretensions." Her smile turned to a frown as she pushed me away. "It is received wisdom that a woman should submit herself to her husband's will & confine her improvement to what would make her pleasing to him. Now look at me embracing you!"

"What kind of god condones a man beating his wife for reading?" She looked down & did not answer. "Have you been forbidden from leaving your farm as well?"

"At first. Then I did not go to church for fear of giving Asa a clue as to the friend you have been to me: For how I could go to church & not glance at you with pleasure visible in my eye?"

"God's teeth, Emily," I was moved by her caring. "If I sell everything I own, would you flee with me & my two little ones to Tennessee? We would be able to buy raw land but no slaves to clear it; we would be poorer than the dirt for years. But I would do everything within my power to make you happy."

She was taken aback by my offer. "Sterling! You...offer... you care that much for me? You have just established your farm with such great diligence & back-breaking industry; you would give up that & every connexion & friend for me?"

"Yes." I had not considered this decision. It had erupted from me, but I meant it.

"I could not ask it of you, Sterling. Besides, I am married to Asa Johnson in God's eyes."

"If God can tolerate the hypocrisy of Preacher Absalom, he should tolerate a woman living with a common-law husband who loves her."

"What do you mean? What hypocrisy? I thought you had come to respect Absalom."

"It is true that Absalom does a lot of good. I own that when Patsy died, he was a sincere source of comfort. At root he is probably a man of some little virtue. I suspect the idea for their dishonesty originated with your odious husband."

I went on to recount what I had learned of Absalom's supernatural feats being contrived—with Asa's help. She was shaken by the knowledge that Asa had been the conduit for Absalom's knowledge of her powerful dream.

"That is how utterly dishonest & dishonorable Asa Johnson is, if it means gaining power—in this case over you."

She sat back on the boulder with a dazed countenance. She looked so sweet & vulnerable—no less for being only in her shift.

"You, on the other hand, have power over me without saying a word." She looked up at me with an expression half way betwixt a half smile at someone who is amiably silly & a plea to let her think…not knowing whether to laugh or cry. I took her hands and pulled her to her feet, back into my embrace. I kissed her as the French are said to do. She returned my kiss as Patsy was never able to do. There is divinity in the harmony with which our lips touch.

Moments of such kissing, tho' meant as an expression of love, yet aroused in me a powerful lust. For an instant, I thought to be embarrassed by it, so tender are my true feelings for her. But Emily kissed me with all the more sweet enthusiasm.

I placed my hands on her soft derriere & pulled her very close to me in an unabashedly lustful way, yet continuing the deliciously, delicate kisses that seemed to join our souls. As my affections were mounting a warmth I had never known, she pulled away from me.

"Sterling, is this right? Is this sin?"

I construed this as the demure protest requisite in any self-respecting Southern belle; I knew she loved me & wanted to be loved. I knew I loved her. I never felt more resolute.

"Yes." I answered as I pulled off my shirt. I yearned to feel her skin against mine.

I went to her and kissed & caressed her deliberately; I did not want this, this feeling, to ever end. I lifted her shift over her head & held her against me. I caressed her dainty white breasts; then fell to my knees to suck & nibble on them as she cradled & caressed my head with her arms & hands. I touched her, her every aspect, with adoring affection. And confirmed my fondest hope of kindred feeling in my beloved…that she wanted me mind & body.

The ecstasy that followed was too intense to be preserved in memory. Alas, if only the carnal knowing of my angel could be so preserved, perhaps I could want nothing further & rest in peace.

Chapter Thirteen

Wed[y] 1 January 1794

Much has occurred in the past 4 months that deserves recording. I have refrained in part because of the exigencies of the farm & family without a wife. (Old Lucy was sick much of November but now evinces her former resilience.) I have refrained in part for fear of discovery of this recorded admission of my transgressions.

Yet the New Year is upon us; I must gather my wits & resolve the proper path to follow. Somehow writing settles & calms my mind. No doubt this journal already contains a surfeit of evidence against me.

Two days after my last entry our tobacco barn burned to the ground, destroying most of the tobacco crop. Eli claims he left it alone during curing for "only a spell." 'Tis a misfortune whose sting was intensified by the good prices tobacco was bringing. (Divine retribution was Absalom's sermon that Sunday.)

Prices are rising for all goods now, deepening our distress. I felt compelled to make use of Kenchen's still to maximize the value of our corn crop. We had hoped to evade the Whiskey Tax as most of our neighbors succeed in doing. But Asa caught us again.

Yet if losing the tobacco crop & paying tax on the corn be the price for consummating what is between Emily & myself, I willingly pay it.

There was scant time during harvest to rendezvous with my beloved. And the safety of the arrangement was as difficult as it was necessary. Hence it was not until Asa went to the Halifax races in late October that Emily & I could meet. All the more sublime for the wait. The spirited vitality in her eyes, her expression, her sweet voice & movements, these render me more alive than anything I have ever known. She is beautiful, demurely sensual, and very true & good inside. How can her husband be so dull & blind as to be insensible to her beauty & virtue?

"Emily, that pudding head whom you must style husband could benefit from Solomon's insight..." I paused all coyness.

"Yes?" I didn't immediately answer. "Of whom amongst us is that not true? Are you going to share which particular of the great Psalmist's insights you mean?"

"'Wisdom maketh the face to shine' said Solomon in the Bible." I paused again. "This be as true of a woman's face as of a man's."

She smiled. "Indeed."

"And you are a case in point: 'tis my view that the cultivated quality of your mind is reflected in your veriest countenance, enhancing your beauty in a thousand illusive ways."

She swatted at me & laughed. "Only you! My flattering gallant. Or should I say rattle?" Shades of vermillion tinged her cheeks, her neck. "Sterling, are you teasing me?"

"No, Emily. I mean it."

"Sterling, I am so unused to the least tincture of appreciation from any corner that I…I…it is hard to credit your beautiful words when the rest of the world seems…so indifferent."

We talked a while bundled in a blanket, for the weather had turned cool. The intensely beautiful red leaves of the blackgum trees were memorable and exactly apposite to our emotions. It was very quiet save the agreeable trickle of the creek. Though our verbal intercourse was deliciously unhurried, she became cognizant of the lust she inspired; it could not be helped sitting so intimately. She giggled pleasantly & took my hand & touched it to her breast. But a few moments elapsed before our only need for the blanket was as an extra cushion on the fallen leaf mulch.

Afterward we talked at length of many things. She had heard nothing of the thousands in Philadelphia who had died of the Yellow Fever in August & September. Nor had she heard of the letter from Hispaniola saying "white people are going out of fashion and black and brown are in vogue."* Nor had she heard of Dr. Gloster's new store opened in Warrenton.

We talked of our affection, nay, devotion to one another. I pressed my offer again to make a new home for us in Tennessee. She spoke compellingly of the loss involved for me in losing the aid & companionship of neighbors & connexions.

"Would it not mean that you would never again see your mother, Kenchen, or Nath' Macon? What a price to pay. There would be none there to help you chop trees & stumps, to build a house, a barn, a smoke house, a corn crib. Many laborious hours in which your affection might sour to resentment. There would be no books or newspapers available to either of us in Tennessee and no time to read them were they available."

I own that my love's sage words rendered me something pensive.

A month later in late November, Emily & I had attempted another rendezvous but were prevented by a formidable snow storm. I had considered recruiting Kenchen as a confederate to my illicit meetings with her. For in the winter when I have the time to be with her, the weather is too foul for a

---

* Referring to the many whites being killed by revolting slaves in Haiti.

satisfactory out-of-doors rendezvous. Proximity & Louisa's natural disdain for Asa made me think of the possibility of using her abode.

Alas, I learn Kenchen has gone the straight & narrow since the beating. I was sorry I raised up the subject, for I could sense the glint of desire for dalliance with Louisa still within him.

I saw her again in early December. It was so cold we both kept our clothes fully on. She had composed a short poem in her head. Imagine not being allowed quill & paper by your husband.

Would that I could be as resourceful in dealing with the abject villainy of Asa Johnson, that odious turkey cock. Nay, a turkey cock is an object of veneration compared to Asa! Of course, murder has reared its head amongst my thoughts, but I doubt I am capable. Unlike my virtuous Emily though, I am capable of entertaining the idea.

To start the year of 1794, let me train my mind on the positive. I have reduced my debt a little. John caught the same sickness as Lucy but has recovered & little Sarah is robustly healthy. Marmaduke, Pris, & Eli behave and apply themselves tolerably. And tho' I do not know how to solve the problem, Emily & I have planned our next rendezvous, and this engenders in me temporary happiness.

Sunday 8 Feb^y

Anger mounts toward Britain, for they run rough shod over all our ships trading with France. Even ships bearing only foodstuffs. And they take by force any of our sailors with the slightest residue of a British accent and press them into slavery upon the British ships.

Even when we trade with *them*, they discriminate against our products with high tariffs. Furthermore, Britain has never lived up to the peace treaty after the Revolution in that they maintain forts in our Northwest Territory to steal American furs & foment unrest amongst the Indians against us.

Many argue that we should join the side of republican France in the conflict. John Macon says each man should adorn the French cockade at this spring's militia muster. (The General Assembly has made Wm. R. Davie Major General of the Militia.)

However a letter from Nathl Macon in Philadelphia urges calm.

"Virtue is with France & villainy with monarchical Britain. Britain abuses us as an enemy while we behave as a neutral. Yet war is too high a price to pay." He says the Yellow Fever fled Philadelphia with the return of cold weather.

Sun' 2 Mar'

The Feb' 12th *N-C Journal* reports the college at Princeton, NJ has conferred the honorary degree of LL.D. upon Sen. Alexander Martin, no doubt for his efforts to end the secrecy of the Senate's deliberation.

Sun' 22 Mar'

At last we managed a meeting. Sweet Emily. She smelled of lavender. I thought aloud of a possible variant of my previous proposal: If the war continues to keep crop prices up, I may be able to reduce my debt substantially. And high crop prices would facilitate a good price for my farm. I conceive of being able to carry my family (including Duke, Pris & their babes) to the wilderness of Tennessee, and once we have constructed shelter, returning surreptitiously to steal Emily away.

"We would still live in fear of Asa." Emily replied. "He would not stand for something of his being taken; he would find us. Besides, Sterling, you have already lifted my life from the ashes. Meeting with you like this & knowing you are alive just a few miles away give me reason to live. I would follow you anywhere, but I fear Tennessee might not be far enough away. I can live with the present circumstances."

I hugged & kissed her. She hath an excellence that would engender affection in any man alive save Asa Johnson. He is indeed 'the veriest varlet that ever chewed with a tooth'. Just as I thought that she said:

"Even Asa seems to respond to my brighter self. He says he's going to take me to the ball the Persons are having."

Sun^y 30 Mar'

We have our tobacco barn nearly rebuilt & hopes of cultivating above seventy-five acres. Fifteen of it will be plowed with hardly any remaining stumps. If the weather & prices are as favorable as last year, then the resulting prosperity can only improve our possibilities. Some talk of war with Britain as inevitable. The cause is just.

Sat^y 12 Apr'

The assemblage at the Ball was splendid & animated, but the talk was of nothing but the war. Our entire Congressional delegation, excepting Macon, has sent an address to the people of the state (thru' the newspapers) speaking warmly of "our republican allies" the French and advising us to produce cotton, hemp, flax & wool as important war commodities.

Nath' Macon's absence from the address was conspicuous; he is known for his republican principles & disdain of all things aristocratical. And who is more aristocratical than Britain? I had a great deal to add to the intercourse, having just received the favor of a letter from him.

"Macon says that Hamilton & the federalists will never allow a war with Great Britain & that they would kiss King George's boot rather than allow war to interfere with the profits of the eastern shipping interests."

Asa Johnson, Absalom Jenkins, Col. Whitaker, and the Hawkins' guest Robt. Goodloe Harper all simultaneously denounced the cynicism of such a statement. All spoke glowingly of their eagerness to assume their duties in the militia and gloriously smite the foul Brits. I could but think selfishly of my time in the militia and the higher taxes the war would require; these are surely the enemy of the prosperity I need to be able to spirit Emily away to the western frontier.

"The people of our vicinage elect Macon as our Congressman with scant opposition," I countered, "not merely because of his integrity, but because they trust him above others to know which way the tree will fall. I've had the privilege of knowing him long enough to place an eminent degree of merit in his words."

From their expressions, I knew my words put me in bad odor with Asa, Col. Whitaker, the visiting Harper, & others who seemed excited by the prospects of war.

Wylie Jones was a voice of caution, in spite of his great pleasure that his horse had won the little informal race preceding the ball: "Though Britain is a villain & the cause is just, war inevitably will enable tyranny & abuse by our own governments against its hard working citizens. You men were too young to properly remember our Revolution & hence are unable to weigh the many penalties inflicted by even a successful war. Our massive debt & the hated Whiskey Tax would not exist had we not had to fight the Revolutionary War. How much treasure, how much blood, how many orphans & cripples is it worth to hurt Britain? *If* we are able to hurt Britain."

None would confront Mr. Jones' wisdom given the history of his efforts in the Revolution & the irrefutability of his logic. But within minutes others could be heard rattling their sabers. It would be a popular war in North-Carolina.

Emily, Wylie Jones, & I enjoyed considerable amiable intercourse; Jones had not seen his former foster child since her marriage. We conversed upon myriad subjects. When Asa joined our group, I pointedly spoke of a novel I had borrowed from Mr. Jones' great library and insisted Emily would enjoy it immensely. Mr. Jones naturally said she was welcome to borrow it.

"I'll be happy to deliver it to you, Mrs. Johnson, on the way back from my next trip to Halifax," I offered.

The knowing smile Emily furtively expresst was ephemeral, effaced instantly by espying Asa's perverse countenance:

"That is a kind offer, sir, but Mr. Johnson has reservations about novels." We all looked at him. I recall about 4 years ago writing in this journal that Asa Johnson was handsome except for a weak chin. When I espy him now I wonder at that assessment. He hath gained weight & the look of one who drinks whiskey too heavily. Have his beady eyes grown somehow closer together? And as goodness marks every line & feature of Emily, baseness & deceit mark Asa Johnson. I own that I am not able to see him impartially.

"I am surely not alone in my reservations." Johnson responded. "Is it not received wisdom, Mr. Jones, Mr. Shearin, that novels do not improve the female sex…in terms of being wives of merit?"

"Ah—," responded Mr. Jones expansively as he tilted his head back. "I see. I have reason to doubt that opinion."

"And why is that, sir?" asked Asa.

"Mrs. Jones doesn't seem to suffer in the least. Why, eager reader of novels that she is, she possesses qualities as a wife that would add grace to any husband."

I smiled inwardly, as I am sure did Emily.

"And more, Mr. Johnson, Mrs. Jones has lately pressed upon me a new novel, *Charlotte, A Tale of Truth*—for it is said to be a true story. *Charlotte Temple*, it is also called. By a Mrs. Rowson. 'Tis so well-liked that it is being published here in America. While it certainly appeals to the tenderest sentiments of the human heart, it is devoted in its every page to morality—& in particular to the morality of the female sex. One chapter begins quoting Pope:

Teach me to feel another's woe,
To hide the fault I see,
That mercy I to others show,
That mercy show to me.

"'Tis a book of quality, which I think all 3 of you would enjoy."

"You certainly pique my interest." I pressed my luck. "If *Charlotte Temple* be not lent out next month when next I visit Halifax, Mr. Jones, might I borrow it for the 3 of us? I'll convey it to Mr. Johnson first that he might ascertain its worth."

What could Asa say? "So kind of you both. I will fetch it. I will probably be going to Halifax soon myself." He would never let on his denial of Emily, the hypocrite.

"Hypocrisy is the homage vice pays to virtue," quoth the great Frenchman LaRochefoucauld.

'Twas an evening full of glee, being in Emily's company with the dancing, the music, much imbibing, the brilliancy of everyone dressed his very best and the luxurious use of candle to illuminate, &c.

Emily wore a gown in a quite new & simpler style without the panniers, which in consequence did not hide her tidy slender figure. The blue trim matched her eyes. It suited her marvelous well.

She & I shared a congo.* I pray our glances were appropriately discreet. I apprehended her aspect to be the true color of health & contentment. Is Asa turning over a new leaf?

I was the object of some flirtation from eligible belles. Especially Margaret Simpson.

'Tis an irony that she became more flirtatious after Emily rendered me incapable of pursuing another last fall. She was merely friendly when I pursued *her*; yet when I ceased to court her, I seemed to have become all the more attractive to her.

After the toast to our hosts, Wylie Jones offered the first toast: "May Liberty, like the atmosphere, pervade—not just France—but every part of the Globe."

Several toasts later, I offered: "To the fair sex—without participation in public affairs, their dominion is the hearts of their countrymen." God help me for I could not resist kissing Emily's eyes for a brief portion of that moment. I pray I was not obvious. Alas, I have turned six-and-twenty & yet still court danger with the foolishness of a child. Yet how alive I feel.

Sunday 11 May

I went to the first day of the May livestock fair in Halifax. I traded a little whiskey on the sly, our winter handiwork (mostly hickory pitchforks), & some linen thread for essentials (we revert to chestnut coffee), a cow & a nice young filly. Aristotle is getting some age on him. *Charlotte Temple* was not there, tho' Mrs. Jones declared Asa Johnson had not been by to borrow it. I borrowed Samuel Richardson's *Clarrisa* instead, which Mrs Jones suggested as having some similarity with *Charlotte Temple*. I had not read it, but Mrs. Jones asserted that women were touched by this classic &

---

* A congo was a fast minuet danced by two or four.

that it manifested much wisdom.

Two or three miles from the Johnson place the bottom fell out. I arrived totally wet from head to toe. I was relieved the book had remained dry in my leather saddlebag; it would not have done so much longer, for rain continued in torrents.

Emily's smile. Alas, I would have swum the Roanoke for it. I espied a slight bruise on one cheek, indicating to me that Asa may not have turned over a new leaf. The ambience was all the more charged for the presence of two of their negroes in the two room house. I wrung out my shirt gently & held it by the fire. Emily stole a furtive look at me, accompanied by a knowing sly smile so evanescent that it might have been the mere indulgence of my fanciful mind. More certain was the suffusion of vermillion that tinged her face & graceful neck.

She said Asa had started out for the livestock fair but a short spell before and it was surprising I did not run into him. She wondered if the rain would not force him back home. I immediately put my damp shirt back on.

I looked for a break in the rain, but none came before an irascible Asa Johnson did. They lent me a deerskin to help me keep my sugar dry & thus furnished another legitimate excuse for my return to their place. Most fortunate, as it rained more before I reached home. Too much rain for the wheat.

News arrives of continued British spoilation of our commerce at sea. Plenty of folks ready for war.

Many in Richmond have died of small pox.

Sun' 22 June

The wheat crop was badly damaged by excessive rain. Very much a hindrance to my plan.

I enjoyed a long conversation with Nath*l* Macon on his return from Congress whence he brought much news.

Consistent with Macon's prediction, Washington & Hamilton have sent John Jay to London to seek peace with the formidable Brits. Hamilton is in complete control with Jefferson retired. Edm. Randolph is the only officer of the gov't outside his sway. Hamilton refers to the Washington administration as "his administration." Rumor has it that he has inquired if the Va. militia might be reliably used to enforce the Whiskey Tax in N-C; apparently no revenue from our State has reached Philadelphia.

Macon had no success in endeavoring to relieve us of this tax. Indeed a Carriage Tax was passed. This will only affect the very affluent, but it strengthens the precedent of the federal gov't taxing the citizens of the individual states directly. Also a tax on snuff & refined sugar.

As Macon says "'Tis the natural progress of things for liberty to recede and government to gain dominion."

At least Macon had success at thwarting four attempts to create a significant standing army.

I returned the deerskin & retrieved *Clarissa* from Emily with Asa present. Something in her subdued demeanor troubles me.

Sunday 6 July

All wears a woeful aspect. Eli, little Sarah, & old Lucy are all ill with a bilious fever. They eliminate bile copiously. One of the three seems to be vomiting every time I turn around. I worry about losing little Sarah & Lucy.

Too much rain ruins the crops. The Roanoke rises. My chances of achieving the prosperity requisite to escape with Emily are severely diminished.

Providence has played a trick on me with regard to *Clarissa*. Now that I have read it, I know it to be the worst possible book I could have gotten for Emily. Little wonder her tone was strange when last I saw her.

To avoid a marriage to which her heart cannot consent, the heroine Clarissa casts herself on the protection of a lover who abuses her confidence; then she pines to death in grief & shame. This well-written book could not have been better designed to render my beloved less trusting of me or less hopeful, more fatalistic.

And now as I recount all the particulars of the scenes which ensue, my heart pounds & my palms grow moist anew:

I arose early on July 4th & tended to my work briskly. The day showed every prospect of being a beautiful day without such humidity as is often the case in this season. I determined to attend the celebration in Warrenton.

The first person I encountered was Margaret with her new husband. I sincerely wished them well. The second was Asa. It took me only a few minutes to ascertain with certainty that he was there without Emily. There were plenty there in Warrenton praising Liberty & France and damning Britain without my help; I quitted Warrenton at once & made haste for the Johnson place.

I pushed my poor horse more than was prudent. We were pretty lathered by the time we arrived in spite of the mildness of the day. A slave cast a suspicious eye upon us.

I asked for some water for my horse & then with feigned casualness asked "Is Mr. or Mrs. Johnson at home?"

It was several minutes before Emily appeared. She was reserved beyond what was necessary for the prying eyes of the nearby slave. I discreetly entreated her to meet me at out private place. She was…reticent. She feared Asa's return she said, but it was obvious there was more to her hesitance. *Sub rosa* I pleaded. I think she finally responded to the pain in my countenance. She acquiesced.

I worried as I waited: This was certain to appear suspicious to the slave. And how long would Asa remain in Warrenton? Had he taken note of my early departure? When she came, I walked back along her path 50 yards or more to insure she had not been followed.

She was still distant.

"Emily, Clarissa was a creature of the England of 50 years ago, a time & place of arranged marriages & wealth by birth. We live in America in a new age: We may love those we marry and prosper by our own industry & diligence. This cautionary tale has no relevance to us."

She simply sighed & looked down. A whirring mosquito landed upon her face, & she reflexively swatted it.

"Emily, I love you. I'm devoted to you. If your happiness requires sending me away, I am at your command."

"Sterling…I. It's what we should…" She started to cry, but then took her hands from her face & ever-so-faintly reached out for my embrace. I held her with all the warmth & tenderness within me. She responded by holding me tightly. I love her so.

After some time, she said to me "'Tis sin, Sterling, but I cannot send you away. I'm miserable without you in my life. I am lost."

"Emily, you are not thinking about this rightly. You were tricked into marriage with a dishonest, cruel man. You are trying to make the best of an odious predicament. You say you are sinning. Just whom are you wronging? Not that villain who is your false husband."

"We said our vows before a minister."

"Your vows were to a man who had hidden his nature from you. A character of invention with little truth in him. A trickster. What other deceit has he been guilty of along the lines of his manipulation with Preacher Absalom…tricking people in search of spiritual truth? A loving God would put no merit in vows to such a deceiver."

She kissed me. "I love you Sterling Shearin." Then, sotto voce, "I'm yours."

I returned her kiss with passion. Passion begot passion. We lay together with conjugal intensity. Blissfully. Afterward, we lay cuddled together like little newborn puppies. I was thinking how this affinity for each others' touch was a great glue for us.

"A penny for your thoughts," said I, wondering if she might possibly be thinking the same.

"Well—"

"Sh! The birds," I interrupted with a loud whisper. "The birds that flew up!" We listened.

"Quickly dress!" I whispered with alarm. "Behind the boulder. Something stirs there." I gestured to the west toward Warrenton.

I got my breeches on & gathered my shirt, shoes, & hat as we moved into the shadow of the biggest of the group of boulders where fortunately Aristotle was tethered to a White Pine, which might also help hide us, positioned as it was there by the boulder. As best my ears would serve, it sounded like a man on horseback. I stroked Aristotle gently to encourage his quietness. The footfall of a single horse thudded closer. I motioned to Emily to cease any motion that would make the least sound. Obviously, she was not fully dressed, much less composed.

Fie upon't! We were done for if seen. If it were Asa returning, would he attach significance to this place? Would he know it as Emily's private spot & hence look about? Surely he would! A pox upon't!

We could not see the rider, but we could hear that he had paused. We heard him sigh. We heard the uncertain creak of his saddle leather. Was he shifting to look about or dismounting? I apprehended that he was immediately on the opposite side of the tall boulder from us. We held our breath. I silently communed with Aristotle with my touch & eye.

The horse took a couple steps & paused again.

"She's been here. The sorry wench."

Emily & I exchanged glances. Asa it was. God's Teeth! Had she left something? I looked her over for what it might be, not that anything could be done. Nothing obvious. Emily turned pale with terror. Her hands trembled. Asa sounded in his cups to a degree. Pray thereby not in full possession of his senses.

There was no sound. He must be looking about him.

There was a loud sound that startled us. That I didn't jump was surprising. That Aristotle did not to react was a miracle. 'Twas flatulence—so loud that it might have been from the horse rather than the man. So close we caught wind of the foul odor. Emily pinched her nose.

The horse took a few steps & sounded to me as if it were turning around. Suddenly, I could see the dappled gray horse's nose through the needles of the White Pine. We held our breath. Time slowed to near stop. No sound. Then a mosquito whined about my ear. Utter concentration to remain still. It lit. It stung me. The sting was almost…well, I knew I was still alive. If Asa had his gun at ready, I might not be momentarily.

We heard a few more steps. Then more. Was he moving away? It sounded like it. He clucked the dapple gray. Still we dared not peek to verify.

We stayed very still, nay, we hardly breathed till he had moved well off into the distance. We quietly finished dressing. My heart would not stop pounding. I peeked at last very carefully.

"I'll go in that direction," Emily whispered. "I can pretend to have gone to check on the slave in the north field. You stay hidden till you hear me well out of ear shot."

Well thought, I nodded.

"Wait," she paused. "Am I presentable?"

I smoothed some hair back under her mob cap & whispered "Exceedingly."

I waited. I heard nothing to indicate mishap. After a while I led Aristotle westward very quietly a ways & finally mounted & rode with some haste & great relief.

Had Asa come some minutes earlier when all my faculties were consumed in the passionate deed, he would have caught us and probably killed us both on the spot.

As I curried Aristotle today, I paused & hugged his neck. My fine old horse knows me so well that he surely gleaned my terror. One snort from him & we would have been done for.

How can this continue?

Sun^y 13 July

At least my family all recovered from their illness. On the other hand Emily was not at church & I have no idea if she is unscathed.

The editor of the *N-C Journal* devoted most of the July 2nd issue to Judge Iredell's long charge of the jury in which he justifies the "energetic role" of the federal gov't. We need a republican newspaper in our State.

It looks like more rain.

Mon 28 July

'Tis woeful to tell. The excessive rain has flooded the Roanoke. To within one hundred yards of our house! My corn crop is devastated. My hopes for absconding with Emily are dashed.

A farmer in Franklin County was knifed to death. A slave is in custody. Marmaduke does well with his gun; Pris & Lucy have knives at their disposal. I trust them but I would just as soon they heard nothing of this occurrence—lest it be in connection with said slave's execution.

Too bad the farmer in question was not Asa Johnson.

Sun', 10 August

I may be ruined. Our crops are devastated by the flooding. If all goes perfectly from now thru' harvest, we may avoid bankruptcy. If I can pay at least half of the interest on the debt, my creditors will have an incentive to work with me.

Have killed great numbers of snakes.

I have had no contact with Emily & fear to initiate it.

As if matters were not bad enough, the arrogant British have managed a great victory over France.

Three slaves in Northampton Co. are accused of murdering their master. How certain events of life clump together. Or did the first give seed to the latter? Maybe Asa's slaves will catch wind of it.

Sunday 24 Aug.

I went to fetch my children from Kenchen & Mary yesterday. Kenchen asked me to help him repair the roof of his barn and during that chore said:

"I have heard a rumor from a reliable source that it was Asa Johnson who burned your tobacco barn last fall."

I was dumbfounded. Then enraged! With all the vicissitudes of nature, for another farmer to destroy so much of my & Marmaduke's & Eli's labor is purely evil. Evil! I could have killed him that instant.

"He suspects you have cuckolded him. Be very careful. He could harm you further."

"Louisa?"

He nodded.

Sunday 7 Sept.

With so little crop to harvest, Eli & I have fished some & carried our catch to Warrenton to sell. A dearth of corn in our flood-ravaged valley makes our fish easier to sell—tho' mostly for last year's whiskey rather than coin. Clearly I have no hope now of paying all the interest on my debt.

The slave in Franklin County has been tried & executed. Those in Northampton are being tried.

Tuesday 30 Sept.

'Twould be a woeful sadness upon me from this day's events, were it not for my fondest possibility coming into view. Instead, 'Tis a checkered agitation. I have lost my beloved horse, Aristotle; he broke a leg & I was compelled to shoot him.

And then occurred what I think the French call *déjà vu*. Asa Johnson was found knifed to death at the very spot where Abner Whitaker was found! Alas, his horse like slain Abner Whitaker's wandered to Kenchen's nearby farm. Could one of his slaves have done it? Surely I am not the only one who hated him.

Chapter Fourteen

Saturday, 4 Oct^r: 1794

With misgivings, I went to Emily right away. 'Twas a strange circumstance; strained, to say the least of it. Emily had no idea of Asa's intentions or destination the day of his death. Nor possesst she any notion of who may have killed him. The sheriff had yet to interview her. The murder occurred in Warren Co., of course, and the Johnson place is just over in Halifax Co.

The newspaper reports Virginia militia on the move in Petersburg. They are ordered to western Pennsylvania where farmers have been noisier in their opposition to the Whiskey Tax than have we here.

Wednesday, 8 Oct^r

We are punctually off our pillows before the cock crows & throw ourselves furiously into cutting trees to be converted to lumber, barrel staves, & roof shingles. 'Tis our only hope to supplement the return from our meager harvest in the face of higher prices we must pay for any thing we purchase. While I work, I cannot help but speculate on the suspects in the murder.

Naturally Kenchen is implicated by the proximity of the body & Kenchen's possession of Asa's horse. Amongst his motives, I hope his liaison with Louisa (not to mention mine with Emily) & the rough beating from Asa shall remain in the dark. Unfortunately the motive of Asa's discriminatory enforcement of the Whiskey Tax against Kenchen & me will surely come out. No doubt the sheriff will see fit to tie this murder to the similar murder of Abner Whitaker.

Amidst this odor of coincidences, the Hawkins' frequent guest Robert Goodloe Harper (now a South-Carolina legislator) was again in the county at the time of this murder.

One could not rule out Louisa or one of Asa's other three slaves. He could hardly have been other than abusive to them, given his character. They might have been clever to transport him away from their farm to this spot to shift suspicion from them. They would have had to do it all late in the night, the darkness of night ever their ally.

Kenchen's neighbor saw Caleb Brown in the vicinity the afternoon the murder probably occurred. 'Twould pain me none were he implicated.

Mrs. Delia Hawkins has died. In spite of her sex, she was a strong

Whig influence in our county who will be hard to replace. She dissuaded Macon's one potential opponent from having his name put forth in the last Congressional election. How discouraging that one generation cannot pass along its knowledge of the adversarial relationship of governmental power & Liberty to the next—as Mrs. Hawkins was not able to pass it to her son, Sen. Benj. Hawkins. I grow sensible that my generation loses that deep understanding possessed by those who bravely fought the Revolution. I hope that her death stemmed from the wear & tear of supporting her substantial size & not from small pox, which is said to be rampant in Virginia. The Hawkins are modern enough & affluent enough to have had the vaccine.

Sunday, 12 Oct'

I went over to Emily's again briefly. One of the slaves persisted in slinking about & eyeing us suspiciously; hence our intercourse was most restrained. I wanted to arrange a rendezvous with her, primarily to assure myself that our relationship endures in spite of emotions conjured by Asa's unnatural end. I could not.

She said the Sheriff was vague but indicated he had several suspects. She mentioned that she told the Sheriff Asa said something about going to Person's Ordinary & then on to Absalom's; this is at odds with what she told me earlier. Is it possible she thinks I'm the perpetrator of the crime?

One could easily imagine Asa's death disturbing her natural view of him as the stinking ogre he was & therefore disturbing her affection for me, attaching guilt to our clandestine relationship. I could discern nothing & am anxious.

She did request me to come back tomorrow when a lawyer & creditors will be present.

Monday, 13 Oct'

It was a beautiful cool clear blue-sky'd autumn day. The leaves of sourwoods, dogwoods, & sassafras were commencing their charm. Alas, I was too agitated on my ride over to the Johnson place to take pleasure in the beauty of the morning.

I was little surprised to find Asa to be more indebted than I am. He spent liberally on drink & fine cotton clothes for himself, gave ostentatiously to the church, & even gambled on the horses & gamecocks. Asa owes a British merchant more than his farm is worth and none of his slaves are free & clear.

Emily will be left with nothing. When they auction everything in two weeks, she will be left destitute without so much as a roof over her head.

As the lawyer & creditors started to leave, I own I felt distresst with a sense of awkwardness, & therefore I quitted the Johnson place as well. My intercourse with Emily was strained with ambiguity, & I was sensible that I was in no position to clarify this, were there privacy adequate to do so.

It lying in my way, I paused at Emily's secret spot. I deliberated for what turned into a long spell. Should I go back, attempt to converse with Emily privately, & discern her mind? Or would it be more fitting to allow more time? I was fearful of the death's effect on her, yet mindful that shortly she would need shelter. I started back toward her house but then turned back toward my place. Yet after 100 yards I reversed again, feeling a sad, conflicted fool. But then as I came around an unusually large sassafras, resplendent in its red & yellow autumnal foliage, I espied her approach on foot.

"You are headed for…your secret spot?"

She nodded.

"Do you mean to be alone?"

She did not reply.

"I don't know," said she at last.

I walked with her. She was sad but reserved, not meeting my eye. When we arrived at our—her spot, I asked if I might remain with her. She didn't answer. A tear ran down her cheek. I took her hand & gently pulled her to me. I slowly embraced her.

She wept quietly. "It's so terrible."

"One thing has not changed," said I.

She looked at me through tears.

"I love you, and when you can see your way to it, I want you to be my wife."

She cried more but did not push me away.

"Will you have me?" I persisted.

After the space of more than a few sobs (it seemed an eternity), she said "you know I will." She kissed me thru' her tears. How my heart filled with glee!

I held her close & then claimed more lachrymose kisses.

"Talk to me Emily. You must have a checquered admixture of emotions clouding your mind, in contrasts to the feelings of pure mourning expected of you. Were I you, there would have been times when I would have wished him dead."

"Sterling, that is exactly my state. And there is none to whom I can unbosome it. What is more, I was uncertain that I could with you. You are so very eligible, & I come penniless."

"Emily, how could you have doubted my earnestness, my devotion to you?"

She talked at length to me & unburdened her mind. I was the happiest man in Warren County to have the barrier between us removed. We eventually turned to pragmatical concerns.

We considered what could be taken from the farm as payment for her years of labor there without causing a stir. Someone will be appointed within a couple of days to supervise the harvest & the slaves, and may well reside there. We settled on a time (mid-morning the next day) for me to come when none of the slaves would be at the house to come fetch her spinning wheel, a couple of pigs & hens, a nice broadax, a gun (for Eli), a shell auger [drill bit for wooden pegs], a quilt, a blanket, some cloth & a couple of utensils. The day before the auction she would take all her thread & personal possessions and her cobb to ride to Halifax. Creditors may well come after the horse, if they reckon it to the uttermost mite.

Emily is confident that she can rely on a fortnight's hospitality at the Jones'. At that time I can bring my meager harvest to market & then fetch her back to stay with Mama or Kenchen & Mary for a month or so.

Gaining at least a two month interval, we will marry quietly. 'Tis hardly adequate; tongues will wag to an eminent degree. Her lack of connexions, her need for a roof, my longing for her—we really should try to figure a way to wait at least 3 or 4 months from Asa's demise.

When I returned home, I found that the Sheriff had been there. No one there for him to question but old Lucy. She is a clever old lady; quite deft at feigning ignorance. Kind of glad Eli was out hunting.

*Monday, 27 Oct*ʳ

Kenchen & I went to the auction. I observed in some vexation when Kenchen made a bid of £38 for Louisa; fortunately she sold for three times that amount to a trader (who will probably transport her away from our vicinage). I declare she looked excellent, yet familiar, as though I had seen her before in a dream.

Kenchen said the Sheriff has been on him hard. He said the Sheriff asked Mary if I had close relations with Asa's widow. And that Mary had to bite her lip to refrain from telling the truth. We are in trouble. Where else have I left grist for the mill of someone sporting with my character?

Our old Sheriff questioned Asa's slaves before they were transported away. They all played old Lucy's game except Louisa, who was insolently uncooperative. In her arrogance, she really seemed the victimized white lady. Her bold "don't tread on me" responses suggested either that she did not commit the murder or that she did & does not care if she's found out.

The Sheriff asked me my whereabouts the day of the murder: of course I was at my farm. He asked my relation with Emily, and I said I knew her through her foster parent, Mr. Jones, & thru' church & had enjoyed merely an occasional conversation with her.

"I *do* have a high regard for her," I added. "I do not know her well, but I have observed her at church to have a kind aspect & a pleasing smile. You must know, Sheriff, that I have children that need a mother. I own that after a decent interval, I may well court her…if she is agreeable."

He said nothing.

"Would you blame me?" said I. He just grunted.

He asked about Asa's punitive enforcement of the Whiskey Tax on Kenchen & me: 'Twas pointless to deny. I hope my inner distress was concealed in some measure. Kenchen manifested (to my knowing eye) palpable agitation when the Sheriff questioned him again.

Wed 12 Nov

With alacrity & yet uneasiness I made the planned trip to Halifax. The news in this place is that Washington & Hamilton led a huge throng of militia from numerous States into western Pennsylvania & there arrested a few poor farmers who asserted their rights to be free from the Whiskey Tax. One wonders at the patience of "Hamilton's Administration" under the kicks & scoffs of the British, yet how they rise at a feather against farmers who proclaim their rights as free men of Pennsylvania.

Given the Sheriff's scrutiny, I had hoped the Joneses would be generous & effusive in insisting Emily stay with them longer. Alas, the Joneses were at their new house at the new State capitol in Raleigh (which Jones was instrumental in locating & laying off) & the house was full of young orphans & some Virginian "gentry"—one of whom made unwelcome overtures to Emily. No one was there to whom she had been close four years earlier; thus her staying longer was unrealistic.

I paid a little over half the interest on my debt, which now swells back well over £140. Many farmers share my plight from the excessive rain, & hence most creditors are making allowances. I wanted to spend two shillings on an engagement gift for Emily, but she would not allow it.

There was small pox in Halifax, & Emily insisted for my sake that we quit that place with haste. For once I managed to put all worries out of my head. 'Twas a cool crisp beautiful day with hardly a cloud. The eight or so hours from Halifax to Kenchen's house (mayhap about four-&-twenty

1794 ≈ SS ≈ 145

WILLIE JONES,
Member of the Continental Congress

Willie Jones, drawn many years earlier during the Revolutionary War in 1780 when he was serving in the Continental Congress. (Courtesy of the North Carolina State Archives) The present day North Carolina General Assembly is located on West Jones St. (Jones Co., NC, and Jonesborough, TN are also named for Willie Jones.)

miles) with my beloved by my side were happy hours. Emily & I talked easily on sundry subjects. Her fortnight in Halifax had been something of an adventure.

"Some of it misadventure. My circumstance was all awkwardness, with no substantial connexions. Tho' in the midst of a veritable multitude compared to what I was used to at the farm, I was very much alone. I am glad you came when you did, Sterling."

"Did you have opportunity to read, now that there is no restraint upon't?"

She laughed. "Yes I did. My new freedom feels strange."

"Did you sing?"

"I had forgotten all about that restraint," she chuckled again. "I had become accustomed to it."

"I'ld love to hear you sing. Why don't you sing something now?"

"No, Sterling!"

"Why on earth not?"

"Well, for one, they would hear." We were passing hard by a farmhouse. Indeed the sweet smell of their apple press pleasingly filled the air.

Even when we had driven out of earshot of the farm, she continued demure, nay, bashful, & I had to prod her mercilessly. She was exceedingly diffident in her singing from the heat of Asa Johnson's criticism. At last she sang "The Ashgrove" for me. Her voice was not full-bodied or broad in range, but very pleasant & sweetly beautiful. What on earth had Asa found objectionable in it? When I stopped going on about how nicely she sang, she asked me to sing with her & she harmonized as I sang melody. I fancy we sounded rather good.

More than once I looked at her & she looked back at me & I thought: There is paradise...right there in her countenance.

She spoke little of what she suffered at Asa's hand, but enough to let me know she mourned him little. I found immense relief in this: many a blackguard seems to gain stature by dying, tho' never to me. She told me of happier reading than *Clarissa* which she managed at Jones' library. She earned a three shillings credit at the store in Halifax working linen for the owner's wife. Can it be true that I shall marry so amiable, so precious a one as Emily & get away with it?

Wed^y 19 Nov

I spoke to Nathaniel's brother John Macon today. He had had the favor of a letter from his brother that rendered him warmly agitated, and most especially agitated with the high & mighty Alexander Hamilton—he that led the throng of militia from sundry states against the poor farmers of western Pennsylvania. Congressman Macon said in his letter that at the New York convention to ratify the Constitution in 1788, Hamilton promised that the Federal gov't would never contemplate "marching the troops of one state into the bosom of another" for any reason. Precisely what he has perpetrated but 6 years later.

Macon's letter also observes that many of the officers of this enormous 13,000 militia were from the ranks of the creditor aristocracy—to wit, holders of government bonds. They were conspicuous in their pretty blue uniforms of the finest broadcloth & mounted on magnificent, matched bay horses. These officers were eager to enforce collection of the Whiskey Tax so that the worth of their bond holdings could be secured, if not enhanced!

Further, Macon reports that right after Hamilton argued (vs. Madison) before the Supreme Court for the tax on chariots as not being a "direct tax," but *before* the Supreme Court ruled on the case, Hamilton dined with Justice Iredell. This gives some color to the stamp of men who style themselves Federalists.

Sunday 30 Nov

We were married yesterday. Emily wore the gown with the blue trim that she wore to the ball in April. Kenchen was my bondsman. 'Twas above 2 months. We debated back & forth waiting till the 1st of the year. How long would we have had to wait to not arouse any talk? Life is short.

We made love for the first time since early July—and for the first time ever without fear of detection. We love each other deeply & are full of contentment.

Sunday 7 Dec^r

News of our marriage provoked another visit from our old sheriff. He questioned us each at length separately. After a spell I followed Louisa's bold lead and asked aggressively:

"Why don't you question Caleb Brown or Robert Harper, who were both seen down that way not too long before Johnson was found?"

"Lots of people were seen near there on the Halifax-Warrenton road."

"Quite a coincidence that Robt G. Harper should be a visitor at the time of both murders, don't you think?"

The sheriff grunted & eyed me malevolently. "Mr. Harper is the friend of the very respectable Hawkins family. He does not readily come to mind as a suspect, Shearin. What link ties this Harper to Asa Johnson?"

"I do not know," I admitted. "My wife...his widow said Johnson was headed to see Preacher Absalom."

"Absalom knew nothing of such an intention and saw nothing of him. Absalom also said you & Kenchen were on none too friendly terms with Asa Johnson."

"Have you asked the widow if Asa had perhaps generated a deep hatred amongst any of his slaves? He had the character of a hard master."

He ignored my last question & continued to look at me as tho' I were guilty. It made my heart pound and my hands sweat.

Thursday, 11 Dec^r

At the rebuilt saw mill, they had an *N-C Journal* with Pres. Washington's speech to Congress. He blames the democratic societies for the so-called "Whiskey Rebellion." "Certain self-created societies" he termed us, as if we needed a charter of endorsement from the government like they do in the monarchies of Europe.

I made a fair return on the lumber: £1, 19 shillings, 3 pence.

Tuesday, 23 Dec^r

Both Pris' young'uns have small pox. My Emily nurses them expertly & without fear. Today is unseasonably warm.

I idly wonder when my beloved & I will ever come to a disagreement. All is harmony & glee—except when we worry about the Sheriff. Emily is unused to the conjugal attention which I lavish upon her. I am sure the flattery aspect of this attention shall wear away. Yet I perceive in her such an amiable nature & such desire to perpetrate kindness towards me, that I am the soul of optimism. At times we engage in a contest for who can be the kindest.

Yesterday I turned around & caught a peculiar smile on her lips.

"What?" I inquired. "Is aught amiss?"

"Nothing" she giggled.

"No, what?" I persisted.

"It's just that, well...the muscles of your...derriere..."

"What?"

"They please me," said she.

I shall never understand women, thought I. Never did I imagine such a thing. Naturally, I laughed too.

"All your muscles please me, my trim, handsome husband," she continued. If 'tis mere invention on her part, 'tis so sweetly expresst. Romeo & Juliet, had their barriers vanished, could never have loved each other (after three weeks of marriage) so well as we.

Tuesday, 28 December

Both pickaninnies improve; Emily has won over everyone in the household. The sheriff came again. To Kenchen's too. He & Mary are in some vexation with worry. Our old Sheriff has always been a careful, plodding man. Slow for fear of a mistake, yet respected as fair. But word has it that Caleb Brown will be a candidate for Sheriff with the Hawkins family's backing. The Sheriff is old and feels pressure.

Chapter Fifteen

Sunday, 9 Jany 1795

We had Mama, Kenchen, & Mary over for Sunday dinner. Distress of mind preys upon Kenchen. The old Sheriff has harassed him further. The Sheriff is under pressure from his rival, Caleb Brown. Caleb makes much of the two unsolved murders. And his candidacy is promoted by Absalom.

My two children call Emily "Mama" already. She sings them lullabies of an evening.

Sun', 23 Jan^y

I went to a democratic society meeting. Very few were present. The censure by Pres. Washington & the excesses of the Jacobins in France have cost us a few members. Members, I might add, who were hardly Tories. No mention of any initiative. Notably no mention of putting forth the name of a more Republican candidate for Sheriff of Warren Co.

Lewis told me he heard that the Sheriff has traveled down towards Enfield in order to question Louisa again. I know not what construction to place upon that.

Sunday, 13 Feb^y

Good & bad news from our General Assembly. Timothy Bloodsworth of Wilmington has been chosen to serve in the room of Senator Benjamin Hawkins. Hawkins' federalist votes for the assumption of States' debts & for the Whiskey excise tax (contrary to his instructions from the Gen'l Assembly) meant his re-appointment was unlikely. Pres. Washington will probably appoint our distinguished federalist neighbor to something with a nice governmental emolument.*

---

* Pres. Washington appointed Hawkins Superintendant of Indian Affairs in 1796, a position at which he excelled until his death in 1816. Hawkins Co. in Tennessee is named for him. He is thought to be the originator of the expression "God willing and the Creek don't rise" in replying to a Presidential summons. (That is, he would come, barring an Indian rebellion.) Hawkins had been Washington's primary French interpreter before the arrival of Lafayette in 1777.

The General Assembly has also outlawed the importation of new slaves into North-Carolina. *Prima facie*, I like this; but it may increase the value of existing slaves. *And* they have outlawed slaves' hiring out their own free time, which renders it impossible for them to buy their own freedom. The two laws together work against a hope I had entertained in the recesses of my mind of Marmaduke & family eventually buying their freedom. Yet these are the least of my problems.

Monday, 14 Feb[y]

"My darling, my creature" spake Emily to me as we embraced in our bed last night. How deeply did these words penetrate into my heart. What I wouldn't endure for her.

Sunday, 20 Feb[y]

Caleb Brown has been elected Sheriff. Woe unto us. Were it not for the necessity of girding her against his inevitable harassment, I would keep this from my loving wife. Aside from this worry, ours is domestic bliss. What sublime pleasure I derive from styling this angel Mrs. Shearin.

Well, perhaps not entirely domestic bliss. Eli is turning out to be a lad of slow parts, but something mouthy. He is a lanky thin 15 year old now with thin straight hair the hue of faded straw, not unlike his sister's. He sassed me so today that I was compelled to slap him. I hope his mercurial nature springs from his stage of life & that it will temper with age. I am bedeviled by the fact that he would rather learn from anyone rather than me. He has much to learn.

Our respected N. Macon has been re-elected to Congress again without opposition.

Sunday, 6 March

Caleb Brown has me in his sights according to Kenchen. He said that Caleb came to his place lately & that most of his questions seem directed at Sterling Shearin's guilt. Sheriff Brown let it be known that he can produce a witness to my friendliness with the former Mrs. Johnson at the Person's ball last spring. And he can produce a witness who says: The day before Asa Johnson was found dead, he left Person's Ordinary for Sterling Shearin's place to investigate said Shearin's conveying whiskey to the Ordinary without paying the tax. These are the stamp of things I expected.

Saturday, 12 March

Maj. John Macon, Lewis, & I received a letter from Nathaniel in Philadelphia. He encourages us to drive some livestock (his & ours) up to Petersburg before demands of spring farming consume us. He argues that prices are still good & that we are all short of grain & coin because of last summer's freshets. He promised hospitality for any of us who continued on to visit him in the premier city of our Union of States.

This is a fruitful idea that Lewis has already promoted. We decided that Lewis, I, two of Nathaniel's slaves, & one of John's would suffice to shepherd the Shearin & Macon stock.

Nath' also said that my acquaintance John Taylor from near Fredericksburg has resigned his Senate seat in disgust. And that Robert Goodloe Harper has been elected to Congress from South Carolina! He promised to follow with some interesting particulars concerning both.

Thurs', 17 March

Alas, what I feared has befallen. The mouth of detraction has been opened against me, & I come foully under blame. This night when I came in from gathering our stock for the drive, I was met by the tidings that Sheriff Caleb Brown (how warmly the combination of that title & that name agitates) had been here.

He questioned Eli at great length. Eli told him that he had seen Asa come to our farm the day before he was found dead. But even worse, he told him there was a lot of blood at & just inside the entrance to our barn. Eli said he had initially accepted my explanation of having to put Aristotle (with a broken leg) out of his misery. However, upon reflection, Eli wondered if there was not more blood than just from Aristotle's death.

When I am hanged, Eli will come to better appreciate me, the master he has condemned. If he is so fortunate as to find another master to which to apprentice, and if he is thought culpable in the burning of a tobacco barn or some such, he will be sure to feel that new master's whip (when he never did from me). Fie! Fie upon't!

I have endeavored to be fair with Patsy's brother. What a reward! Emily & I agreed that my arrest is imminent. My thinking was none too lucid, but after some discussion, we agreed I should attempt to proceed with the 'stock drive. A little ready money will be wanted for hiring a lawyer.

I told Emily to get Suky over from Mama's to help; & I indicated that they should—all of them, even Old Lucy—be working the soil in preparation every spare moment. For I may be jailed in April and unable to carry the burden of planting. They should go ahead with planting Irish potatoes in a week whether I am back or no.

I will start out at dawn.

Sunday, 20 March

So far so good. Emily got word to Lewis & he rendezvoused with me on the north side of the Roanoke at noon yesterday. We camped near the Virginia line last night & covered good ground today; Caleb will not pursue me far into Virginia. Will he?

Lewis was quite insistent on discussing the whole situation. Having learned somehow of Kenchen's beating at Asa's hands, he admitted to having privately speculated of Kenchen's guilt.

"Both times Kenchen winds up with the dead man's horse. Both times the victim is found on the southern edge of his farm. Both times Kenchen Shearin has a decent motive. And the bad cut on his hand back when Abner Whitaker got his. Remember he said a wild turkey did it. Real suspicious."

I thought of how Kenchen had wanted to make up a false story to tell Mary after his beating, but I said nothing. I know Kenchen is innocent.

"Kenchen is a lot more of a hot head than you, Sterling," continued Lewis. "I am pretty surprised that you are about to get pinned with these— even tho' you married Asa's widow like you did. I mean, you're too bookish & practical."

I do reckon Lewis took some little pleasure from our plight, even tho' it does the Shearin name no good. I do not trust him enough to confide. Not to say he is not honest; he is as honest as they come. Nathaniel can & does trust him to look over his farm for these considerable stays at Congress.

Wednesday, 23 March

Petersburg is thrice the town Halifax is because it is a superior river port. Its book store is a good example with twice as many books as Hodge's place in Halifax. A great tempting place to spend money. And to evade the reality of my situation.

I sent half of the £7, twelve shillings I cleared back to Emily and took the rest with me. I am bound for Philadelphia! If I am to be hanged, I will see the golden city first.

Tuesday, 29 March

Philadelphia is everything it is touted to be. Scenes of gaiety & industry abound. Many of the streets are wonderfully paved with stone. The nicest ones are regularly cleaned of horse dung! Macon showed me around the magnificent city & took me to the hilarious *A Bold Stroke for a Wife*, a production of prodigious brilliancy. Macon was a very amiable host and this was a diversion of a lifetime (tho' at all times the worry hangs about me fiercely).

I saw the diminutive James Madison & met Congressman Jos. M'Dowell from Burke County. If only the former were as well-versed a Whig as the latter, our Constitution might be a real guardian of our Liberty. Fortunately, Hamilton's excesses have rendered Madison a decent republican. Also saw one of Hamilton's men, Thomas Pickering, Sec. of War.

We encountered Robt. Goodloe Harper, now Congressman from South Carolina. Once he recovered from his surprise at seeing me, he was full of the wind as usual. He arrogantly denounced North-Carolina's "folly" in not returning Samuel Johnson (Iredell's brother-in-law) & Benj. Hawkins to the Senate. "These very fine federal gentlemen are ever so much more polished than that mechanic."

He referred to Sen. Timothy Bloodworth of Wilmington who is known to have no formal education. But his experience is vast: He has been an innkeeper, doctor, preacher, farmer, blacksmith, wheelwright, & watchmaker. Hence the expression "mechanic." 'Tis no slur in my mind.

From his fine silk stockings & his shoe-buckles more handsome than anything I shall ever own to his hair carefully plaited, clubbed up & tied with a black ribbon, Harper embodies the gay life full of elegance & splendor. If it must needs be that I emulate him to be styled a gentleman, then I am not sure I am meant for it. Nay, tho' I once entertained aspirations of some small degree of improvement in station, I would not have at that moment given you a cherry-stone to be of Harper's stamp.

Mr. Harper avoided any mention of the murders; just as I asked if he knew Asa Johnson, he declared he was late for something & was gone. Maybe a coincidence.

Macon said of him later: "I hope Harper does not represent the future. His first initiative in Congress was to ask for federal money to survey the

Yazoo lands, in which I believe he has a financial interest."

"Did you bring that out?" I asked.

"No. Madison simply pointed out that such a survey would have to extend to all the states to be constitutional. That is, the federal government must concern itself with the *general* welfare—not a *particular* area's welfare. That was the end of it. 'Tis plain tho' that Harper is a harbinger of how future generations will play with the Constitution."

Last night when I got in his bed, Macon gave me a strange look. I looked back at him with confusion & he turned over & went to sleep. I may have been dreaming.

Maybe he was pitying me, for we had just finished discussing my plight. He could not offer much advice except to retain Kemp Plummer, his brother-in-law, as my attorney. If he can free me, how deep in debt will I be then?

Macon gave me directions to the plantations of John Taylor & the deceased Geo. Mason.

"They will both afford you friendly accommodations on your homeward journey. John Taylor resigned his Senate seat in disgust. Too often the best men have no stomach for politics. Just as Wylie Jones observed. That is why I must make it a calling. To persevere for the republican ideal of Liberty."

"The victory is ever to those who persevere," I replied to him. And to myself.

"You can depend on't, Sterling, what you style perseverance, the likes of Harper & Hamilton are quick to call obstinacy. But you must be who you are," said he with a smile. "Aye, persevere we must."

Friday, 1 April

I made good time today & arrived in time to see John Taylor's magnificently beautiful plantation. I cannot imagine a more accomplished agriculturalist than John Taylor. He afforded me a warm welcome. (We enjoyed very tasty Brunswick stew, the best I have ever had without squirrel.) The absence of other guests allowed us to enjoy lively intercourse on many subjects—especially farming & political philosophy.

I commended him on how important his writings had been in informing the people of the nature of Hamilton's system, to wit, the corrupting of the capitalist class into dependents of & promoters of a dominant federal government.

"I hope I had some effect," said Taylor. "The Federalists can be brilliantly devious. The hooks of their fraud & tyranny are universally baited with melodious words like 'checks & balances' of 'public faith &

credit.' I wish we had pushed thru' the plan to sequester our debt payments to British merchants in retaliation for British abuse. Had we done so last fall, I was assured by two New England Senators that the Eastern States would have seceded from The Union. Which would have allowed us to have a confederation of sovereign states more grounded in freedom."

Taylor's farm inspires me greatly. Oh how I wish I could be free of Sheriff Brown & impending prosecution. I could be so happy with my loving Emily & my farm to develop, perfect, & perhaps expand. To follow Taylor's example. 'Tis easy to understand why so excellent a husband to the soil would eschew political leadership. It is as Wylie Jones has said: Few *good* men will be drawn to or endure politics.

All thru' my travels, I have endeavored to apply my mind to the solution of my problem. But my travels have not been useless. I conceive now of the grandness of the world. The possibilities are too multitudinous for me to submit to being hanged over the likes of Abner Whitaker & Asa Johnson.

Sunday 3 April

The events of yesterday have brought about a veritable Revolution.

When I arrived at the inn above Richmond, I was informed by a supercilious innkeeper:

"Supreme Court Justice James Iredell & family occupy one of my rooms & eight other *gentlemen* occupy the other. You may join another farmer on a palate we will put together after the dining & drinking are done, or you can sleep with the slaves in the barn."

Having focused on my plight all day in the saddle, I was the essence of despair: Each step towards home brought me closer to my doom. To be told by an innkeeper that my dress & carriage designated me amongst the lower rungs of his clientele helped none at all. At that moment, the innkeeper's pride in his august clientele hit me more personally than it was probably intended. I dejectedly chose the barn.

I ate little & went straight away to the large barn. Feeling lethargic from despair, I thought I would be asleep soon after resting my head upon my saddlebag. Alas, my mind wandered in a desultory fashion over every aspect of the circumstances I faced at home. And the hard ground beneath my straw was as lumpy as an afflicted cow. After a while I got up & walked out the back entrance of the barn to relieve myself.

When I walked back in I noticed a faint rush light in a stall; I naturally glanced in that direction & thought I saw the word "Aesop" on a book being held close by a dusky hand. Intrigued, I looked closer; yes a tattered *Aesop's*

Fables. I could not see who held the book, but I thought immediately of Sarah and having given her the very same book.

The next few moments, time seemed to stall. By the time I managed to emit the word "Miss?" she realized she was being stared upon & looked up.

"Sir?" she replied.

"Sarah?" I said.

"Who is that?" she asked.

"Sterling Shearin." She appeared as confounded & confused as I felt. She stood slowly. I came closer; I took her hand in mine and touched it to my lips. "Sarah, it *is* you. Are you alright?"

Awkwardly we started to converse. She had aged in some degree but was still handsome, still in bloom. Her speech bore the improvements of having been mostly a house servant in an affluent household. She belonged to the Iredell-Samuel Johnson clan.

She said that she ate much better than she had with the Hawkins & that Mrs. Iredell treated her fairly. She had known some abuse & unwanted attention from the white "gentlemen." She had developed an attachment to a fellow black and become pregnant by him (she thought) and then suffered a still-birth nine or ten months ago. Her owner discouraged a marriage by moving the young buck at that point out of Edenton. And now they were bound for Philadelphia; she was hopeful of a more interesting life.

I assured her that Philadelphia was indeed an exciting city. I told her of my trip and commenced telling her of what had transpired in my life. We were two old friends re-united, perfectly sympathetic to one another. I had no doubt that she had felt tenderness for me when she was my rented slave. She had not been merely opportunistic.

And I told her how I had sought her within my limitations. I hoped I conveyed to her the place she held in my heart.

I fetched us some apple brandy before the tavern closed, and we talked late into the night.

"Sarah, it was said that y'all were sold because of insolence on the part of your Papa. Was that all there was to it? It was so sudden." Never has a conversation taken a more fortuitous turn.

"No. That wasn't it at all. 'Tis very much a story."

"Tell. Tell in every particular."

"My mama delivered Caleb Brown's wife of a baby. The baby was colored. Caleb Brown took the little negro baby out of my mama's arms & told my mama to tell his wife the baby was dead. Mama came & got me. She was very agitated; she thought the overseer was going to leave the little baby out in the woods to die, and she was bent on rescue.

"So we secretly followed Caleb Brown out east almost two miles. Near to where Hawkins' path meets the Warrenton-Halifax road. From a great distance we were stricken to see him dig a shallow grave & then jab his big knife into the heart of the tiny baby.

"But somebody else observed the crime too. A white man. I heard Caleb say 'Abner!' in great shock as he came on him."

"Caleb's brother-in-law."

"I didn't know. They argued. In moments it became fierce and Caleb stabbed the other man to death with the same knife he had used on the tiny babe."

"I still don't understand. Why would he direct all his meanness towards innocent people rather than toward his wife & the black man she had relations with?" I thought out loud. "What happened then?"

"He finished burying the baby quickly. He flung dis Abner over his horse. Just as he climbed onto his horse, he spied us.

"We lit out of there like two rabbits thru' the woods. He started to chase, but we split up & I s'pose he went back to his murder victim. The next thing I know'd, we be on our way to Edenton & new owners."

"Could you describe the spot the baby is buried?"

"Hmn. Let's see. Come up Hawkins path ninety to one hundred yards from the road. Turn left off the path & go forty to fifty yards matching to the Warrenton road."

"Parallel?" I asked trying to demonstrate with my hands.

"Yes. You should see a huge, nay giant, sweetgum tree with a small boulder on the opposite side of the tree from the Warrenton road. Facing the Warrenton road, the grave would be to the right of the boulder."

"Your recall & logical description somehow don't surprise me," I said.

"I will ne'er forget it," she answered.

"You have a good mind, Sarah." How wrong for her to remain a slave, I thought.

She smiled. "I have to be secret 'bout it, but I have sneaked an Iredell book from time to time, and I can write a little."

"Do you know how the post works?" I asked. She shook her head: she did not. "You write on your folded letter Sterling Shearin, Esq., Warrenton, North-Carolina and take it to a post office. I pay the postage cost at the post office in Warrenton in order to collect it." I spelled Warrenton thrice for her.

"Please write me when you get situated somewhere. If I know where you are, some day I may be able to benefit you. Right now I am £140 in debt and wanted for murder. But your insight gives me some hope. The flatteries of hope are ever cheap & we must hold to them."

We were silent for a moment. I put my arm around her shoulders to express some measure of affection and connexion. She put her arms around my waist. In a moment she whispered: "It would please me, if you took pleasure in me."

We kissed deeply. She could feel my lust. I said "Sarah, you know me. It would be pleasure indeed. But..." I paused, searched for the words, & pulled away a little. "I love my wife too much...to dishonor the truthfulness between us. She would not understand that I love her no less for the lust & caring which I hold for you. I must honor my beloved Emily, my wife. I am weak before you, Sarah. Tempt me not."

When we parted in a short spell, I gave her a shilling & kissed her again. I could not get to sleep. The thought of her willing & near was not the least of it. I got an hour or two restless sleep & quitted that place before dawn.

Chapter Sixteen

Tuesday, 7 April 1795

Rain slowed my homeward journey considerably. I own I was surreptitious in my approach to my farm. I sneaked in when Eli was at a good distance from our dwelling house. Emily was the proverbial soothing sight for sore eyes. I had added to her worries by my protracted absence. She threw her arms around me & kissed me & kissed me & lay her face on my neck and said how she had missed me. I love her so.

Caleb had come to arrest me three times. Emily assured him that she had every expectation of my imminent return. She had pleaded with him of her utter certainty of my innocence. Poor Emily.

I told her quickly of the particulars of my journey that signify—most especially of the testimonial of Caleb's murder of Abner Whitaker. I told her & Lucy to say nothing to Eli of my return. I plan to hide the next few days at Marmaduke & Pris' dwelling. There is much to accomplish. On our farm & the attempt to assemble some kind of evidence against Caleb Brown. Can I count on the help of Kenchen & Maj. Macon? Fie upon't. Pray, how do you proceed against the Sheriff?

Friday, 10 April

Everyone was diligent in my absence. The carrots & most of the corn are planted. My absence & the meager harvest of last fall probably created a suitable insecurity in all my dependents. 'Duke grows more autonomous in an entirely favorable manner. If I am ever able to free him, I believe he will do fine.

I confirmed the particulars of a tale Pris told 'Duke before they married that involved Caleb Brown's giving away a little black slave to a free black man. Last night I sneaked over to Kenchen's to enlist him & Maj. Macon in my scheme. The latter proclaimed that I had more tricks than a colt on the first day's breaking.

Monday, 13 April

Well, it is something at least. Nothing to take for granted. It was as Sarah described. Thank goodness. Kenchen & Maj. John Macon witnessed my digging up the little baby's skeleton after hearing what Sarah had told me. In a trial this testimony could be of some value.

Will I ever be able to sleep in my bed again with my Emily without fear of detection? Caleb came again Monday for me. The murderous swine. Emily told me he leered at her as he suggested that I might have deserted her out of shame for my deeds.

"Caleb Brown is a line of vinegar in my milk," said she.

Corn done. Start on cabbage, butter beans, green beans, & peas tomorrow. There was talk in Philadelphia of an amazing machine that will remove seeds from cotton. 'Tis said that it can separate out the seeds from 50 lbs. cotton in a day! Depend upon't, that is impossible. A diligent man or woman might need 3 weeks, nay a month, to accomplish such a task. If there were substance to the talk of this cotton gin, it would certainly behoove us to plant more cotton.

Perhaps I delude myself. 'Duke says a neighboring slave knows I am back. Caleb must know too in short order.

All hinges on Kenchen's trip to Enfield to see Louisa.

I am determined to remain out of gaol long enough to eat some pokeberry salad & pork. And to love upon my Emily at least once more.

Friday, 24 April

I have done what I can & eluded Caleb Brown longer than I hoped. I will sleep in my own bed tonight with Emily & start preparations for moving the tobacco to the fields tomorrow. Time to quit hiding.

Blooming late this year, Sarah's pair of dogwoods still hold their charm.

Sunday, 3 May

Caleb Brown came with a posse (Absalom amongst them). He would have scoured the neighborhood this time and probably have gotten me even if I were still trying to hide.

"At last I have caught this shy cock," said he with a smile & tone that displayed all the true & natural colors of his malice. When I espy him now I wonder that it escaped me before.

During the first night in the dank, foul-smelling gaol, I tossed & turned in the grip of tortured thoughts. The second day & night were but little better, for Kenchen did not come. The inconveniency & discomfort of the place were not negligible, yet they paled beside my worry of all that could go wrong with my plan. Who can ever predict how a man will respond to such a gambit? Finally Kenchen did come.

We made an appointment with Sheriff Brown for a private meeting for the three of us—plus John Macon, Major of the Militia & Senator from Warren Co. to the Gen'l Assembly. The extended private conversation occurred early the next morning; I was subsequently released and joined my family in the fields before Friday was done.

I glory in the bosom of my family and ever henceforth shall glory in it beyond the run of ordinary men. (I missed the marriage of my brother Ab Shearin to Lewis' wife's sister.) I am not out of the woods yet. I must watch my back & be wary of Caleb, but I have hope that my knowledge—known by only the right number—will preserve me.

Sun', 17 May

We have the tobacco to the field. On the very highest ground I possess. Prices remain high for products of agriculture but other prices are rising now. Is this all from the European Wars?

Or the unconstitutional creation of money that John Taylor decries? As Macon says, one of the springs behind our adopting to the Constitution was that it did away with paper money. Now under Hamilton & the Federalists, the power to create a bank that issues paper money is merely assumed! And so again, as in the Revolution, our money loses its value.

Rumors are that John Jay brings a Treaty with him from England. Yet the British still stop & board our commercial vessels on the high seas. They enslave Americans as their sailors.

Maj. Macon, Kenchen, Emily & I know the secret of Caleb Brown. If too many know, its value will diminish as a protector. Hence I hesitate to commit the particulars to paper.

Sunday, 7 June

We are in the greatest glee. The wheat is excellent; my sweet, amiable wife & children & most of my connexions are in good health & disposition. Earlier this spring Kenchen took my filly—well, nearly a mare now—to Macon's stud horse Charlemain and attained results with a single leap.

My plan shows every prospect of working.

Sunday, 5 July

Having sold some wheat, we took advantage of the bankruptcy auction of Mr. Gloster's failed store in Warrenton to purchase Emily a ring, a belated wedding ring.

Maj. Macon reports that Caleb & Absalom took prominent parts in the Masonic Lodge's celebration of St. John the Baptist. Comfortable hypocrites. 'Tis a surprise that a former overseer could gain admission to that high & mighty society. May they perceive his true nature and not become his allies.

The rumors are that John Jay's Treaty is odious & demeaning to our sovereign States. It severely limits where American ships may trade while all our ports are fully open to all British ships. It fails to deal with British impressment of American sailors. All indications are that the Senate will reject Jay's Treaty.

The recent *N-C Journal* reports: "so alarmed is the British gov't at the idea of emigration that all masters of outward bound vessels are obliged to make oath previous to their clearing, that they will take neither mariners nor mechanics of this kingdom, as passenger to another country." Such are the signs & consequences of despotism. 'Tis an oppressive nation that denies its citizens the right to leave.

Sunday 26 July

Much woe. Another fresh: The Roanoke overflowed and ruined much of the corn. We have been busy replanting.

The Senate has ratified the Jay Treaty! Still with secret deliberations. A Virginia Senator sneaked a copy to Benjamin Franklin Bache's *Aurora* or we still would not know what mischief the Treaty entails. If we sell corn to our old allies the French, the British may freely stop the ship & seize it—and a few of our sailors for good measure. Our government agrees to it! Not gunpowder, but corn! The venerable principle of "neutral ships make neutral goods" is totally violated by the British. Might makes right. We hear that great crowds gathered in Philadelphia protesting the Treaty. Cavalry were called out to protect Washington's residence. Surely he will not sign it. Can he have forgotten how essential the French were to our independence? Is the Spirit of '76 dead?

Word is there is a letter for me in Warrenton. I have given Lewis the postage fee; he goes to that place tomorrow. All mine are well. Now if I can manage to keep them fed without going deeper in debt.

Sunday 2 August

Marmaduke was most agitated this morning. He claims he saw the ghost of Mordecai crossing the still-swollen Roanoke. He says just as he was pulling in a catfish, he saw a black shadow emerge from the waters; he declares he saw the flash of Mordecai's knife before he disappeared into the brushes. The runaway slave from Franklin County?

Priss claims that in the legend of Mordecai she heard that Mordecai knifed to death his master & family after said master had beaten him severely. I had not heard that part of it before & found it discomfiting to hear it from her lips.

"Evybody thinks dat freshet flush ole Mordecai out from his home under dem rocks in de river," Marmaduke says. "Evbody sepin you."

"Well Duke, I have little enough understanding of the actions of people— for instance why Priss has yet to uproot & gather the flax seed— & even less understanding of the actions of ghosts."

All are unsettled by the Jay Treaty. How can a few senators & Washington sell us away? Our great Constitution has carried us not so far from monarchy.

Sarah's letter was full of interest & not badly written for a slave girl. They had traveled on to New York where Iredell presided over court. Then they returned to Philadelphia. She had been happy with the excitement of travel to cities, the civil treatment of both the Iredells, the improved allotment of food & clothing, &c. But alas, she has been rented or given to a stern Eastener with whom the Iredells are friendly: Thomas Pickering, Hamilton's Secretary of War. He uses her hard; she hates him. There is no way she would get a letter from me by the post.

Confound it: the rains come again.

Sunday 9 August

We are destroyed. For half a day the most violent storms of wind & rain assaulted us with unabated fury. Yet another fresh of the Roanoke followed. Most of the fodder & corn is destroyed—especially the young corn replanted after the first flood. This calamity is the worse for the prevailing high prices.

We hear of protests of the Jay Treaty from Richmond & Baltimore. Sentiments run favorable to republicans such as Maj. Macon for the annual August election to the Gen'l Assembly. 'Tis a good thing for few us can spare time to apply to it.

My Emily is ever a source of comfort, reminding me of tribulations we have already survived (Asa, Caleb, &c.).

"If it must needs be, Sterling, for us to be together, I shall learn to think homespun preferable to brocade," said she last night to me in bed. My poor sweet beauty with a heart of gold. Now that there is none to stop her reading, she has no time. Yet, ne'er a captious moment on her part. I own I am the most fortunate man on this earth, tho' the flood renders us into poverty.

Sunday 16 August

The water rose yet higher. Within a few feet of our dwelling. We gathered in the wandering hogs that had not already drowned. Now all my family & livestock are here at Kenchen's while water & snakes claim my place. We all work on Kenchen's place to pay for his hospitality and possible future help.

We complain of Hamilton's Jay Treaty to take our minds off our present calamity. The *N-C Journal* reprinted an article from the Philadelphia *Aurora* demonstrating that the Jay Treaty is Hamilton's child. All the Eastern federalists will submit to any indignity from Britain rather than see their interest payments from our mammoth national debt interrupted. Thanks to Hamilton's funding system, they own all of the bonds & we southern farmers pay all the interest. They will get little from me this fall.

Wed^y 26 August

Let me count my blessings—such as they are. We are back in our house; snakes are cleared I hope. We only lost one pig & one chicken. The tobacco might make it if it survives mold. If not, bankruptcy is assured. If creditors go easy, 'Duke, Eli, & I can keep us from starving by hunting.

Our democratic society organized a meeting of protest in Warrenton but toned everything down to attract very respectable folk such as Wm. Falkener, who presided. We sent a mild polite address to Pres. Washington entreating him not to sign the Jay Treaty.

Sunday 6 Sept^r

General Davie, Wylie Jones, & several other gentlemen of substance are organizing a company to build a canal to conquer the rapids that ruin the Roanoke for transport above Halifax. This is a wonderful enterprise, but I fear it will elevate the value of my farm in the eyes of my creditors, at whose mercy I stand.

Maj. Macon's wife Johanna has died! She was but thirty years of age and leaves seven children.

Emily is with child.

Sunday 18 Oct^r

Much hinges on the tobacco. Prices are high, but they are on everything.* A plain coat, not an elegant one of superfine, now cost over 20 shillings. My neighbor on the north of the Roanoke is in foreclosure.

Washington signed the Treaty. His reply to our address was polite. The *N-C Journal* is full for several issues now of Hamilton writing under the name of Camillus. He displays his considerable skill as a writer & lawyer. His essential argument is that the alternative to the Jay Treaty would be war.

The last republican character in "Hamilton's administration" (Edm. Randolph) has resigned under a cloud. The new Sec of State is none other than Thomas Pickering! I have given Nathl Macon a letter to attempt to deliver to Sarah when Congress reconvenes in Philadelphia. I intimate to her that she might achieve revenge on Pickering (whom she despises) and help the republican cause (which I cherish) by reporting to my friend Congressman Macon whatever she might clandestinely observe in the Pickering household. I also suggest to her that Macon might be able to furnish some small compensation to her. Macon's approval was grudging in the extreme as he is no friend to intrigue. It required much persuasion, nay pleading, on my part.

Emily has dug from me much about my relationship with Sarah. This unfortunate knowledge produced little benefit & perchance some harm. There could be no worse time for a barrier to be created betwixt us, for not only are we teetering on the verge of bankruptcy but Emily is with child. 'Tis wretched. Cursed flood. Curse my idiocy. A thousand curses.

Warrenton hosts its first-ever major horse racing this week. Our poverty precludes our attending. Indeed I must sell my promising colt. It distresses me for he is beautiful, a very dark chestnut with red tones, not unlike the hue of my Emily's auburn hair. And ever so spirited. I shall repeat the received wisdom that "wild colts make the best horses" when I take him to market.

---

* From the creation of Hamilton's Bank of the US in 1791 through 1796, wholesale prices rose 72% (*A History of Money and Banking in the United States* by Murray Rothbard, p 69)

Sunday, 22 Nov.

General good tidings. Bankruptcy is avoided, tho' we are now **over £160 in debt**. Macon lent me £10 on security of the colt.

A new Latin school opens near Halifax, and Warrenton Academy & the University both seem to flourish; the dissemination of useful knowledge bodes well for our republics of free men.

The University has been among numerous sites of protest in our State concerning the Jay Treaty. Mecklenburg County in particular produced well-worded resolutions, not only protesting the Treaty, but also decrying the corrupting effect of Hamilton's funding system & national bank. The Mecklenburg militia calls for all citizens henceforth to vote only for Congressional candidates who do not hold bank stock or gov't bonds, as such individuals have a vested interest in more government expenditures and never redeeming the debt. Hamilton tipped his hand when he said "a public debt is a public blessing."

No doubt a few of the Mecklenburg Militia fought against the British with Col. Davie when they caused the village of Charlotte to be styled "a hornet's nest" by the great Lord Cornwallis. 'Tis gratifying to apprehend that they still possess the Spirit of '76. It is gratifying that they clearly perceive how Hamilton's system of a national bank, pecuniary bounties to manufacturers [corporate welfare, in modern parlance], protectionist tariffs, & public debt is calculated to undermine the Republic.

On the negative side, Louisa has been sold far away beyond Tarboro. 'Tis good that Kenchen thereby is delivered from temptation. Yet the poor unfortunate creature is my best proof against Caleb. The hypocrite gets on well with the Masons they say.

I shall not worry. My sweet, fruitful wife & I read to one another by the dim winter light of our hearth.

Chapter Seventeen

Sunday, 10 Jany 1796

Grandpa died at the venerable age of eighty-five. Fifteen children & more grandchildren & great grand children than most people could count. A very fine life. He left Mama & my youngest brother Daniel a slave named Phillis & a few pounds from their share of the sale of his farm, working tools, furniture, & c. He did not free his favorite negro, Tom, as I thought he might but rather stipulated that he could choose his new master.

We are tired of nothing but game to eat.

Philadelphia, 15 Jany 1796

Sir [Sterling],

I succeeded in delivering your letter to your friend [Sarah] during the early days of this Congress. There is much silliness & waste of time at the beginning of each session, as Congress must compose & agree upon an answer to the President's address, & then he replies. Washington & the Federalists are much taken with the aristocratical formalities & pomp of the British.

A few days ago I was in contact with your friend once more and gained some intelligence which—coupled with the discoveries of J.B.—lead me to believe that Sec. of State Thomas Pickering has been involved in nefarious strategems.*

He seems to have manipulated the information that Pres. Washington received to make former Sec. of State Edm. Randolph appear to be in the pay of the French. Disgracing the only remaining voice against the Jay Treaty amongst Washington's cabinet was calculated to wipe away any reservations the President retained regarding the Treaty. A detestable Treaty is made & an honest republican is ruined. Notwithstanding that I abhor the veriest notion of it, your friend's vigilance concerning this scheming Federalist may be of continued importance.

Opinion is so widespread against the Jay Treaty that we should be able to do something in the House about it.

---

* Perhaps John Beckley, clerk of the House of Representatives and a tireless behind the scenes republican activist.

Pray express my good will to all your family, especially Lewis. I am very grateful to him for helping to keep watch on my daughters & plantation.
Your sincere friend,
Nathl Macon

Sunday 14 Feb^y

This letter & other events feed our heads, but we need food for our stomachs. We have had no bread for three weeks, and my wife is in a needful way. Emily is anxious; her history with child-bearing distresses us both.

We live on stews of chicken, rabbit & squirrel but have no flour or corn that can be eaten. We have one or two sweet potatoes left in the heap; Emily shall have them. I will go out hunting a buck early in the morning and try to trade it for cornmeal &c. down in Franklin Co. where the flood did not devastate them.

The newspaper reports that the poor in England suffer great hunger too. Also, the writers there are much persecuted. The reporter speculated that England might be ripe for revolution.

A reprint of an article signed "Franklin" (John Taylor?) used the great Algernon Sidney phrase: "Where Liberty dwells, there is my country."

Caleb Brown seems emboldened by Louisa's distance. Word has it that he commented that Kenchen & I were murderers, tho' he could not at this juncture prove it. I grow sensible that I am the butt of many shafts of calumny. These are cold, dark, insecure times. The gay life full of elegance & splendor were never to be our portion, yet I never conceived that our station would be this humble, this close to desperation.

Sunday 28 Feb^y

Some good fortune. Sold some game to Marmaduke Johnson, whose horse Huntsman won last fall in Warrenton & Halifax. There is no finer horse. Mr. Johnson (no relation to Asa) must have felt pity for us, for he threw into the bargain a couple of leaps for my mare with Huntsman this spring.

The setter puppy I gave my 'Duke last year has turned into a very likely & smart dog.

Lucy & little Sarah are feverish. My head is starting to feel as if I might be coming down with it too. May Emily be spared.

Monday, 7 March

Our sweet child Sarah is lost; the whooping cough came atop her fever and carried her away. John now has it. Resilient old Lucy recovers tho' left weak.

Our heavy clay is so soggy that digging the grave is barely possible. My tears…I must stop.

Wed^y 9 March

There are no pillows in our home not moist with tears of anguish.

Wed^y, 16 March

Little John recovers but Kenchen has lost his youngest. 'Tis utterly woeful all about. Emily is continually worrying. But a matter of weeks now.

I try to be a comfort; but 'tis hardly my talent now, for the loss of our sweet innocent Sarah weighs so heavily. To speak the truth, Emily's spirit is sorely distresst. Having lost two babes, she struggles just to be hopeful. Sometimes I find her weeping; all I know to do is to put my arm around her.

We must think on the good. The soil is finally dry enough to work. I entertain hopes of enough yield from my apple trees this year to have cider to sell. The two cherry trees grow sizeable as well.

Lewis Shearin brought us a little corn & persimmon beer; I will never speak ill of him again.

Wed^y, 13 April

Emily is safely delivered of a healthy daughter! God be praised! Emily is still most anxious and hesitates to name her. I have suggested "Amey" after my Mama or "Seignora" after Macon's younger daughter. I am so relieved. Poke salad will supply us some vegetable component to our diets in a few days. All wears a better aspect.

However, I am concerned that Maj. Macon is courting Caleb Brown's wife's younger half-sister. He could & should do better, tho' there is no denying she is fair. Yet he should be choosing from better stock, and it does not bode well for his guardianship of the secret.

Sunday, 3 July

Nath⟨sup⟩l⟨/sup⟩ Macon is home from Congress at last, & I was happy to see him, in spite of his sorry tidings. The vote in the House to deny funding to the Jay Treaty fell short in the face of opinion throughout the country. Macon asserts that behind the scenes efforts by banks, by companies insuring ships, and even by Englishmen were evident. The skillful demagoguery of Fisher Ames of New England clinched it.

Under the Treaty, all of the cotton we begin to sell to England must be shipped in British boats. And they keep boarding our ships & empressing our sailors. This is all so odious that one naturally wonders if some of the Congress might have had their palms greased.

On a lighter note, Macon observed that the styles in clothing have changed noticeably in Philadelphia. Gentlemen sport uncocked hats with simple round brims in the place of tricorns & pantaloons or breeches that go down to their ankles. "*Sans culotte*" as the French of this new age say. Planters around here have long known long pants (worn inside our boots—leather is tougher than cloth) & uncocked hats to be more practical. Now let us eschew our former homage to aristocratical dress.

"I like the sound of it," said I.

"I'm not one to change with the fashion," answered he, very much in character.

I laughed. "You know, if you fell dead into the river, we would probably find your body upstream. Even dead you'd go against the flow."

He laughed, tacitly acknowledging the merit of my jest.

"Emily will want to know if there are parallel changes in the dress of the ladies."

"Most assuredly," he replied. "But I cannot do justice to describing them. Tell her they have less in the way of hips.—Enough of these things that do not signify, Sterling! I want to see your colt."

I showed Macon the dark liver chestnut colt (on which I owe him) and our little Katie (Kathleen, we named her in the end). Her hair is coming in the same shiny dark auburn color as the colt. They are both beauties. Emily laid in for quite some time and gave us concern but now is working with vigor again.

Macon likes well my name for the promising young horse: "Cato" for the original Roman republican & for the English Whigs who wrote Cato's Letters & inspired our Revolution. I paid Macon £5 of the £10 I owe him. I was able to do this because we enjoyed the finest wheat crop ever. And the beans look promising.

"Cato does not look like he will be a big horse, but how nicely proportioned…a well-knit back & lower-set hips. I collect from his concave nose that there be a drop or 2 of Arabian blood in him," observed Macon.

"Look at his expression, Nathaniel. He apprehends what you say."

Macon laughed heartily. "I think you are right. He is eminently alert. What wild eyes your Cato hath! Spirit in that colt," said he with pleasure in his countenance.

Yet when our discourse turned from horses to his brother John's marrying Sheriff Caleb Brown's sister-in-law, the expression of pleasure disappeared. Naturally, I share his dismay in eminent degree. I debated telling him the secret but refrained.

He brought me a note from Sarah. She continues to suffer abuse at the hands of the high and mighty Yankee, Pickering. She is saving the bits of coin she can come by (Macon gave her 15 shillings) and pleads for my aid in eventually buying her freedom. She remains vigilant.

[no date: late Aug.?]

Newlywed Maj. Macon has declined to be nominated for the Gen'l Assembly. Col. Paine won election in his room; he is a likely & respectable gentleman, but not grounded in Whig principles (frugality, simplicity &c.).

The crops that I bravely planted close to the river could not grow any better. You can literally *hear* the corn grow.

Little Katie thrives. Emily so enjoys our plentiful vegetables (after the situation last winter) that she will be slow regaining her former slenderness.

How trivial it becomes. How easy to love one who possesses such inner beauty.

Sunday 18 Sept^r

The prospects for harvest are excellent. I begin to rest easier that no calamity of weather or critters will ruin it. Pris has successfully produced another son, and looks as tho' she will be able to help again in another day or two.

Mary expresses an intuition that Kenchen strays again. He denies it to me & surely Louisa is too distant. 'Tis probable Mary is simply suspicious, having been previously treated to perfidy.

Pres. Washington has ended the speculation by retiring. Federalists can no longer hide behind the reverence which so many (even around here) hold for the regal & refined old General. Who will be put forward? Some talk of Jefferson. The obvious successor, Vice President Adams has expresst views none too trusting of the people. Perhaps he is right: In the long view liberty

& democracy are not one & the same. 'Tis my hope John Adams is wrong. He was a bit too comfortable presiding over the secret deliberations of the Senate.

Sunday 2 Oct^r

Wylie Jones has announced his candidacy as a presidential elector; we presume he will cast his electoral vote for Jefferson.

Prospects of plenty are upon us. Hallelujah! Emily & I debate what portion of our apples she will dry versus what I will make cider. Mama has so many cherries on her fifty-foot cherry trees that she invites us to come a-picking. If I can put the death of my daughter Sarah out of mind, this year is the best our farm has enjoyed. Ignoring Caleb Brown, my worst problem is little John tearing the cupboard door off its leather hinges.

Sunday 9 Oct^r

Gen'l Washington's farewell was printed in the paper: "'Tis our true policy to steer clear of permanent alliance, with any portion of the foreign world" and only "trust temporary alliances for extraordinary emergencies." Tolerable good sense. Macon said he generally does not write his own pronouncements.

Hodge (*N-C Journal* editor) reprints many articles from other papers which are critical of Jefferson & flattering to Adams. The federalist Pinckney of South Carolina & republican Burr of New-York are also promoted. This is the first election in which we the people get to choose the presidential electors; in 1792 the Gen'l Assembly chose them. Aside from the excellence of our crops, people talk of little else but the election of the new president. Even Emily & some of the women folk to a degree.

N. Macon is not sanguine. He has learned that New-York's Federalist legislature will probably choose only electors for Adams & Pinckney. He suspects Jefferson will get no electoral votes north or east of the Delaware River. He says Jefferson's only hope is in sweeping Pennsylvania, which will have a popular vote like we will. The state has many fine men of republican principles, such as Albert Gallatin, and a diligent organizer, John Beckley. Most prominent men talk always of the evils of party & faction; Beckley says we should accept them as reality. Five years ago I would have styled him a great cynic—but no longer.

Wylie Jones is too dignified and old-school to do anything to bring about his electoral success. And he has made enemies having been harsh with debtors & poachers. Now that Washington is deified in retirement, much criticism is heard of Jones for having shunned him in '91. Both Jones & Jefferson are slandered by many, not merely as deists, but as atheists.

Sunday 6 Nov

I am elated with my harvests & profits. I paid all my interest and reduced my debt to £132. We bought a second window for our house; such a luxury that will be on frigid days in January. We are happy. We hear nothing from Caleb Brown. —Fresh cider is such a treat.

The promoters of Jefferson & Adams sink to scandalous levels of abuse in their criticisms of each man. Robt Goodloe Harper calls Jefferson "a weak, wavering, indecisive character." Hodge prints only the most absurd attacks on Adams, such as the one that he is an "avowed friend of monarchy" and that he has sons whom he might try to install. We await news from Pennsylvania, which voted last week I believe.

Sunday 13 Nov

The French Ambassador has made bold public statements on the eve of the election in Philadelphia! He says the Jay Treaty violates our Treaty of 1778 with France & constitutes an alliance with Britain. He says France will henceforth treat our ships as we have permitted Britain to treat them. "France is terrible to her enemies," he says. No doubt he means to intimidate prosperous Philadelphia merchants into voting for Jefferson electors since Jefferson could more easily re-establish friendship with republican France. A questionable gambit.

The Federalists undermine Jefferson in Virginia by nominating Patrick Henry there (the law forbids an elector to vote for two persons from his own state).

Sunday 20 Nov.

The news from Pennsylvania is that Jefferson may prevail there. Republicans for the first time have won Philadelphia. We may have the French Ambassador to thank, but folks around here resent his "interference" in our elections. Furthermore, it appears Vermont's vote for Adams may be invalidated. Bache's *Aurora* predicts Jefferson 82, Adams 52. The Federalist plans go awry as Eastern Federalists shun Pinckney & Southern Federalists shun Adams.

Wed^y 30 Nov.

Wylie Jones was defeated, but I think most other Jeffersonian electors prevailed in our State. I asked Macon if any of his colleagues had been in touch with Jefferson during the election; he answered that they certainly had not. In fact Madison advised that no one should in this way give Jefferson an opportunity to discourage his election.

Latest word is that Jefferson got fourteen of Pennsylvania's fifteen electoral votes & would have gotten all but that a western county's vote did not arrive in the requisite two weeks.

Wed^y 14 Dec.

North-Carolina's electors just met in Raleigh. They gave Jefferson eleven votes & Adams one. Also six for Burr, three for Judge Iredell, one for Pinckney, one for Washington.

I tried to give Macon a few shillings for Sarah before he left for Philadelphia. He refused & insisted he would take a collection from amongst the gentlemen in his boarding house.

"They are all more affluent than both of us—& certainly less burdened by debt than are you," Nathl said. "I apprehend her desire to buy her freedom. I am pleased that she will possess a proper motive. I will worry less that she be ruled by whimsy. We must educate her well on the dynamics of this philosophical & political struggle if she is to be a useful agent."

"I will write her a long letter (by way of you) and spell out as much as I can. She is very smart," I added.

"I am not keen on this devious spy business—nay, I utterly despise it! But Thomas Pickering is an unscrupulous knave whose self-righteousness renders him all the more dangerous. Your Sarah's being dropped into his home is a gift that could prove crucial." Nathaniel took a deep breath, paused pensively, & then looked me in the eye in his peculiarly honest way. "You still care for her a good deal, don't you Sterling?"

"'Twould be a noble thing to help my country *and* see her go free in the bargain."

Wed. 21 Dec.

    Virginia gave twenty electors to Jefferson & one to Adams. (They showed mistrust of Burr giving him only one, throwing away fifteen votes to the great old libertarian Samuel Adams.) But Adams won Delaware & New Jersey and split Maryland. It appears Jefferson cannot win outright now; the election may go to the House of Representatives.

    My beloved thinks she may be quick with child again.

    Maj. John Macon's marriage does not go smoothly. It is told that his eldest child spat at the feet of Caleb Brown at a Sunday dinner. 'Tis as I feared.

New Years Eve

    Trustworthy sources have it Adams 71, Pinckney 65, Jefferson 61. 1796 ends poorly. Pris lost her youngest three days ago & our sweet little Katie has a similar ailment. **Please** let her recover.

Chapter Eighteen

[no date, probably early Jan. 1797]

We are disconsolate. Little Katie is so sick; she coughs uncontrollably. Mrs. Walker's potion of sumac berries, deer dung, wild cherry bark, & honey seems no help at all. Nor do onion poultices to her feet. Yet she fights. I would be baptized in the icy Roanoke if I thought it would help. Pray let this sweet little one live.

Concerning the Roanoke, they have established the tolls for the prospective canal past the rapids. I must follow this past good year with at least a fair one for Col. John Whitaker (slain Abner's cousin & chief tax gatherer for this vicinage) now holds all my debt. If I cannot pay the full 6% on the £132, I fear he would be after my land. The greater conveniency of getting produce to market will render my land attractive to him.

There is doubt about the actual outcome of the Presidential election, tho' odds are that Adams has won.

Friday, 20 Jan[y]

Praise God! Our little Katie recovered fully. You would never know she had been ill. In a fit of generosity, I am driving old Lucy down to the south of the county to visit her grandchildren tomorrow. She cannot walk that far anymore, & if her grandchildren get passes, they rarely use them to come see her. She has been as loyal as skin to my family.

Adams won: Adams 71, Jefferson 68, Pinckney 50. Three votes! Had North-Carolina & Virginia selected electors via their legislatures (as did New-York & other states) then Adams would not have received one vote from each state and Jefferson would have won 70-69. Or if one of them had done so and Pennsylvania's western county had gotten its vote in earlier, again Jefferson 70-69. "For want of a nail, the shoe was lost. For want of a shoe, the horse was lost. For want of a horse the battle was lost..." Small matters may signify.

Adams is not the worst of federalists. He has a reputation as an independent thinker. Macon says he is not as enamored of Hamilton as Pres. Washington & many others are. We should be optimistic. For certain we have a fine Vice-President.

Sec. of State Pickering has issued inflammatory public messages to the

French on the heels of their ambassador's attempt to influence the election. Late news is that French privateers are now attacking our merchant ships as the British were doing (excepting that they do not kidnap & enslave our sailors).

10 Feb^y

Cato's temperament has improved now that our red Irish setter sleeps in his stall.

Sunday 17 Feb^y

Nathl Macon lifted our spirits on a gray, dank winter's day (and provided me a respite from stump chopping) by paying us a visit. Macon says that a letter from John Beckley indicates that Hamilton contrived to elect Pinckney over Adams by encouraging Eastern electors to cast all votes for Adams & Pinckney. Hamilton assumed that Pinckney would get more votes than Adams in the South and thus be elected President. Hamilton is thought to regard Pinckney as malleable like Washington—in contrast to Adams. Fascinating! Encouraging: Adams sounds better all the time.

Nathaniel also brought news of an assembly [a ball] & festivities in Warrenton to celebrate Washington's Birthday. Emily has been in low spirits from the gray, wet coldness of the past seven days, not to mention bilious morning sickness. We determined immediately we should attend. (Her moodiness never has the shrewish edge that Patsy's did possess. I love her so and fear that she will tire of my affection.)

Friday, 22 Feb^y

We arrived at the ball just behind Maj. John Macon & his wife. They drove in a fine new chaise, apparently undeterred by the new 3 dollar tax on two wheelers. (The precedent of direct federal tax—ignoring the sovereignty of the States—is now established; the efforts of John Taylor & others who believed it contrary to the Constitution came to naught in Judge Iredell's Supreme Court.)

Mrs. Macon & 2 other ladies of some respectability wore extraordinary dresses, carrying the new style that emanated (most say) from France earlier

I started an attempt to draw Maj. & Mrs. Macon (as I remember them at the Assembly) one evening subsequent to the event, but Emily took over the effort the next night. What other hidden talents hath she!

this decade to startling lengths! The 3 ladies wore _thin_ chemise gowns of startling simplicity in white muslin.

"They have no stays or panier or hardly anything," Emily whispered to me with an embarrassed giggle. "Indeed there...is so little to it at all." The dresses are bound just below the bosom & hang down straight as a candle except for the hint of natural feminine curvatures. Mrs. Macon's muslin was remarkably sheer & cut to show much of her copious breasts. It was scandalous. 'Twould have been more so had the gown not been of such exquisite quality of color (an impractical, beautiful white) & fabric & embroidery. Indeed, "exquisite" was the word Emily employed to describe the overall effect, & I own I was somewhat surprised that this reaction overwhelmed the scandal of it. In addition, her hair was cut somewhat short! It curled round her ear with some charm. A feather danced from a headband. One wonders if Mrs. Macon's fine adornments & their expensive new chaise might pinch Maj. Macon's means.

Thus adorned, Mrs. Macon & the others were so impressive, nay, sensual is not too strong a word, that most of us could scarce take our eyes from them. Mrs. Macon is exceedingly handsome. But then so is her brother-in-law, Caleb Brown, handsome. Which reminds one that a vibrantly fresh green husk can entirely conceal an ear of corn riddled with worms.

Dinner was at three at the long room & very fine indeed. Emily & I both ate too much of the pork basted in a delicious vinegar sauce. And also of the pudding rich with pecans. 'Twas a festive affair, brim full of mirth. We all prosper well in comparison to 1795 & '96.

Nath' Macon's was my favorite amongst the sixteen toasts: "To The Univ. of North-Carolina. May it become the nurse of science and the Guardian of Freedom." My least favorite was Solomon Green's, disparaging of France & "Jacobins on both sides of the Atlantic." Naturally all speak of Washington now as a saint and ignore his part in the erosion of the spirit of 1776.

After all the toasts, we were quite ready for dancing. Emily & I enjoyed ourselves thoroughly for a good spell. Then Emily began to feel ill. I took her outside the long room, which had grown hot. It was perhaps foolhardy for her to dance in her condition. Strong drink hardly renders the mind more rational.

Absalom Jenkins happened by & noted that in parts of Virginia married women do not dance at all. (How do they have adequate numbers of women for dancing?) He chided us—tho' in his charming manner—for our absence from church. But he could see that Emily was in distress & did not tarry. I saw him later in a knot of Mason's & federalists: Sheriff Caleb Brown, Col. Whitaker, Solomon Green, & others of that stamp. I had the distinct impression of slanders being communicated.

I was worried about Emily, but after she lay in our wagon for a spell, she insisted she felt better & that we should enjoy the festivities. We went to Dr. Brehon's open house in hopes of some intellectual intercourse with the host or with the Warrenton Academy master. The master has a reputation for considerable use of the hickory stick and for working the boys equally hard in the fields & in the school room. He said the Academy flourishes, & he expects to send one boy to the University & one to College of William & Mary next year.

As we headed homeward, I heard shouting. I stood in the wagon & turned to see what was the matter. It looked like John Macon being restrained from hitting Solomon Green by my brother Lewis. I started to jump down from the wagon when Emily cried:

"Sterling!" Stopping me in my tracks. "I feel really nauseous. Please, let's get home."

She looked wan. The warm altercation—tho' it concerned Maj. Macon—suddenly became trivial. As I scribble now by this dim rush light[*], Emily sleeps badly. We may have been foolish.

Saturday 23 Feb^y

Emily was better this morning but has seemed wan & weak much of the day. At dusk Kenchen, Mary & their children came. I was happy to see them; young John brimmed with delight. Old Lucy rose to the occasion, & Mary was swiftly sensible of Emily's condition & pitched right in.

Kenchen brought a rumor that Maj. Macon & Solomon Green are to fight a duel! God's Teeth! Heaven forbid, what if Maj. Macon is killed? The tragedy would fall heavily on me as well, for my secret then becomes very weak. I would that Louisa were not three days' ride from here—assuming she is still below Tarboro as per last report. Caleb Brown could be behind this.

Wednesday 27 Feb^y

They duel Sunday at an undisclosed site. I doubt I could put my affairs in order with such haste. But then I am not ready to face death & leave my family helpless over some slight.

Well…these duels are for "gentlemen," a status for which I once

---

[*] A rush light was a less labor-intensive, but inferior alternative to a candle, made by dipping the stem of a rush plant in fat.

entertained youthful aspirations. After ten years of toil & struggle, I would settle for simply being free of debt.

I must go see Nathaniel (once I get a bit more fence done) to get the particulars. What on earth precipitated this altercation?

The ground is as wet as it was last year this time when digging little Sarah's grave was so bitter a task. I am writing her namesake in Philadelphia a long letter that Nathaniel will deliver when Congress reconvenes. She should know that a baby was named for her.

Emily was getting better. But then a rabbit ran right in front of her. Alas, she is not totally immune to the belief that such an event will cause the baby to have a hare lip. Pregnancy bears on Emily badly.

Saturday 18 March

I have been very busy with bedding the tobacco & sweet potatoes, planting Irish potatoes, and ploughing my ploughable fields. Consequently no news has reached us of the duel. Kenchen is the only neighbor I have seen in a fortnight & he has been similarly occupied. Hence I stole over to Nathaniel's today. He had just wrung a chicken's neck and was on the cusp of plunging it into boiling water to make the feathers easier to remove. He was glad enough of an excuse to press the rest of the task onto a negro.

There was some good news in Nathaniel's newspaper: A bill passed the New-Jersey House (by one vote) that all blacks born after 4 July 1797 will be free at age 28. An excellent & moderate approach to ending slavery. Yet if it barely passed in New-Jersey where they have few slaves, how shall we accomplish the end of this corrupting institution here, where slaves are so large a portion of all important personages' assets?

This positive was overwhelmed by the negative in the same newspaper: —To wit, further French despoilation of our sailing ships. With the demeaning Jay Treaty and Sec. of State Pickering's harsh words, we have provoked our natural ally, republican France, into becoming our enemy.

Indeed Pres. Adams has summoned a special session of Congress. Many high Federalists who were glad to kiss the British Monarch's boot (with the Jay Treaty) seem ready for war with France.

"Federalist ship owners & merchants have the habit of trading with Britain," said Nathl. "This may explain their reluctance to fight Britain & readiness to fight her enemy. Of course they also distrust republicanism."

Nathaniel had me amend my letter to Sarah to emphasize that her espionage could conceivably play a role in keeping our U. States out of war. He suggested sundry red flags for which she should scan Pickering's papers.

Nathaniel has had to break down & hire an overseer. He is not happy about it. He is also exceedingly disappointed to miss the first major spring horse races in Warrenton (May 13) because of this special Congress.

I have hopes of entering my young Cato in the one-mile heats on the second day. I have endeavored to train him when time permits. He shows an abundance of spirit. Indeed, on occasion just catching sight of Cato darting & fluttering in the pasture lifts my spirit. The thought of racing him is an exciting prospect that distracts me from other worries.

I asked Nathaniel, the most disinterested, objective man of my acquaintance, if he thought my young John resembled Absalom Jenkins at all. He admitted there was a mild resemblance. Hair & eye color at least.

Of course all these things we talked of after I had inquired:

"What of the duel, Nathaniel? I know nothing. Not even how it was provoked."

"Well, Sterling, John rendered some ungenerous insinuations concerning Solomon Green's federalism. Things like that he was a Tory beneath the skin. That Solomon did not think for himself & was a slave to anything approved of by his majesty, Pres. Washington. You know how words can flow with liquor. Caleb relayed these words to Solomon <u>with</u> some enhancement I am told."

"By whom?"

"Absalom Jenkins."

"Hmn—"

"He served as Solomon's second. He was generally helpful."

"Hmn. That's all? Caleb could get his goat with just that?" I asked.

"Well," Nathaniel paused & seemed squeamish, "Caleb claimed John had called a connexion to whom Solomon Green is close a degenerate."

"A sodomite?" I asked.

He nodded affirmatively.

"Who?"

"I do not know. John said Caleb Brown made that up out of whole cloth. Anyway Solomon responded to the baiting by publicly casting several aspersions at John, including one concerning alleged less-than-chaste behavior on the part of Mrs. Macon before her marriage to John."

"She did have her suitors. Still a despicable insinuation to pass the lips of one professing to be a gentleman," I said.

"Yes indeed. Before I could bat an eye, a duel was set."

"Well, okay. So is John alright?" As much as I wanted the details, I could not stand to wait for the crucial fact.

"Well" said Nathaniel, still unhurried, "I made numerous trips between them. And as I said Solomon's second, the Rev. Mr. Absalom Jenkins, was a calming influence. At long last limited apologies were coaxed from both of them. The duel was avoided, but bad blood between them endures. That slandering wretch Caleb Brown deserves a bad end."

"You cannot know how thoroughly I agree."

"He feels like a big man for having captured two runaway slaves in as many months. The first one was for Solomon Green, who in consequence has a degree of confidence in him."

"Some people are exceedingly adept at concealing what knaves they are."

19 Apr.

We just celebrated John's birthnight; he is 8 years old today! How time moves on. (In a few days I will be nine-&-twenty.) Emily loves him as if he were her own, & I can say precisely the same. What I love most about that young'un is his enthusiasm.

Sunday 7 May

We finished planting peas & got the tobacco to the fields. Weather is being reasonably good so far.

N-C Journal tells much bad news. More French spoilation of our shipping. A letter from Europe indicates that many there expect France to go to war with the U. States. Another article cited evidence of French spies over here.

We are diligent in readying our handiworks, hickory pitchforks, linen cloth, candles, pork, &c. to sell on the first day of the races. Then the excitement of racing our very own Cato on the second! Emily calls me "her gentleman of the turf."

Formerly I had thought to have Eli ride him. Yet Eli, now 17, weighs about the same as me & has not my sensitivity to the animal. So I shall ride Cato myself; I hope Eli is not disappointed.

Tuesday 16 May

Our handiworks sold tolerably on the first day of the Warrenton races. In the 3 mile heats, Marmaduke Johnson's famous stallion, Huntsman, led the 1st heat easily through the 1st two miles, but suddenly developed a hitch in his gait. His jockey halted him. Col. Whitaker's grey went on to win in a close contest. And then prevailed again in a close contest in the 2nd heat. Huntsman had suffered a quarter crack of his hoof.

I was obliged to watch Kenchen's cock fight (with fair success) in Absalom's cocking main. Kenchen had the good sense to pick Absalom's game rather than Taylor's. (The roosters are much more often badly hurt under Taylor's unnatural rules.)

I was most agitated that evening, contemplating my actual participation in the races the next day. I slept hardly at all. I was quite awake when a drunken Eli stumbled down under the wagon with me.

Distress of mind continued to plague me right up until the commencement of the 1st mile heat. Amongst my worries was the possibility that the crowd would spook my young Cato. My worries were well-founded.

We got off to a terrible start & were a distant last for most of the 1st half mile. I had to use spur & whip in a fashion against all my proclivities. Yet as a result, we *did* catch up to the pack in the 3rd quarter mile. But then a bird flew in front of Cato, & he veered after it. We finished so badly that I wondered if we would be allowed into the 2nd heat. A mortifying distant last place.

I tried to calm myself, reminding myself that little was expected of us: Cato is a young colt, & both he & his jockey are wholly without experience. Still it was deeply embarrassing. I took some little comfort from the fact that he recovered his breath quickly.

Our start in the 2nd heat was better, tho' we were still 13th out of 13 horses through the 1st half mile. I gave him a couple of flicks of my whip at that juncture; he accelerated nicely & passed a horse. And then he passed a second horse. He seemed to get the point of it. His speed increased a bit more without any prompting at all from me. We took 10th place with a quarter of a mile to go. Cato kept accelerating! Excitement swelled in my bosom. My colt lowered his head. We passed the 9th & 8th place horses on the inside as we entered the straight away for the finish line; he doesn't mind the rail. I apprehended that we were gaining on the leaders. But then the roar of the crowd at the finish line scared Cato. Our momentum carried us by one fading horse, but we lost the charge. We finished 6th. Amongst the admixture of emotions was atonement for our earlier embarrassment & excitement of potential. Middle of the pack may not sound like much to some, but…

Col. John Whitaker's grey, the winner of yesterday's 3 mile heats, had won the 1st heat but was bested by Wm Davie's yellow dun in the 2nd. Thus we had another chance. And Cato regained his breath well again. As Eli & I sponged him during the half hour respite, Eli brought into focus something of value.

"In the heat of the race, could you observe Marmaduke Johnson's chestnut mare make a charge from near the back starting at about the half-mile?"

"Hmn. She almost nosed Whitaker's grey for 2nd."

"That's right."

"Wonder how Cato would do trying to shadow the mare?" There is no finer gentleman of the turf than Marmaduke Johnson. That is in stark contrast to Eli & myself, who surely did not know what we were about.

"Eli, what do you think? *If* we can do it."

We achieved a good start in the 3rd heat. With the benefit of something of a strategy, we were 12th at the turn, positioned right behind Johnson's mare. I worried that Cato might be confused, but with no whip or spur he shadowed the chestnut mare through the next quarter mile. Just beyond the half mile, the mare accelerated with breath-taking celerity. A little whip & Cato did the same thing. Never have I felt such energy in an animal under me! We went by the 9th & 10th place horses with such ease that their riders gave us a startled look (Eli later told me). With less than a quarter to go we were 5th & 6th, Johnson's mare & Cato. My 3-yr-old colt evinced no sign of having run 2 & ¾ miles already this day. Such was the vitality I felt under me. With the mare, we were gaining on the leaders.

Davie's dun decisively passed Whitaker's grey for the lead. We, the mare & Cato, took 3rd & 4th. Whitaker's horse, having been raced over much in 2 days, slowed, ready to give up. I thought we might catch him. Whitaker's jockey whipped the grey wildly. He inadvertently caught the mare's jockey in the face with his whip. His necessary flinch slowed the mare just enough for Cato.

We squeezed to the rail. We got the mare by a neck at the finish line. We both beat Whitaker's grey by more than a length. Col. Whitaker, my creditor, was sorely agitated. Even after I dismounted, he was spitting & cursing & pounding his knee, entirely bereft of his usual genteel insouciance. What did he expect, racing his horse on consecutive days? I stayed out of his way.

I was a happy soul. So happy I used five of the ten shillings we cleared for the 2nd place finish in the final heat to purchase good coffee, molasses, salt, and a novella & a rose-plant for Emily. I was tempted to stay for the third day but thought of the sweet pleasure of bringing the news to my family. Kenchen mysteriously missed the races.

Sunday 21 May

We are all full of delight. I have been so near bursting with glee that those about me cannot help but be infected. Emily was as excited by the rose with its pretty pink blooms as by our success, but nevertheless was quite excited & distracted from her pregnancy anxiety. If possible, we will *all* go to the fall races.

Such a performance in so young a horse as Cato implies that endurance may be his true strong suit. He ran stronger in the 3rd heat than the 1st. It was as tho' once his heart got into it, he would not quit for man or beast. He is eminently easy to love. At 14 ½ hands, Cato is a small horse. His color is nearly identical to Emily's beautiful dark auburn hair, quite dark but with subtle red tones. Without a single marking. Very different from my blue roan Aristotle, much less biddable. Emily warns me not to count prizes & stud fees as yet unearned. Still the burdens of the farm seem lighter: All things wear a happier aspect.

Thurs^y 25 May

A letter attributed to Thomas Jefferson has been published in all the papers. He is supposed to have written it to a Mr. Philip Mazzei in Italy. The letter was translated from Italian to French & then from French to English. Federal editors put it forth to destroy the initial harmony between Jefferson & Adams. Unless Jefferson disavows it, they surely will succeed.

It reads in part: "In place of that noble love of liberty & republican government which carried us triumphantly throu' the war, an Anglican monarchical & aristocratical party has sprung up, whose avowed object is to draw over us the substance, as they have already done the forms, of the British government. The main body of our citizens, however, remain true to their republican principles; the whole landed interest is republican, and so is a great mass of talents. Against us are The Executive, The Judiciary,... all the officers of the government, all who want to be officers, all timid men who prefer the calm of despotism to the boisterous sea of liberty, British merchants & Americans trading on British capital, speculators & holders in the banks & public funds, a contrivance invented for the purposes of corruption & for assimilating us in all things to the rotten as well as the sound parts of the British model. It would give you a fever were I to name to you the apostates who have gone over to these heresies, men who were Samsons in the field & Solomons in council, but who have had their heads shorn by the harlot England."

Washington was the Samson; Adams, the Solomon. It has too much the ring of truth to have been manufactured by a federalist. Yet a very unpolitic thing to have attributed to the new Vice-President. The spirit of party & faction thrive.

Wed' 31 May

 Apparently the final straw inducing Adams to call a special session of Congress was that the French refused to receive our new Ambassador. There is a rumor that Washington misled the previous ambassador, James Monroe (a fine republican by all accounts), such that he had told the French—even as Washington was signing the Jay Treaty—that we would never violate our 1778 treaty with France. The Jay Treaty more than does that.

 This week's paper printed Adams' address to the special Congress: Prepare for war! Macon writes that even some moderate Federalists were startled. Adams called for strengthening the military establishment, especially the navy. A navy is good for getting a country into war since it is not defensive in nature—as the militia is. If it came to war, privateers would function as our navy.

 As unjust as it is that our trading ships are subject to vexations by the belligerent French & British, our government has no business attempting to protect Americans hundreds of miles from our shore. They are gamblers for high profits, venturing amidst the European War. Several republicans have observed that the value of goods a proposed navy might plausibly protect on the broad Atlantic would never exceed the cost to the taxpayer of the Navy.

 Macon has some confidence that Adams' bellicose proposals can be defeated. Unfortunately federalists maneuvered to fire John Beckley as Clerk of the House.

 Infinitely more unfortunate, Sarah was caught snooping at Pickering's desk and delt severe physical punishment. Macon did not elaborate in his letter except to say: "It seems unlikely that Mr. P[ickering] apprehended her trespass to be espionage as he seemed to give no indication that he knew of her ability to read."

 The two uses of "seem" in that sentence provide scant solace. I fear for Sarah. Self-righteously wicked men excel in heinous cruelty. Pickering is such a one if I judge him aright.

 Macon's letter continued: "Before the incident she provided information implying that Mr. P[ickering] is a warm friend to war against France!" No matter how despicably the guillotine has degraded France's republic, France is still <u>the</u> force against monarchical despotism. 'Tis unnatural for her to be our enemy.

Wed' 21 June

 I can still scarce credit my own ears. I was mortified, nay, stunned by the severest harsh words from mid-wife Walker:

"Sterling Shearin, I had never believed those many rumors that I had heard of you. But I can read between the lines of all that Eli, who is in the bosom of your own family, has had to say."

"Mrs. Walker, you know what young people of his age are like. You've raised children. And done an excellent job of it, if you'll allow, in the case of Mary Shearin."

"Don't come at me with your flattery & words of design," replies she, all bitterness. "'Tis you who have dragged down my son-in-law's character, his reputation. 'Tis you who have been a baneful influence upon Kenchen."

I sensed that any reply on my part would merely whet her sharp tongue. Nor did I know how to reply to so broad an attack. She continued to the kill, every word a lash:

"I have no doubt now that you, Sterling Shearin, are a base murdering scoundrel. A murderer! I say! I will have nothing to do with you, or with bringing your seed into this world! Nor will my sister mid-wives, if I have anything to do with it."

My heart fell down in my gut & then out of me. She pointed to her door. "Leave! And never come to my home again!" She slammed her door shut the instant I was outside, as if a more physical assault upon me were needed. I left her dwelling a shell of a man.

My Lord. How can I deal with this wicked calumny, this insidious, stealthy evil that goes on behind my back? How many, unlike Mrs. Walker, harbor the effects of these slanders but express them not?

Sunday 25 June

It has turned hot & dry. Weeds flourish particularly this season, & more so than the crops—except the corn we bravely (or foolishly) planted near the river.

The war scare shows every sign of injuring our freedoms: *N-C Journal* reports a South-Carolina Federalist urged Congress to go into secret deliberation. It took three hours of debate to defeat the motion. (Some fear embargo, which would devastate the prices of our produce.)

The newspaper also reported that Judge Iredell's grand jury is considering indictment of congressmen for circular letters mailed to their constituents which are critical of the government. The rationale is the supposed existence of French spies about in our states endeavoring to separate the people from the government.

The grand jury under Iredell's direction especially pointed at Congressmen Cabell of Virginia. This worthy gentleman has already proven himself: He &

Macon led the successful effort to ameliorate the Whiskey Tax; specifically it is changed from a per gallon tax (which had given advantage to large distillers) to a tax on stills over four hundred gallon capacity. This will put Kenchen & other small corn producers back in operation. If the virtuous Congressman Cabell can be punished for his communications to his constituents, then our Constitution & Bill of Rights are but good as kindling.

Writers in the newspaper call on Jefferson to disavow the Mazzei letter. As he is silent, they assume it to be genuine.

Mrs. Walker's words sink me into utter gloom. I cannot bear the thought of telling my anxious Emily in her condition.

Thursday 29 June

At the special muster of our county militias, Kenchen was distant. God's teeth! Kenchen has been my closest brother & friend. He is with Maj. Macon & Emily the guardian of the secret that protects me from Sheriff Caleb Brown. Surely the rumors have not shaken his belief in the veracity of the secret. He cannot abandon me. I can scarcely deal with the butter churn pounding cruelly in my viscera since Mid-wife Walker's condemnation.

A muster this time of year is an unneeded burden. The damned war scare. Maj. Macon said General Davie defended Pres. Adams, insisting that he is mainly interested in strengthening our negociating position with the French. Maj. Macon declares that Gen' Davie is becoming especially active in organizing Federalists in our state. The war scare favors them. War is ever the friend of energetic government.

On the way home I was to deliver a note from Maj. Macon to his brother's overseer. As I came into a clearing near Nathaniel's place, I espied a well-endowed negress stripped naked with her hands tied above her head to a stout branch of a large white oak. Her breasts were thus sitting up in an excellent comely fashion: I must confess my arousal. Then I perceived the overseer doing his—well, he was rogering her from the rear. Unseen, I receded behind a giant chestnut tree, sensible of arousal, embarrassment, & disgust in equal measures.

I intended to wait there until they were both fully clothed before coming forward, pretending to have seen nothing. But once he buttoned himself up, rather than untie her, he picked up a whip & commenced to whip her unmercifully. With fervor. With pleasure in his countenance. She shrieked in pain. Such appalling, evil brutality! What could she have done to merit this? I thought of Sarah. What could I do? After moments of embarrassed confusion, one of her screams galvanized me: I stepped out into the clearing & hailed the overseer loudly.

"My God, man! What has the wench done?" I tried for a mixture of nonchalant curiosity (that he might save face) & disapproval in my tone.

"You got to establish who is boss with these niggers." It was all he said, but he put the whip aside. Her moans & tears continued, tho' gradually abating.

"To be certain, you have already succeeded. You are Mr. Ezra Blount, aren't you? Nathaniel Macon's overseer?"

"Yep. You are a Shearin, ain't you?" Blount gathered his dark oily hair back into its queue.

"Aye, Sterling Shearin. I have a note for you from his brother, Maj. Macon.

"What does he want of me? Has his wife driven him over the edge?" He was as indiscreet as he was cruel. His scowling face, pitted from small pox & adorned by crooked teeth, was entirely apposite to his character.

I handed him the note. As he studied it with a frown, the negress continued to cry rather pitifully. I loosened her hands, picked up her garment from the ground, & handed it to her.

"You are a bit high & mighty, aren't you Shearin?" The tall, gaunt Blount smiled, his hollow eyes pretending only mild umbrage at my impertinence. One of his crooked teeth was visibly rotted.

"Listen to her." She continued to cry as she hurried away from us. "Surely, she got your message. I'm sorry. I didn't intend to overstep. I thought you were done." I tried to answer mildly.

He returned to struggle with the note, with no thought of offering me or my horse water on this sweltering late June day. I was about to bid him farewell, when he erupted with curses: "Nat Macon can tell me what to do, but not his brother!"

"I esteem them both & credit whatever either of them says," I said, still attempting a tone of mildness. Yet my words were inadequately chosen to mollify. And I am afraid my own countenance could not disguise my true disgust with him. Alas, I cannot feign friendship with the ease that I would put on or off a coat.

"I'll not be told what to do by the likes of you neither. Fie! The high & mighty one, aren't you? A gentleman of the turf just because you have a fast horse. We all know you have skeletons buried 'neath your house. Watch that someone don't break that horse's leg to put you where you belong."

A viler creature I could never have conceived. A worm is an object of veneration compared to him. By comparison to Blount, Caleb seems human; at least he has an excuse.

Slavery is a curse. I vowed on my way home that Sarah shall live free if it is the last thing I do.

Chapter Nineteen

Tuesday, 4 July 1797

I encounter disrespect from all sides. Eli & Marmaduke seemed to have played while I was at the muster & respond with surliness to my remonstrances. Emily is too much with child to tend more than the house & kitchen garden, but old Lucy confirms that 'Duke went fishing & Eli spent much of the day on Cato. A wise master would make an example of one or both of them; I haven't the heart for it after what I recently witnessed.

Well, we all skipped the festivities of today. Eli, Prissy, 'Duke, little John, & I sweated from dawn to dusk and made some progress on the weeds. I hung my whip on the wagon prominently & got less lip. I am thankful that my lack of resolve to use it was not apparent.

'Tis hot & dry. The corn begins to suffer. It takes very little to stir up dust, which seems often in our throats. A plethora of mosquitoes & flies afflict us.

I have written to Nathaniel Macon concerning his overseer; Lewis promises to deliver it to post in Warrenton tomorrow.

The *N-C Journal* has articles indicating that Nathl has served as second to Congressman Blount, delivering a duel challenge to Congressman Thatcher of New England. Rumor has it that the New Englander had the bold rationality to simply refuse the challenge.

After great victory in Italy, the French armies have gained peace with Austria. The French grow yet stronger. A letter in the paper from Europe indicates that everyone there expects France & the U. States to go to war.

Sunday 16 July

At last the rain; the earth has enough, but more is wanting for streams & springs. More good news. Maj. Macon wants his name placed in nomination for State Senate again. The tattle is that he wishes to get away from his wife. She is said to be more than a little ill-tempered & not merely a poor manager of their household but even a spendthrift.

I wonder if Maj. Macon will ask my support, given the injurious stains upon my public character.

Sunday 23 July

'Tis a mark of how badly my reputation suffers that Maj. Macon has not asked my support. The incumbent, Col. Paine, *and* Solomon Green! will also be nominated.

All the tobacco on our mature land is backward. We barely get this red clay to the state of being ploughable and now it is worn out. 'Tis received wisdom that tobacco is the worst in this regard. If time allows, we will manure a part of it this winter; if money allows, we will buy clover seed for the rest. I should rest it a year, but the exigencies of my debt require our farm to produce: maybe peas. Corn thrives by the river but threat of flooding is ever present for that low land.

Emily is much beset by anxious thoughts concerning her swollen state. She is less rational than her normal self. In a rare fit, she berated me for spending so much time with my beloved Cato. I went from her & shared Eli's whiskey jug with him as we both curried our fine young stallion.

'Twas a peculiar evening. I felt despised by all—even my wife. I sought some rapprochement with Eli. Yes, with him who supplies the mortar for the brick wall of slander that condemns me.

"Eli, you were vexed by not being Cato's jockey at the races, weren't you?"

He merely nodded affirmatively. He pretended a casual air, but, all things considered, I warrant that he was exceedingly disappointed.

"I hear the Warrenton races will have four-mile heats on Thursday & one-mile heats on Friday."

"What about Saturday?"

"Well, sweepstakes of unknown distance. We can't afford to enter the sweepstakes. Of course I speak the obvious." After a spell I offered: "Suppose you ride the first four-mile heat on Thursday & I ride the 2nd?"

Eli's face brightened perceptively. He was delighted. With the whiskey as a lubricant, our conversation grew warm and easy. Eventually he said:

"I guess I owe you an apology for the trouble I have caused you with the sheriff." I thought to myself: if your false words were confined to the sheriff I could tolerate it.

"Old Lucy jumped all over me," he continued. "She said any other master would have beaten the stuffing out of his apprentice for speaking against him like I did. She said the truth was that when Asa Johnson came to the farm that day, you & he got into a scuffle. That Aristotle was trying to come to your aid just as Asa had picked up an axe. That he swung the axe at you, missed, but with his momentum swung round & broke Aristotle's front leg with the axe."

"I loved Aristotle as you love Cato. Asa deserved his fate. He was odious scum," I blurted, victim of a thousand invading passions. "You know little of his sins, how he abused Emily, how he burnt the tobacco barn that you got blamed for."

Eli reacted in astonishment. To Asa's burning of the barn or my overly warm words? Liquor had weakened my brain. Eli was taken aback. I had spoken with too much vehemence.

"No I didn't know," he replied. Did I imagine his reaction? Damn my jackrabbit mouth.

I took a deep breath. I stuttered, "W-was that all Lucy said?"

"Well, she said Asa was stunned at what he had done. He got on his own horse right quick without apologizing & rode away."

"You can see why I'm not unhappy that someone killed him?"

"And he burned the barn? Sure enough? How do you know that?" Eli espied me with some little wariness even as his tone of voice was on my side.

"It is from one of his slaves. In spite of that, it is very reliable information," said I.

I thought too late of the Bard's words "Have more than thou showest; speak less than thou knowest." Whatever I can do to ease old Lucy's life must be done forthwith. I extracted from Eli, that having learnt the truth, he would communicate the same to mid-wife Walker & c.

Sunday 30 July

Emily & I reconciled sweetly after those rare coarse words. But she worries herself sick, and I cannot seem to dissuade her from it. Rather she persuades me to worry. If she will merely come thru' this childbirth well, I will accept my fate as pariah without complaint.

Unwanted by Maj. Macon, alienated from my closest brother, Kenchen, and my neighbors, I was feeling most isolated today and quite ready to converse with someone, if only to get some news of the outside world. I was glad of having offered to carry old Lucy to see her progeny again today. (I also fetched her extra lemon balm for flavoring & for bettering the smell of her pillow.)

After delivering Lucy to her folk, I visited Isham, whose farm is hard by. My watermelon & I received a sorely-needed warm welcome.

His wife is pregnant also, but she never has trouble. Goodly portions of his crops are backward from worn out land too, but his plan is to rent a slave this winter & clear some new land.

An astounding bit of news! It seems that former Sec. of Tres. Alexander Hamilton has been exposed for having a sexual liaison with a certain Mrs. Reynolds, the wife of the very James Reynolds, who with his inside knowledge, bought Kenchen's certificate for a trifling portion of its value!

Isham said Kenchen's bad luck continues. He gambled much of what he had won in the cockfight on the lottery (a lottery to raise money to start a cotton manufactury in Halifax) & won nothing.

Other news: Congressional Republicans have beaten back Federalist efforts to loudly rattle our swords & provoke mighty France. Macon's time in Philadelphia is not in vain. New negociators have been sent to France.

As I was leaving, Isham's wife obliged me in great measure by saying candidly that I was "too gentle a soul" to have killed two men & that she did not believe the slander & that she did not think most people did.

12 August

I went to Warrenton to vote, & of course to trade, and found Solomon Green indulging in a vulgar enticement. He provided a barbecue to all voting freemen. He spoke warmly of our need to arm against "Jacobin France" & promised the men gathered that the government can do all manner of things for them. At next year's election, perhaps he will stoop to running an advertisement in the newspaper soliciting votes. The shameless offering of chicken pie & drink for a vote! How unseemly! How lacking in disinterestedness & rectitude!

I perceived a coolness from many there towards me. I begin to doubt that Eli followed through on the extracted promise to clear my name. Awkward for him perchance. Or maybe people more readily believe ill than good of one. As it is received wisdom that want of suspicion betrays innocence, the opposite must surely be true: To wit, people generally have guilty hearts & are hence readily suspicious. Sheriff Brown & his friends continue to besmirch my name no doubt.

Kenchen has been scarce. Worms & grasshoppers plague the tobacco & keep us fully employed. We will make little on it this time. At least we cleared a few shillings on beans, peas, & watermelon in Warrenton. Copious drinking loosens the purse strings on Election Day.

The perhaps uncleansable smears on my public character would pain me a good deal more if they were not overwhelmed by my concerns of losing my Emily to childbirth (she is filled with foreboding) & losing our farm to my creditor.

Sunday 20 Aug

The dog days of August brought their usual sicknesses & I tell myself Emily's is just such. God, we are miserably fragile & needy. And all crops beg now for rain; the heat is infernal.

Solomon Green won. Maj. John Macon came in third! Tho' nearly tying Col. Paine. A wretched event. We of republican principles are on the defensive. Fie upon't.

Only Cato's strong running at twilight provides us optimism. More & more I am sensible that his forte is going to be his bottom. Eli & I have determined a four-mile course on which to train him. We have no clock but he feels so strong.

Tuesday, 29 August

Emily is somewhat better but still poorly. The heat renders her condition miserable. The crops are not especially good but should make the interest payment & taxes—if no disaster befalls in these last few weeks. We must reduce the debt, for our situation is most precarious. 'Tis as Macon says: "Whoever is much in debt can never be free. Be it a nation or a man." We are exceedingly vulnerable to our creditor, the unsympathetic federalist Col. Whitaker. In the recesses of my mind, I entertain hopes of Cato as our salvation. (The filly sprung from Marmaduke Johnson's stud shows promise also.)

In a fit of loneliness I went yesterday to seek out Kenchen; he was not there. His wife was her friendly self. However, after a spell she confided that her mother, Mrs. Walker, & many a one hereabouts speak ill of me.

"Is Kenchen among them?" I asked.

She hesitated. "He does not speak to me much about anything...I would swear he is at it again."

"Louisa is far, far away from here. Nigh 80 miles I'ld think. It's not her."

Mary Shearin sighed in despair. She herself had lately recovered from a bilious August sickness & I suggested this had likely jaundiced her perception. I expresst how much we missed both her & Kenchen and begged her to attend Emily in her delivery.

"Even if I were as guilty of the worst slanders, why should my innocent wife suffer?"

Worthy woman that she is, she promised.

The only other bit of news she imparted was that Maj. Macon is bitter, and is contemplating selling out for a move to Tennessee! This is ominous.

Friday, 8 Sept^r

Maj. Macon has placed a notice in the *N-C Journal* that he is "determined not to pay for any articles that may hereafter be contracted for by my wife" except with a written order signed by himself. Alas…

Sunday, 17 Sept^r

"Have you heard the latest news?" Nathaniel Macon greeted me with the utmost good-nature. It was my turn to give Cato his twilight training; on a lark, I took the path to Nathaniel's instead of our normal course. I had heard nothing from him since his return from Congress. Surely my old friend would not shun me. I needed to know.

"What news? Concerning what? I know little. I have been isolated," I replied.

The high & mighty Alexander Hamilton has responded to the exposition of his illicit affair & his giving out privileged government secrets: Responded by writing his own long pamphlet. He confesses explicitly all the unsavory details of his protracted amours with Maria Reynolds in order to refute the charges that he gave out advanced knowledge of the treasury plan to buy all the States' revolutionary certificates at face value.

"How else could James Reynolds have been in North-Carolina before anyone here knew, buying certificates for a tenth their subsequent value?" I asked.

"How indeed? Fortunes were made." Macon laughed. "That he would go to such lengths to vindicate his public honor in itself suggests to me that his behavior as Sec. of Treasury was pregnant with corruption."

"You say the pamphlet is lengthy?"

"Indeed. He goes on to attribute all criticisms of himself to evil designs against the national interest. He blames all on the 'spirit of Jacobinism.'"

"We've heard a lot of that around here from Federalists like Solomon Green & Gen. Davie. They love to hate France & any republicans they can tie to her."

"Hamilton contends the spirit of Jacobinism is the worst threat the world has ever known. That it threatens the overthrow of the political & moral universe, of which Hamilton naturally is the mainstay." We laughed.

"He continues that he is caught in the Jacobins' conspiracy of vice against virtue, namely the slander of upright men."

Suddenly I identified a bit with Hamilton. Nath[l] continued "The irony is that it is Jefferson who is the true victim of slanders & he bears it all in silence. While this agent of corruption 'doth protest too much'; his quill full of venom."

Macon smiled. "'Tis good that it all comes out. And 'tis good to see you, my poor Sterling." His cordial friendliness warmed my heart. "Like Hamilton & Jefferson, your public character has suffered difficult blows. But where free enquiry & free speech subsist, the truth will rise in due course like cream to the top."

"Your optimism—& even more, your friendliness—cheer me more than you can know, Nathaniel."

Macon went right past my warm thanks: "Hamilton is a dangerous man. His system flows from principles clearly adverse to liberty. But for the recent work of Gallatin*, Hamilton would have successfully hidden from us that instead of reducing our unnecessarily bloated debt, Hamilton had been adding roughly a million dollars new debt during each year of his regime. 'Tis a great thing that the public gain more knowledge of his true nature."

"Surely, this folly will end his ambitions to power," I said.

"You would think it. But Hamilton is intelligent, resourceful, energetic…& persistent. He is full of invention & design, ever to be feared. Even now he wields great influence. All the rich Federalists are beholden to him for their gains by way of the National Bank & the national debt.

"Many owe their government jobs to him. We have confirmed from clandestine sources such as Sarah—she is invaluable—that all of Pres. Adams cabinet secretly consult with Hamilton! May you be as resourceful as Hamilton in dealing with your difficulties."

"I thought I had been resourceful. But alas, it all collapses. Your brother John, whom I thought to render my shield, sells his plantation and will be gone after harvest."

"Aye. To Tennessee. I could not talk him out of it."

"My public character is so besmirched, I fear I will be easy pickin's for the Sheriff without him." I spoke to him of my secret & how John Macon aided my cause. He mulled what I told him with a troubled brow.

"I can understand your refraining from doing more than holding the secret over his head; you could never convict Caleb Brown on such a basis. Yet this confidence you have reposed in me is a wretched one. For it presents no honest or just resolution."

He looked at me in silence, & I wondered if I would lose even his friendship. Honesty & straight-forward dealings are the essence of his nature. How many times now have I pulled him from his natural course with what he would call my designs?

"Perhaps I could get you to notarize a statement from your brother before he leaves?"

Nathaniel grunted ambivalently.

"Well…I have more immediate concerns: my debts and Emily's deliverance from her troubled pregnancy. A mind hath not capacity for but so many worries at one time."

---

* Congressman Albert Gallatin of Pennsylvania initiated the Ways and Means Committee in an attempt to supervise the "utterly undecipherable form" with which the Sec. of the Treasury directed the country's finances.

He chuckled. "You do have more than your portion. Every life has little rubs & vexations, but I would not trade places with you." He didn't seem on the cusp of rejecting me.

"Has Maj. Macon a good bid on his plantation yet?" I asked.

"I don't think so. That might keep him here awhile." He turned his gaze toward Cato. "Sterling, one good thing…You do have a fine looking animal there. I don't regret lending you money on that one."

Nath[^l] loves horse-racing like the rest of us & has lately taken up fox hunting with some of our aristocratic Virginian neighbors (John Randolph of quarter horse fame, for instance).

Tentatively & with trepidation, I brought up the subject of the overseer. He had left Philadelphia at the end of the special "war" Congress before my letter arrived. I elaborated what I had apprehended.

"Well, Sterling, I appreciate your candid information. I hate the sound of it. I must own that I am conflicted. Ezra Blount has produced a fair harvest considering our want of rain. I have not favored the whip, but…I need to talk with certain of my slaves & deliberate on the subject."

"What can you say regarding Sarah? Is she receiving pecuniary reward? You called her invaluable."

His answer was vague & unsatisfying. My esteemed friend becomes too pragmatical regarding slaves.

"She must be freed. She is in jeopardy. I fear this Pickering. A righteously cruel man can be the worst. She assumes great risks to preserve our freedom; 'tis very little for her to ask."

"I believe you love two women, Sterling."

"'Tis but justice."

Tuesday, 17 Oct^r

The Roanoke began to rise; hence we harvested our best corn from the lowland early. None too soon, for we subsequently suffered a freshet. 'Twas not as bad as in 1795 & our diligence limited the harm.

However, it was not until today that I had opportunity to visit mid-wife Walker—even tho' Emily should give birth any moment. Mrs. Walker was callous & obstinate; Eli had not even talked to her. The graceless varlet! A pox on him!

I am afraid to leave her for the races, but at least I could attempt to secure the services of Dr. Brehon there. I will go fetch Mama tomorrow.

Friday, 20 Oct'

 I left my poor swollen Emily with grave misgivings. It helped that she, Mama, & Mary Shearin gave encouragement as they worked the flax.

 We sold a goodly amount of produce Thursday morn, and I took it as a good omen. I must admit I had very high hopes for Cato; young John must have picked them up from me for he talked gaily of Cato beating all comers. Little did we know.

 There was reason aplenty not to be sanguine. The race-meeting was only 2 days with 4 mile heats the 1st day and 1 mile heats & a sweepstakes on the 2nd. Tho' Cato is now nearly four & tho' his bottom rather than absolute speed is his strength, I did not wish to race him in the 4 mile heroic distance. I would have preferred 3 mile or maybe 2 mile heats. Especially when more than 2 heats are necessary to establish the winner, it can be brutal on the strongest of horses. I saw a horse die in a fourth 4 mile heat once. And proper training for the 4 mile distance simply requires more time than Eli or I can spare. Yet I chose the 4 mile event on the first day because of Emily's condition.

 In the first of the two four-mile heats, I kept my word to Eli by letting him ride. But not before obtaining a commitment to keep his earlier promise before the end of October—or there will be hell to pay!

 Eli & Cato started poorly & trailed the entire field for the all first mile. Beginning the 2nd mile, as they were attempting to pass the next-to-last horse, Eli caught some grit in his eye. They dropped back into last, & I feared they would be distanced & disqualified. But they recovered a little. As they finished the second mile I observed Cato's gait still looked smooth & efficient, his eyes still alert. They caught & cleanly passed the 10th place horse. And then Macon's beautiful black stallion. Beginning the 4th mile, Cato was running the fastest yet and passed 2 horses to take seventh place. With half a mile to go, he was just about to pass for 6th when Macon's black charged by them both. It seemed to take something out of Cato. He dropped back. Eli whipped & spurred him as I never would have. But to no avail. They finished 8th out of 11 horses. (Macon's black finished 2nd.)

 Cato's condition was something dreadful. He took so long to regain his breath that I decided not to run him in the 2nd heat. But then it was announced that the normal 30 minute period would be extended to 45 minutes. With Eli, John, & I lovingly sponging him and the extra time, Cato brightened & regained a sense of himself. When the call to the post came, I mounted him gingerly. I apprehended no hesitance on his part to join the line. I determined not to spur him at all (not least because Eli had wounded him) & to accept distant last place if that be our portion.

 Nine of the 11 horses answered the call. I made no effort to start well.

We settled with another horse about 3-4 lengths behind Macon's black, who ran 7th. We held that position for more than a mile & ½. When Macon's black took 6th, the horse he passed drifted back to us. For the first time in the race, I gave Cato a bit of whip. He picked up his pace & seemed to enjoy passing this horse. We gained to within 2 lengths of Macon's black.

I brightened as we moved into the 3rd mile for Cato was evincing bottom of eminent degree. He was maintaining a formidable pace 2 lengths behind Macon's black. Both of us over-took another horse that slowed. We entered the fourth mile 5th & 6th about 15 lengths behind the leader, and my horse was not done.

We maintained pace as the 4th place mare drifted back to us. We passed the mare with less than ½ mile to go. Macon's black attempted to mount a charge; Cato attempted to follow without much prompting from me. He did not match the black's charge, but he finished very strongly, over-taking one more horse for 4th place. (Macon's black gained 2nd again.)

No prize money. But I was inwardly pleased with the strength of Cato's performance. And with the unbridled joy the 2nd heat gave my ebullient son. John was in the greatest glee the rest of the afternoon.

Not long before dusk as we were preparing to quit Warrenton, Mary Shearin arrived to tell me Emily was in her travail. As she spoke I was overcome with a sense of foreboding. A cloud of a thousand fears fixed itself upon me. I had spoken to Dr. Brehon earlier in the day of this possibility of her travail; we immediately solicited his attendance on Emily. When we arrived late into the night, poor Emily was still moaning in pain, still undelivered. And thus she remains this morning. She is pitiful. I fear Dr. Brehon's patience & sympathy are being taxed as a good midwife's would not: I heard him grumbling beneath his breath about missing the one-mile heats.

I humbly pray to God to spare my poor Emily.

'Tis late evening. The world is closing in on us. The clouds render the night exceedingly dark. The specter of death is all around us.

The life flows out Emily. The moans of pain are low now such that I do not hear them from outside. Dr. Brehon speaks of cutting her. Mary has gone to plead with her mother, Mrs. Walker, to come & give the benefit of her long experience; she would have done so earlier except they suffer an estrangement of more than half a year. (Perhaps this colored Mrs. Walker's vehemence towards me.)

Eli stayed for the races & is just back now. He is full of telling of them. Col. Whitaker has a new horse he calls Avenger which won the sweepstakes.

What does any of it matter now? I write because there is nothing else to be done. At least John & little Katie sleep peacefully at 'Duke & Prissy's place.

21 Oct^r

Mrs. Walker came in the middle of the night. At dawn she & the doctor aggressively removed the babe, a dead boy. Emily hangs near death. They tell me to expect no better than that. To speak the truth, they hath given her over.

They left me alone in the middle of the morning with her. It was a very gray, foggy morning. The fog was so thick it seemed to float into the windows so that we were surrounded by tearfulness. I asked Emily, so pale, if there were any thing I could do, anything at all. She didn't reply. I listened close to assure myself she still breathed.

"Emily, can you take a little cool water?" I asked. "It's right from the spring." Her nod was barely perceptible. I held her a little more upright for her to drink. It seemed a great effort on her part. She was so weak.

I sat & held her clammy hand for several minutes. Just as I closed my eyes, she asked me in a weak whisper to sing a song of her youth. I did my best. I didn't know all the verses. I sang a second song that I know better, her favorite hymn, *O for a Thousand Tongues to Sing.*

How oft have I heard her quote the Revelations inspiration for the hymn "I heard the voice of many angels, numbering thousands upon thousands" after delighting in its melody & poetry. Listen to those angels now Emily, not to the utter anguish which no amount of will can efface from my trembling voice…the hymn too poignant to bear.

"He breaks the power of cancelled sin
He sets the prisoner free…"

Alas, I bawled. I broke down into uncontrollable weeping. Holding it back through 4 verses was like damning the flooding Roanoke. Why could I not be strong for her? I cried in my weakness. She was too weak to cry.

She could barely lift her hand to touch my head. She whispered for me to hold her. I lay beside her & held her, choking back tears.

I held her close & put her limp nearly lifeless arm around me. I held her as close & cradled as humanly possible and cherished these last moments of touch; cherished these last moments of smelling her smell, bereft as it was of any enhancements of her herbs, yet ever so familiar & sweet to me. I cherished these moments, tho' the tears welled in my eyes. I tried to accept that this was the end. Then she grew so still. So lifeless. It was over. I broke down again and cried loudly.

She stirred! Thank God! There's hope. I had awakened her from needed sleep.

She whispered "Bring Katie. Please let me see her once more."

"Of course, Emily, of course. But please, please don't think of it that way. If you give up, we shall all perish too without you."

I went straight away to fetch Katie. No one was at 'Duke's place. I searched all about in vain. My God! I thought, Fie! Fie! at least let me do this one simple thing for Emily. Please! she cannot die without seeing her child. I thought they might all be fishing on the Roanoke. But before I could find them I stumbled upon a negro man, woman & baby, attempting to conceal themselves. The woman was Louisa! What events doth Providence visit upon us.

Calamity upon calamity.

Chapter Twenty

Sunday, 22 October 1797

So wan & weak was Emily that I was afraid of it scaring little Katie. Yet if Emily…died…Emily managed somehow to rise upon this event & to give Katie a little smile, tho' she could not sit up to hug her. Still I drew encouragement from the smile. I am also encouraged that Mrs. Walker thought it worthwhile to return. She speaks the obvious: "Emily is barely hanging on."

In time the women grew weary of my sad face. Or was it that the household is woman's particular province?

"Sterling, she knows of your love & caring," said a patient Mary Shearin. "There is nothing you can do. We will tell her we urged you to see to your farm, if she gets a good conscious spell. And the distress & anguish which your countenance fails to conceal might not be the best vision for her if she does become alert."

So utterly routed were my senses that I doubted my ability to deal with any matter. I could not order my thoughts beyond the inescapable knowledge that my beloved was dying. Who is so undeserving of this fate as she? Nature bleeds from every pore. What could be more utterly wrong?

I went to chopping wood for the physical action of it. Once I had worked a good sweat, my mind calmed to the point of thinking: Well, what can I do at this moment that will help anything? Something must be done about the dangerous predicament of the fugitive slaves.

When my muscles were some little fatigued from the axe, I fetched some corn cakes & cider and headed back to their hiding place near the Roanoke.

Staying in motion, doing something helped somehow. I sought to lose myself in action lest I wither in despair. The fog & clouds had been cleared by cool winds; it had started to turn cold. As my sweat dried, I started to feel chill. Nay, this was no bad omen. I chose to see the bluing sky as a good omen.

I found them by the river where I had left them. I reckon they had believed me when I said I would not turn them in. Perhaps Kenchen had familiarized Louisa with my character. More likely, they were lacking good alternatives. They were gaunt with hunger and devoured what I brought them. Their story was a desperate one.

Louisa had succeeded in escaping her role as paramour through the good offices of her last owner's wife & the new church they joined. The wife went to great lengths to encourage Christianity & good behavior amongst the slaves as well. Indeed, Louisa married the light-skinned negro George who now accompanies her, in a church!

Unfortunately, in an occasional weak moment, the owner himself would take advantage of Louisa. George bore it badly, but bore it. The baby is darker than either of them, so it is probably George's progeny rather than the owner's. But what happened next was too much to bear.

The owner's degenerate brother debauched George! (He is a fine looking high yellow & an appropriate consort for the handsome Louisa.) After the fourth instance, poor George dared to plead his case to the owner. The owner reacted in horror, refused to believe George, & attempted to convince him of the unreality of it by having him beaten nigh unto death.

Once George recovered, they patiently planned & slyly executed their escape. It had taken them three weeks to make it to this place. I have not seen a newspaper to know if a reward notice has been placed.

As if I did not have enough woe, they now come to share theirs with me. Should I be discovered harboring fugitive slaves, Sheriff Brown—how ironic in this case—would have my sweet derriere. Hmn, or would he?

I drift about as if in a nightmare dream. That I care a fig for their plight, or my own if Emily dies, is only because I cannot imagine life without her. It can**not** happen.

Even if I lose Emily, I will have to go on. For my children. I must repeat this to myself. I must use my faculties, tho' if I lose Emily, I do not see how I can live. Parting with her will tear my flesh, my bones, my mind asunder.

Louisa's plan of escape was clever for getting them away from Tarboro. And they had the necessities for fishing, flint for an occasional mid-night fire, &c. However, hope of succor from Kenchen was the last & most dubious aspect of the plan.

I repeated to them that my wife was on the cusp of death & that they were by comparison a minor concern for me. But I vowed not to turn them in & I vowed to contact Kenchen on their behalf. I told them their hiding place was a relatively good one but that they should exercise every caution. They must avoid detection by Eli or my blacks. I shewed them a little nook where they can fish unseen & shewed them areas along the river to avoid.

I pray to & plead to God for Emily.

Tues' 24 Oct^r

Emily hangs at death's door. She takes a little nourishment at least. I have but hope.

Wed' 25 Oct'

Emily rallied. She sits up in bed. I am on the wings of ecstasy.

Isham's wife has come to relieve Mary. I told Mary it is imperative that I speak to Kenchen.

This morning brought the first hard frost of the season. I need to take my remaining harvest to Halifax & pay the interest on the debt—before Col. Whitaker gets impatient.

Thur' 26 Oct'

Needless to say, Kenchen was stunned. Neither of us possesst a notion of how to proceed. What a complicated set of springs acts upon each of us in this predicament. Neither of us for an instant contemplated turning them in to the Sheriff, reward or no. We carried them some corn cakes & talked with them to apprehend their thinking & resolve. For now, it was decided that they stay put. We will determine if the *N-C Journal* or *Virginia Gazette* has run an advertisement concerning them—to wit, discern if their escape be well known in this vicinage or parts north.

Fri' 27 Oct', Halifax

I am sick with worry. Emily was better, but as I left for market, she came down with fever. Please, dear God, don't let her come down with what Patsy had.

Sat' 28 Oct'

Too bad my harvests were not more bountiful, for the prices they fetched were more than tolerable. I was able to pay down our debt by an even £12, buy all the gunpowder, salt, sugar, &c. (we've grown accustomed to homemade chestnut coffee), and save aside £9, 10 shillings for taxes & contingencies. The dresses in the French style are all about now; how fetching one would look on Emily.

I encountered Mr. Wylie Jones and enjoyed most animated intercourse with that fine gentleman. He evinced heartfelt sympathy for Emily. He expresst great commendation for Macon in thwarting the Federalist war party, though he says the French in their excess have departed severely from republican principles.

We discussed Cato & horse-racing at some length, and got on so famously that Mr. Jones concluded by inviting me to come to his house during the Halifax races next month. He said he would give me some seeds for love apples [tomatoes], which he claims are good for more than ornament: —to wit, they are actually not poison to eat & their juice is excellent to cut odor. Even that of a skunk. I could only think of the putrid odor of the disease that killed Patsy.

Alas, I was delayed by the difficulty of getting up with that damned puff'd-with-importance Col. Whitaker to pay him. Hence I am sleeping here under the wagon this frosty night mid-way betwixt Halifax & home. When I folded a blanket some moments ago for a pillow, it smelled faintly of her. I wept uncontrollably.

The weight of what I may find 10 miles from here, at home, descended on me so that I began to tremble. And then I could not stop trembling. I wanted to cry again to regain that brief momentary frisson of cleansing calm, but I couldn't do that either. Am I so weak? I must regain control. I must deploy my wits for all those who depend upon me.

Please, dear God, spare my Emily. Can you not see she is the essence of virtue? How can you take such a one as Emily?

Mon' 30 Oct'

When I arrived Emily was still alive, yet in great perspiration. Mrs. Walker has discontinued onions to her feet & her favorite tonic (which smells to me like three-fourths apples brandy) because they have been so ineffectual. She suggested I fetch Dr. Brehon back; however, on our earlier trip together from Warrenton, he admitted to me that he is rethinking his entire approach to Medicine & Physic (to wit, purging, bleeding, & c.) and I must say that his magnanimously confessed uncertainty inspires no confidence. We settled on lots of spring water & broth of sorrel & bits of chicken. Significantly, the putrid smell was absent.

Wed' 1 Nov'

Halleluia! The fever broke. Emily is still very weak, but she is plainly better. She has an appetite & speaks to me as if she expects to live. I am so happy I could leap over Cato.

I must turn my attention to the problem of the fugitive slaves. Kenchen was here briefly; he was the soul of worry. We could not come up with a plan. We agreed to wait another week to make sure no notice of the escape appears in the Halifax paper. George said that their owner probably expected them to make for New Bern (instead of this direction) since he was from there.

I acquiesced to the extended imploring of Eli & John to their entering Cato in the 3 mile heats of the Halifax races. I think that distance is best suited to him. Am I a wantwit to allow them to take him without me?

Perhaps I dream beyond reason, but if the field in Halifax is not over strong, Cato might place & gain us a few shillings. As he matures, might he even be a contender? A horse for whom some might pay a few shillings in stud fee for a leap? That Emily can smile even weakly gives me the flatteries of hope. I am all hope.

With Eli gone, I intend to put George & Louisa to work around the house. Loyal Lucy can be trusted.

I must devise a plan.

Mon' 6 Nov^r

Fie upon our bad fortune! Friday Sheriff Caleb Brown descended upon us without warning. He claimed to be looking for an escaped slave from Franklin Co. True to our prior planning, George hid in the woods at the first warning by our dogs of visitors. I am guardedly confident the Sheriff did not see him.

I talked to the Sheriff loudly outside our house to give Louisa time to hide under Emily's bed in case he insisted on coming in. Louisa had been skillfully massaging flax towards being linen while keeping company for Emily.

I assured him I had seen no such slave. After supplying him and his horse some water, I excused myself from inviting him in, to avoid disturbing my convalescing wife. Just as he was turning his horse to leave, Louisa's baby could be heard to cry from inside our house. My viscera jumped up into my throat.

He turned back suddenly. "I thought I heard you had lost your baby," he said.

"Yes" I replied. "'Tis a slave's baby, what Lucy's watchin'."

He looked at me suspiciously. He eyed me for what seemed like 20 or thirty pounding heartbeats. But then he turned in his saddle & clucked his horse. Was he unaware of Louisa's escape or did it not occur to him? Would it? A few questions on his part could determine that it was not Prissy's baby or Lucy's great grandchild. A solution must be found quickly.

Emily recovers slowly. She is weak & probably vulnerable to new illness.

Yet there are some good tidings: The field at the race-meeting in Halifax was diminished by the foul weather (& the course was sloppy). In the 2nd heat, Eli rode Cato to a third place finish! John was all happiness in his enthusiastic way. (He is such a likely boy, be he mine or no.) I split the 10 shillings with Eli. He has at least squared things with Mrs. Walker.

Sun' 12 Nov^r

To make matters worse, a notice appeared in the Halifax paper describing George, Louisa, & baby. After discussions with all involved, we all decided on a plan. I will pretend to have rented George from an unnamed source in Halifax. He will stay with Duke & Prissy. And I do mean stay at that place, avoiding all contact with outsiders and sharing nothing of the truth with Duke or Prissy.

Louisa & baby will go with Kenchen under similar pretense & even stricter guidelines—lest someone recognize her. Indeed, they will sequester themselves *entirely* in Kenchen's kitchen. Thus separated they can lie low through the winter, at least till people are less mindful of them.

Perhaps we can get them up as far as Petersburg as part of a livestock drive in the Spring.

The fair Louisa asked me how extensive her services to Kenchen need be. Neither Kenchen nor I have ever been in want of passion flower;* no doubt Kenchen will be tempted. I considered the difficulty she would be for me if she were in my care, given that I am not sure I will ever be able to enter Emily again. The best answer I could give her is that our commitment to helping them does not depend on it.

Sun' 19 Nov^r

Sheriff Brown came back. He asked questions relating to Louisa & C. He wanted to see the baby that cried. I said it was my servant Prissy's. If he pursues this, how will I explain this to Prissy & will he believe a three year old made the sounds rather than a six month old? I do not want him to see George who is at Prissy's.

---

* The pulverized root of this wild flower, Passiflora incarnata, was used to treat impotence et al.

As he left Sheriff Brown commented malevolently to me "Maj. Macon will be gone in a few weeks you know."

Emily is recovered after a fashion; she is still too weak to do more than thread work. I look over at her now sitting by the hearth licking a thread to thread the needle. She looks up & smiles and says "Yes?" She lives; life's other vicissitudes I will handle.

Chapter Twenty-One

1 January 1798

We enter the New Year of 1798 happily, safe & well. All save Eli who has a painful swelling behind his lower back teeth. Emily, tho' not strong, is recovered, and has resumed her place as Mistress of the household. We owe Mama, Mary Shearin, venerable Lucy, & several other womenfolk hereabout more gratitude than we may ever be able to repay; we will try.

Sheriff Brown returned in November & wanted to see the crying baby. I sent young John to Prissy's to fetch her youngest without explanation. The Sheriff commented that it had sounded like a younger child to him. He told me to spank the pickanniny to see what its cry sounded like.

My insides were considerable agitated. If Sheriff Brown catches me at this, 'twill be my undoing. Maj. Macon is no longer here to bolster the story I hold over the Sheriff. To cover my deep anxiety, I responded aggressively: I told him to go to hell. I told him to cease pestering me lest he could tell me some meaningful purpose.

"Have you forgot your own vulnerability?" Never mind my diminished ability to enforce it. —My boldness worked: He left & has not been back in the intervening five weeks. As Virgil wrote: Fortune favors the bold.

Duke & Prissy were so relieved I was not selling the young'un that they did not question my bogus explanation. George deftly throws himself into the deception of our design: 'Duke & Prissy question not that he be rented. George has been a real help in manuring the weak fields; he earns his keep. As long as he can rendezvous with Louisa in the black of night once per week, he does not complain.

I got a written testimonial from John Macon before he left. I had hoped to get Nathaniel to witness it, but he had already left for Congress in Philadelphia.

7 Jan^y

Eli finally got some relief after we lanced the angry swelling. Poor boy suffered greatly.

Lewis had a letter from Nathl in Philadelphia. He writes that party animosities have never run higher. Federalists call republicans "Jacobins"— or worse, whisper of their being agents of France. Outside Congress, Nathaniel has seen more than one member cross the street to avoid touching his hat in greeting to another of the opposite party. It is essential that our new envoys to France, John Marshall et al., manage to ameliorate our relations with France.

"War is ever a great threat to your liberty—whether you live in a republic or a monarchy," writes Congressman Macon. "If the war threat may be calmed, there are enough honest Whigs in this house to protect our rights; I judge us to be at rough parity with the Federalists."

8 Feb^y

A letter writer from Paris opined in the *N-C Journal* that France & the U. States would be at war in three to six months.

Emily is herself again. I catch her eye now as she sits with spindle & distaff. I smile at her, and she gives me a little smile as fine as a bee's wing. I keep looking at her with unguarded pleasure in my countenance. She giggles & then shakes her head to express how silly she deems me. I am afraid to do more than hold her.

Eli is having the problem in his mouth again.

18 March

We are just returned from carrying Eli to the doctor in Warrenton. His face was more swollen on the left side than ever, & he was hot with fever. Dr. Brehon made an incision in his cheek, draining copious amounts of pus. Then he plied Eli with whiskey & laudanum (the cost of which ate up all Cato's stud fees thus far) and extracted his backmost tooth. It appeared to be a perfectly sound molar, but Dr. Brehon said he suspected it was keeping another tooth submerged.* Poor Eli has suffered mightily.

In Warrenton, I encountered Mr. Wylie Jones, who honored me exceedingly by asking me to join him as he shared drink with Marmaduke Johnson & Benj. Hawkins' brother. I expected them to be talking horses since Johnson & Jones are gentlemen of the turf beyond compare. But I concluded shortly that Jones' main mission in Warrenton was to reassure investors of the viability of the Roanoke Canal enterprise. Paradoxically I learned what a daunting project it is. I could not help but wonder as I listened if Mr. Jones would ever live to see it completed; he has declined perceptibly in vigor. He grows frail & suffers a stye in one of his eyes.

Mr. Jones is a paragon of virtue: He spends much of his time promoting this canal & the cotton manufactorie, which will benefit us all around here

---

* Presumably, an impacted wisdom tooth.

more than himself. And nobody has done more for the Univ. of North-Carolina—unless it be General Davie.

The conversation took a troubling turn when Hawkins brought up the Lyon-Griswold affair. Congressman Griswold of Connecticut had called Congressman Lyon of Vermont a "low-life" & "coward" at the back of House chambers. Lyon retaliated by spitting in Griswold's face. Whereupon the genteel Federalist Griswold attacked Lyon in his seat in Congress with his cane! Lyon escaped his seat & defended himself with fire tongs. A motion to expel the rough republican Lyon followed and barely failed to command the required two-thirds vote.[*]

Tho' Hawkins is as federal as Jones & I are Whig, we all deplored the asperity of partisan conflict. But then Mr. Jones began to defend his friend Jefferson, who has been attacked in Congress with distortions of the Mazzei letter. Those distortions imply that the Vice-President is trying to undermine the government.

"Congressman Cort avers that Jefferson is a criminal if he believes there exists an aristocratical faction which wishes to impose the substance & form of British government upon us," said Mr. Jones.

"Well?" replied Hawkins.

"You think of a man as a criminal because of his quite plausible beliefs?" asks Jones.

"Well, time will show, I suspect, that Jefferson is an agent of the French."

"Fie, sir! You accept the ridiculous slander put forth by Robert Harper?"

"Harper is quite a formidable leader now," replied Hawkins. "He is one to be reckoned with. I am proud to have hosted him in our home."

"Philemon Hawkins! You know him. Robert Goodloe Harper is glib & sophisticated, but without a system, without principle. He is, in his way, more dangerous than Hamilton!

"He is a patriot. He does not in stealth tear down the government as our Vice-President does." Hawkins replied. "'Tis plain that Jefferson is ever full of invention & design,".

The conversation descended from there. In a short spell Hawkins & Johnson departed with mere grudging politeness.

"Sterling I am afraid we are losing this battle. I think M'duke Johnson, and many previously apolitical fellows of his stamp, are being driven into the federal camp by the excesses of the French."

---

[*] In the debate over expelling Congressman Lyon, Congressman Macon was Lyon's main defender.

"What irony," I replied, "that we sign a treaty agreeing to be Britain's lapdog in order to avoid war with her, only to provoke a more unjust war with France."

We conversed in perfect sympathy for a spell & when I walked with him back to his fine coach (I do not believe his health would allow him to ride a horse), he gave me a new fangled plow with a curved mouldboard. 'Tis the same one which Nathaniel had spoken of, the invention in the good sense of the word of Thos. Jefferson. He had intended to show it to the gentlemen but deemed it inapposite after Hawkins' ungenerous pronouncements.

"You should justly be the first in Warren County to use it, Sterling. With your clear vision, you are as likely to promote this useful knowledge as they are. Take this hickory one. My blacksmith is making me three iron ones."

I was overcome by this supreme compliment from my genteel friend. I am afraid Lord Chesterfield[*] would have found me wanting in my effort to express my heartfelt gratitude with the proper refinement. However, I truncated my awkwardness by noting to Mr. Jones how the smoke from the chimney rose very slowly & the odor from the nearby ditch swelled. The rain storm these signs foretold might make the road to Halifax difficult for his carriage; thus he departed without further ado.

1 April

In an imperfect world, I am most blessed.

My Emily has regained her health. The crow's feet around her eyes only make her more beautiful. And finally last night we had relations. 'Tis near ten months. Mrs. Walker believes that during her time of month, no babies can be created. I pray she is right.

The weather has been favorable, and with George's diligent help, we will cultivate the largest acreage yet. I wish that I could keep George. Another visit from Sheriff Caleb Brown effaced from me any such temptation. His suspicious, malevolent gazes agitate my insides.

Jefferson's plough with the curved mouldboard does indeed turn sod more efficiently than our straight stick plough. With it I expect to have a quarter of our fields ploughed into beautiful rows.

Finally, my children, young John & little Katie, are healthy & easy to love. Eli recovered & all our livestock—most especially Cato—thrive. I am blessed.

---

[*] *Lord Chesterfield's Letters* was a very popular book for manners among those who aspired to polite or genteel society. The word "genteel" had no sardonic or negative connotations in the 1790's but was entirely complimentary.

Sir [Sterling],

I regret not seeing you before leaving for Congress. We have accomplished little & enmity between the two factions has been nearly as severe as between Tory & Whig during the Revolution.

But the plot may be even now thickening: We in the House were near to passing a bill curtailing our swollen diplomatic corps (we now even have envoys in Portugal & Prussia—the latter, the President's son!) & wasteful executive patronage generally, when Pres. Adams reported to us that (1) French navy will seize our ships carrying British goods—to wit, behave as the British navy does—and (2) the French government will *not* receive our new envoys!

Adams calls upon us for swift action to provide authorization & <u>revenue</u> for augmenting the standing army *and* the navy. "Prepare for war" he seems to say. Astonished Republicans called for the President to allow free examination of the actual messages from the envoys, hoping 'twould reveal the irresponsibility of the President's analysis. 'Tis a bad omen that most Federalists voted for the call as well. I would like to have had opportunity to consult S[arah] first. By the time you receive this epistle, a crucial turn in our States' history may well have occurred.

You should be gratified that I at last acted upon your urging & let my overseer go. It was a very difficult decision, for my yields for the year were quite respectable. But in truth I detected great ill-will & discontent amongst my negroes. Please tender my appreciation to Lewis for his attentions to Buck Spring [Nathaniel's plantation].

My dear singular friend Sterling, I thought of you & your wife lately when reading the following lines from Mary Wollstonecraft's **A Vindication of the Rights of Woman:**

"The man who can be contented to live with a pretty, useful companion, without a mind, has lost in voluptuous gratifications a taste for more refined enjoyments; he has never felt the calm satisfaction that refreshes the parched heart like the silent dew of heaven—of being beloved by one who could understand him."

May a miracle occur such that I may watch you ride Cato in the Warrenton races the 10th of May. Such a miracle would imply that peace has been preserved.

      Yr mst obt srvnt,

         Nathl Macon

2 April 1798, Philadelphia.

Macon honors me & girds me against lustful imaginings which Emily's & my carnal limitations engender. I love my wife for so many reasons in addition to Wollstonecrafts's sublime one. Yet my guilt & discomforting arousal when encountering or thinking of one such as Louisa...And how I miss when we could be like puppies & never mind if it led to a carnal connection—such a fine thing between man & wife. —God's teeth! What a servile ruffian I am to need reminding of Wollstonecraft's eloquent truth.

Selfishly, I pray this war may be avoided: This year at last I have hopes of progress on our debts (some small measure of thanks to George's diligence).

The dogwoods bloom with profuse beauty. Especially Sarah's pair. Vernal hope.

7 May

My insides tremble now to think of it. I was working toward mid-day out in our south field, lost in thought. Appearing of a sudden out of the woods on horseback was Sheriff Caleb Brown. I walked out of the row to see what he wanted as he dismounted.

He was ill at ease & seemed to stumble over the disjointed questions he asked. Finally he just stared at me oddly.

"Sheriff, mayhap you should let me get back to work," I said as I turned away from him to pick up my hoe. Just as I put my hand on the hoe, I heard from a distance Emily yell:

"Sterling! Sterling!"

I jumped. When I turned back, Sheriff Brown was putting his knife back in its sheath. "What's this!?" I asked as I put the end of my hoe between us.

"Shearin, you & I will speak again," said he as he remounted his horse. He tipped his hat to Emily & John, who were bringing me my mid-day meal, and rode away casually as if nothing had happened.

John had not seen it clearly. Hence Emily whispered it to me privately: "He was going to knife you to death, Sterling. You would be dead now had we been a moment later."

What can I do? How can I be rid of this sword of Damocles? And with the weighty stone of the runaway slaves about my neck. I must strengthen the case against the Sheriff somehow & then gain one or more respectable gentlemen to share the secrets. Then perhaps Sheriff Brown will—at least—see little gain in my death.

10 May '98

All goeth awry. Torrents of rain damaged our new crops, damaged all the mills on the Roanoke, & interrupted travel & the post. And the last communication to cross the Roanoke before the excessive rains was a veritable thunderbolt.

In complying with the House's demand, the President revealed that the French gov't refused to accept our new envoys and dealt with them in an appalling manner through minor personages designated Messieurs W, X, Y & Z. Adding injury to insult, X, Y, & Z attempted to solicit huge bribes for the mere accomplishment of the envoys being officially received. Even worse, Monsieur Y threatened to use "the diplomatic skill" of France & "*the French Party in America*" to lay blame for the failure of the negotiation on the American envoys.

So corrupt do the French reveal themselves, if these reports are to be believed, that anyone with the least French association will feel tainted. The very word "republican" is blackened. Adams, Harper, Pickering, & the warmongers will have their way with us.

"Sterling!" Emily greeted me when I came in from surveying the rain damage, "Sheriff Brown's horrible man was here. It was most unnerving. A leering, vulgar countenance...rather well-suited to his behavior. He rifled through our barn. Lingered by Cato so that I went into the barn & demanded he leave until you returned, or at least wait out under our oaks. He just looked at me as if he contemplated violence toward me. I was relieved when Eli came up."

"Who was he? What's his name?"

"Ezra Blun or Blunt or something. He mumbled half of what he uttered." Macon's discharged overseer!

"And he is a Sheriff's deputy now?"

"Apparently."

"God's Teeth! Emily. He is not to be trusted. He's Macon's former overseer, whom I exposed to Macon as the blackguard he is. I spared your ears the worst of him, dearest. Keep a weapon by you should he come 'round again without Eli or me here." I embraced her, inwardly cringing that such a one should be in position of authority.

"Where is he now?" I asked.

"He left half an hour ago. All he really said to me was he was looking for runaway slaves & that he would be keeping an eye out 'round here. He talked to Eli a spell."

Alas, Eli could not or would not add anything. Motives of the purest benevolence are not always the spring which moves Eli. His very demeanor often suggests old wounds lying fallow, just waiting for the turn of the plow.

12 May

I discussed our danger with Kenchen. Then I wrote to Nath' in Philadelphia. Naturally, I encouraged him to hold to his convictions, to defend our liberty, tho' such action should label him a Jacobin. Alas, Nathaniel Macon is not one to be untrue to his principles merely because they want friends. Never has our country needed such firmness more. And of course, I inquired of Sarah. Then I asked in vague terms if he could help orient a family of freed negroes.

I told George of my plan. We must work furiously from dawn to dusk to get the planting done. Our personal jeopardy is as great as our country's.

29 May

We got the last of tobacco & beans in the ground & we leave in the morning. Except for letting Eli run Cato in the three mile heats—the field was large & the competition stiff: his achieving 5th in the second heat was respectable—everyone here has been required to be the model of diligence. Young John thinks I am an ogre for not letting him go with Eli.

I have instructed Eli & Marmaduke to beware Ezra Blount, for I believe no deed to be beneath him. (How much worse if he apprehends my role in his dismissal by Nathaniel.) Especially they should stay near to the womenfolk & to Cato. Mama's servant, Sukie, (on whom we have a little claim) will help Emily &c. move the sweet potatoes, weed, & so forth.

2 June

Prices were favorable in Petersburg; Lewis will be pleased with what his three large steers fetched.

We drew no suspicion in driving the stock up. Indeed, why would fugitive slaves be helping a livestock drive? But I worry about the remainder of the trip: So fair a mulatto woman with an eighteen-month-old child & husband, traveling with two yeoman farmers...well...it may appear incongruous to sheriff patrols geared to keeping slaves in the proper places. We must hope that the runaway slave advertisement did not circulate this far north, or if it did, that it is forgotten by now.

The news at this place is of continued violence committed by the French on the seas against our merchant vessels. Great numbers of "patriotic" addresses are being composed & sent to Pres. Adams by towns & counties throughout the States. Even in Virginia, many are gripped with war fever.

5 June

It happened mid-way between Richmond & Fredericksburg. We were detained by a Sheriff's patrol. His questions seemed to go on & on. He had a vague recollection of a runaway slave advertisement matching Louisa &c. He deliberately espied the rough weave of our clothes (indeed we wore sad-colored stuff of our own spinning) and the mediocrity of our horses, saddles, &c. His questions became aggressive & rude. He implied that Kenchen & I were of too low a station to be traveling with this particular combination of slaves.

"Sir, you judge us too much from superficial trappings. We believe in republican simplicity in manners & dress." I bit my tongue. Federalism is so on the rise. "Especially on the dusty road. As the bard wrote: Have more than thou showest; speak less than thou knowest." I was squirming. He looked at me brim full of suspicions. Surely I sounded more genteel than I looked. Might not all of my reading to improve myself just this once stand me in good stead? I went into our prepared story, referring to Louisa by the name "Seignora."

"I assure you, sir, these are my slaves. I have been offered a handsome price for them, as a family, by a prosperous but sentimental planter near Baltimore. The woman Seignora is the daughter of this planter & his favorite slave. No doubt you can apprehend from her complexion & her features that her father was a white man. Now that the planter's wife is dead, he wishes to please his favorite." I shewed him papers of ownership I had forged.

After he examined them slowly, he espied me deliberately, all suspicion. I think he could sense my inward tension, nay my cold fear. Either that or he just simply enjoyed his power as Sheriff. With each second of his oppressive stare, I felt more desperate.

"Sir, I beseech you to cease this; we have a vast long way to travel."

He spat some tobacco juice on the ground. And then I had a thought.

"Sir, do you know John Taylor of Caroline County, Virginia, formerly a Senator for this State? I dare say he is prominent in these parts. I have the good fortune to be on warm enough terms with that superlative gentleman that I flatter myself he would immediately vouch for me. Indeed we will likely sojourn with him on our return."

Perhaps he could detect the truth of this last ploy of mine, that I am on warm terms with John Taylor. Perhaps it was that, yes, this was easy enough to verify & hence less likely to be false. His expression softened & he let us pass.

Heaven be praised! Kenchen & I could have been ruined! We were all so afflicted with fright that we traveled all through the night & all the next day before resting at this place. I pray the sheriff is not too inquisitive, or if he is, is not inclined to give chase.

9 June

We were questioned again by a Sheriff's deputy in Maryland, but not with the suspicious prejudice of the Sheriff back in Virginia. He seemed to accept our story. A cloud burst came on suddenly & soaked us all. In a matter of minutes we were all wet skin out. If this deputy had any thought of challenging us, the storm drowned it.

The face of the country here is pleasant: Some farms indifferent but many are beautiful.

All hereabout are violently federal and anti-"Jacobin." There are sarcastic references to the "diplomatic skill of France" & the need to be on guard against the traitorous "French party." I can imagine what Macon contends with in Congress. The farmer we are boarding with tonight said that Gen'l Washington, who will head up the new army, says that there should be no "democrats or mobocrats" (as he refers to republicans) in its ranks. Rumor has it there will be a standing army of 25,000! Whither go our freedoms & our treasure? Rumor also of a sedition act.

We hope to make Philadelphia by nightfall on the morrow.

11 June

"By my soul, Sterling, I am so glad to see your friendly faces. I have been feeling lonely & deserted," said Congressman Macon.

"'Tis as bad as the rumors?" I asked.

"Aye. Numbers of Republican Congressmen have gone home in despair—especially Virginians. Or gone over to the federal side. To stand & speak for liberty—that is to say against a too energetic government—is to invite scorn, worse—to invite being branded a French-loving traitor."

"From all I have heard, Nathaniel, I am little surprised. Don't let it distress you too much. Your neighbors, those you represent, we know you. You are so respected that no Federalist will dare to run against you, even in these strange circumstances."

"I need such reassurance. There are but a handful of us secure enough to raise the voice of reason against the tidal wave of war. Gallatin of Pennsylvania, Nicholas of Virginia, McDowell & myself from North Carolina. The pompous, syrup-tongued South Carolinian Robert G. Harper is the man of the hour."

"Is it futile?" I asked.

"Well, we got the size of the odious standing army down to 10,000. Alas, the republic is but ten years old, and already weighted down by a *standing* army.

"'Tis so unnecessary" I interjected. "I've seen four different militia companies drilling. Philadelphia seems part military encampment."

"On one issue I am sensible of a degree of satisfaction: The Federalists, especially Harper, tried to make it impossible for immigrants to become voting citizens. Naturally all the Irish & other refugees of European tyranny incline in a republican direction. I was instrumental getting the waiting period* & fees back to within the realm of normal.

"Sterling, can you conceive of it? Several Federalists suggested that only those born here within the States should *ever* be allowed to vote."

"Well then Nathaniel, your efforts are not in vain. —We heard yesterday of a sedition act which would make it illegal to criticize the President or Congress," I said.

"Exactly so. 'Tis in the works. Take notice: Vice-Pres. Jefferson *can* be legally criticized. And you can be sure he will be. 'Tis fully in the teeth of the Constitution."

"Indeed!" I agreed. "Does not the First Amendment say precisely Congress shall make no law abridging freedom of speech or of the press?"

He threw his hands in the air: "Exactly! Sterling, what could be clearer? We are surrounded by people now with all sensibility & no sense. Words do not mean what they were written to mean.

"Let me quote Robert Goodloe Harper on liberty of the press: 'It is no more than that a man shall be at liberty to print what he pleases, provided he does not offend against the law, and not that no law shall be passed to regulate this liberty of the press.'"

"I don't think people will stand for it," I said.

"Suppose they declare war & extend the hysteria? They'll accustom the people to standing armies, to restricted speech, to heavy taxes—all in the name of patriotism."

"It must be fought," I said.

"Indeed."

"What of Sarah?" I asked.

Nathaniel paused. "Well, she confirms that Sec. of State Pickering is the worst of the war hawks. Even that he desires an alliance with the British! She provides evidence that all of Adams' cabinet is more loyal to Hamilton than to Adams!"

"To Hamilton?!"

"Quite so. Just when scandal should have damned him to oblivion, his star ascendeth. It appears that he will be the actual General of the new standing

---

* The waiting period to become a naturalized citizen had been 5 years. Rather than eliminate the right of immigrants to become citizens as Federalists wanted, Republicans got Federalists to compromise with a 14 year waiting period.

army, since he will be Washington's second in command—at Washington's insistence. And Washington's role is likely to be that of a passive supervisor. If we go to war successfully under Gen'l Hamilton, I could easily conceive of Hamilton ending up our emperor. It is his type of ambition. He is a man to be feared."

"How is Sarah? Is she getting some payment?"

"Oh, and trust not the post. All the postmasters are Washington & Adams appointees & hence Federalists. Sarah says Pickering has some mail addressed to Thomas Jefferson."

"One stunning revelation after another! The rule of law vanquished by the rule of faction. Our world turns upside down. I guess I should not be surprised. But again, how is *Sarah*?"

"She looks well. Apparently chaste: no pregnancy. She serves us well. We have paid her a few shillings. Less than she is worth in this precarious time."

"I want her freedom, Nathaniel. If she helps us keep our freedom, she should gain her own from it."

"Fairly spoken, Sterling. Tho' you know you are talking about a fair sum, probably £65. Tomorrow even' is the appointed time of rendezvous; I shall take another collection among my colleagues. We will do better by her. —Now what news of home? And what of Kenchen being here with that family of slaves?"

"Therein lies quite a tale, Nathaniel. Two tales, actually, one of which is critical to the survival of me & my family." I commenced to tell him.

12 June

We got Louisa & family situated with some free blacks here in Philadelphia with papers of manumission that I forged. Their gratitude for our promises kept was palpable. Nay, visible: Louisa kissed & hugged Kenchen & me right in front of George as we departed from them. (My incorrigible brother later commented he would give £3 to have her just one more time; she is fetching in a uniquely sensual way, a view enhanced in my case by virtual celibacy. Knowing Kenchen, the fortnight since we left home feels like celibacy to him.)

There are enough free blacks & few enough slaves in Pennsylvania[*] to presume in their favor if they mind their business properly. I pray the papers in my possession with Louisa's "X" on them (witnessed & notarized by N. Macon) are of some value.

---

[*] All persons born after 1780 within Pennsylvania were free, such that by 1790, 63% of Blacks in Pennsylvania were free.

I worry about my family & my fine stallion. What foul deeds might Sheriff Caleb Brown & his odious lackey Ezra Blount visit upon us? Will there be evidence uncovered or fabricated to convict me yet of murder now that Maj. Macon is gone? Or evidence to convict me of abetting escaped slaves? Continual worry is my portion.

The troubles awaiting me at home & the belligerently federalist, militaristic atmosphere of Philadelphia make it hard to enjoy the glories of this magnificent city. Kenchen is better at it than I: On the heels of Nathaniel telling us how at the theatre each night they sing songs glorifying Pres. Adams & war and how heavy-drinking throngs roam the city at night looking for "Jacobin" spies, or even someone still sporting the red, white & blue cockades (which we all wore three years ago)—on the heels of hearing that, Kenchen suggests we find the prettiest whore we could find & lie low in our room. Given my poor Emily's situation, 'tis a tempting thought.

I bought Emily some fine cotton cloth, which is exceptionally well-made & yet well-priced —thanks to the new cotton gin. Also bought her ribbon & a novel, *Amelia* by Fielding.

Nathaniel bade me to take his place tonight for the rendezvous with Sarah. I suspect she will be most surprised; I am warm with anticipation.

13 June, wee hours

To walk about in this great city of Philadelphia, thronged as it is with people, enterprise, bustle, & commotion, created in my bosom such an admixture of agitation & exhilaration that I cannot find the words to adequately convey it. Add to that mixture the alacrity with which I anticipated seeing Sarah again. I was not calm.

I arrived at the public well first, but my wait was not long. I saw her before she saw me; my heart jumped in my chest. When Sarah espied me, her countenance grew at once confused & eager. But she recovered from her surprise more quickly than I could have. Slavery teaches the talent of deceit. She had the good sense to sidle up beside me where I leaned against the well, with superbly feigned casualness, without so much as a greeting or hint of recognition that a bystander would note our acquaintance. I asked her quietly, without turning to look at her—for all that I wanted to badly, if she were at leisure to follow me circumspectly to my room at the Inn where we might converse at length unobserved. She said yes (I learned later that Mr. & Mrs. Pickering were out to the theatre).

She followed me at 15 to 20 paces through the darkening streets. But once did I hazard looking back. Her dark eyes, vivid & alert, made me think of a fire laid, just ready to be lit. How different she looks now than the girl I knew: very neatly dressed with her hair very short & neat up under her mobcap. All the more beautiful in this more mature & polished visage. As best I could discern, none noticed our entry into my room, but subsequent events fill me with doubt. I had not discussed with Kenchen my thought of bringing Sarah to the room, but in any event, for good or ill, he was not there.

And so we were alone.

We visually beheld each other with some little pleasure & uncertainty on each side of it for half a minute. At last I broke the silence: "You look well."

She suddenly threw her arms around me & kissed me fully on the lips. How could I object? Her kiss is so perfect. Her body against mine was quickly agitating to my blood.

I parted us:

"Sarah, you are as passing fair, & fine as ever. 'Tis pleasure to see you, dear friend."

"Master...Sterling...you are a sight for my sore eyes."

"Are you being treated as well as your looks imply?" I asked.

"Master Pickering has let me be the past three months. Since he got the buxom white servant. I'm doing pretty good, all considered."

I gave her the fifteen shillings Macon had given me & five more from me to make an even pound. That gave her a total of £13. We both reckoned she would need above £65 to purchase her freedom.

She hugged and kissed me again, making my unsubsided manly state worse. Grabbing her arms, I said: "You'll make a dishonest man of me."

"You are the one in the world who deep down cares 'bout me."

"I do Sarah. I do...too much...but there is my wife whom I truly love & have pledged to honor. Please don't tempt me. You're too..."

Like a fool I went on to describe my predicament...to wit our virtual lack of conjugal intercourse because of our fear of Emily's deathly pregnancies. I said this to make clear my particular vulnerability to her sex.

I changed the subject to her espionage. What she could tell me made little sense to me. We needed Macon there to provide context. I assured her that what she was doing was of value to people who loved liberty & that I have dedicated myself to her gaining *her* liberty.

"I'll come be your hand maiden for a year if you do. I would serve you & your wife anyway I could." It was so heartfelt.

The thought took my breath. Suddenly I leaned towards her, kissed her, & cupped her breast. Her mouth fitted mine like they were made for each other...with utter concinnity, the touch of our lips & tongue, light &

sublimely attuned. My hand was over big for her fine little breast but the nipple felt so interested in the center of my palm.

Alas, I regained control & apologized. I looked away from her. I stayed turned slightly away from her to lessen the visual temptation. I diverted our minds: I asked her of her life in Philadelphia. Was she able to avail herself of books or newspapers or any of the advantages of the great city? Had she good friends here?

She said she was able to do a little reading, but very carefully, for she reminded me: She was the better spy with Pickering not knowing she was able to read. (I apprehended that her speech had grown more refined—even a tinge of Yankee in it.) She said they worked her hard and gave her scant opportunity to be about the city. Outside a window once she had listened to enchanting music... "Do you remember calling me enchanting?" Music that made her cry with its beauty and then thrilled her with its excitement. She pestered a number of people there till one declared it to be the music of one named Mozart. Sounds German, but there are some of them hereabout. She wanted to spend time in Philadelphia when she was free.

I told her of Louisa, George & the free blacks that have a strong colony here.

"That's good news. 'Cause I've no friends. The white serving folk look down on negroes as bad as any master. If 'tweren't for hard work & the spying, I would be pretty lonely. I have considered the propositions of an Irish blacksmith."

"Be patient, Sarah. I am low of pocket. Nay, more: I am quite insecure with debt, but I will contribute as much as my harvests will allow. And you should not be shy about asking Macon for pay. Amongst the Republican Congressmen are the means to pay you."

She did not say anything. When I turned she had taken off her petticoat and cap. She looked me in the eye as she loosened her bodice & removed it. She untied her shift. She uncovered one shoulder. Then the other. Her shift fell to her feet. She was as much a vision of loveliness as ever. A light-brown goddess. I looked at her with a lustful sense of awe. I was at her mercy. I was her slave & she, my mistress.

With sensual deliberateness she took off my clothes, then knelt & took me in her mouth. Ecstasy demolished any lingering thoughts of guilt. She pushed me down on the bed & mounted me, holding my wrists down above my head, symbolic of her power over me.

I confess to magnificent explosions of animal passion. Yet the aftermath of our naked bodies lying comfortably together was robbed of some of its sweetness: As much as I care for Sarah, as personally alluring as she is, as satisfying to my imagination & viscera as this had been, guilt weighed heavily. I knew I loved Emily no less, but I knew that if she saw Sarah & me so intimate, she would feel wronged.

I attempted to cover my emotions with kind words for Sarah. In a few moments, I put on my shirt & gave her my written account of what she saw Caleb Brown do to his infant & Abner Whitaker back in December 1787. I admired her naked figure (I would that Emily's were as well preserved) as she read over it. No sooner had I obtained her signature at the end of the account than came a rude knock at the door.

An insistent "Sterling Shearin!" roared from opposite the door.

I considered not answering but feared the vaguely familiar voice would come on in. Getting my britches on, I shouted back that I was indisposed & who was it?

"Robert Goodloe Harper, Sir!" Was it my imagination or could I detect the rich odor of his boot polish through the thin door?

I read in Sarah's alarmed countenance that Congressman Harper was a frequent enough Pickering guest to probably recognize her. Fie! How more vulnerable could we be!

"Give me a few moments, Mr. Harper...Why don't you wait for me at the tavern across the street. I'll be there shortly."

A terrible silence ensued. Through the door I could smell the suspicion in his malignant, puff'd up bosom. I continued to dress quietly & looked about the little room for some way to conceal Sarah.

I felt he was on the cusp of breaking down the door.

"I'm not entirely well, Mr. Harper. But if you will give me a few minutes, say 10 or 15, I shall endeavor to meet with you at the tavern across the street. Could I beg the kindness of you to request chamomile tea for me?"

Several seconds of silence. The suggestion that there may be kindness in Harper's breast might be confusing to him, especially with the mood implicit in his tone. The longer he delayed, the more hopeful I grew that he would not barge in.

"Hmph...Alright. Please be swift as you are able. My time is valuable," said he at last.

I let out a deep breath in relief. But I was hardly swift. It took me a spell to regain my composure & concoct a strategy of dissemblance. Sarah was to stay put until I could ensure her undetected passage away from the Inn. I looked for Kenchen without success. When finally I went across the street to the tavern, Congressman Harper had just quitted the place. He left no message. Then I found Kenchen & got him to help me get Sarah out of there, keeping an eye out for Harper at every turn. Our parting was done with unsatisfactory haste. I thanked her for her "kind ravishment" of me. I told her that Macon was the honestest man in Philadelphia & should be turned to if she required help. We leave at dawn for home.

Concerning Sarah's intelligence, Macon thought it might imply that Secretary of State Pickering could not be counted on to clearly convey to Pres. Adams all communications which cast France in a less belligerent posture. To wit, if France becomes more reasonable & makes peaceful overtures through the Sec. of State, will Pres. Adams get the message?

With this admixture of tonight's sensual feast, the intrigue, the war fever, my feelings of guilt, the worry of what awaits at home, how shall I sleep tonight?

I told Nathaniel that Sarah may be in danger if she was seen with me. 'Twas only for a few moments at the well & then entering the Inn that we were together; otherwise she followed at a discreet distance. Yet if Harper saw us enter the Inn…In all probability the dangers awaiting me at home, or even on the way, are greater.

Chapter Twenty-Two

Friday 22 June 1798

Great numbers of concerns masked my inward guilt when at last Emily's sweet & welcoming countenance was before my eyes. I squeezed her in a long tight embrace to express how I missed her these three weeks & to preclude her studying my face too closely.

The Sheriff & Ezra Blount had come a-calling to question me & had been informed that I had gone up the country after taking livestock up to Petersburg.

"Sterling, they had a severe, serious attitude. Sheriff Brown kind of let Blount do the talking. Brown himself hung back & looked about slyly. Blount makes me anxious just being in his presence. He hath dissemblance & malice in every angle of his pox-pitted face & in every intonation of his speech." Emily had had these worries contained in her for much of my absence with no one to whom she could unbosome them. I felt distresst for my guiltless sweet-tempered wife.

"Honey, your instincts are sound."

"I think they mean to arrest you, tho' they did not say that explicitly."

"Did they question Eli?"

"Yes. Off from us, separate. He wouldn't say much about it, even as I beseeched."

She has suffered enough disquiet over these matters which she cannot affect. I tried to reassure. I focused on our blessings. Indeed, none of my apprehension about harm to Emily or to the farm or to Cato had been given substance. Everyone at this place is in good health, & the crops were helped by yesterday's drenching rain.

These rains had delayed me on the last day of my journey. I had many items that needed keeping dry: the documents signed by Louisa & Nathaniel; the Fielding novel, the ribbon, & the cloth I bought for Emily, the paper I bought in advance of the new Federal tax, &c. Kenchen had traveled on in the rain.

Eli makes himself scarce. After the barest greeting, he went to muck the stalls unbidden. They were verily in want of such attention, but this particular initiative & his quietness suggests…guilt? He is possesst of a mercurial nature, sometimes his tongue wagging like our Irish setter's tail when he is happy to see you, other times quiet & withdrawn. Mayhap it is nothing.

Kenchen came over today in a warmly agitated state and quickly produced the same in me. He has heard a rumor that we are both to be arrested. The sorry state of the country mirrors our own: The Sedition Act is certain to pass. Any who dare criticize the government will join us in gaol. And even North-Carolinians do not object. They are overwhelmed with the war talk. They are frightened by Congressman Harper's latest speech, to the effect that the French will invade the South with an army of blacks from St. Domingue [Haiti], thereby inciting a slave insurrection.

Sunday, 24 June

I risked spending all day yesterday attending to the farm (they have done alright in my absence), and headed for Warrenton before dawn. I was exceedingly fortunate in my timing. I deposited the original documents with Nathaniel's brother-in-law Kemp Plummer. (He is the only lawyer I know who possesses a reputation for integrity approaching Nathaniel's.) When I returned home, I learned that the Sheriff "had come for me" while I was away. What can I do now but attend to the farm?

Mr. Plummer read from a newspaper that John Marshall, one of the envoys the French treated so impolitely, has received a hero's welcome beyond compare. How intriguing that on such a basis doth the country offer incense to a man. Great throngs lined the streets in New York & Philadelphia to glimpse him.

"The streets, the windows, even the tops of houses were crowded with people desirous of seeing the great John Marshall & welcoming him home. Church bells pealed a continuous welcome that lasted well into the evening." The officers of the New-Jersey militia assured him they were resolved "to enforce by the sword, those injured rights which the milder means of negociation have failed to secure."

Addresses from all the States (including North-Carolina: Halifax, Scotland Neck, Salisbury) continue to pour in to Pres. Adams. They praise him & urge him on to "valiant action" against the French. The addresses he returns to them are disturbingly bellicose. We all expect a declaration of war at any moment. Our country goes to ruin & despotism like so many before it upon the frenzied wings of war. (I found one note of encouragement in Adam's reply to the students at Princeton: His observation that "the Borgias & Catalines* will always defeat well-meaning persons who have little reading in the science of government" displays an inkling of the Whig mind.)

---

* The Borgias were infamously ruthless Renaissance politicians. Cataline conspired to overthrow the Roman government in its early republican period; having read Cicero and Voltaire, 18th-century Americans often referred to traitors as "Catalines."

Thursday, 28 June

Kenchen & I were arrested yesterday. I got word to lawyer Plummer. But I have heard nothing. Kenchen is not greatly calmed by my plan. I despair.

29 June

Still no word from Kemp Plummer. All the talk here in Warrenton is of war. (Mercifully, the visitors of our mates, who are in for their debts, & the lady who brings us our meals are all very chatty.) All expect us to go to war with France any day now. Former members of the Democratic Society, like me, wisely keep their contrary view to themselves. I would that I had previously so followed the dictates of Prudence.

Many around here who met Robert Goodloe Harper on his visits to the Hawkins are excited by his celebrated toast at the banquet for John Marshall in Philadelphia: "Millions for defence, but not a cent for tribute." 'Tis oft repeated. Often followed by "I'm proud to have made the acquaintance of the esteemed Mr. Harper."

At least the weather has been favorable for the crops. Still the flatteries of hope are difficult to muster. My insides could have churned good quantities of butter in these three days in gaol. Where is Plummer? How Emily must worry. If we succeed in getting out of here, I vow that my deportment ever more shall have a perpetual view to her happiness & improvement.

30 June

Three weeks away from my family & then snatched forcefully from them. My faithful as skin wife, my darling little daughter, John...I am overwhelmed with loneliness for them, love for them. I am unworthy of Emily. I despair. No word from Plummer. A thousand flies in this dank place do the office of deepening my sense of menace.

1 July

Kenchen & I had regained our intimacy of some standing on our long trip to Philadelphia & back. Indeed, I was especially touched by information he shared with me—however unwillingly—as we rode our horses southward through the Maryland countryside. I had made an aimless, flippant remark about young John's probably being Preacher Absalom's son. Kenchen answered:

"John's not Absalom's son."

I looked at him dumbfounded. "How do you know that?"

"I just do."

He said nothing more. After several minutes I spoke forcefully: "How do you know that Kenchen? You've got to tell me. 'Tis hardly a trivial matter to me."

"I told you already. I just do. You'll get no more out of me about it, Sterling. It wouldn't do for you to know."

What construction was I to place on such a sentiment? For a full hour I pried relentlessly in an effort to have him unbosome himself to me. Without success. As we approached the Potomac, I was on the cusp of threatening him when finally he spake thus:

"On occasion I have had some friendly intercourse with Absalom's wife." He paused.

"Friendly intercourse with Mrs. Jenkins? Hmn. Please continue."

"Preacher Absalom has no carnal interest in his wife." He paused again. "Nor in any woman."

Absalom a degenerate! How this deceit, which ordinarily should provoke disgust, soothes me & makes me long to hug my son lovingly. (Curiously, my previous antipathy toward Absalom melts into pity for the plight of one whose apparent nature must be cloaked in such utter hypocrisy. He is a man of parts, for I am sensible that in spite of his deceits, he serves our church community ably & with good-will in his heart.)

I had the sober discretion to press Kenchen no further on the particulars of his being allowed into the confidence of Mrs. Absalom Jenkins.

Yet now, 5 days in gaol has aroused malignant passions in Kenchen towards me. He is convinced my plan will fail & protests louder & louder that he is guilty of nothing warranting incarceration save being my brother. I pray my plan will work. Dwelling in this abject place for 5 days without word from lawyer Plummer renders me meek-spirited, to express it with understatement. Why has he abandoned us?

Monday, 2 July

Yesterday Mr. Plummer finally came. Alas, he had been in Halifax. We managed a private conference with Mr. Plummer, Sheriff Caleb Brown, Kenchen & myself. Ezra Blount was pointedly excluded. Then I laid out my hand:

I produced the description of the events of Dec. 1787 signed by Sarah, former slave of the Hawkins, & notarized by Congressman Nathaniel Macon.

The events of course were the murder & burial of Caleb Brown's infant and the murder of Abner Whitaker; the perpetrator, Caleb Brown.

Next I produced the written testimonial of Maj. John Macon that he found the remains of an infant exactly where it was described by the eyewitness to the murders, Sarah.

"Why" I asked, "did Caleb Brown kill his own baby? For the same reason that he gave away an earlier baby to a black family in 1786 to be their slave. This boy is currently the mulatto slave of the Persons.

"Quite an odd thing to do, this giving away a slave child. Unless it is borne by your own white wife. Since both these unfortunate babies **were** borne by Sheriff Brown's wife, we naturally ask 'why there has been neither retribution against his wife nor the negro man who presumably cuckolded him?'"

I paused. Caleb Brown looked uncomfortable but said nothing.

"There has been no retribution because Mrs. Brown has been faithful to her husband. Her mulatto husband! Who has all these years been passing for white!"

Sheriff Brown said nothing. He furtively looked at the respected lawyer Plummer & then at the ground. Then he fought back: "This is one hell of a cock & bull story. I have a child, who is white."

"One white child out of how many children conceived?" I replied.

"I will not stand for more of these insults, Sterling Shearin!"

"If you wish to hear no more of them, Sir," said I, "you had best hear them this once from me."

Then I had Mr. Plummer hand me the last document. On it was a statement from Louisa that Caleb Brown was her brother, that they were both the progeny of a white slaveholder & a mulatto slave, and that her brother Caleb had been passing for white most of his life. Below that, Nathl Macon wrote that he witnessed Louisa's X and that he confirmed the strong physical resemblance between Louisa & Caleb Brown.

Kenchen chimed in "There are a number of people who will see the resemblance once it is pointed out to them." I thought back to that Sunday when Caleb had berated Asa Johnson so for bringing Louisa to church.

"Need we point it out to them?" I asked.

Saturday, 14 July

The Alien & Sedition Acts pass. Benjamin Franklin Bache, grandson of the great Franklin himself, is arrested already! Not content to demean our most eloquent & outspoken republican writer as "Lightning Rod Jr.," the Federalists now have him a prisoner in gaol merely for writing truthful criticism of the government.

Meanwhile his newspaper's rival, the *Gazette of the U.S.*, spews out such slogans as "He that is not for us is against us" and "It is patriotism to write in favor of the government—it is sedition to write against it." Alas we follow the path of Rome's short-lived republic; our experiment in Liberty fails as quickly as did their own.

'Tis two weeks since we were released from gaol. Oh how I cherish my freedom! How I cherish my own home & my place in the bosom of my family! More than anyone can apprehend who has not been denied these pleasures. All the more for how uncertain it all remains.

I hold secrets over Sheriff Caleb Brown's head, but they render me all the more profoundly his enemy. Our health & freedom are not out of jeopardy. I own that I am not as yet easy on these matters. For what stratagem might his tortured & determined mind devise?

The weather turns very hot. All the crops thrive, but there is much work to catch up on. Emily & I had sanguine relations last night, the third time since her near death. My twinges of guilt must be dealt with in a constructive manner. I love Emily with all my mind...& my heart. Tho' I feel something akin to this for Sarah, mulatto tho' she be, I belong to my loving wife. I am not so sorry for it, but I vow never more shall I fail my Emily.

25 July

The republican editor of the *New-York Timepiece* was arrested for sedition. The critics of the Federalists shall be silenced.

30 July

Nathaniel Macon arrived home today & had much to tell. Sarah has experienced no repercussions (Pickering has not had Harper over to the house either). A few days after my visit, Sarah reported seeing a letter Pickering was writing to his son saying "The Rubicon is passed: War is inevitable."

Then other sources tell of a caucus of the Federalists at Sen. Wm. Bingham's mansion on July 1st. (I saw Bingham's fine mansion there in Philadelphia; like Robt. Morris, he made a vast fortune off government contracts during the war & gov't bonds ever since.) They met there to confirm that they had the votes for a declaration of war. They had the votes in the Senate. *But* they fell a little short in the House.

"So they merely kept pushing for longer enlistments—to wit, a more permanent army—& more ships & so on; they succeeded in adding two more regiments," said Macon. They are militarizing our country. Even worse, they mean to create an army in which all the officers are Federalists & then station it in the South to make us toe the line.

"And by sending armed ships out on the high seas, the Federalists enhance the chances for war. We republicans willingly voted to strengthen the militia: this is truly defensive, with no danger in it beyond expense. But sending out an armed navy to tangle with French ships is to wage offensive war! 'Tis provocative. Strategically, Federalists wish France to declare war."

"The *N.-C.Journal* reported of the direct tax on houses, land, & slaves," I said.

"Well yes, the army & navy, these engines of Federalist patronage, must be paid for," Macon replied. "I proposed instead increasing tariffs on luxuries like large looking glasses, prints, hair powder, umbrellas, watches, &c. 'Tis a woeful day when a Whig proposes a tax, but it is more honorable than burdening our children with more debt. But I am not too unhappy that the Federalist majority encroached instead on the States' sources of revenue. The pain will be felt broadly & hence be broadly unpopular."

"These direct taxes will be *very* unpopular," I said.

"Yes, but will it work upon the people in time to prevent war? War sentiment is so strong. Tho' I must admit it is less so in Virginia than in Pennsylvania & Maryland. What is the word in our vicinage?"

"Well," I replied, "I have not heard of anyone being run against you."

"That is a great relief."

"And a profound compliment. But for the General Assembly of our State, no good Whigs will suffer their names to be placed. Federalists are sure to carry the day."

"This could never happen in North-Carolina except for the XYZ fiasco & the saber rattling."

"The *N-C Journal* stirs Federalist sentiment. That also is a factor."

"Yes, our few newspapers in this State are all Federalist. The Sedition Act will not trouble them." Then Macon asked "Have they printed anything about Hamilton's being head of the Army?"

"No." I spit on the ground.

"On the other hand, Wm. R. Davie is to be a brigadier general," Macon said.

"A smart move that will counter peoples' reaction to Hamilton."

"It will not mollify the Virginians tho'. You will not be surprised when I tell you the talk at John Taylor's place."

"You stopped there on the way back from Philadelphia?"

"Yes. Taylor & Giles & other Virginians of note are talking of Virginia & North Carolina seceding from the Union! They make the strong case that the Constitution has ceased to have meaning."

"They are right," I replied. "But they will be as disheartened as I am by the Federalist ascendancy in North-Carolina. It looks like Virginia stands alone to fight this madness."

"Well they are not of one mind either. Taylor said Jefferson has written him dissuading exiting the Union. He writes that we must have someone to quarrel with, man's nature being what it is. If Virginia & North-Carolina seek a separate existence, they will soon quarrel with each other. Better that we keep our New England associates for that. Tho' we are now completely under the saddle of the Eastern States & tho' they ride us hard, yet 'a little patience, and we shall see the reign of witches pass over, their spell dissolve, and the people recovering their true sight, restore their government to its true principles!' "

"The flatteries of hope from the great inventor of my excellent curved plow."

Sunday, 5 Aug.

How small, of all that human hearts endure,
That part which laws or kings can cause or cure.
——Samuel Johnson

Emily read this to me before we went to bed last night. The failure of the great republican experiment is largely beyond our ability to affect—like slavery. And indeed we presently have many blessings.

Our crops over all are the best since I started our farm. Plenty of rain & not brutally hot so far. That portion of our worn fields we were able to manure show good effect. And prices are good—in spite of, or because of, the depredations by the French *and* British upon many of our trading vessels.

Young John grows into a good farmer, tho' all his passion is for horse racing & the cocking mane and none for the written word. Little Katie is a loveable darling. Emily is my best friend. Her memories of her near fatal pregnancy fade, but not so much that her oblique suggestion of our having relations involve anything more than her altruistic regard for me. She is a saint.

Not only is she a saint, but she has started to make the finest butter of any in these parts & takes a deserved pride in it. I look up now at her and relish the sight of her at the churn, a purposeful look upon her face. She catches my gaze & smiles. Let me take a turn.

Friday, 10 Aug. 1798

I strained to observe some silver linings yesterday in Warrenton. John Ward outdid Solomon Green in bribing voters with grog & barbecue. Perhaps both these Federalists will bankrupt themselves in so dishonorably endeavoring to buy a seat in the General Assembly. I tolerated listening to imbibers sing "Adams & Liberty"* & such and sold them some produce.

Late in the day, Nath! Macon came to vote, & afterwards a group of us who formerly were members of the democratic society gathered about him & asked him about how Congress came to inflict the taxes, the standing army & navy, the Alien & Sedition Acts &c. upon us.

Robt. Goodloe Harper, Harrison Gray Otis of Massachusetts, and John Allen & Joshua Coit of Connecticut—these Federalists' names deserve to live in infamy. Their ears were deaf to the well-reasoned arguments of Gallatin, Joseph McDowell (Burke Co., N.-C.), Edw. Livingston of New-York, John Nicholas of Virginia, and our own Nathaniel Macon.

For instance when Macon & Nicholas emphatically asked for some explanation of how the Sedition Act could be passed in the face of the express wording of the 1st Amendment, Otis lamely offered mere assertions that the act did not infringe upon the Constitution. "Freedom of speech & the press involve precise technical phraseology. They must be regulated."

Macon answered Congressman Otis powerfully: The best way to be sure of the meaning of the various parts of the Constitution was to examine the opinions put forth by its proponents in the State ratifying conventions.

"Not a single member of any ratifying convention gave an opinion that the Central Government had any right to regulate speech or the press. Indeed, I quoted current Supreme Court Justice James Iredell to the effect that, even before the First Amendment, the Constitution would not allow it.

"Back then Iredell said: 'The powers of the Government are particularly enumerated & defined. Congress can claim no other powers but such as are enumerated. In my opinion, the government is excluded as much from the exercise of any other authority [such as regulation of speech] as it could be by the strongest negative clause that could be framed!'

"I went on to quote similar statements by members of Congress when the 1st ten amendments were being discussed in 1789. After quoting numerous statements of those creating our Constitution & 1st amendment

---

* The song "Adams & Liberty" was to the tune later used for the "Star Spangled Banner."

to the effect that regulation of speech & the press are beyond scope of the Central government, I asked my fellow Congressmen what had come to pass to make them think we had any right to legislate on this subject.

"The federal government seems to forget that it owes its very existence to the State legislatures. It moves steadily to consolidate us all into timid provinces."

"I have to like your reminding Justice Iredell of his earlier utterances," I said. "It should make it hard for him to rule the Sedition Act constitutional."

Macon chuckled. "We'll see. —Anyway, our arguments won over three Federalists, but the thing passed 44-41."

"Close enough that the Republicans like Giles who gave up & went home early might have made the difference," I offered.

"A good point, Sterling. In Giles' defense, I think he is thinking secession. He quit Congress to enter the Virginia legislature. Rumors abound that they will take some action."

29 August

Every way we are beset. I am sorely agitated & worried. The hot, humid weather does not help. Until this late hour, my clothes, my face, my hands & arms were all too wet with sweat to allow me to write.

At dusk the heifer [young cow] looked up at the heavens & flared her nostrils. I confirmed this sign by checking the bee tree: Indeed the bees seem to be staying close to the hive. And Emily noted the swallows stayed close to the ground. Three signs of rain make for a certainty, & sure enough now I hear thunder to the west. More rain is the last thing the tobacco needs.

Equally a source of worry is my reckless initiative yesterday afternoon with Emily. I had long wanted to describe all that Sarah had taught me of the use of the mouth in relations between a man & woman; of course I had never dared.

It was oppressively hot & hence not too unnatural for me to entice her to the swell in the creek, where years before Sarah & I had done those unspeakable but memorable acts. For a dip.

Together in the water we kissed & held each others' naked bodies. Sensing my arousal, my pretty wife said, with some hesitance:

"Sterling…I'll…chance it. It's not natural for a man & woman not to cleave unto one another."

We had made love three times in a year & a half. All during her time of the month. "Emily maybe there is a safer way."

She looked at me uncertainly. I ushered her onto the bank. Down onto the homespun tow cloth I had brought to dry us. I parted her legs & started kissing her there. I was most afraid of her reaction. Her reaction was startled, then shame?, then pleasure? The moans became regular & I relished the pleasure I grew sure of. Then she made sounds such that I thought I was hurting her; I stopped.

"No! Please…I…"

"Does it hurt?"

"No! 'Tis…scary. But you don't have to stop."

And so I continued. Unhurried & greatly aroused by her visceral music. Until this music reached a great crescendo! What spasms!

"My God, Sterling" she panted. "Are you the devil? Where, in God's name, did you learn this…this wicked…ness?"

"I'm not any kind of devil. I'm a man who loves you with all his heart and soul." I lay on the cloth beside her.

"I love you too," she said sheepishly. She started to mount me, but I guided her to use her mouth. She tried awkwardly for a few moments. It was too unnatural for her. Her mouth is not over large. I was helpless when she put my member between her legs. "Where it belongs," said she. So now I worry to no end that she will get with child.

Of less personal concern, but still discouraging, seven of the ten Congressmen whom North-Carolina elected publicly espoused federalist views. And Federalists dominate the General Assembly.

And then there is Sarah. Lewis flattered me with the great kindness of paying the postage & bringing her letter from Warrenton.

She was unhappy for weeks after my visit. So wretched was she that she stole away to where George & Louisa stay. (She thought Louisa beautiful; they spoke well of us.) She discussed running away for good. From Pickering & Iredell? Two of the most powerful men in America? Pickering is in a mean spell. Yellow Fever has hit Philadelphia again. Obvious exacerbations.

She begged me to help her gain her freedom. This was the central reason for her letter, rather than the secrets it contained. Her unhappiness was palpable. Were she isolated with other slaves away on a remote plantation, it might be more bearable. The possibility of a good & free life is too vivid in her mind for her to know contentment as a self-righteous ogre's slave.

Her intelligence: (1) Pickering spends each morning reading newspapers looking for writers to prosecute under the Sedition Act. (2) He has initiated exploration of an alliance with Britain! The monarchist! (3) Gen. Alexander Hamilton conspires to use the great army we build—once war with France is declared—to attack Florida & Louisiana and perhaps eventually even Mexico. From such as he are the grandly despotic Julius Caesars of this world made. This great empire-building would necessarily be in conjunction with the mighty British navy and South American revolutionaries under one Francisco de Miranda.

"I hate intrigue!" cried Macon when I showed him Sarah's letter. "Not just Hamilton's, but my own involvement in this espionage with your Sarah. If our noble republican experiment were not at stake, I would have none of it. Providence help us." Macon paused. "Surely President Adams is no party to the British alliance. Does he know what his Secretary of State & the General of the Army are up to? Do you reckon?"

I shook my head in despair.

"These are dire times; every way we are beset. You probably haven't heard: Matthew Lyons has been arrested for Sedition. He was merely writing in a Vermont newspaper what he had previously spoken in the halls of Congress."

Our republic appears doomed.

Macon also shared this confidence: Jefferson secretly indicated that the Virginia Assembly will take some action against the General government's destruction of the Constitution & wished to know of the possibility of North-Carolina's legislature doing so as well—perhaps first. Has Jefferson changed his mind on secession? Alas, our fickle state is in the grip of Federalists.

Here comes the rain.

Chapter Twenty-Three

Sunday 23 Sept. 1798

As I pick up my journal this night, the buzz of Emily's foot wheel [spinning wheel] assumes a soothing character. Much that we had worried over these recent weeks wears a better aspect. Most especially that Emily is having her time of month. 'Tis a great relief.

And it has rained no more since 29 Aug; a few more dry days & our tobacco crop will be at least a moderate success. The corn & cotton look very good. It should lie in our way to reduce our debt substantially. Or send Sarah substantial money for buying her freedom. Pray, how do I broach this subject with Emily?

Thurs' 27 Sept.

The indian summer has extended the sickly season. Emily watched the night with Lewis' wife's mother last night. Nathl Macon was by with news of the ague [malaria] in Halifax & Edenton and considerable death in Philadelphia from Yellow Fever. Benjamin Franklin Bache died of it (in gaol for Sedition). My family has been blessed during this sickly season except for Prissy's youngest having taken a bilious illness.

Macon's main reason for visiting was to inquire whether Sarah's letter had appeared to have been opened before it reached me; he worried that a postmaster (they are uniformly Federalist appointees) might have read her explicit missive. Unfortunately, I have received so few letters & was so excited by the event that I did not take particular notice of the seal.

We diverted ourselves with conversation of a pleasanter nature. The goodness of the crops, particularly. Macon said his are so good, he intends to paint his house after harvest. As prosperous & refined as Congressman Macon is, I would have expected him to have already done so years earlier. Macon's older daughter Betsy will be reaching courting age anon.

We all anticipate warmly the coming horse races in Halifax & Warrenton. Eli went on & on about having seen Col. Whitaker's splendid new stallion he calls 'Avenger'. Apparently a spirited chestnut with white blaze & stockings, a full 16 hands high at the withers. According to Eli, to look at him, you'd wager he could be a match for Medley.

"Have you ever heard the stories of Wylie Jones' little colored jockey who would crouch low over the horse?" Eli, in one of his talkative moods, asked Macon.

"Oh yes. He rode Trick-em. He & Wylie endured some little ridicule for him not assuming the more genteel, upright position," replied Macon.

"Exactly how did he do it?" I asked. I had never heard of the curiosity.

"I think he had shorter stirrups on which, I would say, he put most of his weight. His derriere stuck up in the air in a most ludicrous fashion. His head he held low against the horse's neck."

We all laughed.

"Of course he won several shorter races. Trick-em had no bottom but was fast as the blazes."

"Why was he styled 'Trick-em'?" Eli asked.

"Ah, so you don't know the story. It was back before the War got started good. I was at College of New Jersey at the time, but it was all the talk when next I returned to North-Carolina. Mr. Wylie Jones, whom both Sterling & I esteem in eminent degree in his present maturity, was a man in his youth of some design, nay, perhaps that is too mild a description of him when horse racing was the object." He paused cryptically.

"Tell us!" we all demanded.

"Well, there was arranged a one-on-one quarter-mile contest between a celebrated horse of Jones' & the powerful Virginia racer 'Mud Colt' at Tucker's Path in Northampton County right on the Virginia line. Back in that day before we had the luxury of mile oval courses, the fashion was to race just 2 horses on a quarter-mile straight. A huge crowd assembled, 4 deep all around the straight. They both brought their horses in carts so that they would be particularly fresh. But as it turned out, Jones' colt was too tall for the rules that had been established. Jones had his hooves shaved twice but to no avail. Looking down at his fine colt's bleeding hooves, Mr. Jones appeared visibly upset at his mistake. Quite visibly for him.

"'It is a shame that so many have come sundry distances to see a horse race for naught,' said Jones' friend by his side. 'Rather than default, might Mr. Jones substitute some other horse that is small enough to qualify?'

"Mud Colt's owner hesitated. He could claim a large prize by way of the default, but not the substantial gain to be had by way of wager for himself & his assembled friends.

"Mr. Jones looked about him. 'The horse what pulled the cart is small,' observed he. He turned to his groom who had just shaved his stallion's hooves & asked: 'Austin isn't he of tolerable speed? Do you think that horse might have a chance?'

"The groom replied 'Massa, he'd have a better chance than a hoss wid no feet.'

"Mud Colt's owner laughed heartily. But never one to act quickly, he then pensively walked twice around the cart horse. Jones' cart horse was not an impressive animal: In truth, he was a rough-coated, shaggy beast, not even decently groomed. Naturally, the assembled crowd all attempted to bet on Mud Colt & they found few takers save the gracious Mr. Jones & a few of his friends. And only then at steep odds.

"Sterling, Eli, Master John, Miss Emily…let me tell you, the race was not even all that close. Jones' horse beat Mud Colt by more than 2 lengths. It was only at that point that someone asked Jones what he called his small stallion. 'We call him Trick-em,' answered he with a smile."

What a tale! What an intricate ruse. And then Macon went on to tell us of an equally intricate stratagem played by Jones with Trick-em before the War down near the town of Kinston*. This is a facet to Mr. Jones of which I had not been sensible. Mayhap some of those voting against Jones when he stood as Jefferson's elector remembered losing such a wager to him.

"Sterling, you know the jockey."

"I do? Who?"

"Austin Curtis."

"What?! Marmaduke Johnson's mulatto trainer? But he's a freed man."

"That's right. Wylie Jones freed him about a decade ago. Perhaps in part because during the War, when Cornwallis came through—claiming to free all the slaves in his path—slave Austin Curtis was the one who loyally hid all Jones' horses from Tarleton's marauders."

We all have high hopes for our horses. I beat Macon & Eli in a little two mile impromptu race. Macon is much heavier than his jockey. Eli rode young Freshet (the progeny of Marmaduke Johnson's well-bread Huntsman) & led at the one mile turn.

Tuesday 23 Oct^r

Our harvests are bountiful & prices are still good. Tobacco fetched thirteen dollars per hundred weight! Kenchen has gotten himself completely

---

* *The Life and Times of Sir Archie* by Elizabeth Blanchard and M. W. Wellman asserts that Willie Jones' brother Allen was the owner of Trickem and perpetrator of the Tucker's Path ruse. His Northampton County plantation Mt. Gallant [near present day Gaston, NC] was certainly very near Tucker's Path. Henry Lewis in *North Carolina Historical Review* 51 (April 1974) makes the same assertion. However, letters (thought to be from nephew Allen Jones Davie) to the *American Turf Register and Sporting Magazine* (December, 1831, p.193) seem to provide good evidence that Willie Jones was the perpetrator of both involved ruses.

clear of debt. Lewis is in still better shape; he has the down payment on a possible new slave. I have paid off £28 1/2 of our debt; more controversially, I have laid aside £20 to send to Sarah. My discussion of such a thing with Emily caused *great* consternation, nay, vexation. I am not certain I can do it. I hope Emily will warm to the idea—no more honorable, altruistic idea has ever hatched in my bosom—once she is assured I have no designs to ever have more intercourse with this, my former paramour. Still she would have every right to object to this use of our resources when we are still much in debt.

In the 1st three mile heat at the Warrenton races, Eli rode Cato & achieved a quite respectable 5th place out of 20 horses. In the 2nd heat, I rode Cato to a third place finish! Tho' I must admit that we were several lengths behind Col. Whitaker's hulking chestnut which took 2nd in both heats. (Of course Marmaduke Johnson's Medley won both heats to preclude a third.) The Warrenton races were great fun for everyone. John was wild with excitement. I gave Emily the 10 shillings from my third place finish.

"Spend it gaily & gleefully," said I.

I sought out Austin Curtis after the race, naturally congratulating him on Medley. Mr. Curtis is ever the soul of affability & courtesy, and all the more so basking in Medley's glory.

When I asked him about the crouch, he was intrigued by my interest & talked with me about it at length.

"I won't d'only one to use it. We called it the quarter crouch. Evbody's forgot 'cause quarter racing be out of fashion. I 'spect it be a might tiring for three 4-milers."

"Perhaps one could use it for the end of the race. For the charge."

"Mr. Shearin, I tried to get Mr. Johnson's jockey to use it that way. He was sot in his ways. Thought he'd be made fun of. If you be interested, they's right smart a little 'culiarities to it."

"Mr. Curtis, I am. Might I buy you a cider after we both get done with things?"

He warmly agreed.

When we met later, he brought with him a light, short-stirrupped saddle that he had used with his 'quarter crouch.' He sold it to me for a few pence, saying it was going completely to waste as it was. He told me to get Cato, of whom he was complimentary, so nicely trained to race & so nicely attuned to me that I need not wear spurs, for the location of my heals would be unfavorable for their use. He told me of other wrinkles; I listened in rapt attention to this knowledgeable colored man. I asked if he would take note of my horse & me in the Halifax races, if his duties allowed, & give me the benefit of his advice. He seemed complimented by my request. He said he would try.

Austin Curtis seems true to his excellent reputation for being as good a man as ever wore shoe leather, tho' he be a small man of color & born a slave. He is liked & respected by all. Look what he has overcome. Surely there is hope for the likes of me if my attitude is sufficient to the task.

In spite of the general plenty this fall, there was some grumbling about the new Federal taxes. And tho' some made statements about the necessary preparations against a French invasion, I am sensible that the former jealousy of our liberty may be re-emerging. In Virginia, many counties have held meetings protesting the taxes & the Alien & Sedition Acts.

This year at last our apple trees produced truly delicious cider. I have many blessings.

This evening I experimented with the Austin Curtis' quarter crouch. I apprehend that it makes for less resistance to the wind. The balance is very different, perhaps better. Cato seemed fine with it. We all are determined to go to Halifax for part of the races there.

Sunday 4 Nov

Excepting for the absence of Marmaduke Johnson's Medley, who dominated yesterday's 4 mile as he dominated the 3 mile at Warrenton, the field was larger & stronger at the Halifax races. Hence my hopes were not high. Yet Eli achieved a respectable 6th out of 25 horses in the 1st heat. I have prevailed upon Eli to be more subtle in his prompts to Cato; he argues with me about it tho', instinctively wanting to flail away in the last half mile.

It does me good I suppose, this being forced to observe rather than direct Cato: Tho' my small horse's stride could be longer, his running action is flawless. I am sensible also that he holds to the rail better in the turns than some horses. Avenger, winner of the 1st heat, went rather wide on the turns, but was so powerful on the straights as to not be hurt by it.

During the rub down, I changed to the diminutive saddle Curtis sold me. Cato recovered pretty well with our assiduous ministrations to him by the end of the half hour.

In the 2nd heat with me in the saddle, Cato manifested all the strength & bottom I could have imagined for him. We kept a steady fast pace through the first 2 & ½ miles that put us in striking distance of the leaders in about 6th place. Then Cato mounted a beautiful charge, easily passing the 2 horses directly in front, fighting off a charging gelding from behind, & getting by the famous paint from Edenton by a nose at the finish. Third place! tho' 5 lengths back from the winner.

Col. Whitaker's big Avenger won the 1st heat but not the second. Hence there would be a third heat. I wondered how my horse would handle this difficult challenge as we sponged him down. He was in much greater distress after running a total six miles, taking longer to regain normal breathing & focused eyes. I determined not to push him over much lest he showed a will to run.

He started slow, but so did most of the horses that returned to the post for the 3rd heat. Yet by the backstretch of the 1st mile, Cato let me know he wished not to be bettered by these horses. But he also seemed to remember the 3 mile length to which he was now growing accustomed. He set a steady fast pace as in the 2nd heat. I marveled at the intelligence & heart of my beloved steed.

Coming out of the 1st turn of the third mile, I had barely used my whip or heels. We passed a horse on the backstretch to take 5th place. Entering the last turn, we were no more than 5 lengths behind the leader, Avenger. God's teeth! We were in striking distance.

I gave him one swat to his rear & adopted the head down position. With my head down on his neck, Cato heard my urgings intimately & responded thrillingly. We powerfully passed 2 horses (including the paint from Edenton) for third place, going to their inside on the final turn. We were gaining on Avenger, now running second, but I doubted we would catch him, so powerful is his long stride. That is, until at the very last when we nearly did. At the finish line Cato's nose was at least even with John Whitaker's chestnut, but the judge gave his horse second & us third. As far as my relations with the man to whom I owe £92 are concerned, perhaps this was the better outcome.

Austin Curtis clapped for me when I came into his presence. "Mr. Shearin, I lubs de way you let yo little hoss run fo' de love of it. You're my kind o' jockey. You got the right idea. My main advice be to use dat hoss's talent for holdin' dem turns." He went on to say I need to build his wind & stamina with a great deal of training—have I that kind of time?—but not too much training to make him think it a chore.

Two third place finishes earned us ten shillings each & mayhap some stud fees next spring. And what we have learned of Cato's redoubtable bottom & heart. An eminently worthwhile trip to Halifax. A happy trip for us all.

The harvests in the Roanoke Valley this fall have everyone feeling prosperous, & hence the frugal Emily had difficulty finding bargains upon which to spend her £1 ½ (5 shillings to Eli). She got candles in Warrenton. In Halifax, she studied a print & an oil cloth, quite refined & prestigious improvements for our home. However, what she purchased was more consistent with her natural prudence: some ready-made cotton cloth of excellent quality & some other little elegancies such as sugar & coffee.

Some of this fine cotton she will employ no doubt to make herself a gown of the newer style (all forget its French origin), which is more charming on her than any seen in these parts in my humble opinion.

I grow sensible of some diminution of war talk in preference for grumbling of the taxes. All of the Supreme Court Justices have let it be known that they view the Alien & Sedition Acts as not only constitutional but also good & proper. They are all Federalist appointees. What hypocrisy on the part of James Iredell!

John Marshall rides upon his great popularity to stand for Congress in Virginia. He is the rare Federalist who is not enthusiastic about the Sedition Act, but even he views it as constitutional.*

Many have died of Yellow Fever in Philadelphia. Macon is glad Congress does not commence until December.

Sunday 25 November

Two nights away from Emily, little Katie, John, &c. heightens my love & appreciation for my family. I was very glad to be home from the muster where General Davie set the Federalist tone. Company commanders were required to read to the men newspaper stories of the French conquests in Europe.

And I had to endure slandering whispers. I am sure I did not imagine the subtle disdain in my fellow militiamen. Kenchen says that Ezra Blount & the Sheriff stir up the old rumors of my murdering Abner Whitaker & Asa Johnson and further demean me for my manner of riding Cato. 'Tis hateful. How my character bleeds on every side of it.

Saturday 30 November

Macon came with items of considerable importance. The best news was of the British destroying the French fleet on Aug 1st in the Battle of the Nile. Pray tell, how are the truculent French to invade us now?

Then Macon asked why we were not at the Person's husking frolic. I had to say the bold truth that we were not invited.

Weightiest of all, Macon brought a letter to me from Sarah. He feels certain the seal had been broken! Sarah related that Sec. of State Pickering is aggravated that Pres. Adams will not give him *carte blanche* to enforce

---

* John Marshall was to become the first famous Chief Justice of the Supreme Court.

the Alien & Sedition Acts. More significant, when Adams asked his cabinet for advice on his speech to open the new Congress in December, they all held a meeting *with Hamilton* before replying. Hamilton complained of slow progress in the building of his army, emphasized the need to maintain a war footing, & proposed a law be passed encouraging the President to declare war with France by August. This ambitious man will be our monarch yet, if we do not regain that jealousy for our liberty which drove the Revolution. It would be very worthwhile to somehow render Adams sensible of Hamilton's secret & pervasive influence—and his ambition to build an empire.

Sarah went on to say that Louisa was among the fatal victims of the Yellow Fever. Thus far George is trying to keep his child. "The city's orphanages over-flow. George is a very fine man. I wish I were free to help him. I wish I were free. I would do anything to be free. I have £13, 18 shillings. I am anxious that someone will find its hiding place. Please, please help me. I will do anything to be free. You worship freedom like it was a religion. Can you know what it means to me?"

Sunday 2 Dec'

I read Emily Sarah's letters & endeavored to describe her circumstances, hopeful of eliciting Emily's natural sympathetic instincts. For two days this knowledge fermented in her loving mind & at last produced sweet wine. We agreed to send £15 to Sarah. She insisted we buy the oil cloth she had admired & some store-bought cloth for curtains, and keep the remaining £3 1/2 for contingencies. And Emily wants to go to Washington's birthnight ball in February.

I went over to Macon's with this considerable sum. His jaw dropped. With my encouragement, he promised to take another collection from the Republicans who are privy to this espionage. Against our instincts, we agreed to put it all in the Bank of the U.States in Philadelphia in Macon's name to get a little interest. After all I am paying Col. Whitaker 6%. It will give Sarah hope.

Macon shewed me a newspaper account of the Kentucky legislature passing Resolutions vigorously protesting the Alien & Seditions Acts: The States "…constituted a General Gov't for special purposes, delegated to that Gov't certain definite powers, reserving each State to itself the residuary mass of right to their own self-government; and whensoever the General Government assumes undelegated power, its acts are unauthoritative, void and of no force…"

Well said. Have we established a Constitution in which the Federal government is the final arbiter of the extent of its own powers? 'Twas not our intention.

10 Dec^r

The Richmond *Examiner* reports resolutions of citizens of Dinwiddie County opposing the standing army, the expensive navy, the federal government's power to borrow money, & the Alien & Sedition Acts. They also oppose our allying with any foreign nation & the practice of maintaining ministers resident in foreign countries "...because it adds still more to the already enormous mass of presidential patronage." Thank God for the Virginians.

The frosty breath of Winter is upon us most early this year; I remember not when it was so cold so early. Cuddling under our blankets last night, Emily & I slipped up. Now we will worry again.

As a master, I am a wretch. Both Marmaduke & Eli give me considerable trouble.

Wednesday 26 Dec^r

The cold weather eased & Lewis had us all over for a barn raising on Christmas. A very fine large barn. Eli did a headstand on the barn's ridgepole & scared us to death. Trying to impress a girl. The occasion was full of glee & good fellowship. Thank goodness for family.

I drew comfort from all the news. The Virginia legislature followed the lead of Kentucky in passing resolutions protesting the constitutionality of the Alien & Sedition Acts; John Taylor introduced them. Virginia went further and ordered more arms for her militia.

Philadelphia is all astir over the return of Quaker Dr. Geo. Logan from France. He endeavored to serve as an informal liaison with the French government to restore the severed diplomatic relations between us. The Federalist press made much of his having a letter of introduction from Thos. Jefferson, but of course one must have such letters for safety, for a passport, for entrance to the company of personages of import. The Federalists are warmly agitated that Dr. Logan brings news of a friendlier attitude by the French.

Sir [Sterling],
On Saturday Dec. 8, with Genl Hamilton & the British minister et al.

seated on the dais, Pres. Adams delivered his message to Congress. He had lost several teeth since last year, but he read his message more forcefully & clearly than would many—Jefferson, for instance. He said that tho' France had not repealed its laws so harmful to our commerce, it had indicated it would welcome an American envoy. Federalists were troubled by this, & hence Adams soothed them by saying we should not relax our military or naval posture.

Republicans refrained from protesting the ceremonial reply to the President's message this time; Congressman Lyon, formerly a prime objector, is in gaol under the Sedition Act. Our very partisan Speaker of the House removed me from the Chairmanship of the Committee on Unfinished business. I had been virtually the only Republican with a committee appointment of any significance.

Early on in the session, Robt. G. Harper moved the printing for dissemination of several thousand copies of the Alien & Sedition Acts. We flummoxed them by agreeing & moving that the Bill of Rights be printed with them. Federalists eventually buried the whole idea.

Sterling, have you read in the newspapers of Dr. Geo. Logan's return from France? Were it not for Logan & Pres. Adams' son, it is doubtful Adams would have received France's recent conciliatory message thru' Pickering's State Department.

Well, now Congressman Harper has inspired the perception of a plot in which Logan was co-ordinating a French invasion with Republican assistance. Without a shred of evidence against Logan, the Federalists worked themselves into a frenzy over the supposed conspiracy. Harper declared as a certainty that the representative of the "French Party" (Logan) had advised the Directory to make conciliatory gestures in order to strengthen his party at home. Preparations for French invasion would then be made. Jefferson was implicated as contriver of the mission. I challenged them in debate to offer proof, that such a person (as they painted Jefferson) be removed from office. If they had no proof, it is "a strange way of supporting the constituted authorities, thus to calumniate a man whom the people have thought proper to place in so high a station."

No doubt you have read of the Logan Act, which they have fashioned to stifle future efforts of private diplomacy. In spite of our exertions, the Logan Act is likely to pass.* What an irony that for a private citizen to provoke a war will remain unpunishable, while a private citizen attempting to facilitate peace with a foreign government will be punishable as a felony.

S[arah] was greatly encouraged by the money. Initially she was reluctant to allow me to bank it, but she came around yesterday. I spoke to her about

---

* The Logan Act passed and is still a Federal statute.

the danger of using the government's mail to write you. I reminded her of her observation that Pickering had some of Jefferson's mail. I must tell you that she had been recently beaten for sneaking off late in the night to see George.

Her intelligence helped to confirm Gen'l Hamilton's imperial designs. Once his army is built & war is declared with France, Hamilton envisions invasion of Florida, Louisiana, & Mexico in conjunction with actions by the British navy & South Americans under Francisco de Miranda. Hamilton & Pickering agree that all measures to encourage war are desirable. They have received assurances that no State legislatures will follow Kentucky & Virginia in protests because various recent elections have been much influenced by war fever (as in North-Carolina).—Also, Hamilton wishes Virginia divided into two smaller states that it may be more easily subdued. They discuss stationing much of the army in Virginia to discourage resistance there. One perhaps encouraging note: Adams is no party to these schemes of Hamilton & the cabinet.

Please relay my high regard & esteem to all your family. I remain
   Yr mst obdt & hmble srvnt,
     Nathl Macon

Philadelphia
December 31, 1798

Chapter Twenty-Four

Monday 4 Feb^r 1799

I feel more than a little wasteful: The problems with 'Duke & Eli fester, fire wood needs cutting, numerous repairs & amendments are ever about me; and yet I dally with the latest political news. I talk, read, & even write about my devilishly imperfect god, Liberty. That god which those with lust for power are ever ready to subdue. Yet if I cannot dally in the hoary cold days of winter, then when? This is how I begin the last year of the century, 1799.

I bought a used copy of the *Cato's Letters* (our sixth book) & found much wisdom on this second perusal. Should we regain our republic from the aristocratical Federalists, will we ever be able to rid it of the cursed flaw of slavery?

What sort of an animal is man, to value his own freedom as he values his honor & yet to impose slavery upon the sons of Africa? Is it the specious name Christian that gives us the right over what we arrogantly call a Heathen world? Is blackness the divine mark of servitude? Be there a God of justice, mercy & universal beneficence, He must deliver us from this wolf we have by the ears and

Brake the dire chain, that holds the slave,
And heal those wounds the tyrant gave.

So I wrote for anonymous submission to the newspaper. My understanding wife supported my impractical use of time and agreed with my sentiments entirely. But she added the natural observation of how little above subsistence we would be without our servants & Eli. We would not have six books, two glass windows with curtains, or a smokehouse well-stocked with salted pork.

In the news, the N.-C. House of Commons passed a resolution requesting repeal of the Alien & Sedition Acts, but the N.-C. Senate rejected the resolution. New Jersey & Maryland also rejected the protest which Kentucky & Virginia initiated. There was a long article on the conquest of Switzerland by France. Corn is fetching a good thirty shillings/barrel.

19 Feb^r

The *N.-C. Journal* printed a long piece by Pickering in which he attempts to fan the flames of war fever. In reference to France's late conciliatory gestures, the Sec. of State warns "that the Tyger crouches before he leaps upon his prey."

Eli & I have worked out an agreement. He will stay thru' this year's harvest (he will be twenty in August), if I agree to give him Freshet (a valuable well-bred animal) & £5 at that time. His future plans remain undivulged.

Emily eagerly anticipates Washington's Birthnight Assembly. With some misgivings & fear, I do as well. At Lewis' on Sunday, we all learned the new dance which an Italian dance master taught in Halifax of late. Those who had learned it from the Italian said that he spoke at such length regarding the carriage of the head & shoulders that they wondered would they ever learn the steps. This new "cotillion" is most intimate, as two couples dance together, rather than the entire assembled company as with normal dances. (Kenchen struggles with his newly acquired fiddle.)

Tuesday 5 March

Mathew Lyon has been re-elected to Congress from gaol! A scheme of lottery for raising his Sedition fine of 1000 D. [=$, which was not yet in use] has been issued "to ransom him from the oppressive hand of usurped power."

Washington's birthnight Ball at Mr. Hopkin's Long Room was, as the *N.-C. Journal* stated, "graced with a brilliant company of the fair, whose beauty of person and elegance of taste appeared to the greatest advantage." Indeed, the general prosperity was well-displayed. All the fashionable young men wear the round hats now, many having cut their queues. All the young women wear the high-waisted gowns, which were initially called the French style but are no more. Some few of these gowns are remarkably sheer, and I own they provoke in me an admixture of pleasure & discomfort. While not so sheer, Emily's gown, which she made from a very fine white *purchased* cotton cloth they call muslin, looked marvelous well on her.

Emily & I tasted all these sights in the highest degree. She was able to visit with numerous friends, including one she had known as an orphan in Halifax. Tho' we are both by nature as timid as partridges, after we armed ourselves with imbibed fortification, we were among those who danced the new "cotillion." What a stir it caused! Perhaps that contributed to what later transpired, for all I know. But to say the truth, we had a most excellent evening, for jollity & mirth prevailed. That is, until just before we were to depart.

A ball was being set on foot by way of subscription for the Warrenton races in April. Just before we left I attempted to subscribe. Solomon Green answered me in a voice none too delicate:

"Sir, you are unworthy of being admitted as a subscriber."

At first I was unable to credit my senses. As the embarrassment, nay the mortification, descended upon me, my thoughts were too disordered to respond. Have the Sheriff & Ezra Blount set such a stamp on my character? Solomon Green has long despised me as a "Jacobin" & friend of the Macons, but he would not be so bold had I not forfeited the good opinion of numerous persons of note. I have yet to tell Emily. I am mortified. Pray, what can I do?

6 March

Some say that there is nothing so good for the inside of a man as the outside of a horse. I am training Cato in earnest. I take some little comfort from a couple of particulars I learned at the Washington birthnight Ball regarding the spring races. After it became known that Marmaduke Johnson's[*] Medley distanced all competitors at the vaunted Newmarket course at Petersburg last fall, it was determined that his horse would not be allowed to race in Warrenton or Halifax. Furthermore, rules will stipulate that all horses must carry 11 stone[**], eliminating these diminutive 90 lb jockeys & helping normal size owners who wish to ride their own horses. And Freemasons will officiate. All these factors make me hopeful for Cato. Who is not excited & hopeful when anticipating a horse race?

"Sterling, you should not raise your sights too high," Emily cautions. "Think of the breeding & care of the horses of Mr. Jones, Col. Whitaker, Davie, Capt. Dancy & others." I cannot bring myself to tell her of our embarrassment. It weighs upon me in eminent degree.

13 March

All are electrified by the President's action. He has nominated our consul in Holland to be envoy to France. Republicans are pleasantly surprised; Federalists are mortified.

---

[*] Marmaduke Johnson's son William Ransom Johnson was subsequently the owner of the illustrious American-foaled champion & sire, Sir Archie, and perhaps the nation's premier horseman/gentleman of the turf (grass was more or less the surface of all tracks until the Union Course in New York in 1821) for the first 3 decades of the 1800's. (He was also a legislator in both North Carolina and Virginia.)

[**] 11 stone=154lbs

I believe I have mollified Marmaduke & Prissy. Whereas I had previously allowed them one hand of tobacco per month for their own consumption, I will now provide a good number of plants from my protected bed that they may grow in their own plot. I am sensible that they derive a degree of status from selling or giving tobacco to other blacks. Marmaduke is a diligent man: he has made little cedar tubs so that each member of his household has his own plate like all refined folk. They no longer all dip their wooden spoons into one common bowl of corn mush & milk the way everyone did in our grandfathers' day.

I am filled with anticipation of the races. I make Eli (on Freshet) race Cato the three mile distance; tho' Freshet regularly leads at the one mile mark, at three miles Cato wins by an overwhelming margin.

Cato had learned the game of the 3 circuits of the mile oval last fall… well, by the end of that last heat. But in contrast to extravagantly trained horses like Avenger & Darcy's mare, we have only indulged the time to go to the race course in Warrenton once to train there in the 5 months since the last Fall race. I fear he will suffer disadvantage.

I have yet to tell Emily of our insult.

Sun^y 24 March

We are just above the want of fire. The redbuds bloom.

Macon returns from Congress & says the Federalists are back in the saddle. They robbed Pres. Adams' initiative of its thrust by bringing about nominations of two additional envoys—one of them being the venerable Patrick Henry, who could never make the voyage. And further assurances are required from the French before we send any mission to France. Huge delays are inevitable. As a practical matter, they have assured no rapprochement with France until our navy & other malignant forces have caused war. Furthermore, Pickering has gained control of the coming census, & Federalists continue to study methods of rigging the electoral process.

2 April

Today like many another, I was patting Cato & nuzzling his neck. He nickered in response. I own that I love my stallion. I was speaking to him in soft tones when Eli walked by. He laughed heartily at me.

I wax more certain that there is advantage in the quarter crouch. Initially I thought perhaps the relief I felt in going into it—after the first 2 & 1/2 miles with my knees bent so uncomfortably—was what made everything feel so good. Indeed, the somewhat shorter stirrups make the conventional upright position a strain. But more experience manifests to me that the balance is a distinct advantage somehow over the normal upright riding position. There is no doubt that Cato really likes it. And he has learned that it means the climax of the race approaches; 'tis a better prompt than my whip. I feel as if we are of one mind.

18 April, Warrenton

Freshet came through with a very respectable showing in his first day of racing. Eli rode him to seventh, sixth, & fourth places in the 3 one-mile heats. I will not sleep well tonight because of my anticipation of Cato's races tomorrow.

Last night I finally told Emily of the insult of our exclusion from the ball here in Warrenton. Naturally she was distresst. Yet she bore it well. She suggested that we should go ahead & expose the Sheriff as a mulatto. I am restrained by the fear that Caleb Brown & Ezra Blount could hand over evidence (to whomever succeeded as Sheriff) tying me uncomfortably close to Asa Johnson's death—especially what Eli told. Would it signify to rehabilitate my good name? It would not stop Ezra Blount's calumny, his odious slanders.

The Federalists take full possession of their legal monopoly to publicly slander in the newspapers. The infamous Robt. G. Harper writes that the new French mildness is "a trick, contrived and executed for the sole purpose of producing an effect upon the people of America, of lulling this country... into a fatal repose, of encreasing our division, of furnishing the French party with pretenses for opposing all our measures of defence and preparation, and of raising a clamour against the government..." Yet they have prohibited the Whigs & Republicans, whom he demeans as "the French party," from "raising a clamour against the government." And Justice James Iredell was quoted approving the constitutionality of this—the First Amendment be damned. Will such an unjust one as he ever consent to sell Sarah?

19 April, Warrenton

It was a very fine day of the stamp that can only be had in April. Beautifully cool with a blue sky, dogwoods still abloom & tiny little light green leaves everywhere emerging. I remember it well, not for its beauty as much as for the moment of the particulars that follow.

I estimated my primary competition to be Col. Whitaker's hulking (easily 16 hands high at the withers) chestnut styled Avenger, Capt. Dancy's blue roan mare—she fondly reminds me of my old Aristotle—& Jones' light copper-red sorrel. But there were horses from as far away as Edenton—all dark horses to me. The big field manifested the general prosperity. Without a doubt, I was the poorest (in money & public esteem) with any chance to win. Well, at least in my mind there was a chance.

We got off to a poor start in the first heat & spent the 1st half mile in the dust of above 25 horses. But at the one mile mark I was sensible that we were gaining a little on the leaders (Whitaker's chestnut Avenger & a bright bay from Virginia), and I waxed sanguine. I passed Capt. Dancy's mare before the 2 mile mark to move into fifth place! As I caught up to Jones' sorrel, he made his move to catch the two leaders. I tried to go with him. Just as the sorrel achieved Avenger's flank, he was thrown off by a hole or Whitaker's jockey's whip, and that in turn threw us off & wide of the turn. The sorrel recovered better than we did, but both of us were passed by the charging Dancy mare, who challenged the leaders. The three of them made a race of it, nearly distancing the rest of us. Avenger won; we struggled to maintain sixth. I had let my hopes rise too high. The 3 top horses were formidable. I was exceedingly discouraged.

During the 30 minute space for breathing & rubbing down our horses, Emily's soothing words steadied both me & Cato for the second three-miler.

"Sterling, Mr. Jones observed to me that Cato has a pretty motion…a smooth gait. And that a sixth place finish is quite good for your horse in this competition." She did not say then what she told me later, that Mr. Jones went on to say: "If he were a bigger horse with a longer stride, I'd wager on him to place or show."

Twenty-three of the original 27 horses answered the call to the post for the second heat. We started much better. Indeed, when the word was given, Cato dashed forward with the whole body of horses without the least motion of my heels to his sides, as tho' he understood this game now without any guidance from me. I thought to myself how remarkable the enthusiasm of these 23 horses after already having run 3 miles, for they took to this 2nd heat with all the pleasure they had exhibited in the 1st. They hung together—"like roses on the same stem shaking in a gale-force wind" in Emily's words—for well over a quarter mile.

But by the first half mile, we had spread a bit. The Virginian bay & Avenger had confidently assumed a healthy lead; we were about 15th, but not far behind Dancy's mare. I slowly caught & commenced to shadow the mare, who gradually started moving through the field. We were 7th & 8th at the mid-point of the race, but so far off the strong pace set by the Virginian,

Avenger, & Jones' sorrel, that I thought it unlikely we had a chance. Would Cato even be able to respond when the mare made her charge?

We gained on them in small measure in the next half mile. After the 2 mile mark, Jones' sorrel dropped back to us, but the Virginian bay & Avenger maintained redoubtable pace. Their lead was such that I had scant hope; there was no prospect of me claiming a third place & winning a little coin & glory amongst this competition. It got worse as a black gelding, whose jockey seemingly held back in the 1st heat, charged by us. Had I misjudged that the mare would make a well-calculated late charge?

With less than a half mile to go and our running a distant 6th behind the Dancy mare, the mare made her move. With my giving Cato the least touch of heel & whip, my small stallion seemed to know my plan & stayed right on the charging mare's inside flank. We caught up to the black gelding & we three went by Jones' sorrel decisively. The thrilling celerity with which we charged was wonderful to experience whether we could catch the leaders or no! The throng of spectators audibly took note of our charge with a roar.

Up ahead of us, the Virginia bay seemed to tire a bit & give Avenger space. And confidence. The gelding caught up to the bay, but just as he did, the gelding lost his balance & fell into the Virginian bay, causing it to also suffer a floundering fall. The crowd was electrified (to use Franklin's word) by this event & exclaimed with five thousand voices. The increasingly confident Avenger jockey turned to look back at what the multitude perceived. In the ridiculed crouch low behind Cato's head, I spake an intimate loud whisper in his ear: "Now Cato!"

He lowered his head & bolted by Dancy's mare, which was perhaps distracted by the accident, going through the small space on the inside, a space only he would have fit. What a reserve! What a heart hath Cato! We were sure to secure 2nd. Avenger had lost pace, assuming the race won. We were making such a charge, that I knew we could pass them if we had an extra 30 yards. Cato accelerated all the way to the finish line. We were flying at the finish line! We got Avenger by a nose!

We came from nowhere to win by a nose! I won, I won, I won the most exciting three-miler there ever was. This moment was so fine, inexpressibly fine. What can compare? Lest it be that moment when first I heard Emily say she loved me. Tempered only by Col. John Whitaker's hateful, haughty stare.

With 2 different winners of the 2 heats, a third heat would follow in another half hour. Would Cato have anything left after that? Would the veriest effort hurt my fine stallion? His ribs heaved as he endeavored to regain his breath. Sweat poured down his sides; his eyes were glassy. Wagerers gathered around us to gauge how to bet. I thought it unlikely that they would find encouragement to bet for us by what they observed. My creditor, Col. Whitaker, arrogantly walked by & glared at me as I rubbed Cato down. He looked at me with the countenance of one who has bitten into the most bitter of crab apples. The intimidation he aimed at me, his debtor, his inferior, filled me with no little discomfiture.

Little by little, Cato regained his breath. His eyes regained focus. He did not complain when at the end of the 30 minutes I remounted him & guided him to the post. My stallion has an abundance of heart, but would he collapse on the 8th or 9th mile I was asking him to run this day?

Only 9 horses answered the post for the 3rd heat. Avenger immediately took the lead, much whipped & spurred by his hired white jockey. He tried to discourage us by establishing a distancing lead. I think he & Col. Whitaker felt certain that Avenger was the superior horse and wished to leave no doubt he had been beaten by fluke. Jones' sorrel, Dancy's mare, Cato, & the 5 horses behind us did not pursue but bunched together in a slow pace. I collect that all the horses were very tired.

On the backstretch of the second mile, Avenger's white-stockinged legs slowed to a virtual canter, in spite of the urgings of his jockey. Sorrel, mare, & Cato went by the big chestnut easily coming out of the far turn. We opened a little space on the other 6 horses now starting the 3rd mile. The light copper-red sorrel held the lead till the mare made her charge, again making her move with about a half mile to go but with perceptibly weaker acceleration than in the previous heat. But she passed the sorrel decisively. I gave one swat to Cato's behind and crouched, flattening my back & dropping my chin into his mane. He accelerated & moved to the inside flank of the sorrel. The sorrel fought us all the way around the far turn. Racing each other, we both re-caught the blue roan mare. The mare had drifted ever so slightly out from the rail, such that I had a little space to squeeze but the sorrel did not.

With that momentum, we pulled even to Dancy's mare. We ran neck & neck, eyeball-to-eyeball, all the way down the stretch. Cato gave it every fiber of his being & could not go any faster. The mare gave up 40 yards from the finish, allowing us to win by half Cato's length. What heart, what bottom hath my Cato! He nearly killed himself doing it. I despaired, as I thought he would never regain his breath.

£12 worth of prize money! We bought Emily the print she admired. As the Spaniards say, "Living well is the best revenge."

Sunday, 21 April

We had Lewis, Kenchen, Isham, their families, Mama &c. over for the finest Sunday dinner I would ever hope to host. We splurged, but nothing inappropriate for so happy a celebration. All admired our print upon the wall with its moral lesson of diligence versus dissipation. All admired Cato, but Kenchen asked if 'twere actually necessary for me to adopt so unmanly a riding position for the final half mile. Naturally I observed that I only adopted it in two of the three races—the two I won. At least amongst my close kin, I can enjoy fully the good fortune of Cato. At least these successes must vex those who slander my name.

Isham said his neighbor told him there was a letter for me at Warrenton. Sarah? There is no possibility I can spare the time to fetch it, given the time away from the farm for the Halifax races. Emily & I shall dance at Halifax & hold our heads high.

Wednesday, 24 April

Macon came; he brought the letter from Sarah. She has been found out! Harper? A Federalist postmaster? Her note was brief. She has been whipped severely, confined in movement, starved, &c. She pleads for me to buy her. Her last bit of intelligence was that Pickering, [Secretary of Treasury] Wolcott, [Secretary of War] McHenry, & Gen. Hamilton plot to replace Pres. Adams with Pinckney or Ellsworth in the next election. This is particularly significant for it confirms (1) Adams' sincerity in appointing new envoys to France & (2) that there is a real division in the Federalist ranks.

I asked Macon how much help we could get from Republican congressmen now that she will be of no further service to them.

"Well...I will not even be seeing any of them again till December. Beckley has no money. The other two who are cognizant will view it as a pretty cold charity by that time. I am ashamed to say the kind of money she needs will not be forthcoming. From us. I am ashamed of my part in this devious espionage business, & I am ashamed of the way it ends."

"If Cato wins the three-mile heats overall in Halifax Friday, I will have over £20 to give you in her behalf. Can you kick in something & help to tender the offer?" I asked.

"Sterling, you sanguine cuss," exclaimed Macon. "What an optimist you are. Halifax will have a very strong field. You will be lucky to come in second or third in one of the heats & clear a pound over your entrance fee. But let us flatter ourselves that you win outright as you did in Warrenton. £20 plus what she has yields £49. I will chip in £2; that is £51. You need £65 or more to buy her. Suffer me to say unto you, Sterling, you aren't going to be able to free her."

I had never looked at my esteemed friend with such disappointment in my countenance. He felt it.

"I will talk to Wylie Jones at the races. He is on more familiar terms with the Iredells than am I. He might sympathize. If so, he might arrange to buy her & let her work for him till you can raise the full price."

Later I discussed all this with Emily.

"Sterling, if we were out of debt, your altruism would be more admirable. Our own family's circumstances are too precarious to think of giving more towards her freedom." How could I argue against her? Indeed, my family's future, uncertain indeed, must take precedent. Emily also was not easy on another particular: the idea of her coming back to this area as a slave. With uncharacteristic coarseness, Emily said that if Sarah came around me again she would "pinch her nipples off." I love my wife.

27 April

What a great throng of people & animals! Every man, woman, & child, black & white, for miles around were gathered about that race course. Not since Philadelphia have I seen such a festive multitude as was there in Halifax. I would that it could have rendered me as buoyant as it did John & Emily; alas I was not sanguine.

Macon was correct: The Halifax races brought together the finest assemblage of horses I have ever seen. Eli & Freshet did well to achieve middle of the pack finishes in the one-mile heats. (By the bye, the horse of Macon's Virginian friend John Randolph won.) I slept better that night than in Warrenton because my hopes & aspirations were appropriately lowered.

Before the 1st heat, Kenchen & I discussed the possible stratagem of holding Cato back in the 1st heat amongst this stellar group of horses, in the hope that the really fast horses would lose their edge in exertion & Cato's excellent bottom might work for him in the 2nd heat. A highly touted dun from Tarboro & a dappled gray from below Petersburg (who was 2nd to Medley at Newmarket last fall) were thought to be the favorites. My chief rivals at Warrenton were thought to have only outside chances. This astounded me, for as I conversed with Kenchen, I could espy nearby the intimidating Avenger, well over 16 hands high with massive chest & shoulders, a long waist. His coat gleamed in the sun, a testament to his careful conditioning. My more compact Cato must take 6 steps to cover what Whitaker's massive chestnut covers in 5. I found it unbelievable that we had bested that horse in Warrenton little more than a week ago. With the help of the accident. And perhaps with the benefit of Col. Whitaker's or the jockey's bad strategy in the final heat. Avenger's wiry white jockey gave me a nasty, mischievous smile.

"One danger of such a ploy though, is you might accidentally teach Cato to think he is inferior to these horses. To not think himself capable of beating them in the later heats."

"Kenchen, I have the same fear."

As it transpired, we might have been accused of such a stratagem.

Thirty-four horses lined up at the post. At least as a consequence of having won at Warrenton, we were not consigned to the 2nd row at the start. Still I was distressed at how poorly we started. The Virginian bright bay & the dun from Tarboro took a commanding lead & set a punishing pace, distancing the rest of us during most of the 2nd mile. The Petersburg dappled gray & Capt. Dancy's mare caught up to them during the last mile. The pace was so fast that it never seemed practical to catch & shadow the mare as I had in Warrenton. The mare & the estimable dappled gray, named Brutus, made a valiant charge. The 4 horses approached the finish line all within a length of each other, having set a record time for 3 miles in North-Carolina! Brutus beat the bright bay by half a length. How mortifying to the Halifax spectators to have Virginians take 1st & 2nd (after also dominating the 1 mile heats). We finished 10th behind Avenger, who may have adopted our same approach. At the end of the heat, his jockey gave me another sly look, upon which no precise construction could I place.

In the second heat, I endeavored strenuously to be within striking distance of the leaders at the half-way point. Cato responded well. The Tarboro dun & Brutus traded the lead several times during the 1st two miles at a slower pace than the 1st heat. I passed the apparently fatigued Virginian bright bay just before the 2 mile mark & positioned right behind Dancy's mare in 6th. Jones' sorrel & Avenger just ahead of us made a move together on the leaders, which caused the leaders to enhance their pace. (Just then I painfully caught some grit in my eye.) I gave Cato a little whip then for fear the leaders would distance us. With half a mile to go, I saw we had no chance. Capt. Dancy's jockey made the same judgment. We had to hope someone could beat Brutus so that a 3rd heat would be called for. The Tarboro dun got him by a length, thankfully. Another length back, Jones' sorrel beat Avenger for a very respectable 3rd.

During the 30 minute interval for breathing & currying, I whispered to Cato of my love & regard for him & of the greatness that was in his future. I am a man of one-and-thirty now but still the dreamer.

Only 14 of the 34 original horses answered the call to the post for the 3rd heat. The Virginian bright bay that was 2nd in the 1st heat was among those missing.

Brutus & the dun set a slow early pace & were challenged at the mile marker by Avenger, who then led them at a respectable clip. Indeed, the pace was difficult for the rest of us. Avenger is an impressive stallion.

I positioned again behind Dancy's blue roan mare with much uncertainty in my mind. For most of the 2nd mile, the 3 leaders distanced the rest of us, & I despaired of any possibility of our catching them. I wanted to make a move, but respected the racing sagacity of Capt. Dancy & feared the charge of his mare if I moved before him. Then a little into the 3rd mile, the leaders began to slow. With this minimal encouragement in view, the mare & Cato picked up their pace. Little by little we gained. With a half mile to go, it looked like we might catch them. And the horse I felt under me saw his quarry too.

I went into the ridiculed crouch. I said into Cato's ear "Now Cato! 'Tis your time! Go boy!"

Decisively, we went by Dancy's mare on the inside. So decisively that I sensed it startled her—to our advantage. We passed the fading dun with a quarter mile to go at the top of the far turn. My stomach was flat to Cato's withers, face pressed into his mane; my body curved along the ebb & flow of Cato's body. Our speed was thrilling…all I could ask of my beloved little stallion. The dicing Brutus & Avenger were catchable at this charging pace, *if* we could keep it. At least I felt we could get a 3rd place.

Brutus was about to retake Avenger when he may have caught Avenger's damned jockey's whip in the face. For he slowed noticeably. At 150 yards from the finish I thought I could get by Brutus for 2nd. Yet I was sensible of Dancy's charging mare right upon my tail! We got by Brutus. My God!

We caught up to Avenger. With Avenger still ahead by a half his length his jockey turned & spat tobacco juice at us. But I had seen enough of that varlet's wild whip. I had kept some little space that made him miss. We were nose & nose with Avenger with 20 yards to go. But Dancy's charging mare was there too & might get us both. It was too close to call! It was pandemonium. The many thousands of spectators roared in appreciation. A deafening roar, unceasing! So thunderous I warrant they might have heard it 40 miles away in Warrenton.

The judges declared Cato the winner by a nose, & the mare 2nd by a whisker over Whitaker's Avenger. I was so proud. Whitaker hotly protested. Brutus' owner protested the whip incident.

Poor Cato. The sweat rolled down him now. He struggled so for every choppy breath. His ribs heaved. And now crowds of interested wagerers crowded around him as well as the other 2 heat winners to gauge what action to take. I had to ask them to give him space. Ten minutes into the rubdown, Cato still struggled for breath, which caused me great concern. His eyes had no focus.

Marmaduke Johnson's son & Austin Curtis, knowing me, took the liberty to step closer & speak to me.

"Mr. Shearin, my father wishes to wager on your horse, your being from our county & all. I love Cato's smooth gait, his obvious heart. I apprehend you've trained him superbly. But I am sensible that his shorter stride & breathing aren't strengths," said the handsome young Master Johnson, hoping I would offer some insight.

I did not respond. Kench, Eli, John & I busied ourselves sponging down Cato. For all our sponging, the foamy sweat rolled down his flanks. Nine miles had taken a toll.

"Master Johnson," I responded after a minute, "I don't wish to appear rude, but I don't know what to say. I *am* concerned about Cato's breathing. I pray all the protesting might extend the 30 minute rest period."

"Master Johnson, les you & me tell the judges that in the interest of a good finish to this race, they ought to 'xtend the rest to 45 minutes," suggested Austin Curtis.

"Once again I'm in your debt, Mr. Curtis," said I.

"I cannot conceive that the other 2 owners would object," said Johnson in agreement.

Mr. Curtis returned shortly with a couple of buckets of water, which he suggested pouring upon Cato. My liver chestnut gradually recovered & I recovered a glimmer of hope for him running 3 more miles.

Capt. Dancy joined those studying Cato. With Kench, Eli, & John continuing their ministrations, I turned and spoke to him.

"Sir, let me be the first to acknowledge that your mare would have beaten us with another 30 yards of race length."

"Mr. Shearin, I won't dispute you. The decisiveness of your pass was so unexpected that it threw my horse & jockey. After Warrenton, we should have been more wary of you, but were focused on Brutus. Congratulations & good luck in the run-off. All of Halifax will cheer for you over the Virginian Brutus, as will I." Capt. Dancy, a respectable planter from Northampton Co., was not happy, but he returned my effort at magnanimity in kind. And I appreciated this from so formidable a gentleman of the turf as he, in view of the stains painted upon my public character.

I thought to say to him 'I owe your mare a free leap with Cato' but thought better of it & bade him farewell. I wondered could my small horse represent the Roanoke Valley as well as Dancy's formidable, well-bred mare surely would have.

For all the glory of having won a heat amongst this august competition, the bold truth was that the real prize money would go to the winner of the run off. I was brought back to that reality by the heated glare of my creditor,

Col. Whitaker. His intimidating presence now joined the group of interested wagerers gathered there about us.

Having spent himself so in the third heat, I girded myself for the possibility that Cato might have nothing left for this run-off, the fourth three mile race in one day. Cato had never run four in a day. What planter of my level could afford the time to run a horse such distances in training? Of the three horses in the run-off, we were the most local, and I had some little concern about an embarrassing performance disappointing everyone.

When at last the 3 heat winners lined up at the post for the run-off, the great noisy crowd grew completely silent. Yet when the signal was given, they erupted into a full-throated den. I warrant this helped all three horses get going again.

Yet, the three of us set a wary slow pace for most of the 1st mile. During the 2nd mile the Tarboro dun attempted to up the pace, but after maintaining a solid lead for a half mile, faded completely from apparent exhaustion & was ultimately distanced. The dappled gray Brutus & Cato warily paced themselves for the final half mile. As we approached the backstretch of the 3rd mile, I was possesst of a modicum of confidence. For Cato was sustaining this pace well after running 11 miles & did not seem on the verge of giving up; I judged that Cato had something left.

I thought to wait for Brutus to make the first move. Yet when it had not come approaching the far turn, I (already in the crouch) signaled Cato to enhance our pace just a little to insure we took the turn to the inside. Brutus matched our pace, running the turn just to our outside, where Cato could see his competition nearly eye to eye.

We entered the homestretch ahead by a neck. Brutus' little black jockey began to whip him fiercely. Brutus responded. He pulled even to us. 200 yards. With me up over his neck & moving with him, I gave Cato a couple of whips to his rear. He lowered his head yet more & accelerated. Brutus did not quit, but he knew he was beat. We won by most of a length. What bottom my formidable, beautiful dark liver chestnut has! A total £22 & 10 shillings prize money.

Our afternoon in Halifax was a triumph beyond my dreams. All acclaimed me as the Roanoke Valley champion. (The slanders against me were doubtless less well known here as compared with Warren Co.) I had bested the highly touted horses of Virginia, Tarboro, Edenton, &c. I demonstrated local prowess on the turf. More than one complimented me on being the rare owner to ride his own horse to victory in an important race. Only John Whitaker dared look down his nose at me this day.

We bought Emily imported spices (vanilla!), a rose plant, & a book. We purchased a regular subscription to the *N.-C. Journal* & some metal tools &

nails. Spent right at £3. Never have I spent so profligately.

 The particulars of the evening that followed were as brim full of portent as the events of the afternoon. Amongst the splendid assemblage at the more inclusive ball at the Long Room, Emily & I consumed libations & danced as celebrants should. Early in the evening it seemed as if some Federalist ladies & gentlemen (Col. Whitaker, for instance) were scandalized by the intimate cotillion, but as the consumption of punch & whiskey proceeded, their reserve diminished, and all were overcome by increasing glee & conviviality.
 General Davie himself toasted us & our fine steed. Federalist leader tho' he be, such magnanimity from him in these tense times did not entirely surprise me; he is married to Wylie Jones' niece & Mr. Jones has from time to time made mention of his virtues in contrast to his politics. Indeed, Genl Davie was a veritable hero in the Revolution & has lately been elected Governor. His magnanimity in any event was exceedingly welcome; I thanked him profusely & spoke in praise of his own excellent horses. Mrs. Davie knew Emily from her days as an orphan, such that we were very pleasantly immersed in agreeable converse for a spell. Until Mr. Jones & Col. Whitaker interrupted the pleasing harmony.
 "Our society will descend into chaos if anyone may write or say anything they wish!" cried Col. Whitaker.
 "Not as long as reason may counter false or errant statements," replied Mr. Jones with intensity.
 "Our judges to a man reckon the Sedition Act proper & consistent with the Constitution. Our own respected James Iredell does."
 "Yes, & that sticks in my craw as much as the act itself. For upon my honor, Col. Whitaker, I remember at the Hillsborough Convention where we rejected the Constitution— rightly for its lack of a Bill of Rights—Iredell argued that, even without the explicit 1st Amendment, Congress would have no right to restrict the right of free speech. General Davie must confirm as much," said Jones.
 While too meek to say this myself under these circumstances, I was glad to hear Mr. Jones say it to the Federalists gathered there. So bitter is sentiment betwixt Republicans & Federalists these days that little real debate occurs. Jones & Davie, connected not only by marriage, but working together tirelessly on the establishment & development of the Univ. of North-Carolina, on the fixing of the capital at Raleigh, & on the effort to build a canal on the Roanoke, &c.—perhaps these 2 can discuss the issues as they deserve without rancor...and have reason, which is on our side, prevail.
 And fie upon't. How can one read the 1st amendment, to wit, Congress

shall make no law abridging the freedom of speech or of the press, & view the Sedition Act as constitutional? As Mr. Jones said to Macon & I earlier, "To assert it is to betray a degree of intelligence that would disgrace a set of drovers."

Davie nodded somewhat sheepishly.

"We were too sanguine in those days, Wylie. I will own that we were mistaken. To speak the bold truth, 'tis much easier to alarm the people than to inform them. And many the Republican alarming them—present company excepted—is almost indistinguishable from a French Jacobin," said Davie.

"Many the American who is, in so many words, indistinguishable from the enemy!" added Col. Whitaker with warmth. "In what they write & say, they aid the enemy. They are seditious!"

Macon & Jones frowned at Whitaker; yet Davie's countenance expresst that he could not disagree.

"Could it be, Col. Whitaker, that you identify our country too closely with its government?" I asked. "Villainous the French may be, but they haven't harmed North-Carolinians or Americans in general in any manner justifying War. Or justifying our destroying our natural liberties. Or justifying so much bitterness betwixt Federalist & Republican."

Before Davie or Whitaker could answer, Mrs. Davie spoke. "Mr. Shearin, you are at least right in your last statement. And may I make a suggestion, prompted in part by the return of the musicians? In years past, your sweet wife & the former Miss Sitgreaves over there & I used to sing as a trio from time to time. Would you be so kind as to indulge us presently to do at least one number?"

"It would be a great pleasure, Mrs. Davie," I replied, actually relieved, for as much as had I wanted to reply to Whitaker, I feared I had merely fanned the flames. I held my glass up and toasted "To the harmony of beautiful music." Everyone in our group joined in the toast, but I noted Whitaker's brittle countenance. As if he had rusty metal in his libation.

I was very proud of Emily's singing. She harmonizes superbly. All that brilliant assembly praised their singing.

Later this subject flared again in another part of the Long Room & blows were nearly exchanged. By that time, I had imbibed to the point that the Spanish proverb "living well is the best revenge" ruled my aspect. I listened in amusement to an exchange amongst General Davie, Mr. Jones, & the dancing master over the curriculum at the University. Genl Davie was explaining to the dance master that he & Wylie had put an end to the University's putting on entire plays "because we want the students to become men, not players." On the other hand, they had gone to great lengths to engage a dance master for the students "because it is imperative that our students be gentlemen. The master we obtained is something weak on the English dances, but very good on the minuet, the congo, & this new cotillion."

Near the end of the evening, Mr. Jones visited upon us honor & burden.

"Sterling, Emily, it has started to rain more than a little. Are you put up anywhere?"

I shook my head that we were not. Our plan was to sleep under our wagon.

"Well I have several guests, what with the races, but I think I could find some room for you & Emily. It may be a something makeshift in the parlor."

"Thank you very much Mr. Jones. That would be exceedingly kind of you."

Then he obligated me yet more deeply:

"You are very welcome. Very welcome. Sterling, on another... perhaps delicate subject, Mr. Macon has told me of your circumstances & aims regarding an Iredell slave lent to the villain Pickering. He says you have about £50 but that it will take a good £65 to £70 to get her.

"Having known Mrs. Iredell since her youth, I will take it upon myself to buy the servant through her. If I must, I'll acquaint her with the mistreatment this Sarah suffers at Pickering's hand. I will lend you what is necessary at no interest, to be paid at your convenience."

Was there ever a more worthy gentleman than Wylie Jones? What could I say? What could Emily say?

I gave Mr. Jones my share ere we quitted Halifax this morning.

Chapter Twenty-Five

30 May 1799

    The wheat crop is looking weak & none of the news is good. The "friends of the government," as Federalists style themselves, made several gains in the congressional elections in Virginia in late April.

    The famous John Marshall was one of the winners (at least his margin was small). No man has benefited more from the unpleasantness with France than Marshall. Macon tells me Marshall received a fortune in compensation for his failed mission to France; he received three times his previous annual earnings as a Richmond lawyer. How perfectly natural for him to be a "friend of the government." And his status as hero greatly exceeds that of Congressman Harper, Pres. Adams, & other beneficiaries of the war scare.

    Associate Supreme Court Justice Iredell's explanation for approving the constitutionality of the Sedition Act in the face of the First Amendment was printed as part of a long direction to a grand jury in Philadelphia: Iredell says he was mistaken in 1788 & now adopts the English view that as long as there is no prior restraint on publication, freedom of the press has not been abridged. "But to punish any dangerous or offensive writing, which, when published, shall...be adjudged of a pernicious tendency, is necessary for the preservation of peace & good order..." All the federal judges engage in this kind of prejudicial political discourse to their grand juries. Those in power use us ill.

    I have heard nothing more concerning Sarah. I pray that the Iredells have sold her to Jones. On the road home from Halifax after the races, Emily asked Macon if he was emphatic in talking to Wylie Jones to the effect that we wish to free Sarah, not to own her.

    "I was not emphatic," Macon replied, "but I think I expresst that plainly." He did not sound confident.

    'Tis a worry. Miscommunication is an easy thing. And Jones made no mention of the remarkable act of a farmer of my status making such a sacrifice to *free* a slave.

10 June

    Since last Summer's war fever highlighted the federalism of North-Carolina's handful of newspapers, Macon has been attempting to recruit an honest Whig to start a newspaper in our State. He views it as essential if we are to shift our state back to its more natural republican view in time for the presidential election.

Today Macon brought the excellent news that he has enticed an English refugee in Philadelphia, a Mr. Jos. Gales, to initiate a newspaper in Raleigh this fall. Even better in my view, tho' perhaps not in Macon's, Mr. Gales opposes slavery.

Macon's wheat does as poorly as our own.

20 June

I was weeding corn near the house when he came. Col. John Whitaker, my creditor & formidable federal tax gatherer, came, he said, to reassess our houses, land, & slaves for the federal tax. With deep, malicious jealousy evident in his visage, he did eye my Cato over much.

The only thing pleasant he had to say to me during the hour he was here was that Marmaduke's house was one of the finer slave quarters he had ever seen. Considering tho' that this comment came from a tax assessor, it would have been pleasanter from anyone else.

'Twas an hour of dread. An hour of ominous foreshadowing, fully warranted by its conclusion. Col. Whitaker, gentleman in the old style with his plaited, clubbed up hair & silk stockings, for once did not affect his normal air of debonair insouciance. No pretentiously deft use of his jeweled snuffbox this day. He looked at me as if he might curse me till the leaves shook on the trees.

"Shearin your tax will be higher this fall." More than once, when I reflected on his jealousy of Cato's besting his chestnut stallion Avenger, I considered the likelihood of such a consequence. But what followed was more woeful, nay... it was to the quick.

"'Tis said that you have murdered two men, one of whom was a kinsman of mine," Col. Whitaker continued in a voice dripping with contempt. "'Tis said that you harbored escaped slaves, the property of a respectable citizen of Tarborough. I am entirely persuaded by the common view of your stained character. You, Sterling Shearin, you are a despicable knave! A designing blackguard. A God-damned poltroon!

"In consequence, I am no longer disposed to act as your creditor. If you fail to pay me in full, interest & principal & tax, subsequent to this fall's harvest, I shall ***take your farm***."

1 July

We are ruined. How can I raise that kind of money? With higher taxes & the interest, we need well in excess of £100. Has Wylie Jones used my £20 to purchase Sarah yet? How mortifying to have to ask him.

There will be no ready money from the wheat crop. Between a backward year & the weevil, we will be doing well to have bread for our own consumption for a few months.

6 July

The embarrassment of my question to Wylie Jones is pre-empted.
The deed is done. She is freed for £70.
How can I rejoice in this good turn when it is so tied to our own ruin? Not only have I given well over £40 to Sarah if 'twere added all together, but now I owe £20 to the one man (Wylie Jones) to whom I might have turned for a loan. Either the money given or the loan would make such a difference to our plight.

10 July

It has been exceedingly hot these last two weeks & the corn starts to suffer from want of rain. We hear at least that our governor, General Davie, has been named one of the envoys to France in the room of Patrick Henry. However, no word of when they will set sail.

25 July

The hot dust is in our throats. Our shoulders ache from the neck yokes by which we tote pails of water to keep our plants alive. Our eyes are weary from the absolute necessity of vigilance against copperheads. Such is our portion.
Poor old Lucy has lost the last of her teeth & has only poor eyesight. Little Katie loves her as much as she does us. We all have affection for her. If we ever get rain, I will get Emily to ride her down to visit her favorite grandchild.
What will become of us? Even with good rains & abundant crops, we are likely done in. With poor crops, 'tis hopeless.
Tonight I was sure I could read Eli's thoughts: "I should take off with Freshet now, for Sterling Shearin will not have the £5 he promised me come harvest time."

1 Aug'

It is so dry that there are not even any mosquitoes.

3 Aug'

I received a letter from Sarah "north of Philadelphia." In spite of her oppressive circumstances in those last months of service with Pickering, she learned that Pickering & Sec. of War McHenry are attempting to disrupt communication between the President & the French by instructing our only official conduit, the consul in Holland, to address all official business to Pickering's State Dept. Pickering intends to put every road block in the way of our envoys sailing for France. Furthermore Pickering intends to prosecute every leading Republican paper in all the States. Sarah also overheard it said that Genl Hamilton & Theodore Sedgewick[*] have urged stationing much of the new army in Virginia to quell Virginia's independent spirit. Fortunately, Adams has resisted them thus far.

She spelled Theodore Sedgewick (a name which could hardly be very familiar to her) correctly; her letter evinced a steadily advancing intelligence. I am compelled to enter her last paragraph that I may savor its poignance when, as it so frequently does, life visits nothing but frustration & failure upon me:

"I want you to know that I lernt these things at some danger to me & sind them to you as some payment for my debt to you for what you have done for me. Tho' every moment I expect some one to tell me that I should awake from my dream, that I am steel a slave & always will be. You have given me my life, my freedom, & my bleef in the goodness, the possible goodness of a man. If you never do nothing else in your life, Master Sterling, you have done one thing that was very fine. I am forever in your debt. You have my undying love & admiration."

10 Aug

'Twas cloudy & the signs foreshadow rain. Hence I knocked off toting water for the crops today and gave Cato a good run over to Macon's to show him Sarah's letter. He was in a rare black mood; his crops all parch like everyone else's. And his promising colt has a severe case of the bastard strangles.

"The prosecutions of the newspapers proceeds apace" said he after reading Sarah's letter. "Pickering will have every major Republican paper shut down for next year's election."

"How can elections have any meaning if the shortcomings of one set of candidates may not be mentioned?" said I.

Macon shook his head dejectedly. "Even if we should miraculously

---

[*] Senator from Massachusetts; later Macon's opponent for Speaker of the House.

prevail in these elections, the spirit of 1776 is *gone*. The Whig understanding of the nature of power, the nature of government...the new generation has lost it.

"Twenty years ago, 'twas commonly understood that all governments thru' out history have degenerated & abused the powers reposed in them. 'Twas understood therefore that gov't must be limited to protecting the liberty, lives, & property of the people governed from violence...limited to that well-defined task. Otherwise there is no hope of countering government's natural proclivity for becoming big, wasteful, corrupt, & abusive.

"The Whig writers fade from view. —Even the tolerance of Deism is out of fashion. Fifteen years ago, no respectable gentleman would have branded Mr. Jefferson an atheist in an effort to discredit him."

It was troubling to see the steady Macon, perhaps the best leader of the cause of liberty, so pessimistic. I tried to offer some sanguine thought: "What about the young Congressman from Tennessee?"

"Andrew Jackson? Well. Mayhap one exception. But in truth, probably not. Very few of this generation have read the literature of liberty upon which my generation was nourished. Jackson probably has read very little of it, but is rather a man of good instincts. Instinct will not serve against the vicissitudes of political turmoil; a well-girded intellect & resourcefulness in an eminent degree are also required."

"Adams is a man of the 1776 generation," said I. "'Tis said that during the Revolution he wrote that a 'Free Press will maintain the Majesty of the PEOPLE.' Has he changed so much?"

Macon sat in silence for a few moments as if contemplating my question. He sucked on the inside of his cheek. Suddenly he said: "Let us write to him and spell out all the scheming of Pickering, General Hamilton, & the others."

We set to it, debating only whether to sign it "Anonymous." Doubtless Pres. Adams will dismiss it as a Republican stratagem to create dissension within his administration. In spite of the likely futility of such an effort, at least we had the satisfaction of doing something.

It threatened rain several times, but alas never did it rain.

27 Aug.

At last we got a little thunder storm. Just enough to lend hope. Everyone hereabouts is upset about a slave uprising in Southampton Co., Virginia. A number of whites were viciously murdered; I rationalize that they treated their slaves barbarically.

5 Sept^r

The Sheriff & Ezra Blount presented their intimidating presence at my front door today. "Shearin, we hear that you let your slave keep a musket or a fowler. Is that true?"

"No," I answered perversely. "I have given him a *rifle*." For some reason, I took pleasure at Blount's raised eyebrow that my slave should have, not just a gun, but a gun of some refinement. (The one I inherited from Papa.) They insisted that I take possession of it. Had they been nicer about it, I might have acquiesced, rather than merely promising to think on it. People are scared. Perhaps rightly so.

They took great pleasure in telling me that Marmaduke Johnson's great dominating horse will be allowed back into the races this fall. The 11-stone rule for jockeys is also rescinded.

7 Sept^r

Praise to Nature's God! A little gentle rain. And all my family has come through the sickly season whole.

Still I see no way to raise the money to keep our farm. I am reduced to inquiring of everyone where I might borrow the apposite money—with my farm and slaves as collateral.[*]

Emily & I have resolved to observe Marmaduke, Prissy, & any company they entertain with a sharp eye. It is some reassurance that when we questioned old Lucy—somewhat obliquely—on the subject of hidden violence that 'Duke & Prissy might hold in their hearts for us, their master & mistress, she said: "I cain't say 'bout Prissy, but 'Duke, he lubs y'all." I trust Lucy as much as my wife. I have known this ancient colored woman all my life. She knows things about me…that I don't know. If I cannot trust her… then mayhap I have no place in this world.

I thought about what Whitaker said about Marmaduke's abode being the finest of slave dwellings. 'Duke never took it for granted in the first instance. I said to him, what, 8 years ago now "This is your home now." He behaved in that manner, investing himself in it & enhancing it. He may not love us, but I think he is sensible of my respect for him & my effort to treat him with a degree of fairness. But one never knows how a slave views the world. Pretension & invention are natural devices for them, strategies of survival.

1 Oct^r

'Tis a bad year, tho' it looked to be even worse back in that hot, dry,

---

[*] There were no banks in North Carolina until 1804.

hateful month of August. The tobacco survived better than the corn; there is a little cotton, which is in constantly increasing demand since the invention of the machine [cotton gin, i.e., engine]. Some cider of middling quality. We will carry it all to Halifax and try against all chance in the races.

Macon, Lewis, & Kenchen have committed to lend me £15 between them. If Cato could somehow repeat his sweeps of the three mile events at Halifax & Warrenton & I could get £40-50 for my crops, then surely the Scotsman in Halifax would lend me the balance.

18 Oct^r

The British monopoly on our trade begins to depress the prices. We sold everything, leaving no corn or cider even for our own consumption, and cleared only £33 & 11 shillings. How ridiculously futile we are to hope Cato will come through tomorrow; the field is huge & Marmaduke Johnson's horse has never been beaten.

21 Oct^r

M'duke Johnson's animal is verily superlative a horse. He won the first three-mile heat handily. And with the rule change regarding jockey weight, we could not match the sheer speed of Dancy's mare, Brutus, nor Avenger. But Cato never gave up & we nosed by Jones' sorrel for 5th.

In the second heat, Cato's run was valiant. He just kept running. He made a brilliant charge (me in the crouch) shadowing Dancy's mare. We beat Whitaker's Avenger by a length & Brutus by a whisker to achieve a thrilling 3rd place. A length behind Dancy's mare & 5 lengths behind Johnson's dominating stallion. This at least was very satisfying for me & my spirited son John. Were our need less dire I would not be at all unhappy. We cleared 10 shillings above the entry fee.

What will become of us?

On the way home, Macon confided in me receiving a letter urging him to be his usual prompt self, to wit, to be at the first day of the new Congress: It has been gleaned that some moderate Federalists are unhappy with the extreme partisanship shown by the past speaker & expected from the proposed Theodore Sedgewick. If they support an alternate on the first ballot & the right mix of late arrivals exists, Republicans hope to elect Macon Speaker! What a mark of esteem for my friend & neighbor.

24 Oct^r

Utter, utter tragedy. Unutterable despair is our portion. I cannot go on.

Chapter Twenty-six

(1800)

Dear Sterling,
Dear friend & neighbor, no one ever deserved such tragedy less than you. I wish I could lend you strength in some way to help you overcome it.

I can report some glimmers of hope from this place—tho' only glimmers. You have heard no doubt that Sedgewick prevailed on the 2nd ballot to become Speaker of the House. And he has been as partisan as anyone might have conceived. We continue to fight off extension of Pickering's power over the coming census & other bills by which Federalists would attempt to control future elections.*

We have attempted without success to reduce the large standing army, necessitating as it does higher taxes & more debt. What would we think of a father who would run in debt & leave it to his children to pay? The "friends of government" held firm. Even for regiments & companies yet empty of soldiers, Federalists insist on keeping the officers so that they may make use of the patronage. Yet here is one of the glimmers: Petitions come from all over now complaining of the taxes & the standing army.

As you may have read in the papers, I led the charge for repeal of the Sedition Act. I reminded my fellow Congressmen that the members of the State ratifying conventions explicitly declared their understanding that no power was given to the federal government to make a law abridging freedom of the press. Later when the Bill of Rights was debated in the House, many argued against the necessity of the 1st Amendment on the grounds that the Constitution precluded the possibility of legislation on the subject—by not specifically granting Congress that power.

Yet Congress & the people removed all doubt by way of the Bill of Rights: (1) The 1st Amendment says no law on the subject of freedom of the press is permitted; (2) the 10th Amendment confirms that the federal government may not assume powers not spelled out in the Constitution.**

And how, pray tell, are we supposed to have elections if one side may not be criticized? How are we supposed to ever impeach an officer of the gov't— as the Constitution allows—if that guilty officer cannot be criticized?

---

* The Ross electoral count bill would have set up a Federalist-dominated committee to decide on whether to allow the electoral votes of any state where there was any dispute. It passed the Senate & very nearly became law.

** *The 10th Amendment: "The powers not delegated to the United States by the Constitution… are reserved to the States respectively, or to the people."*

I believe that we won over a couple of moderates with our logic, but the Federalists still prevail. But here is another glimmer: I believe that laws of restraint, like the Sedition Act, operate in a contrary direction from that which they were intended. The people's suspicions are aroused when the gov't shows it fears free discussion. They know the truth is not afraid of investigation. I grow sensible of the people coming in our direction. The more so since new Whig newspapers such as Gales' Raleigh Register are now printing our Congressional speeches. With a modicum of good fortune & much work, we can elect Mr. Jefferson this fall & restore liberty.

I pray you to maintain hope.
     Yr mst obt srvnt,
      Nathl Macon
12 Jany 1800, Philadelphia

Dear Sterling,

I fear my recent letter was poorly fashioned to do what I intended—to wit, to cheer you. And hence I write again to express my regard for you by way of a lighter, gossipy epistle.

You, sir, & Miss Emily would be much in fashion here in Philadelphia with your curly hair. One's own rather than wigs are so much the better. Sterling, you & Kenchen would be much—I beg your indulgence—aroused by the immodest dress of many young ladies at the balls. They expose the greater part of their breasts; wear no stays or bodice; and their dresses are so loosely draped as to show much of their natural shape. When some of these belles curtsy, every head in the room is turned.

The wonderful new Argand lamps are brighter than the oil lamps—to wit, they are unimaginably brighter than candles. 'Tis indeed a new century. Many folks say such brightness is against nature & will cause sickness amongst those often exposed.[*]

We will miss Philadelphia exceedingly when the gov't moves to the new Federal City. Halifax is more of a city than the new capital from all I hear. Among the plethora of things we will miss about Philadelphia will be the many excellent stone-paved streets. This hit home in late December when Washington's funeral procession took well over an hour to go a short distance because of an especially muddy street. The mud was so thick that several gentlemen's shoes were sucked off.

---

[*] Oil lamps appeared about 1798; they burned more evenly and brighter than candles. The Argand lamp was even brighter, using costly, refined whale sperm oil, the precious commodity hunted for in *Moby Dick*.

We must wonder if Adams has read our letter. S[arah]'s information confirms that he is not from the same cloth as Pickering, Hamilton &c. Thus we may hope he considered its contents. Probably he interpreted it as some concoction of scheming Republicans & simply threw it straight into the fireplace.

I must say, I like Pres. Adams' response to one bit of slander making the rounds in Pennsylvania. An early misguided eruption of the presidential election this year no doubt, the story avers that Adams had dispatched Gen'l Pinckney to England in a U. States frigate to procure 4 pretty girls as mistresses, 2 for Pinckney & 2 for himself. 'Tis said that when Adams heard this tale he quipped "I do declare upon my honor, if this be true, Gen'l Pinckney has kept them all for himself & cheated me out of my 2."

I saw S[arah] briefly. She said she is married to G[eorge], who also owes his freedom to you. I did not spoil her obvious happiness by communicating to her the degree of your sacrifice & your subsequent misfortune. May you derive a certain satisfaction from this very dear good turn.

Yr mst obt srvnt,
Nathl Macon

20 Jany 1800,
Philadelphia

1 March 1800

'Tis a new century. I would that I could leave more of the pain in the last century.

Still let me dwell upon the many blessings that are mine. The greening of the grasses, the beautiful little purple violets blooming in profusion by the river, the tobacco & yam sproutings in their protective beds, the sparrows & doves building their nests—all these reassure one of spring's dependable rebirth. My remaining family is healthy. I owe great debts of gratitude to Macon, Kenchen, & Lewis; sustaining friends they were.

Three days after the Halifax races, *my* son, my John took Cato for a ride. Against our counsel, John was playing the horse racer, *assuming my crouch* & urging Cato on to his greatest speed. Tragically, he did not observe a copperhead occupying the path; Cato's abrupt halt flung John head first into the trunk of a stout oak. He died quickly at least.

I was devastated. I thought surely I would die with him, for my heart was broken. I remained in paralyzed despair. Emily was sooner able to act than I. She took the initiative to deal with our impending bankruptcy. She suggested that we sell Cato.

"Sterling, every time you go into the crouch, will you not think of your son, John?"

I *wanted* to die at that moment. I wanted to be able to go to my son to tell him how much I loved him. At least one more time. Why did I not do it more when he was alive?

"Otherwise, dear husband," Emily continued gently, "we will lose our home. We will lose what you have created with 12 years of difficult labor & diligence. John is gone. But I know you love Katie & me. I know you would not have us starve. Nor others who depend on you."

Macon & Kenchen sold him at the Warrenton races. Lewis took the proceeds of Cato & the harvest & negotiated a loan from the Scotsman in Halifax. He thereby paid my taxes & my debt to John Whitaker. I am indebted to Lewis as I had not the fortitude required for these dealings at that time, nor his talent for them at any time.

The needs of my wife & daughter are what kept me alive. Having sold virtually all our food, Marmaduke & I hunted for game to keep us fed. I threw myself into clearing new land. Four months of hunting and heavy axe & saw work have fed us, paid the £5 I borrowed from Lewis & the £5 I promised Eli, & dulled my grief.

Remaining debt: £10 to Nathl Macon
     £5 to Frederick Kenchen Shearin
     £35 to the Scotsman @ 9%
     £20 to Wylie Jones

8 March

Through the good offices of Macon's brother-in-law, Kemp Plummer, I have had placed in my care 2 orphans, Lucie (9yrs) & William (12yrs). These children have known a difficult life during the last years of their father's sickness; he died of consumption [tuberculosis]. They will be, I hope, a salutary burden. I suspect their labor on our farm will outweigh the burden of their care, for they have not been pampered. They seem likely children.

The entrusting of these orphans to us suggests that my reputation recovers somewhat. Mary told Emily that Eli has let it be known that we dealt with him honorably in the face of great difficulties. Naturally I am cheered by this.

I resolve from this day forth to maintain irrepressibly the best attitude that may be conceived. Indeed, I resolve to excel all men in attitude. One can expect a full measure of tragedy in life. I resolve to make life as good as it can be in the face of all disappointments; to enjoy the small victories such as Sarah's freedom even should the country descend into despotcy;

to enjoy loving my wife & daughter tho' one or all our lives be painfully brief; to take pleasure in dealing well & fairly with those who depend on me—from old Lucie to young Lucie, tho' some several may be depended upon to disappoint in due course.

18 April

Heavy rains shorten the dogwoods' spell of beautiful blooms & drive us inside. 'Tis reported that Thos. Cooper has been arrested for sedition; it will be interesting to hear what he said or wrote to provoke the prosecution.

Half a year's interval dulls the pain of losing my son John—tho' being needed by my wife, daughter, & extended family hath been more ameliorating than the elapse of time. The concern exhibited by the actions of Macon, Kenchen, Lewis, & other connexions also had an incalculable salutary effect. In any case, I once again care about my country; I miss my beloved Cato; & I am as beset & victimized by lustful urgings as ever. My dear Emily & I occasionally take a chance. For all my resolve about being possesst of the most excellent temper, the most positive disposition, in the face of all vicissitudes, if I lost Emily—or charming little Katie, could I persevere?

What irony that many prominent Baptists would follow their natural urges & seek pleasure outside the matrimonial bed with a slave, concubine, &c., confident that their God will forgive them by way of a timely repentance; whilst I, the deist, am more effectively prevented from giving in to these powerful urges by the dishonesty & dishonor it would express to the one who has softened & warmed my heart. I shall never fail Emily or myself again.

Permit me to dilate upon that previous thought. I have known some fine Christians; Macon, ne'er a slave to fashion, now seems to incline that way. But the few deists I know—I'm put in mind of Wylie Jones, for instance— are more honorable & trustworthy than the Christians who are constantly vocal about their Christianity. Such Christians wax these days. Already criticisms of Jefferson on account of his deism commence in prospect of this fall's election.

2 May

On Sunday we went to visit Lewis. We carried a goodly quantity of venison; I can never repay him fully for past kindnesses. Their new baby, Nathaniel Macon Shearin, thrives. There was a good deal of other news:

Eli is apprenticing with a blacksmith in Warrenton. Alas, he has taken up with Ezra Blount's sister.

Lewis had a letter from his new son's namesake in Philadelphia where Thos. Cooper is being tried for sedition. Macon attends some of the trial. Sec. of State Pickering sits on the bench with Judge Chase, who exceeds Iredell in his Federal prejudice. Robert G. Harper is also there.

Macon said that Cooper was marked for prosecution by a famous piece he wrote in which he merely pretended he were a president who wished to increase his power at the expense of the governed. What would such a one do?

A usurping president would first undermine the Constitution either by expanding its grants of power so as to encroach upon the rights of the States or by explaining away the plain & obvious meaning of its words. For example he would restrict liberty of the press.

His next "instrument of despotic power" would be a standing army & a naval armament. In no instance in history has a standing army failed to render the governing powers independent of the people. By making the militia idle, useless, & contemptible, a standing army would provide the partisans of the ruling party with arms, at the same time disarming & paralyzing its opponents. If no reason existed for the maintenance of a standing force, a usurping president would invent one. An army & navy would gain him support of the mercantile interest, would attract other supporters through offices & contracts, & furnish the means of suppressing his opposition.

A usurping president would have his partisans charge all who opposed the measures of his administration as enemies of the their country; the opposition would be branded as dangerous & seditious, as disturbers of the peace of society, and as desirous of overturning the Constitution.

Tho' not a direct criticism of anyone, this thought experiment really must have hit close to home.

10 May

Our scoundrel of a deputy sheriff, Ezra Blount, paid us an unwelcome visit. He seemed to take some little pleasure from eyeing the jade of a broken-winded horse which I now ride in lieu of Cato. I imagined similar pleasure in his tone when he conveyed the news of Thos. Cooper's conviction for sedition: Six months in prison, 400 dollars fine, & 2000 dollars bond for good behavior. Further ungenerous insinuations seemed to accompany his assertions of what good friends he was becoming with Eli.

Yet the real point of his visit was to say that, in light of last summer's unpleasantness, everyone in the county agreed that no slaves should be allowed firearms. He felt sure that I would have the good sense to comply with the consensus. I did not say how indispensable Marmaduke's hunting had been to keeping everyone fed this particular winter; I did reply with feigned casualness that having 'Duke shoot a crow now & then was a mighty effective way of keeping them out of the corn.

15 May

We did not attend either of the spring horse races. They dredge painful memories of John; he loved them as much as I did. We hear Cato finished in the middle of the field in the 3 mile heats. —Weather continues favorable for vegetation.

A lump in Emily's left breast (of which I had become sensible earlier) seems to grow. Naturally to my worrisome mind, this conjures the horrible death of the woman near Halifax from a sickness of the breast. I speak not of it to Emily.

25 May

President Adams has dismissed Pickering! And McHenry as well. Macon brought the news. We could not help conjecturing of some effect from our letter, at least perchance confirming other bits of information Adams may have received.

And more exceedingly encouraging news: Thru' the great energy of Aaron Burr & others, Republicans have won a narrow majority in the New-York legislative elections. New-York chooses its presidential electors by its legislature! This is a major coup for Mr. Jefferson!—& hence for the hopes of regaining liberty.

As I pause & look up at my sweet amiable Emily at her wheel & my beautiful Katie—4 is *the* cutest age—I am full of hope & appreciation of my blessings. Our crops have never looked better. (Unfortunately prices, esp. tobacco, are down.) Tho' today young William got into a fight with 'Duke's oldest, he & Lucie are at least as much benefit to us as they are trouble. Lucie is good with Katie.

I have done nothing with regard to Marmaduke. Emily thinks him trustworthy, but is sensible of a possible malicious influence on the part of his wife Prissy. Prissy can be designing & devious, and there is no discounting a wife's influence.

4 June

The Federal government has arrested a writer (James Callender) for sedition *in Virginia*! A troop of the standing army accompanies Judge Chase in Richmond—where they must surely comb the populace to assemble a sufficiently Federalist jury.

There is a rumor that Gov. John Jay will call into session the old Federalist-dominated New-York legislature so that it may change the method of selecting presidential electors & prevent the newly elected legislature from awarding them all to Jefferson.* The aristocratical party is unscrupulous.

On a positive note, the French have received our envoys. Macon conjectures that with Iredell deceased & Davie in France, the Federalists will be less well-organized in our state.

9 June

Numerous Virginians (esp. John Taylor) came to the aid of the unfortunate Mr. Callender. But the lawyers who defended him were so persistently contradicted & over-ruled by Judge Chase that they withdrew. Naturally he was convicted. How will his poor family be fed?

Alas, we who would criticize the Federalists are intimidated, while the most scurrilous venom spews forth against Jefferson.

28 June

How uncertain art these times. Can it be true as reported that Jefferson is dead after a sudden illness? How flimsy our hold on life. How pointless become the articles branding him a French infidel & atheist (one of those by a man who was a known deist but a decade ago).

The growing numbers of Methodists & Baptists are as anxious as the rest of us. I received a letter signed by Preacher Absalom & the pastor of the new Methodist church imploring me to take Marmaduke's gun from him. Perhaps they are right. At least until these fears of insurrection subside.

Emily may be with child.

---

* Alexander Hamilton wrote to Gov. Jay making the request in a letter dated May 7, 1800.

3 July

We have the most excellent wheat harvest ever (almost 8 bushels/acre)*; 'tis my hope to pay each of my creditors £2.

7 July

Emily is sure now. We must pray for good fortune.

9 July

Well, Ezra Blount for once brought good tidings: Jefferson lives. 'Twas a plot by Federalists to diminish the many July 4th toasts to the author of the Declaration of Independence.

But then he spoke of most troubling things indeed:

"Sheriff Caleb Brown is not going to stand for re-election next month. He is leaving for Tennessee." With good reason. "And I mean to replace him." A bad enough prospect in itself. But it is worse. He spoke of his chumminess with Eli & of Eli's special knowledge of my shortcomings.

"I am puzzled by Sheriff Brown's tolerance toward you. Don't expect it from me. Toe my line or I will be on you. For starters, you will take back your negro's gun."

---

* A typical yield seems to have been 5-6 bushels/acre. The average yield/acre in the United States in 1992 was 39.3 bushels. In 2010, in particularly favorable or irrigated fields, wheat yields exceed 80 bushels/acre.

Chapter Twenty-seven

10 July 1800

I rode over to Marmaduke's with a tentative intention of asking for his gun. But it was simply beyond my capability: I could not deal my faithful servant yet another virtual kick in the teeth. When I arrived at their dwelling, he was being simultaneously ministered to & berated by Prissy. The poor fellow had been in a fight with a slave from across the Roanoke. He got the worst of it; he had numerous cuts & bruises, & worse yet, had lost a 2nd upper fore tooth!

Whether the offending negro had a pass to be off his farm or what the fight was all about I did not ascertain; 'Duke was vague & too pitiful to press.

17 July

'Tis very hot & the plants want rain. Poor Emily suffers (as it is her nature to do) at this stage of her pregnancy. I could never coax one detail of his fight from Marmaduke, save that his adversary was quite large; this may be cause to worry.

Farm produce prices, esp. tobacco, go lower still on account of the British having a monopoly on our trade. People are quite properly attributing this to Adams & the "friends of the government."

Still the abuse spews forth upon the head of Mr. Jefferson. He is called an infidel, an atheist, an impractical philosopher, a lover of France & her radical democracy, a Jacobin, and a coward—this last because as Governor of Virginia in 1781 he very reasonably fled from the British troops. Also, because he resigned Washington's cabinet under fire.

No one has stepped forward to oppose Ezra Blount for sheriff; this poses more dire consequences for me & mine than the Presidential contest, tho' the latter is nearly the only topic of conversation.

28 July

We received a much needed rain; now my worries concentrate on getting someone other than Ezra Blount elected. (Emily seems relatively well & I cannot tell that the lump is any different—tho' I try not to be obvious in my touching. What a fine thing the touch, the hug, the near presence of my Emily in bed beside me.) I went over to Macon's to solicit his thoughts on the matter. How grateful I am that he was well ahead of me:

Being well aware of the shortcomings of Blount, Macon & his brother-in-law Mr. Kemp Plummer have persuaded a respectable farmer & honest Whig from the other side of Warrenton to allow his name to be placed in nomination for sheriff. I assured him that I & my brothers will do our part in promoting him & Republican legislative candidates in our vicinage. Macon will devise a schedule for several of us to work the polling place on Thursday & Friday—especially to keep Blount honest.

We fell to lamenting the scurrilous pamphlets & newspaper articles criticizing Mr. Jefferson:

"The viciousness & breadth of the slander seems to know no bounds," I said sincerely.

"Have you read some of the claims of his 'lust for power'? In particular Robt. Goodloe Harper—but not only him! They claim Jefferson is determined to reshape the country in the image of France. If he is elected, the country will be flooded with every seditious, demoralizing, atheistic publication which industry & wickedness can produce."

"Followed shortly by the execution of aristocrats, the death of religion, & the extinction of industry & commerce," I interjected.

"Depend upon't, the Federalists are shameless. You get a better taste of what we've had to put up with in Congress since the XYZ affair," said he.

"I declare, I think they believe their claims. The particular pamphleteer I was just quoting asserted that Jefferson would overturn Hamilton's sorry funding system, which surely would be a revolution."

"No doubt that has more effect north of Virginia where all the holders of gov't bonds reside," responded Macon. "The irony of it is that in practice Jefferson's character is quite mild & given to compromise. Perhaps too much."

5 August

Eli came by; his visit was more than a little unsettling. He calls Blount "his friend" & claims Blount's opponent is "debilitated" by the ague.* This certainly is not an encouragement. He also had nasty things to say about Jefferson, dredging up that old Mazzei letter again. I would wager that deep down Eli just wants to evince his independence of me. Fortunately, he has

---

* The ague was malaria, which was characterized by recurrent spasms of fever, chills, and weakness—that is, "debilitating" fits.

yet to acquire sufficient property to vote. He made quite a lot of what a prize he has in Blount's sister; indeed, she seems to possess all the merits of female character in an eminent degree.

Crops are mostly thriving; alas, so are the tobacco worms.

13 August

The voting for Congress, the General Assembly, & sheriff commences tomorrow. We must hope that the ague does not detract too strongly from the honest reputation of Blount's opponent. I cannot help but worry. Emily is well & helps us with the tobacco worms. She also leavens my natural melancholia saying things like:

"Sterling! Look at all the swallowtail butterflies on the Purple Boneset flowers.* There must be 50. Isn't that an agreeable sight?"

Then she gets me singing with her & pushes disquiet from my mind.

14 August

It rained all day today; 'tis unlikely that many voted. My turn to work the polling place is the period immediately before it closes at sundown. Whether Blount can be defeated or no I cannot hazard a guess. Neither man is a well-known character throughout the county.

Emily read to me tonight where Mr. Thomas Cooper continues to write for the republican cause from gaol. "What spirit hath the man," said she. A heroic model for us all. I resolve to write a vindication of Mr. Jefferson to the *N.-C. Journal* as soon as there is breathing space; one could hardly be prosecuted for that.

18 August

Virtually all the voting was done on Friday. I believe I may have encouraged a man or two to change his vote away from Ezra Blount. Eli was cocksure his "friend" would prevail. It was very close; so close that it was recounted 4 times. Blount lost by between 6 & 18 votes. At last I think we are safe.

The degree of imbibing going on when I left Warrenton was in excess

---

* Purple Bonset: Joe-Pye Weed or Eupatorium purpureum.

of the typical Election Day spectacle. Thus I was not surprised to hear of a couple of fights breaking out. But I was surprised by the consequences of one of the fights:

Today Macon (who was naturally re-elected again without opposition) brought me a young man to nurse who was beaten to the point of being nearly unrecognizable. I think he will live, but one of his eyes has been gouged out; he is most pitiful. 'Twas Eli. He was the victim of Ezra Blount's fierce temper. The poor fellow received no comfort from his fiancée, who is after all Blount's sister & who probably will find it easier to love a man with 2 eyes; they do tend to be better providers. Poor Eli had nowhere else to turn.

1 Sept^r

The crops thrive, tho' it is a little wet for the tobacco's quality. And Eli mends albeit slowly; he has been walking around unassisted the past 2 days & I hope he'll be able to help with harvest in 3 weeks or so. The poor fellow's spirit is understandably low. In one woeful moment he spoke of taking his life. We all endeavored to deflect this line of thought. I own it was my sweet Emily who succeeded.

11 Sept^r

Many have slandered Mr. Jefferson on account of the letter he wrote confidentially to Mazzei in 1796; 'twas roughly translated & publicly printed in '97. Jefferson unbosomed himself to his Italian friend with trenchant observations on the aristocratic, pro-British orientation of the Federalists under whom he served. The remark about men "who were Samsons in the field & Solomons in the Council, but who have had their heads shorn by the whore of England" is seized upon by the Federalists as a great insult to the deceased Washington. Critics couple Jefferson's public praise of Washington with the Mazzei letter to brand Jefferson as duplicitous & hypocritical. They say it demonstrates his lack of character & his want of personal firmness. Further, 'tis asserted that the letter's originally being written "in the vile French tongue" is proof of Jefferson's French bias.

I have spent too much precious candle these past three nights endeavoring with my quill to make the case that the glorified Washington deserved these criticisms. Ever do I cut against the grain.

"Sterling, do not get your hopes raised that Mr. Hodge will print your letter," Emily said to me tonight. "I've read precious little in the *N.-C. Journal* favorable to Mr. Jefferson."

I told her I must do something. She bears this pregnancy a little better than the last & keeps her fears to herself. We have not mentioned the lump, but the horrible death of the woman in Halifax 2 years back, after a surgeon removed her infected breast...I cannot extinguish it from my thoughts. I remind myself that it is ever my nature to be beset by a thousand fears.

13 Sept'

Eli is still a bit weak but has expressed an encouraging interest in earning his keep. If we can get 2-3 weeks of dry weather, we will have one of our best crops ever; if prices were higher, I declare we might be able to nearly pay off our entire debt. "Ifs" galore.

The latest is that Republicans won 8 of our state's Congressional seats & that Federalists won 4. Several races were close. Better than 2 years ago, but apparently much of the state is still affected by the XYZ affair. Or is more Tory than I could ever have imagined. Too many of our people are unschooled & are hence too easily swayed by the many lawyers who gravitate to the legislature.

18 Sept'

Rumor of a sizeable slave revolt in southside Virginia puts fear into us all & ruins the calm of this beautiful clear September day.

21 Sept'

The 21st of September 1800 was a fine day with only a few clouds & a light pleasant breeze. Yet my mind was occupied in such a manner that I had ceased to take notice. For some little time before we finished working the west field, I had almost on impulse sent William over to fetch Marmaduke & have him bring his gun with him. I still had not decided for certain to tell him to surrender it but was possesst of that inclination. Now that I had finished the field, I was sore conflicted.

In a short spell I started home. The painful particulars that followed derive in part from my being oblivious to all around me. I was thinking in terms of: "Marmaduke, it would give me some peace of mind to hold your gun for a few months till the hubbub has quieted down. I want to give you this fat hen to soften the insult you might feel, tho' none is intended." How, I wondered, would he accept that? Had I not been engrossed in those thoughts, I might have noticed that something was not right as I approached our home.

I walked up our little apple tree avenue with my head down in thought. When I walked between the 2 big white oaks, 2 negroes, one of them a hulking buck, bounded from behind an oak & knocked me to the ground! A third black man ran out of my front door with a formidable knife & threw them a rope with which to bind me.

It became clear quickly that resistance was futile.

"We've killt us 'least 8 white folk a'ready," blurted the man with the knife. "I kinda like the smell of it." He grinned at me as the other two tied my hands. "You gonna do 'xactly what I say."

"Where's my wife?" I prayed there was not as much terror in my voice as there was in my bosom.

"You see 'er soon enough." At least he was true to these words. They threw me down in the corner of our main room where she was; Emily was bound like I was and a little blood flowed from a corner of her mouth.

I looked in her eyes to ask "You alright?" Her expression suffered me to infer that nothing really bad had happened yet. I attempted to gather my wits, to assess the possibilities. How pathetic, how tragic for our lives to be ended in such a manner.

I saw 4 black men & a negress; old Lucie was trying to assure them we were good masters. The fellow with the big knife, a stout high yellow with alert dark eyes, answered her roughly that we would die like the rest unless we were mighty helpful. The hulking one said "less eat now dat dis'un"(gesturing at me) was accounted for.

'Big knife' glanced at me & then grunted okay; he seemed to be the leader. Another black woman carrying a baby & a young negro boy came down from the loft where they had kept little Lucie & Katie quiet; it became clear that our 2 little girls were up there bound with rope as Emily & I were. Was Eli up there too? My gun was not over the fireplace & none of these desperate negroes seemed to have it.

They ate & drank everything within easy reach. I gleaned too little from their garrulous conversation. One Gabriel's name was oft repeated. The hulking one spoke familiarly of Prissy. Marmaduke's Prissy? He seemed to be from just across the Roanoke; the rest seemed to be from Virginia. Nor were Emily's whispers helpful. I thought I understood her to say one of them had been lifting her skirt just as they espied me coming; she seemed to rethink my need to apprehend this item & would not repeat it. She whispered something about Eli, but I could not hear what; she was too fearful of their hearing this sentence to repeat its substance. I hung some hope on the uncertainty with the respect to him.

The leader & the smaller of the 2 who accosted me between the oaks finished eating first & returned their attention to me. They wanted to know where my gun was. I lied that I had lent it to one of my brothers. The leader gave me the back of his hand with all his might; I could feel the blood run down from my lip. I stuck to my story. He struck me again with such enthusiasm that I immediately dreaded how much worse this was likely to get. I yelled in a voice that I hoped disguised my utter fear: "I'm telling the truth!" He hit me again so hard that it was obvious I was nearly knocked senseless.

They threw some water in my face to revive my attention. My mouth filled so with blood that I had to spit some of it upon the floor. The leader put his knife against Emily's throat & made plain his desires: They wanted my gun, my powder & ammunition, and careful instruction in its use & the use of the other gun they had stolen north of the river. There would be more after that, but if I did not comply immediately, they would slowly cut Emily up before my eyes in a manner to torture; then they would do the same to me. His bitter, angry dark eyes left no doubt of his venomous sincerity.

I looked at Emily to say you "are going to have to tell me if you know where my gun is?" Just as she got a syllable out of her mouth....there was a distinct though tentative knock on the door. The big one jumped to the window.

"It's a runt," he said. He quickly went to the door & opened it. As soon as he did, the "runt," William, saw him & wisely bolted at quarter-horse speed; the big one gave chase. The leader went to the door. What he saw did not calm him, & he waved for someone to follow him. They all followed, save one of the women who merely went to the open window. Old Lucy very slyly left her stool, and with a butcher knife she produced from the folds of her petticoat she cut my bindings. I took the knife, & in the instant it might take to pinch out the flame of a candle I had the knife against the back of the negress at the window, with the words "Move a muscle & you are dead!"

Emily miraculously sprang to her feet & with her shoulder slammed the door to; old Lucy somehow managed the bolting board into place. A blink later I heard someone hit against the bolted door trying to get in—the woman with baby: she screamed.

At that moment I saw that Marmaduke had stepped from behind the barn with his gun pointed at the leader. Behind him came young William with my gun and Eli with our new metal pitchfork. To add to the sorry runaway slaves' dismay, I yelled from the window that I had a knife to the back of this black bitch & that she would die if they did not give up.

The 3 I could see looked about in confusion. Eli bravely came at the leader with the pitchfork. They sparred for a several seconds. God's Teeth, thought I, Eli, with your one eye, take no chances. These slaves are bloodthirsty killers.

Then William shot the leader right thru' the chest. Bravely done! He collapsed to the ground. One of the men fled; the other, the husband of the woman with the child, yelled that they gave up. I learnt in a short spell that the big brute lay mortally wounded on the back side of the barn where he had pursued young William—but found Eli's pitchfork & the stock of 'Duke's gun. The latter had the pleasure of claiming revenge on the man who knocked out his second fore tooth & who (if I may liberally construct what I have since heard) possibly cuckolded him.

It turns out that Eli had gone out earlier in the day with my gun to see if he could hit any game with only one eye; alas, to his great dejection, he could not hit anything. To our great good fortune, our incredible good fortune, he observed my capture from a great distance. He started for Kenchen's but encountered 'Duke & William, and—with some uncertainty—decided to trust Duke.

Tomorrow night we shall have a great feast of thanksgiving: To old Lucie, to Duke, to Eli, to William, & to Providence. 'Tis surely as if someone were looking out for us. May I ever behave in such a way as to merit the numerous turns & twist of good fortune that leave me & mine alive & well this night.

A substantial group of darker clouds had formed above us, tho' out in the distance in at least three directions it was mostly blue sky. "Sterling," said Emily, directing my gaze toward the clouds with her own. "The shadows of the Angels' wings?" I hugged her and kissed her cheek.

Chapter Twenty-eight

1 Octr 1800

 Gabriel's rebellion has the militias of much of Virginia & a few counties of North-Carolina very active; successfully so, for no more whites have been reported murdered for at least a week. Our captain excused me from this duty because of our ordeal. I still pray daily to God for our being spared. I have taken old Lucy down to spend a few days with her grandchildren & doubled the size of 'Duke's personal garden plot for the coming spring. It goes without saying that his gun belongs to him as long as I live.

 'Tis troubling that so much hate should exist betwixt master & slave. 'Tis plainly indicative of how foul is the institution (slavery) & at the same time how impracticable is its cessation.

 We are very excited by the prospects of our crops. Cotton gins for cleansing cotton are being offered for sale in this state. I shall definitely plant more cotton next year.

16 Oct^r

 37 leaders of Gabriel's rebellion (including Gabriel) have been hanged. 'Tis said they all met death with fortitude. Macon has it thru' his friend John Randolph that they "exhibited a spirit, which, if it becomes general, must deluge the Southern country in blood. They manifested a sense of their rights, & a contempt of danger, & a thirst for revenge which portend the most unhappy consequences."

 The event has temporarily upstaged the Presidential contest. It is very unfavorable for Mr. Jefferson's prospects. It conjures injurious thoughts in both the mind of the slaveholder (who remembers Jefferson's earlier criticisms of slavery) & in the mind of the Easterner (who look upon the Southern planter with condescension). 'Tis also discouraging what we hear about Genl Hamilton having organized the military officers for the coming elections.

 I must accept that the *N-C Journal* will not print my piece. I must take solace from the several vindications of Jefferson printed in the *Raleigh Register*. And from yields of 15 bushels of Indian corn per acre! More than 3 bushels better than my previous best.

20 Oct^r

 Today I went to the Ordinary for a modest drink to celebrate the success of our crops (even tho' the prices are poor), & there I encountered John Whitaker. He that hath more than once designed to render me mortified & obsequious. It suits me excellently well to no longer be in debt to the arrogant Col. Whitaker. He has never been known as a flincher at the bottle & on this day had imbibed considerable. No doubt he purposely baited me by loudly asking "Do you believe in this strangest of paradoxes—that Jefferson the spendthrift, the libertine, the atheist, should be qualified to make your laws & govern you?"

 I could not let this go by with several respectable gentlemen, including Marmaduke Johnson, present. I ignored "spendthrift": So many farmers & planters are indebted that this slur carries no weight hereabouts. I spent a couple of sentences countering that his calumnies of fornication & atheism were not based on any firm information, anymore than is the story of Pres. Adams having dispatched Genl Pinckney to secure them concubines.

 "Indeed, Col. Whitaker, I could match your slanderous characterizations by dwelling on Pres. Adams' tremors, his toothlessness, his poor eyesight, & so on, but the truth is I admire Mr. Adams on a number of accounts. Indeed, he is an exceedingly well-read & learned gentleman. Had he not condoned the excesses of his party, he would be more than tolerable."

 "Hrmph," Whitaker muttered.

 "I ask you, sir, whom should we wish as our President if we wish for the preservation of the rights of the States? If we wish for a government rigorously frugal & simple? If we wish to restrain the dangerous standing army commanded by that would-be Caesar, Hamilton? If we wish for freedom of religion & of the press? If we wish for commerce with all nations—that is to say, decent prices for our products—but political entanglements with none? If we wish for an end to these burdensome taxes? If we wish for these reasonable elements so essential to a free society, who but Jefferson should we choose?"

 Whitaker was taken aback by the momentum of my response & had no ready answer. Three of the other 4 men present applauded; the apolitical Marmaduke Johnson insisted on buying me an apple brandy. Whitaker left in a huff. A minor triumph. Yet the coming vote is what matters.

22 Oct^r

 The *N-C Journal* printed a letter from Charleston saying that it was certain that Jefferson will not get Georgia's vote. 'Tis essential that he receive all the southern votes to win. Less than 2 weeks now till the citizens of North-Carolina vote for the Presidential electors. Much attention will be upon our state as we are one of the rare states not to choose its electors essentially by way of the legislature: we get to vote for the elector from our district directly.

29 Oct^r

I am elated that I have paid down my debts so well: I now owe just £3 to Macon, £10 to the Scotsman, and £5 to Wylie Jones. That most sublime of gentlemen forgave half my debt to him when he learned lately of all the particulars by way of Macon! How unfortunate that his health declines as it does.

Halifax is all abuzz with the prospect of the Presidential vote. The grumbling about the taxes, the standing army, & the low tobacco prices bode well for Jefferson. (The dearth of complaint about the Alien & Sedition Acts shews, said Wylie Jones, that the old Whig sensibilities that fueled the Revolution are dying out.)

The election can easily go either way. Macon predicts Adams will get 4 of North-Carolina's electors! If either Georgia, as is rumored, or South Carolina, the home state of Adams' running mate Gen'l Pinckney, goes primarily for Adams, then Adams will prevail. Pennsylvania & Maryland are big question marks as well.

I view this article from the *Raleigh Register* with some skepticism but do not mind its being circulated:

"At a large party at dinner at New-York a few years ago, Mr. Adams & Mr. Jefferson were present. The former declared his opinion that it would be better for this country if it were under a hereditary ruler. There was a silence for a few minutes, but the conversation was closed by the following observation from Mr. Jefferson.— 'I once traveled in Germany, and came to a university, where the chemistry professorship was hereditary. The then professor held the office in that way... and a precious chemist he was!' The relater of this anecdote was one of the party present, a gentleman well known in this city (Philadelphia)."

3 Nov., 1st Monday

After voting today, I learnt of a thunderbolt! Alexander Hamilton has written a 54-page letter scathingly critical of President Adams! Printed in the paper was supposedly one of the milder passages: Adams "is a man of an imagination sublimated & eccentric; propitious neither to the regular display of sound judgment, nor to steady perseverance in a systematic plan of conduct; & I began to perceive what has since been too manifest, that to this defect are added the unfortunate foibles of a vanity without bounds, & a jealousy capable of discoloring every object." According to the paper, the broadly circulated letter goes on to allege many instances of Adams' blunders, fatuities, & inconsistencies. Probably too late to affect the selection of many electors; but then it may have an influence on some few of the electors. I am dumbfounded.

10 Nov.

The elector for Jefferson won our Warren-Halifax district handily. The Edgecombe-Pitt Co. district went for Adams & the New Bern district probably did too. No more results are known.

I am sure the lump has grown; Emily complains not of tenderness. However, the pregnancy goes better than last time.

14 Nov.

I have seen the full Hamilton letter in pamphlet form. It reveals confidential knowledge of the fragmented Adams administration, confirming many of the things we had learnt from Sarah. Upon reflection, one might infer that Hamilton was provoked by hearing that Pres. Adams had referred to him as a member of the "British faction" & "a man destitute of every moral principle"—indeed, that hearing these charges, his injured vanity then overrode every other consideration. Surely Hamilton exposed at least as much unattractive about himself as he did about Adams. Jefferson & Republicans can only benefit.

The electors meet in their respective State capitals on the 4th of December to cast the votes for President & Vice-President.

17 Nov.

Nathaniel Macon had a large corn husking yesterday, an affair full of mirth & conviviality. It appears that Macon was correct; if all the electors cast their votes as expected, North-Carolina will award 8 votes each to

Jefferson & Burr and 4 votes each to Adams & Pinckney.

"The present purpose of the intriguer Hamilton & his High Federalists becomes clear," Macon said. "They push for all of the North, where Adams is strong, to support Adams & General Pinckney equally; they leave unstated their belief & hope that South Carolina will give all its votes to Pinckney but few or none to Adams. In this case Pinckney becomes our President. Hamilton's apparent fall-back strategy, and the probable reason for his recent publication, is to influence one or 2 electors to switch their votes away from Adams. He seems determined to have Pinckney & cast Adams aside—even if it increases the risk of electing Jefferson."

"'Tis discouraging that Adams got 3 more votes from our state than last time," I offered.

"One of those votes will be offset by Virginia's electors being essentially chosen in a block by their legislature. So Jefferson will gain one there over last time. The paramount thing is that the New-York legislature must follow thru' & give all their votes to Jefferson; 'tis no certainty for their legislative majority is small."

Macon's brother-in-law, Kemp Plumer, said he had read that Pennsylvania's legislature was so evenly divided that their vote may be with-held.

"I for one am relieved that Congress managed to reduce Hamilton's army a little right before adjourning," commented Lewis. "That beast must be reduced to a minimum, kept on the frontier away from the capital & generaled by a less ambitious man than Hamilton. Otherwise the history of this country as a republic will be brief."

Macon leaves immediately for the new Federal City for the first session of Congress to be held in that place. "Cities are always home to much depravity & villainy, but I confess I will miss many fine attributes of Philadelphia."

1 Dec^r

It turns unseasonably cold. We turn to indoor crafts & try to improve the tightness of our abode. Emily may well deliver in a fortnight. Her spirits are good & she shares the great general interest in the Adams-Jefferson contest (& in truth it is a contest upon which hinges our experiment in liberty), certainly more than do most of her sex. I love her more every day. She hath such a nicety of temper, soft as the finest shawl.

9 Dec^r

The votes of Virginia (21 for Jefferson, 0 for Adams) & North-Carolina

(8-4) are now known at this place. First day in a week that it was not cold enough to snow. Most unusual this early in the winter.

12 Dec^r

Maryland split 5 for Adams & 5 for Jefferson; Federalists set the woods afire in a strong Jefferson district & succeeded in keeping many honest farmers from voting. New-Jersey, Delaware, & Connecticut awarded all their votes to Pres. Adams. It stands: Jefferson 34, Burr 34, Adams 28, Pinckney 28.

14 Dec^r

Pennsylvania split almost evenly, but Massachusetts gave all 16 of its votes to Adams, putting him ahead 51 to 42. All electors thus far are voting for Adams & Pinckney or Jefferson & Burr equally. Hamilton's plan is very much a possibility.

17 Dec^r

Kenchen & I were so agitated to know the fate of our country that we went to the Halifax-Warrenton road & sat working on leather shoes until a traveler came by with some definite news of the election. Finally a peddler coming from Halifax said New-Hampshire, Vermont, & Rhodes-Island have given all their votes to Adams & Pinckney. (We had hoped for one from R.-I.) Kentucky's 4 votes went to Jefferson as expected. Adams 65, Jefferson 46. If South-Carolina goes against Jefferson, or if Georgia goes against him, or if a mere 4 votes is lost from the new state Tennessee, from Georgia , & from South-Carolina in total—then our hopes are dashed; for then it will be up to the *old,* heavily Federalist Congress to elect the new President, to wit, should Adams & Pinckney get 69 votes.

'Tis very cold & gray. The frosty breath of winter is upon us. Old Lucie says she can smell snow.

19 Dec^r

Lucie's nose was true. And I feel as tho' pandemonium's fury hath broken loose in celebration of the defeat of the cause of liberty. Bitterly cold wind drives mixtures of fine snow & ice that stings the skin of all who are out in it—as I, of necessity, have been.

Whilst I was trying to provide for the livestock yester even, Emily sent William with word that it was definitely time to fetch the midwife. Regrettably, it is far too cold to attempt to gather in the neighborhood women. Still it will not be so lonely a birth, for we must all of us—old Lucie, little Lucie, little Kate, William, Eli, & me—huddle in this room with the fireplace, with Emily & midwife Walker. (This very ink was frozen solid in the room without a fire but 3 hours ago; even on the far side of the room from the fire we shiver when the wind blows hard, tho' as wrapped as we can be.) We have hung a little oznaburg partition, and my poor brave wife stifles her expressions of pain & anguish, endeavoring to spare Katie & Lucie from fright.

21 Dec^r

We are delivered! I am the most grateful, the most favored of men! Emily has given us a healthy boy, which we have with premature optimism named Luke in honor of old Lucie. Mother & babe fare well. 'Tis a little warmer; soft large flakes of snow fall upon the hardened, crusted, frozen snow on the ground.

When I went to fetch Mary Shearin, Kenchen gave the happy news of the *Raleigh Register*'s report: South-Carolina, Georgia, & Tennessee have given all their votes to Jefferson & Burr. They each have 73 to the 65 for Adams & Pinckney. Our jubilance is tempered by the realization that the tie between Jefferson & Burr may allow for mischief on the part of the old Congress.

We must busy ourselves with preserving a number of animals who were lost to the cold. Otherwise I would love to be in Warrenton where great celebration is a certainty.

25 Dec^r

Emily is not well this Christmas day; perhaps I am over-reacting but I went forthwith to fetch Mrs. Walker. (She can treat Eli's canker rash too.) Kenchen was there & told of the great rejoicing in Warrenton over the election. One wag asserted that all the rich Eastern Federalists will surely have such long faces that their barbers will be forced to raise their fees for shaving them.

26 Dec^r

Mrs. Walker's clister of milk, water, & salt seems to have helped Emily, tho' Eli's "putrid malignant sore throat" (as Mrs. Walker calls it) is worse.

27 Dec^r

Emily does not improve swiftly; so I went to ask Mary Shearin to help with the baby & sit the night tonight. Kenchen said Lewis had fresh received a letter from Macon full of foreboding & intrigue: Macon writes that even tho' the votes from Tennessee & Georgia are not yet officially received in the new Federal city, a tie between Jefferson & Burr is a known certainty. There is some reason to suspect Burr of being a party to this by telling electors in various states that someone else was going to drop a vote to insure Jefferson got the first spot.

What is known on a firmer basis is that Federalist Congressmen are making plans to make Secretary of State John Marshall the new President after going thru' the motions of several deadlocked votes in which neither Jefferson nor Burr gets the necessary votes in the House to be elected President! What an unanticipated calamity is this tie vote of the electors.

30 Dec^r

Emily is worse. I am sick with worry. I go now to fetch Mrs. Walker.

1 January 1801

Never did a year begin more woefully than this. My poor sweet Emily is hot with fever, very weak, & in considerable pain down low. The dreaded foul smell is there.[*] The utter fear is a knot of pain in my own gut. This afternoon for fear of weeping in front of her, I had to leave. Repeatedly. 'Tis unbearable. Dear God, how can you take one so virtuous & unoffending as she when the world is so full of villains?

She asks for Katie & for the Methodist minister.

Emily, my heart breaks.

---

[*] Emily presumably had Puerperal fever, the major cause of death associated with child birth. It is caused by the same streptococcal bacteria that caused Eli's strep throat.

Epilogue

Dear Sir (Sterling),

I think of you frequently as I persist in this cause that you & I believe in so fiercely. But more I think of you for having suffered losses parallel to your own. It is my conviction that I can say little of value to help your sorrow; but I want you to know that you are in my mind & my heart. Please keep your hand on the plow; I, your family & neighbors, we need you.

The story in this place is one full of intrigue, drama, & moment. Except for recent events, it would be of great interest to you; I hope that under the circumstances, it will be at least a positive diversion.

The balloting in the House of Representatives began on the frigid, blustery afternoon of 11th of February. On the 1st ballot Jefferson won 8 states; Burr, 6 (N-H., Mass., R-I., Conn., Del., & S-C.). Maryland & Vermont were unable to reconcile differences in their delegation & thus cast blank ballots. Actually, had it not been by state, Burr would have won 55-51!

26 more times we voted without any significant Congressmen changing their votes. The vote was as frozen as we were—the chamber was unheated & the wintry northern wind pierced it so that we were bone cold. All thru' the night we went with nothing but high tempers & futile negotiations to warm us. Tho' bound not to adjourn before electing a President, at 8 o'clock in the morning the session was "suspended" until noon. We trudged thru' considerable snowdrifts & icy winds to breakfast & fires at our respective lodgings. I hoped at that juncture that Federalists members were hearing some of what I was hearing—to wit, that Gov. Monroe of Virginia & the Gov. of Pennsylvania were being urged to ready the militias of their sovereign States in the event the Congress tried to essentially over-turn the recent Presidential election.

When we returned I believe they were focused instead on the weakened condition of my great friend Jos. Nicholson of Maryland, who was unable to sit & had to lay in the ante-chamber on a cot. Without his vote, Maryland would cast for Burr. There was every prospect he could die there on that spot. After the next ballot, Federalists spread a quiet rumor that some Republicans were about to give way to Burr, a rumor which I did my best to counter. After 2 more ballots, a move was made to postpone the next vote until March 3rd, the day before the scheduled inauguration; that was defeated, but tensions continued to mount. Messages came in from President Adams, from the Senate, from department heads, &c.; but by rules that I helped frame, we were not allowed to consider any business but the selection of a president. After the 33rd ballot, we suspended again until Monday the 16th.

On Sunday I took solace from continued rumors of the readiness of nearby militias to enforce Jefferson's election & from the firm information that attempts have been made to obtain promises from Jefferson in exchange for Federalist votes. If the Federalists could muster the votes & the temerity to appoint Marshall President, would they not have done so already? Yet Burr had not withdrawn as he properly should have, & possible trimmers had been solicited on his behalf by Congressman Bayard of Vermont—with promises of federal appointments. Disgusting! How little better is a republic than a monarchy!

But then yesterday on the 36th ballot, Morris of Vermont withdrew his vote from Burr, leaving the vote of the famous Matthew Lyon to carry that hitherto split state for Jefferson. The Burr votes in Maryland also refrained, giving Maryland to Jefferson. Jefferson is elected by 10 states! The spirit of 1776, the spirit of liberty—it lives. Will we need a revolution every 25 years to maintain it?

Naturally the favor of your reply is impracticable. I hope this excellent news is of some benefit to you. My sympathy & highest regard.

    Your mst obedient srvnt,
      Nathl Macon

18 February 1801
Federal City

1817

I found this old Journal of my uncle's a couple of years ago. My father, Frederick Kenchen Shearin, complains that it gives no very good account of him and disputes much of what is said with reference to him; however, he attests that otherwise it is true. At this historic moment when President James Monroe visits our county & our Senator Macon, it seems appropriate to fill in some loose ends:

Nathaniel Macon was elected Speaker of the House of Representatives in December of 1801 & re-elected in each of the next two Congresses; he was the first to serve in that capacity three times & the first to be universally acclaimed for his impartiality & fairness as presiding officer (in marked contrast to his two predecessors). He might have been selected again in 1807 but for the death of his oldest grandson, which he said left his heart "fit to burst," & his own severe illness which together rendered him three weeks late for the session. One of his famous acts as Speaker was breaking the tie to allow the 12th Amendment (providing for the presidential & vice-presidential candidates to share a ticket). Presently he serves as our Senator. Mothers name their children for him, and men speak of naming places for him.* There are few men in all our States who command more respect.

Thomas Jefferson's administration was true to all of its promises: freedom of the press was restored; internal taxes were eliminated; the army, the navy, & the diplomatic corps were all reduced to a minimum; the government's stock in the national bank was sold; the aristocratic levees of Washington & Adams were abolished; & other trappings of monarchy such as the President personally addressing Congress & then receiving their formal reply were all abolished. Commerce with all nations but alliances with none has been adhered to with difficulty. Liberty & its handmaiden, frugal government, were achieved. The main failure, not constitutionally limiting the Federal government's ability to borrow money, may be blamed on the necessary Louisiana purchase.

Sterling's wife Emily died of childbirth fever in January of 1801 & a few days thereafter Sterling lost two finger of his right hand (in an accident involving a cider press I believe) so that he no longer attempted to write. He remarried a few years later. He sold his farm after the first year of the 1805-1806 droughts & moved to Tennessee. When my father last heard from him in 1814, Sterling was quite prosperous, presiding over a 600 acre farm & a considerable family. Apparently, he did keep his hand on the plow.

Ezekiel Shearin

---

* Macon, GA, and Randolph-Macon College in Virginia are named for him. Also Macon, MO, Ft. Macon, counties in North Carolina, Illinois, Missouri, Georgia, Tennessee, and Alabama, and a World War Two transport vessel.

Afterword

The Secrets of Sterling Shearin is deeply researched historical fiction. Both professional historians who read the manuscript commented that there was probably too much history in it for commercial success. But alas, it is fiction. Although Lewis Shearin did help Nathaniel Macon with his plantation and the Shearin brothers fought at the Battle of Guilford Court House, a great deal about that family is fictional. Similarly, Col. John Whitaker was a Revolutionary militia officer, a Federalist delegate ratifying the Constitution in Fayetteville in 1789, a "tax gatherer," and a generous benefactor of the University of North Carolina, but all his villainy was invented for the sake of the story. In the same vein, apologies may be due to Federalist James Iredell, for his description through the voice of libertarian, anti-Federalist diarist Sterling emphasizes the negative traits mentioned in Willis P. Whichard's biography *Justice James Iredell* and not the many positive ones.

I wish to thank Kate Ferrell, Rachel Rees, Velma Brown, Gail Curry, Roberta Pearson, historian William S. Price Jr., Lennis Loving, George Machen, Susan Deese, and Carol Cox for their help and encouragement in this project. The cover and illustration on page 179 are the artistry of Anna Lyon.

I was born and raised in Halifax County, North Carolina, attaining degrees and some knowledge from Weldon High School, North Carolina State University, UNC, and UNCG.

       Willard (Will) Doral Ferrell
       Kernersville, NC

Made in the USA
Charleston, SC
10 June 2014